PARKS PAT MYSTERIES

PARKS PAT MYSTERIES

CASES 1-6

P.D. WORKMAN

ISBN: 9781774683989 (Paperback)
ISBN: 9781774684009 (ePub)

He Never Forgot

She Was At Risk

He Drowned in Memory

Their Walls Were Empty

They Came for Him

They Sought Vengeance

She Was Their Target

Kenzie Kirsch Medical Thrillers

Unlawful Harvest

Doctored Death

Dosed to Death

Gentle Angel

Rushin' Death

Posed for Death (Coming Soon)

Death of a Corpse (Coming Soon)

High-Tech Crime Solvers Series

Virtually Harmless

Stand Alone Suspense Novels

Looking Over Your Shoulder

Lion Within

Pursued by the Past

In the Tick of Time

Loose the Dogs

AND MORE AT PDWORKMAN.COM

STYLE NOTE

Since my largest readership is in the USA, I have chosen to use US spellings throughout this series. That includes the Americanization of centre to center, even where it is an actual place name, just for consistency's sake. I apologize to my Canadian readers for this.

I have chosen, however, to use Canadian grammar, particularly for Canadian voices. If you see what you think is a grammar error, it may just be Canadian, eh?

CONTENT

Contains discussion of Canadian Residential Schools and other other institutional abuses of children. There are no graphic depictions of violence against children or others, but some readers may be sensitive to these topics.

OUT WITH THE SUNSET

PARKS PAT MYSTERIES #1

To the survivors
Strength and peace

CHAPTER ONE

*M*om, you've got to be kidding me! Are you serious?"

Margie winced at Christina's complaint. Up until her phone ringer had shattered their quiet morning preparations, the day had been going well. Bright sunshine streamed in through the kitchen windows of the small house. The rich odor of brewing coffee filled the air. Christina had been blow-drying her long black hair, the hum of the dryer providing a soothing white-noise background as Margie prepared her breakfast and reviewed the day's plans. Everything had been peaceful despite both of their 'first-day' anxieties.

"I know, honey. I didn't plan this. You know I was going to take you to school today and help with your schedule and getting settled in. But…" She gave a dramatic shrug and grimace, "you know I can't control when someone gets murdered."

"Couldn't someone else take this one? You *promised* me."

"They need me. Others in the department will be involved, but this is my first lead, and I can't turn it down."

"You could."

Margie took a deep breath in. Her stomach felt hollow and heavy. She knew she had promised Christina that she would be there for her first day of school. It wasn't fair to expect her to do everything by herself while Margie went off to a murder scene. She was brand new

5

in the Calgary homicide department, and her coworkers would be watching to see how she took on her first case—watching for her to make a mistake. To see whether she was competent, or was just a 'diversity hire' for a department that needed Indigenous representation on the team.

Christina was right, of course; she could turn it down and ask them to make someone else the primary. But what message would that send to the rest of her team about her commitment and ability to handle both her personal life and the rigors of the job?

"Maybe you could start tomorrow instead," Margie suggested. "I could call the school and let them know that you won't be starting today, but you'll be there tomorrow."

"No way!" Christina's response was immediate and emphatic. "I'm starting the same day as everyone else. It's bad enough that I'm the new girl; I'm not going to have everybody looking at me because I didn't start the same day as everyone else. Like I've got some kind of... privilege."

Like Margie's, Christina's black hair, bronze skin, and facial features showed her Cree heritage clearly. Neither one would ever be mistaken for white. But others often saw Indigenous people as lazy, looking for a handout, or expecting compensation for what had happened to them over the generations. Christina wouldn't want to be branded as one of *those Indians*.

"Well, those are the only two options." Margie looked at her watch. "I need to get to the scene. You can go today and get your guidance counselor to help you get everything set up, or you can wait until tomorrow when I can go with you."

Christina slammed the door to the bathroom and started the water running so that Margie couldn't talk to her.

Margie swept her long hair back with both hands and divided it into sections. She deftly braided it and pinned it up into a bun so that it would be neat and out of the way. The coffee machine finished brewing and she poured her coffee into a travel mug.

After making sure she had everything else she would need, including Staff Sergeant MacDonald's directions to get to the site, she knocked on the bathroom door. "I'm going now. Are you okay?"

"I'm fine," Christina snapped. What she said after that wasn't as easy to make out, but it was something along the lines of "Not that you'd care."

Margie sighed. "Love you, sweetie. I'll see you after school. Give me a call if I'm not home and let me know how your day went."

"You're really going to go take this case and make me go to a new school all by myself?"

"I'm sorry. I can't do anything about it."

Christina slammed something down on the bathroom counter. Margie knew there wasn't anything else she could do or say to smooth things over. Christina was old enough that she could manage. She wasn't a shy or anxious child. She was a strong young woman. She would be able to navigate a new school. Margie had actually been surprised that Christina had wanted her to be there. Usually, she was embarrassed by her mother and didn't want her anywhere close to her teenager peers.

"Goodbye. Love you."

There was no answer from her daughter.

Margie picked up her coffee and her shoulder bag and got into the car. She stuck the note with Sergeant MacDonald's instructions on the dash. After starting the car, she waited for the GPS to boot up. She put Fish Creek Park into the GPS, but the route it popped up was nothing like the directions she had been given. She studied the picture on the small screen. The green area was massive, covering many blocks. So there was undoubtedly more than one entrance. She would have to go by MacDonald's instructions and hope that they were detailed enough to get her there.

She pulled out of the gravel parking pad in the back of the house and found her way out to Twenty-Sixth Street. There was a long multiuse path along the ridge above the irrigation canal, or 'the ditch' as it was known as in the neighborhood. There were always people walking dogs, running, or biking along it. Even late at night or early in the morning, she could almost always count on seeing people on the pathway. She was looking forward to taking Stella out to explore and meet other fur-babies. In September, the trees were still green, with just occasional yellow leaves fluttering to the ground, and there were a lot of parks and green spaces throughout the city. The grass along the path was more yellow than it was green. She hadn't realized before moving to Calgary how arid the city was. The summer temperatures were nothing like they were in Manitoba, but it was still hot and dry. She had thought that it would be a lot more temperate in the shadow of the Rockies.

She found her way to Deerfoot Trail and kept one eye on MacDonald's instructions to make sure that she didn't miss any exits or turns.

Despite the traffic, she pulled into the east entrance to Fish Creek Park in under twenty minutes. There had been no need for lights and siren. The man wasn't going to get any more dead.

There were more cars in the parking lot than Margie would have expected, and she wondered how many of them could be associated with the investigation and how many were typically there every weekday morning, like the walkers on the path along Twenty-Sixth Street. She supposed that if she lived close to a big park like Fish Creek, she would try to get over there as often as possible. She pulled on a face mask, got out of her car and looked around, trying to figure out which way to go. MacDonald had only given her directions to the parking lot; he hadn't told her where to go from there. She had hoped to be able to see the crime scene from there, but all she saw were trees.

"Detective Pat—er—Patter…" A man in a gray uniform shirt, dark pants, and gun belt approached her with his hand outstretched. He had a bandana-style mask.

Margie reached automatically to shake, then drew back and gave him a little wave. "Patenaude," she told him, pronouncing it clearly for him, "PAT-en-ode."

"Oh, that's not so hard." He gave an embarrassed laugh. He dropped his hand to his side. "French?"

"Yes. Métis."

"Sure." He gestured toward her face, indicating her dark skin and whatever he could see of her nose and other features above the mask. "I should have guessed. We don't see a lot of Natives in law enforcement. Sorry."

Margie shrugged it off. "I guess if you know my name, you know what I'm here for."

"Yes," he seemed far more comfortable with this topic. "You're here for our body."

He said it possessively, maybe even a little affectionately. *Our* body. She glanced at his gray uniform. Not the black shirt of a Calgary Police Services uniform. "What department are you with?"

"Alberta Parks. I'm one of the Conservation Officers here. Dave Barnes."

"Okay." Margie nodded. "You know the park well, then."

"Very well. Come on; I'll take you to the crime scene."

She followed him to an electric golf cart and took the passenger seat. Margie looked around her as Barnes drove down one of the bicycle paths, slowing and occasionally tapping his horn as they passed cyclists out for a morning ride.

"The park looked pretty big on my GPS screen. How big is it?"

"Thirteen and a half square kilometers with ninety kilometers of trails."

"Whoa. I'm glad you've got a cart."

"Me too. But we don't have too far to go today. We're just headed to Hull's Wood."

Margie watched the sunlight filtering through the green leaves, creating dappled shadows on the pavement of the pathway. It all seemed so peaceful and idyllic, people walking and running, some with dogs or companions and some alone, the occasional bicycles thrumming along beside them. A paradise in the middle of the busy city. She had been impressed by Calgary's long list of parks, both city and provincial. She liked to walk and bike. She was hoping to be able to ride her bike to work, taking the new bridge alongside Blackfoot Trail, then through Pearce Estate Park and along the Bow River Pathway to get downtown. It would be much better for her than always driving her car. Once she got settled in and more familiar with the route.

"Here we are." Barnes's words drew her attention back to the present and to the not-so-idyllic scene she was there to see.

Tape had been looped around several trees to cordon off the area. Sunlight streamed down on a small clearing. Bright green grass against the dark trunks of the trees. The grass and wild plants had a fresh, sweet scent. There were more gray-shirted conservation officers and a few dark-uniformed Calgary Police officers hanging around. A crime scene truck was parked outside the cordoned area, waiting for Margie to review the scene and give them the go-ahead to collect forensic evidence.

She dismounted from the cart and looked slowly around before advancing to the crime scene. She looked at the spectators rubbernecking nearby, all hoping to catch a glimpse of something exciting or disgusting to brag about to their friends and family.

No one who seemed out of place. No one who appeared to be anything other than curious as to what had happened. But one never knew. Sometimes killers returned to the scene or stayed around to watch the discovery and investigation go down.

Margie approached the crime scene truck and nodded at the techs who were suited up, face shields on and ready to go.

"Hi. I'm Detective Patenaude. New in town. You guys been here long?"

A couple held disposable cups of Tim's coffee, looking like they had been waiting for her for a while.

"Half hour," one of them commented, thumbing his phone to check the time.

"Okay. Sorry to keep you waiting." Margie pulled on her own protective gear, trying not to fumble or look incompetent in front of them. It wasn't her first rodeo and she didn't want them thinking that she was inexperienced. "While I take a look, do you think you could get pictures of the bystanders?"

One of the men holding a Tim's cup raised an eyebrow. "The bystanders?"

"Yeah. If you could just do that sort of unobtrusively, so we've got a record if one of them ends up being a witness or suspect?"

Most of the observers were not wearing masks, which was lucky.

One of the unfortunate effects of mandatory masking policies was the increased difficulty of reading and recognizing faces.

The tech exchanged a look with his coworkers, then shrugged and nodded. "Pictures of the bystanders. Roger."

"Thanks." Margie finished with her protective gear and lifted one of the lines of tape to duck under it. She made her way over to the body with great care, watching for any footprints or crushed vegetation.

One of the uniformed cops nodded to her. He wasn't masked and kept his distance. He had a medium build and a round face, hair thinning on top. "You the primary?" he asked.

"Yes. Hope I didn't keep you waiting too long."

"He might have gotten a degree or two colder while we were waiting, but it's not like he's going to get up and walk away."

Margie chuckled. "No," she agreed. She looked at his name bar. "Officer Smith. You want to walk me through it?"

"Found by a dog walker this morning. As you can see," he tilted his head toward the spectators on the pathway, "there is a lot of foot traffic here, even very early in the morning. Dogs are really good at smelling out bodies. The riper, the better."

"But this one hasn't been here very long," Margie observed. The body hadn't been there long enough for her to detect any decomp.

She gazed down at the crumpled figure. Looked like a male, but he was face-down, so she wouldn't be able to verify until he had been moved. Tall and slim. He seemed deflated beneath the wrinkled jacket and pants. The vegetation in the area had not been trampled down; Margie couldn't see any sign of a major struggle. And there was not a lot of blood and gore. Most of that would be underneath him.

"Has anyone touched him? Moved him?"

"Just to verify that he didn't have a pulse and check for signs of violence."

Margie raised her brows questioningly.

"Stabbed," Smith informed her. "Center mass. Probably too low for the heart, but could have punctured a lung or caught the aorta. Not just a heart attack on his morning constitutional."

Margie stooped briefly to feel for a pulse—never hurt to have it verified more than once—and to evaluate the temperature and rigidity of the body. Someone from the medical examiner's office would be there to take the liver temp and make other observations, such as rigor, but Margie wanted to know for herself as she began the investigation.

"He's been here a while," she observed. "I don't think it happened this morning. More likely last night."

Smith didn't disagree. "The park closes at night. But that doesn't mean someone didn't stick around and avoid being seen. A place like this, you can't check behind every rock. The CO's do what they can to keep anyone from setting up camp here, but still come across homeless encampments now and then hidden in the bush. It's a big park."

Margie looked around. "I guess we don't have the luxury of surveillance cameras like we would if this happened on the street."

"Actually, there are some. I don't know where they all are."

"Probably the parking lots."

"There are wildlife cams too, though. And some of the trails are probably monitored. You can ask the CO's what video they have. Maybe you'll get lucky."

"Not lucky enough to have a video of the actual murder," Margie posited. "That would be too much to expect."

Smith shrugged. "Yeah. You're probably right."

Margie looked around at the ground for anything that was out of place. "Is the knife still in him? If not, did you take a look around for it?"

"Not in him. I kept my eyes open while we were deciding how much area to rope off. I was hoping it might have been dropped close by. But we didn't see anything. We can take another look, now that it's daylight. It was still pretty dark when we got here."

Sunrise had been around seven o'clock the last few days, Margie knew. Of course there had been runners and dog walkers out before that. People trying to get their workouts in before heading to office or retail jobs starting at eight or nine.

So when was their victim killed? During the small hours of the morning before opening? Or late at night when he shouldn't have even been in the park? She hoped they would be able to narrow it down quickly.

"Did you get all of the contact information for the dog walker who found him? And what about him, did he touch the body?"

"Dog might have contaminated it. Owner kept his distance after bringing the dog under control. We got everything we needed from him, down to the dog's name and morning routine. You can give him a call and talk to him or request an interview any time today. He's eager to help."

"Great. Thanks. Do we have an identity for our victim yet?"

"Haven't searched him. He's fully dressed—you know, not for running or something—so he probably has a wallet on him, unless it was a robbery. We figured we'd let the techies do that part."

Margie nodded. It was a good call. They might even have a missing person report on him already if he had a family and should have been home the night before.

She looked around some more without moving her feet, but couldn't see any other clues and didn't want to be guilty of contaminating the scene any further. She looked toward the crime scene investigators and nodded to them.

"Let's get out of the way and let them do their thing," she advised Smith, raising her voice a little for everyone within the cordoned-off area.

CHAPTER THREE

hile Margie got out of the way to allow the crime scene techs to do their job, she wandered casually toward the bystanders. She wasn't wearing a uniform but, of course, it would be apparent to everyone there that she was a police detective. They wouldn't have allowed just anyone to get that close to the body. But no one peeled abruptly away from the group or attracted her attention.

"My name is Detective Marguerite Patenaude," she told the onlookers in a friendly, pleasant tone. "I wonder if anyone here happened to see anything this morning? Not necessarily him," she motioned back toward the body, "but anything that's out of the ordinary for the park. Most of you probably walk or run here several times a week?"

Most of them nodded automatically. A few looked away. Maybe they had just been called by their friends to come to see what was going on, in hopes of being able to see something brag-worthy.

"So? Anything unusual? People or activities that you don't normally see? A strange noise or smell? Anything that made you take notice?"

No one stepped forward to offer anything. Most shook their heads and made negative noises. Margie hadn't actually expected to get anything from them. More than likely, the murder had happened many hours before, and the people who walked the park in the morning were not the same ones who walked it in the evening.

"Anybody want my card? In case you think of something or hear anything from someone else?" Margie pulled a stack of business cards out of her pocket and held them out, offering them to each person. A couple people took one. Maybe hoping she'd be able to help them out of a speeding ticket at some point. No one met her eyes or gave her the impression that they would call her later when they could speak to her without witnesses. "All right. Thank you. You can move along, you can't see much from here, and we'll be around for a while. You might as well finish your workouts."

Most of them moved on. Only a few lingered. None of them did anything to make her think that they might know what had happened. No one started asking her questions about the murder. There was no one who appeared to be from the press, though she was sure they would be there within the hour. Even if there were nothing to report, they still had to get some shots at the scene and report that there was nothing to report.

BEFORE LONG, a couple of the other homicide detectives from Margie's team made it to the site. Margie tried to remember their names and what she knew about them. She'd only had one brief meeting with the team so far, when she had been introduced to them and read in on all of the usual policies and procedures. She had filled out her tax forms and been assigned a desk and told when she would be on duty. Even though she had known she would be on duty on Christina's first day, she had made arrangements not to be at the office until later in the day once she got Christina settled at the school. None of them had anticipated that they would be called to a homicide early that morning. That was just the way that it went. You couldn't plan.

Detective Cruz would have played a good Hispanic cop on TV. Olive skin, hair turning to salt and pepper, a short mustache now hidden behind a mask, and a bit of a paunch. But he'd made it clear when they met that he was Filipino, not Hispanic. Margie had been surprised to find such a large Filipino community in Calgary. She had thought Calgary's demographics would skew a lot more white—and redneck—but there was a surprisingly multicultural population. Half of the people in her neighborhood seemed to be either Asian or Polynesian. Cruz was an older cop, probably ready for retirement before too long. Homicide was not an easy job. People didn't stay there for more than two or three years, and Cruz had been there at least four.

Riding with Cruz was Detective Kaitlyn Jones. Margie had been happy to discover that she would not to be the sole woman on the homicide team. She could hold her own; she'd always been able to fit in as "one of the guys," but it was still a relief to know that there was another woman there who would have her back in case of any sexist or harassing behavior. Boys would be boys, but she was not going to put up with any garbage.

Margie filled them in on her arrival on the scene and everything they had done before Cruz and Jones arrived.

"The victim did have a wallet. It gives his name as Jerry Robinson, and his face matches the picture on his ID." She read off the address from his driver's license. "I guess that's not far from here?"

"Deer Run," Cruz said with a nod. "Not far at all. Might have walked in."

"The CO's haven't seen any abandoned vehicles, anything left overnight, so he probably did."

"Any background on him yet?" Jones asked. Her blond hair was pulled back into a bun, and despite the blue mask over her face, Margie could still tell by the cheer in her voice and the fan of laugh lines around her eyes she was smiling. "Wedding ring? Business card? Family pictures?"

Margie laid out what they had. "Union card; apparently he is a welder. Don't know about family or kids yet; his phone is locked. No wedding ring, but that might just be so he doesn't injure himself on a job site. We'll have to do some background and find out if he has a family, make a death notification to the next of kin. I haven't checked social media yet, but that might be a good place to start."

"So it wasn't robbery," Cruz mused. "Everything appeared to be in his wallet? Cash? Plastic? Jewelry wasn't stolen?"

"Doesn't look like robbery. He could have had a watch or necklace or something of value, but we won't know that until we talk to people who knew him. There's no mark on his finger showing that he typically wears a ring, but he could still have one and only wear it some of the time. Cash and credit cards in his wallet. Not a lot, but if the motive had been robbery, I would have expected at least the cash to disappear."

"Okay. Makes sense. Any sign he's been in a fight?"

"We'll have to wait for the ME's report, but nothing obvious. Hands are scarred from working. No split knuckles or broken nose."

"Then what happened?" Jones asked, shaking her head. "Usually, it's pretty obvious. Robbery, fight, drug or gang connection. In a park like this, at night, it could be drugs, but...?"

But Margie hadn't mentioned anything that would give them that idea. "Nothing that I could see. The body certainly doesn't scream drug dealer or addict."

CHAPTER FOUR

nvestigating even a major crime like homicide, there was a lot of 'hurry up and wait.' They would have to wait for the video surveillance. For the medical examiner's report. For the techs to crack the code on Robinson's phone if he didn't have a family member who knew it.

By the time they got to the duty room, it was already midafternoon. Phones rang, people banged away at their keyboards and chatted with each other in voices that were a little too loud for Margie to concentrate. Her desk was out in the bullpen, not behind a closed door, and she found it a little distracting.

And she had promised Christina that she would get home early.

"It's my daughter's first day of school," Margie told Jones, hoping she would be the most sympathetic. "Would you mind screening Robinson to see if we have anything on him or if you can find him on social media, and I'll check in with you later? I'd like to pick her up at school or at least take her out for a burger once she gets home. I had promised to go in with her this morning and then I couldn't."

"Sure," Jones agreed. "How old is your daughter?"

"She's fifteen—a terrible age to uproot her and come to Calgary, her first year in high school. I mean, she was in high school last year, but grade nine was high school in Winnipeg, and the high school here starts at grade ten. So even though she had her first year of high school in Winnipeg last year, she's the little fish again this year. In a new school. In a new city."

"That's tough," Jones agreed. "Which school?"

"Forest Lawn High."

"Oh."

Margie tried to interpret Jones's reaction. She didn't immediately tell Margie what a great school it was, even though the principal had really talked up the school and its programs. But it wasn't like she had badmouthed it either. Maybe she or a friend had gone there for high school.

"Where did you go?"

"Oh, I wasn't in Calgary during high school. Ft. McMurray."

Northern Alberta. Where the tar sands were. Margie nodded. "Cold there?"

Jones shuddered. "Oh yes, it was. No Chinooks there."

"I'm looking forward to experiencing a Chinook wind. We don't get them in Winnipeg. Once it gets cold there, it stays cold all winter."

"One of the best things about Calgary," Jones agreed. "Though it wreaks havoc with the roads. And sometimes the trees, if they think it is spring before it is. And migraine headaches."

Margie nodded, her attention no longer on the subject. She gathered her things. "You have my cell number in case you need to reach me? Sorry to be ducking out early on my first homicide, but I'll be in bright and early in the morning, and you can reach me tonight if you need me."

"Go take care of your daughter. We'll be fine."

※

MARGIE DIDN'T QUITE MAKE it in time to pick Christina up from school, so she hurried back to the house instead to beat her there and try to smooth things out for when she arrived. She let Stella out to run in the yard for a few minutes, tidied up the living room and kitchen, and tried to decide what they would do for supper. She didn't call or text Christina while she was on the bus, which would probably just irritate her. And she didn't want to inundate her daughter with questions as soon as she got in the door. But she also didn't want to look like she had just been home relaxing while Christina dealt with school and the bus ride home.

Eventually, Christina got home. Later than Margie had expected. Maybe she should have gone to the school to pick her up after all. Christina pushed the door open with a loud bang, then stepped in and slammed it behind her. She ripped off her mask.

Margie kept her temper. Of course Christina was tired and irritable after a long day at school, and she wanted to show her displeasure with her mother for letting her down. Margie forced a welcoming smile. "Hi, honey. How was it?"

If looks could kill, she would have had to arrest her own daughter for murder. Or one of the other homicide detectives would have to, since Margie herself would have been dead. Christina dropped her backpack on the floor and flounced down onto the couch.

"Was it that bad? I'm so sorry. Tell me all about it."

"We should have stayed in the Peg. I don't understand why we had to come here. Your job there was just fine, and I had friends and knew my way around the school and the bus system and everything else there. We should have just stayed. Couldn't we have stayed until I was done school? Three more years? Would that have been so bad? Then you could go wherever you wanted to, and I could go to university or start working. Why did we have to come here?"

Christina was one of the reasons that Margie had wanted to move away from Winnipeg. Yes, Christina had friends there and knew her way around, but that was part of the problem. Margie hadn't liked Christina's friends, and there was a lot of violence and drug culture in Winnipeg. As a cop, Margie knew the statistics about murdered or missing Indigenous women in the Peg. She hadn't wanted Christina to become another statistic.

"What happened?" she persisted. "Did something bad happen, or is it just because it is difficult getting used to a new place?"

"I hate it. Why did you move us to the hood? We had a nice place in Winnipeg. Here, we're in the ghetto!" She kicked at her schoolbag with a thud.

"Ghetto? Calgary doesn't have a ghetto or a hood. This is a nice area. Lots of families and retired couples that have been here for years."

"It's the *hood*. That's what the kids at school say. Forest Lawn is the hood, and everybody who goes to the school is in a gang."

"We aren't in Forest Lawn. We're in Southview. And I checked out the crime statistics before we came. It isn't bad. There is crime all over; you can't escape that. There isn't a lot of gang activity at the school. Maybe some kids there are in gangs, but that was true in Winnipeg too. The crime rate there was *much* higher than here. I don't think you need to worry that you've been dumped into the middle of a war zone."

Christina shook her head irritably. "I should have known you wouldn't listen."

"I am listening." Margie tried to tone it down. Christina needed to know she was being heard; she didn't need her mother arguing statistics. "Tell me more about it. I'll try to keep my mouth shut and just listen to you. I didn't mean to argue. Did you make any friends? Meet anyone interesting?"

"At home, everybody was First Nations or Métis. It's different here. Everybody is white. Or Asian. Or Black. There aren't that many Indigenous kids."

Margie nodded. "I know. The demographics are a bit different. Calgary has lots of immigrants."

"So I'm, like, I stand out. I look Cree, so everyone thinks that I'm… I don't know. Just there for a free ride, or drugs, or to steal their stuff. They look at me like I'm…" Christina shook her head, at a loss for words. "I don't know. Like I'm dirty or a criminal."

Christina threw her head back against the back of the couch in frustration.

"Oh, honey." Margie hoped that Christina was just overreacting and being dramatic. She had found so far that Calgarians treated her pretty well. But she was an adult with tough skin and a badge. Not a sensitive teenager. "I'm sorry you felt so much like an outsider."

Christina nodded vigorously. "Exactly. Like an outsider. I hate it. I just want to go home."

"Is there any way I can help? We're not moving back to Winnipeg, but is there anything else I can do to help make it better?"

"The school is huge. I'm so lost. And everybody already has friends. I don't have anybody."

"Give it a few days. I'm sure other people are new, and people who are looking for new friends. They'll be coming from all different junior highs, so everyone will have to meet new people, and friendships will be changing. Maybe we could look at some clubs or after-school activities that will help you get in with a group sooner."

"I don't want to do sports or photography or any other stupid hobbies. I want to… hang out with friends like I did in Winnipeg."

One of the things that Margie hadn't liked in Winnipeg was how much unsupervised time Christina and her friends had for hanging around, looking for new ways to get in trouble.

"I'm going to be connecting with the Métis community here. I'm sure you'll be able to make some friends through the Métis Nation or Friendship Center so you won't feel so different."

Christina shrugged. It wasn't an objection, so it felt like a win— score one for Mom.

"And when we visit Moushoom, we can see if he has some other suggestions. There are probably cousins we don't even know about here. Not as many as at home—in Winnipeg—but you might be able to connect with someone."

Christina's head went up. "When are we going to go see Moushoom? That's one of the reasons you said we should move here. Well, we're here, so when are we going to go see him?"

Margie didn't even have all of their boxes unpacked. But she was glad that Christina wanted to see her great-grandfather. Other kids might roll their eyes and say they didn't want to visit some old person in a nursing home. Though it wasn't a nursing home. It was an independent living facility. Margie and some of the cousins had been worried about his still living on his own. It was hard to tell from so far away whether he still had all of his faculties or whether he should have more care and supervision. Someone looking after him and making sure he took his pills and ate what he should.

"I was going to suggest that we go out for burgers to celebrate your first day of school and my first homicide. Or… commiserate. I don't suppose 'celebrate' is the right word."

"Yeah? And then go see Moushoom? Maybe we could take him a burger; I bet he would like that."

Margie hesitated. "I don't know if he is on a special diet. We'd better find that out before we take him any food. But we could get some supper and then go see him afterwards."

Christina nodded her approval at this. "Where are we going to go?"

"I don't really know what's good. There are a ton of ethnic restaurants on Seventeenth Avenue. They call it International Avenue. But if we're going to go see Moushoom, maybe we should just get something quick, so we're not stuck waiting for an hour for our food. There's an A&W. You like their burgers."

"Do they have a veggie burger?"

Margie frowned at her. "A veggie burger? Maybe, I don't know."

"I decided I want to be vegetarian."

That was a bit of a shock. Christina had always enjoyed her meat. And even hunting. Margie hadn't seen that one coming. Her brain immediately spun into high gear. Was Christina flirting with an eating disorder? Looking for ways to cut her food intake or calories? Would she be able to get the protein she needed on a vegetarian diet? Teen girls needed plenty of iron if they didn't want to be anemic.

But she answered as calmly as she could. It was probably just a passing phase. This week, Christina would be vegetarian, and next week, she would be ordering a rack of ribs.

"I'm sure they must have a veggie burger." Stella barked from outside the back door, and Margie took a couple of steps toward it to let her in. "Why don't you look it up on your phone and make sure they have what you want? Then we can head over."

She opened the door and let Stella in. She scratched her floppy ears and cuddled her black and brown face, asking, 'Who's a good girl?' Then Stella noticed that Christina was home and launched herself at her. Christina squealed and laughed and wrestled with Stella. Margie smiled at the two of them. Stella was good therapy at the end of a rough day.

A&W did have a veggie burger, and it was pretty good. Christina gave Margie a bite and, despite her hesitation, Margie found that it tasted pretty much just like a regular beef burger. This made her wonder how much beef was in a regular beef burger and how much was fillers of some kind. You wanted breadcrumbs or something to help give it a good texture and moisture, but not too much.

"That's great," Margie observed. "Maybe I'll get one next time." She nearly patted her stomach and commented on getting too thick around the middle, but stopped herself. She didn't want Christina to start worrying about her weight or to model her own thoughts about her body after negative comments her mother made.

Christina finished her burger in a few more bites and dabbled some remaining fries in the puddle of ketchup. "Where does Moushoom live? Is it far away?"

Calgary was the big city. Not like the population of New York, of course, but it was bigger than Winnipeg, and it sprawled over hundreds of square kilometers. It could take an hour to drive across the city. Margie smiled. "He's very close. We'll drive over today, but you can walk there from the house. You can go see him any time you want."

Christina smiled broadly at that. "Really? That's awesome."

She loved her Moushoom. They cleared away their garbage and went back to the car. Margie used the GPS even though she knew it was close. She didn't want to head in the wrong direction. Once she had been there a few times, she would be able to get there without instructions. For a descendant of Cree women and explorers, Margie had a terrible sense of direction.

MARGIE SCANNED the signs on the door to the building. They were, of course, required to wear masks while visiting. There was a hand sanitizing station to wash before going up to the living quarters and upon leaving, to protect both their loved ones and themselves. There was a long list of symptoms. *If you have experienced a new cough, fever, upset stomach, trouble breathing…*

But no unexpected rules. Nothing about having to quarantine for fourteen days if they had come from out of the province. That was a relief. She had been secretly worried about it, even though she had told Christina that she could visit whenever she wanted to. They already had their masks on, so they rubbed gel into their hands and continued on to the elevators.

Moushoom was sitting in an easy chair, watching the TV when they arrived. He hollered for them to come in rather than getting up to answer the door. When he saw they were visitors rather than staff, he sat up straighter.

"Who's there?"

"It's Margie and Christina, Moushoom," Margie informed him. Christina stepped forward to hug him, but Margie touched her to prevent her. "We have to be careful of infection," she reminded.

Christina shook her head. "I'm going to hug him! I'll hold my breath, and I just washed my hands. I'm not going to infect him!"

Moushoom eagerly accepted a hug from Christina. "Is it really little Christina? But you were just a little girl the last time I saw you!"

"That was two summers ago. I… grew up."

"Yes, you did." Moushoom released his hold on her and looked her over. "You are turning into a lovely young lady. Your mother must be very proud."

"Isn't she?" Margie agreed. She drew a couple of chairs over so they could sit close—but not too close—to him. "We have a surprise for you."

"A bigger surprise than this? I didn't think they would even let people travel right now. Everything has been so crazy with the pandemic."

"A bigger surprise than this."

Margie looked at the old man with great affection. He still looked just the same as she remembered him. He wore his buckskins, bead-work, and sash proudly. He was always reminding them of their heritage. Telling them not to forget their history and where they had come from. It was all important. It wasn't just where they had come from; it was a piece of who they were. Maybe he was a little shrunken, a little more gray than she remembered him, but other-wise, he looked exactly the same. Her own Moushoom.

"What could it be? What is it?"

"We bought a house just a few blocks from here," Christina burst out. "So we can come and visit you all the time."

His eyes widened in surprise and delight. "Are you pulling my leg? How could that be? You lived in…" It took him a minute to dredge it up, "in Winnipeg."

"We did," Margie agreed. "But I got a job with Calgary homicide. And now we live here."

"That's great!" Moushoom enthused. "It will be so great to have you close by!"

CHAPTER FIVE

Margie wasn't thinking that it was so great when she was driving downtown before dawn the next morning to get a head start on her investigation. She felt guilty about having gone home so early the day before, leaving the rest of the team to handle the investigation while she went home to be with her family. No one had complained, but of course they would be watching her to see whether it was a regular thing and whether she was going to take advantage of them. They probably figured that she would have some special privileges, being female and Métis, because if they complained about her, they could be accused of being sexist and racist, of not understanding how difficult things were for her as a single mom and a minority.

She didn't want to reinforce those stereotypes. She had always been a hard worker. She hated to be classified as a 'lazy Indian' and did everything she could to avoid being seen that way, even if it meant putting in more hours and effort than anyone else on the team. Even when it meant driving to work while it was still pitch black outside, with not even a sliver of light on the horizon.

Calgary's cold and changeable weather destroyed the roads, the water seeping into cracks and then expanding when it froze there, widening the gaps even more. It was too difficult to do roadwork when it was thirty below. As the joke went, there were two seasons in Calgary: winter and construction. So Margie avoided the potholes, lost her lanes due to construction pylons and tape, and followed detour signs until she finally made it downtown and pulled into the underground parking. The lighting was dim, but what could be safer than a police parkade? There wouldn't be anyone lurking around there looking to cause trouble.

She sat down at her desk and checked her physical and electronic inboxes to see what had come in the afternoon before or overnight that she could start working on. She saw that videos had been loaded onto the server space for the new case. Lots of video. That was great, possibly giving them a way to narrow down the time of the murder and who had been in the area at that point. And it was also bad because it meant that she would be staring at the screen for a long time, processing hours of videos from various camera feeds.

Detective Siever had sent her an email outlining what video had been uploaded. She tried to remember his face. Middle-aged, round face, buzz cut. He had seemed like a nice guy when they had been introduced.

Camera feed 8302 is the camera closest to the crime scene. Start with that.

Bless you, Detective Siever. Margie started with the video prefaced with 8302. It ran from midday until about the time that Margie had reached the scene. That was what, eighteen hours of video? Margie breathed out slowly, trying to figure out how to approach it. She wasn't going to start at the beginning. Midday was way too early. There would have been a lot of people and dogs through the park at that time. Since the body had not been discovered until early the next morning, she had to assume that Robinson had been killed either shortly before or sometime after the park had closed. Referring to the park's website, she found that to be ten o'clock.

She started at the end of the video and began scrubbing backwards. She watched as all of the emergency responders backed out of the scene and the frame was empty except for a man and a dog. They reversed off the screen. Margie could not see Robinson's body with the distance and angle of the camera location, but she could see approximately where it was. Not right on the pathway, but a ways into the woods. She scrubbed backwards some more, watching for anyone else walking along the pathway or through the camera frame. There was one passerby in the wee hours of the morning, and she stopped and played the video at normal speed to watch a homeless man push a shopping cart loaded high with garbage bags past the camera. He didn't leave the pathway or deviate from his course. Margie made a notation of the time and a short explanation and continued to scrub backwards.

No golf carts. No other homeless people. No sign of Robinson himself. Back, and back, and back, until she crossed the time stamp for ten o'clock. Margie hesitated, wondering if she had missed something. But it was possible that the homicide had occurred before ten o'clock, so she kept going. She started to see the last few stragglers before the park had closed. She froze the video and took screenshots, getting the best pictures she could of the people leaving the park, walking toward the camera. She made notes of the timestamps and quick descriptions of the people. Woman with dog. Couple walking hand-in-hand. Man in hoodie. Cyclist. Skateboarding kid. Then she reached a point in the tape where there were people both coming and going, which made it more complicated. The last few people who had taken their late-evening walks on that pathway. Some of them she recognized because she had already seen them leave. The couple walking hand-in-hand. Skateboarding kid.

Then the victim. Margie watched him walk by the camera. His back was to it so that she couldn't see his face, but he had been wearing a coat. It was getting chilly in the evenings. Down to six degrees lately. She paused the video and searched for the photos taken at the scene to compare the man's attire to Robinson's. It was him, or someone dressed exactly the same way. She noted the time. She now had a much better idea of the time of death. Sometime after eight-thirty. Probably between eight-thirty and ten. Unless the killer was the homeless guy she had seen after ten. There hadn't been anyone else around. Not visible on that camera.

She watched Robinson walk down the path and wander off into the woods. Not taking pictures. Not, as far as she could tell, meeting someone else. Sneaking off to relieve himself? Just enjoying the green trees and lengthening shadows? Going to a favorite clearing to meditate or walking to the edge of the river she had seen when scouting the area earlier?

He didn't come back into sight after disappearing off of the screen. He had been killed out of view of the camera. Margie let the video play forwards, watching each of the people who arrived and left the park after Robinson. Was one of them the killer, or had he managed to avoid cameras? Was it a planned attack? Had the killer scoped out all of the cameras first and then avoided them? She thought about the injury. A single stab in the middle of the body. Not multiple wounds. Not someone who had gone for the throat or had been aiming for the heart. What did that signify? A professional hit? An accident? A lucky shot? It didn't strike her as a crime of passion. Not that a death in the middle of the park sounded like a crime of passion anyway, but she hadn't ruled it out completely.

As the video rolled forward, she made sure that she had noted the arrivals and departures in her list and hadn't missed anyone. She scrutinized the faces she could see. Anyone who was upset? Angry? Overwrought?

She didn't like the people whose faces she could not see. People with masks, baseball caps, the guy with the dark hoodie. She wanted to be able to see their expressions, to be able to identify them if she saw them again. She wanted to compare the faces to those she'd had taken of the bystanders in the morning. Had one of them stuck around to watch what happened once the body was discovered?

"Patenaude. Detective Patenaude. Pat. Hey. Patenaude!"

Margie pulled her focus from the video to the room. People had arrived without her taking any notice of the fact. Cruz was leaning close, trying to get her attention. When she finally heard him and saw him, Cruz chuckled and shook his head at the rest of the team.

"Now that's focus!"

"Sorry, I was lost in my own little world," Margie apologized.

"We have a morning briefing. You ready?"

"Uh… yeah. Give me just a minute." Margie looked at her watch and then at the papers and notes scattered around her. Morning briefing, and it wouldn't just be MacDonald briefing the team, but Margie briefing him on what they had accomplished so far, sharing progress with the rest of the team, and making assignments. It was one reason she had wanted to get there as early as she could to get a head start on the work she had left incomplete the afternoon before.

"Five minutes," Cruz advised. "And Mac doesn't like people to be late."

"I'll be there."

Margie tried to gather her notes together in some semblance of order. She looked at herself in her phone camera to make sure that she looked presentable.

"Funny time to take a selfie," Jones commented. "You should be getting a move on it."

"Not a selfie. Just making sure I look okay."

"Look fine to me. Let's go." Jones motioned toward the conference room. Margie took a deep breath and preceded Jones into the room. She was momentarily disconcerted by the fact that everyone was standing around the table, no one sitting down. Was this some kind of chivalrous behavior? The men waiting until the women were seated, or showing Margie respect because it was her case or her first briefing? She reached to pull one of the chairs out, and Jones put her hand on Margie's arm.

"No, it's a stand-up meeting."

"A stand-up meeting?" Margie repeated stupidly, trying to process it.

"MacDonald says we think better on our feet. It keeps anyone from falling asleep and ensures that meetings are as quick as they can be."

"Okay, then." Margie put her papers down on the table in front of her and waited, like everyone else, standing around the table.

Staff Sergeant MacDonald entered the room. A tall man with short-cropped gray hair, thin-rimmed glasses, and a deeply lined face. He looked around at the team and nodded briskly. "Let's get to it, then. How are we doing on the Fish Creek Park case?" He consulted his notes. "Jerry Robinson."

Everyone's eyes turned to Margie. She cleared her throat. "We are still waiting for the full postmortem results, but apparent cause of death was a single stab wound to the abdomen. Robbery does not appear to be a motive. No missing person report had been filed and there was no answer when Cruz knocked on his door, so we suspect that he lived alone; no partner or children. I have been going through video. I'm still just beginning my review of the video, but I believe I have identified Robinson entering the area at 8:23 p.m."

There were murmurs from the team.

"If it's him, that helps quite a bit with the time of death."

"Yes. We'll get confirmation from the medical examiner, but I don't think she'll be able to narrow it down any more than that. I've been making notes of everyone else that I can see entering or leaving after Robinson's arrival—looking for any aberrant behaviors, emotion, someone who is running or appears distressed. Nothing so far. I don't see anyone who seems to be out of place or behaving strangely."

"No one covered in blood?" Cruz joked.

Margie shook her head. "Sorry, no. No one covered in blood. No one who seems to be in too much of a hurry. There are not a lot of park-goers there after Robinson, so it isn't a huge pool of suspects, but of course, it's going to take some work to identify them all."

"They're probably mostly regulars," Jones suggested. "If we were to go back there around the same time tonight, we could probably get ID's on a good number on them, and maybe some suggestions on how to find the others from the regulars. These are probably people who are local who use the park all the time."

Margie nodded. "Good idea. You're probably right. We might be able to narrow down the suspects that way—if it was me, and I had killed someone in the park, I probably wouldn't go back there. Not for a while, anyway."

MacDonald gave a nod. "You may be right there. Let's get some people canvassing there tonight. Who is available?"

Margie indicated she was. Christina would be home from school. There would be time for supper and for Christina to get settled in on her homework. She was old enough to be left alone while Margie went back out to canvass the park for a couple of hours looking for witnesses and trying to match faces to names. Most of the rest of the team indicated that they would be able to help. A dedicated bunch. No one complained about not being able to spend the evening with their families or watching the NHL playoffs.

They had a lot of work ahead of them if they were going to crack the case.

CHAPTER SIX

*C*hristina was less angry when she arrived home than she had been the first day of school, but she was still sullen about having to move there and obviously not enjoying the new school yet. Margie had been hoping that she would have made at least one friend, which would help her to get through the first few weeks of school until she started to feel more at home. But apparently, that was not in the cards. Maybe in another day or two, Christina and another new girl would gravitate toward each other, or she would be admitted into one of the already-established circles of friends.

These things took time.

They had a quick meal of tacos made with microwaved beans.

"I'm going to take Stella for a quick walk out on the pathway," Margie told Christina. "Do you want to come with us?"

Christina hesitated. Margie didn't push it. The last thing she needed to do was make Christina think that Margie wanted her to go with her. That would just convince her to shut herself in her room and refuse to go out. Margie stayed casual about it, going to the door to put on her shoes and calling Stella for walkies.

"I guess I can come," Christina said eventually. "I don't have that much homework tonight. It's too early for them to be assigning anything big. They have to figure out where everyone is first. Since people are coming from all different schools," she pointed out.

Margie nodded. "That makes sense," she agreed. "They'll need to do some remedial stuff and to get everyone on the same level first, won't they? At least with some basics."

Christina petted Stella and scratched her soft brown ears before picking up her own shoes. "We should get some moccasins like Moushoom's."

"I don't know how they would fare on the pathways. You wouldn't want them to be ruined."

"They're meant to be worn outside."

Margie nodded. She was glad to see Christina showing some interest in the traditional clothing. She didn't expect Christina to start wearing a sash to school, but she liked that Christina was aware of her culture and felt positive about what she saw Moushoom doing. A lot of kids might have just thought him a funny old man.

Margie clipped on Stella's leash, and they headed out the door. It was only a couple of blocks to the pathway. Most of the houses in the area were older, built in the late fifties or early sixties. The little bungalows all looked pretty similar. But with a view of the city skyline in the distance, and the Rocky Mountains beyond that, the lots along Twenty-Sixth Street were only fifteen minutes from downtown. Professionals were beginning to buy the little post-war houses, razing them to the ground and replacing them with designer mini-mansions. And why not? As the city council forced people to build up instead of out, people had to find a way to build their dream homes within the city limits.

"Look at that one!" Christina pointed to one of the big houses fronted with lots of tinted glass. She whistled and shook her head. "I can't believe anyone would spend the money to build something like that in the middle of the hood."

"I told you, it is not a hood."

Christina rolled her eyes.

Stella was enjoying herself, sniffing at the grass and weeds beside the pathway, wandering out as far as Margie would let her.

"It's an off-leash area," Christina told her, watching another dog playing chase with a ball. "You should let her run."

"Maybe when I know the area better. Right now… I'm not sure how responsible other people are with their dogs. You wouldn't want her to get hurt because someone else lets their dog off-leash when they shouldn't."

"Nothing would happen."

"That's what everyone always thinks. But some people are not responsible, and animals can turn in an instant, do something completely out of character because they felt threatened or excited by something."

They walked for a while in silence. There was a little viewing platform up ahead—a sort of a look-out point. Margie decided to check it out.

They stood looking down at Deerfoot and the Bow River and out at the city skyline glowing orange from the setting sun and, in the distance, the shadowy mountains.

"Isn't it gorgeous?" a man said. "No two sunsets are alike. I've heard that Calgary has some of the best in the world. I'm no world traveler, so I don't have much to compare it to, but this…" he gazed out at the city. "I never get tired of it."

Margie nodded. She studied his profile as he looked at the sunset. He wasn't wearing a mask. Mid-thirties or early forties. Good looking. Friendly and outgoing, apparently. A guy who probably would have shaken her hand before the pandemic. At his side was a large dog—a mutt like Stella, not something that Margie could classify.

"It is beautiful," she agreed. She looked at her watch. She should be heading back to Fish Creek Park to help canvass for witnesses and identify the faces caught on the tape.

"Oscar," the man said. "And this is Milo." He indicated the dog.

"I'm Margie. And this is my daughter, Christina, and Stella."

"You're not old enough to have a teenage daughter," Oscar challenged in a teasing tone.

"Well, that's a nice compliment. But believe me, I'm old enough and I feel it!"

Christina rolled her eyes as if she were being disparaged. "She was really young when she had me." In an *it's not my fault* tone.

"I don't remember seeing either of you here before. Do you live around here?"

"Just moved into the neighborhood," Margie agreed, making a motion back the way they had come. "Christina's been complaining about it, but I really like this." She looked out at the sky and the river. "And Fish Creek Park. I was just there this morning, and it's beautiful. Amazing to have such a big park right in the middle of the city."

"We're lucky to have these green spaces," Oscar agreed. He turned and pointed behind them, across Twenty-Sixth Street. "I'm just over there. If you cross here, there is a little park. There's a pond, a little waterpark for the kids, and volleyball courts with sand. A little gem hardly anybody knows about."

"Can we go over there?" Christina asked, moving away from them toward the crosswalk.

"I need to get home," Margie told her apologetically. "We can check it out tomorrow. But I have some work I need to do tonight."

Christina gave a heavy sigh. Life was hard for the kids of cops and working mothers.

CHAPTER SEVEN

ish Creek Park had a different feeling as darkness started to fall and closing time approached. It was quiet. Voices carried, so people whispered or spoke in lowered tones as they walked. It was a slower pace, and the tang of wood smoke hung in the air from the campfires of earlier in the day.

Margie watched the shadows, thinking, drinking in the atmosphere. The weather conditions were almost the same as they had been the night Robinson was killed. She arrived at the same time as he had. She looked for the faces she had seen on the video surveillance, which she had carefully studied before arriving.

How easy would it have been for Robinson to be followed there by someone who intended to do him harm? He had left the pathway. She didn't know if he had still been visible from the path before he was killed. Maybe they should try a scene reconstruction just to test it out. Had his attacker gone there with the sole purpose of killing him? Had it been a drug deal or blackmail gone wrong? A quarrel between friends or lovers?

It wasn't robbery, that was about all Margie knew for sure. That, and it didn't look like a crime of passion.

She stopped a couple walking toward her, keeping the prescribed two meters away since they were not wearing masks. "Excuse me. You were here two nights ago?"

They looked at each other, nodding automatically but then not sure if they should talk to her.

"I'm a homicide detective," Margie explained, pulling out her ID and showing it to them. "There was someone killed here, did you hear about it?"

"Yeah, we did." The woman, blond, a little shorter than Margie, nodded again. "I couldn't believe it. That happened in our park, where we walk, around the time that we were here." She said it with a tone of disbelief, as if it couldn't possibly be true.

Margie murmured confirmation at this.

"We didn't see anything suspicious." The woman looked at the man, getting a nod from him. "It was a night just like any other. Nothing… There wasn't anything that alarmed us."

"Anything out of the ordinary that night?" Margie asked. "Sounds, smells? Someone you don't normally see walking around here? Someone who seemed out of place or lost? Sick or afraid?"

The man put his arm around the woman and tightened his grip, pulling her to him protectively. "No," his voice was strong, slightly challenging. "Don't you have any leads? How could something like this happen here? I assumed that… it was drugs. A gang. Something where they knew each other. You always hear that in police reports. 'The victim was known to the killer.' They knew each other, right?"

"We are still very early in the investigation. We're hoping that you can help us with some background. Identify the people who normally walk around this time, help us to narrow the scope."

"Like what?" the woman asked. "What do you need us to do?"

"First of all, if I could get your information. Name, address, phone number, in case I need to contact you with further questions later."

They were a little reluctant. People were brought up not to share their personal information with strangers. They grew up watching cop shows on TV where people were suspects or were framed by the police. It was scary for them to be part of an investigation.

But also exciting. She could see their excitement at the novelty of being part of the investigation. A homicide investigation. Something most people had only ever seen on TV or read about in books.

Margie took down their information. Elise and Roger Erickson. Married ten years and still walking hand in hand every night in the park.

"I have some pictures on my tablet. I wonder if you could look at them, tell me who are regulars. What you know about them."

"Sure." This was the good part. The part where they could help her to break the case. They looked intently at the tablet as Margie moved a bit closer and brought up the first of the pictures. "Oh, that's Bob," Elise said confidently. "He doesn't like bicycles."

"Bicycles?" Margie repeated, not understanding.

"Bob is the dog," Roger laughed. "I think the detective wants the name of Bob's owner."

Margie chuckled. "Yes. That would be helpful."

"I don't know his owner's name... I just know Bob's name, because I hear him calling him, especially when Bob wants to chase after a bike."

Margie wrote down the information she had. "They walk here often?"

"Most nights. Most of the people who walk at this time of night are regulars. Day-trippers come during the day. Family reunions and parties in the late afternoon and evening. The people who walk late at night or early in the morning, they're all pretty regular."

Margie swiped to the next person on the tablet. Elise and Roger studied it.

"I've seen him," Roger said, "but I don't know anything about him."

"You said you thought maybe it was something to do with drugs or gangs," Margie said. "Is that because you've seen drugs or gang activity in the park? Graffiti? People congregating? Something that makes you think that is going on?"

"No, I've never seen anything," Roger admitted. "I'm sure it goes on... it goes on everywhere, doesn't it? But I've never seen any drug deals going down or gangs. Or anything that I thought was. I just hoped... it isn't some crazy person, attacking at random..."

"I don't think that was the case here," Margie assured him. Very few homicides were random attacks. Maybe a robbery, someone with jewelry or a coat that made them look like they had a lot of money, but not random murders. "And if it is a serial killer, nobody has identified any pattern. Nothing that they had seen across a number of homicides."

They looked slightly reassured at this. Though Margie was kicking herself for using the words serial killer. That was only going to make them more worried, and they might use it when talking to other people, spreading the rumor that it was, in fact, a serial killer, when there was absolutely nothing to indicate that it was.

"If you could look at a few more people here..." She showed them the tablet again, swiping through the various people, most of whom they recognized. But they didn't have names to attach to a lot of them. At any rate, if they were frequent walkers in the park at that time of day, Margie would talk to them sooner or later.

She displayed the picture of the hooded figure. Elise shuddered. "Black hoodies always make me think of... Darth Vader or the Sith. Creepy, you know?"

"Do you recognize this person? We didn't get a very good picture of the face." Really, they hadn't captured anything of the face, just the hood and the shadows beneath it, as the hooded figure walked with head bowed past the camera. Margie didn't like it either. Not because it reminded her of the Sith, just because she didn't like anyone who appeared to have a reason to hide his face.

Who needed to hide his face in a park? Especially at night, when the shadows were already falling?

Maybe someone with a disfigurement. Otherwise, Margie couldn't think of a good reason, other than to avoid cameras and hide his identity.

"I've... I'm sure I've probably seen them here," Elise said slowly. "Not a lot, but a few times over the last week or two? Not every day. Or maybe he comes other times of the day, and not at the same time every night."

"Man or woman?" The figure was slim and could be either.

"A boy," Elise offered. "Not an adult. Maybe, sixteen? Umm...

black. Not just brown, but very dark skin. I don't know..." She looked at her husband. "Maybe that's what made you think of drugs or gangs? Young Black man in a hoodie… if you watch much TV, it's sort of a trope." She shrugged, embarrassed. "I'm not racist; I'm not saying every kid in a hoodie is a drug dealer."

"I don't think it was anything like that," Roger protested, raising his hands in a 'stop' or 'surrender' motion. "I just wondered about drugs or gangs because it seems like that's where a lot of the violence stems from. Not because I saw him." He jerked his chin toward the hooded figure on the tablet and scratched the back of his neck. "I'm not judging anyone."

"We'll follow up on every possible lead. So you don't know his name or what area he lives in? Was he ever here with someone else?"

"No." They both looked at each other for confirmation and shook their heads at the same time. "No, we never talked to him or left at the same time. And he's always alone."

Margie thanked them for their time when they were finished looking through all of the pictures. Even though she didn't have many names or details, she felt like she was making progress. Lots of the people whose pictures she had clipped would be walking through the park just then. Margie would find them and talk with them, slowly gathering identities and alibis and sorting out who she felt was suspicious and warranted further attention.

THE CANVASS SLOWED TO A TRICKLE, and then a stop. There was no one left on the pathways but the detectives themselves. They converged and began comparing notes as they walked back to their vehicles.

"Some nice folks out here," Jones commented. She seemed to be walking a little gingerly, and Margie watched her, trying to figure out whether she had turned her ankle or had blisters or something else. "Reminds me that I don't take advantage of the parks around here often enough. We complain about being stuck in the city, but there is all of this… wilderness right here in the middle of it."

"I was really excited about that when I started to look at Calgary," Margie agreed. "I like walking and hiking and biking, and I'm looking forward to being able to check out the different parks and pathways in Calgary. There are so many places to go."

"I *think* that I like walking until I'm actually on my feet for a few hours like this," Jones said. "And then my feet start to hurt, and I start to chafe, and then I realize that I really *don't* like it very much at all."

Margie laughed. "Don't go right from being sedentary to walking for a few hours. Do it gradually; your body will adjust."

Jones smoothed her hands over her broad hips and grimaced. "Yeah. One step at a time," she agreed.

"Who on your list do you want to follow up on?" Siever asked. "We still have lots more video that we can check. Spy on people the whole time they were at the park."

"There are a few I'd like to look into further," Margie admitted. "Of course, everyone who wasn't here tonight, but the man with the pit bull and the young man in the hoodie in particular."

"Don't tell me you have a thing about pitties," Siever challenged, "sweetest disposition you ever saw…"

"I didn't say anything in particular about the dog or the breed," Margie said. "Everybody has their own opinion about that. I just mean I'd like to take a closer look at the owner. He rubbed me the wrong way. I want to explore the possibility that he might have gotten into an argument with Mr. Robinson."

"Could have," Siever agreed, nodding. "He didn't look like the most laid-back guy."

"But why would he come to walk in the park if he was that irritable?" Jones asked. "If you're spoiling to pick a fight, why go to a park? Why not a bar or somewhere else he could have blown off some steam?"

Siever shrugged. "Maybe he didn't want to get in a fight. Maybe he was trying to work off whatever stress he was feeling so that he could relax and *not* get in a fight."

"I suppose."

"Walking somewhere like this is peaceful. Get in touch with your serenity. Put all of the stress of the day behind you."

Jones nodded. "Okay. Maybe."

"I'd still like to look into him further," Margie repeated.

"Of course. We'll see if we can spot him on some of the other video, follow him back, see where he came from and went to and the times. Everyone we have pictures of was here at roughly the right time. We can't eliminate anyone just by having one conversation with them."

No, there would be a lot of footwork and further discussions to eliminate people from their lists. Like all police work, it was long hours of tedium, followed by moments of intense action or terror. It would take a long time to look through the videos to find everybody and identify their movements, and then try to find any connections with Robinson other than that they had just happened to be in the park at the same time.

Could anyone put them together? Did they walk together? Have a business? Were they friends? Lovers? Enemies? In a club? Share a vice? Lots of questions to be asked.

Margie was watching videos again the next morning. The camera locations had been plotted on a map, which was helpful, so that she could try to find people again after they walked off of one camera. Follow the trail until it came to another camera, and then watch for them to appear there. If they didn't appear, then look at some of the places it might branch off to a different location. Or had they gone off trail completely, and wouldn't reconnect with it again for several hours?

It was tedious work, but she created a profile for each person who had been at the park at the same time as Robinson, included their picture and, if they had it, the person's name and any other details they had. She ignored, for the time being, anyone who they had gathered identification and contact details from. It was more important to track down the people who hadn't come forward or returned to the park as usual. Those were the people who were more likely to have had something to do with Robinson's death. Someone who hoped that by staying away for a few days, or permanently, that he would be able to distance himself from the investigation and maybe stay below the radar.

She had identified the man with the pit bull by following his images on the videos back to the parking lot and getting the license plate from his car. That was a lucky break. With the name on the car's registration, she was able to look up his driver's license and confirm that it matched the face on the video. They would gather his contact information and pay him a visit.

Margie was having a more difficult time with the boy in the hoodie. She peered at the screen, trying to track him as he moved from one camera to another like a ghost. His dark outfit blended in with the shadows, and he drifted rather than walked along the pathway.

"Any luck?" Cruz's voice at Margie's shoulder made her startle. She looked around at him, blowing out her breath.

"You mind not sneaking up on me? Next time I might go for my gun."

He raised his brows, knowing full well that her gun was locked away while she was at her desk, the same as everyone else's. It wasn't really much of a threat. Margie shook her head.

"Working on it. Fitting together one piece of the puzzle at a time."

"You think this kid had anything to do with it?" He indicated the screen.

Margie took a deep breath, studying the young man on the monitor as if it were the first time she had seen him. "I really don't. What reason would he have to be involved with someone like Robinson? An adult. A welder. Not the kind of person he would have hung out with. No sign that it was robbery or drugs. A random attack? It's possible, but I don't think so."

"But you're still going to track him down."

"Of course."

Cruz nodded. "Have fun."

"You're welcome to take a video any time you like. I don't mean to hog all of the fun stuff."

He grinned. "No, no, you're the new one here. You should have the opportunity for as much investigative work as you want." He straightened his shirt, a bold pink color that apparently was no threat to his manhood.

"There's plenty to go around. I promise."

"I've got other files to work. This is your first, so you can put your full attention into it," he told her sagely, smiling but no longer joking. "See what you can dig up."

Margie went back to work trying to track the hoodie boy.

AFTER TRACKING the boy's walk through the park, they needed more. He had not taken a vehicle into the park, but had walked in. Video from traffic cams, security surveillance, private householders, whatever they could get. That meant Margie and the other detectives getting out on the street to spot all of the cameras they could and to track him half a block at a time as they backtracked his arrival and then requesting the video from the owner. The footage taken in the daylight hours when he had arrived was much easier to see than the nighttime footage after he had left.

More than once, she asked herself why she was doing it. They had a lot of people they hadn't yet eliminated. She was working on them too. But the boy who had arrived on foot with his face hidden was suspicious. He wasn't there with friends, wasn't there to work out, and appeared to be intentionally hiding his face from the cameras or the other patrons of the park. What was he doing there?

"Got him!" Jones said, banging her keyboard and sitting back in her chair.

Margie looked over at her. "Got him?"

"The boy. I have him coming out of a house." Jones smiled like the cat who caught the canary, then gave Margie the address.

"Shall we go check it out?" Margie suggested.

"You want me to come?"

"You're the one who got the address. I think you should. Unless you don't want to…"

"Oh, I want to!" Jones pushed back from her desk. "Let's do it."

MARGIE LOOKED at her watch as they arrived at the house. It was afternoon and, if they were lucky, the boy would be home from school. Back in Forest Lawn, Christina would be getting on the bus. It would be half an hour before she was home. Hopefully, this boy's school was within walking distance of his home. From what she had seen, though, the newer areas were farther away from schools. Or the boy might be one of the kids accessing online schooling during the pandemic and was therefore home during the day.

She raised her hand and knocked loudly on the door. A good, authoritative knock. The kind that made people take notice instead of deciding that since they weren't expecting any friends or deliveries, they would just ignore the door and hope that the salesperson or missionaries went on to the next house.

In about half a minute, she could hear footsteps from within, and a man came to the door. Tall and skinny. Taller than the boy on the footage. Not a teenager. His skin was very dark, just as the boy's had been reported to be. Margie decided to go with it.

"We're here looking for your son, is he home?" she asked.

He looked confused. "My son?" Then he gave his head a little shake. "Oh. Yes. Abdul."

Abdul. Margie made a mental note of it. The man had a thick accent. She wasn't sure where he was from. "Is Abdul home?"

"No. He's not back from school yet." The man looked to the side as if studying something. "He is not working today, so he will probably be home in… about half an hour?"

"Could we come in, please? We should probably talk to you before he gets home."

He looked down, frowning. Searching for a way to tell them no. He didn't want the police in his house. He didn't seem curious to know what they wanted with his son; he just wanted them to leave. Wanted a way to tell them to go. But after standing there silently for a few uncomfortable seconds, he stepped back and opened the door farther to allow them entrance.

Margie and Jones stepped in. The living room was plainly furnished. An older couch and some easy chairs. A TV on a stand. A colorful tapestry hung on the wall, and another draped over the couch, but there were no paintings or prints. The man made a motion toward the couch. Margie looked around once more. She didn't hear anyone else in the house. She didn't see any sign of drugs, weapons, or anything else that raised red flags. She met Jones's eyes to make sure she felt the same way and didn't see any concerns there. They sat down.

"What's your last name?" Margie asked, pulling out her notepad and writing *Abdul* on a fresh page.

"Paul."

"Paul is your last name?" she checked. "Not your first?"

He nodded. "Sadiq is my first name."

"Sadiq Paul?" Margie spelled it out as she wrote it, and he nodded his agreement. But the way that his eyes stayed on her face, she wondered if she had spelled too fast and he was still trying to catch up with her. English was not his first language.

"And is that Abdul's last name too?"

"No." He shook his head. "Abdul's last name is James."

"Got it." Margie wrote it down. "Did he take his mother's name, then?"

The man gave a shrug that Margie wasn't sure how to interpret. Yes, it was his mother's name? Or there was some other reason he had a different last name?

"Can you tell me where Abdul was three nights ago?"

"Three nights. He was here. He is always here. This is his home."

"Before bed," Margie clarified. "Say, between school and bedtime. He wasn't here the whole time."

"No. It takes time for him to get home from school. And some nights he works." This time, Margie saw the schedule on the whiteboard he had been looking at previously. Her eyes went to the night of Robinson's death. No shift was noted for Abdul. He should have been home.

"Where would he have gone if he wasn't working? He doesn't come straight home."

"He comes home for supper. Always home for supper, if he's not working."

"And then he goes out again after that?"

"Sometimes," Sadiq agreed.

"Where does he go when he goes out again in the evening and he doesn't have work?"

"I don't ask him. Sometimes, just walking around the neighborhood. Maybe to a friend's house. Sometimes to the park."

"Fish Creek Park?"

"Yes." His head turned in the direction of the park. "It's a good place to walk. To… reconnect with yourself after a long day."

"Do you go with him?"

"No." Sadiq shook his head firmly. "I don't get in his way. He wants to walk alone."

"I see. So you don't supervise him and you don't ask him to account for where he has been."

Sadiq shook his head and didn't offer any explanation. Maybe that was normal in the culture and background he came from. Many Indigenous parents let their children explore on their own and take care of themselves much more than their white counterparts. It taught interdependence with the land. Learning to live in harmony with others and the environment. Perhaps it was the same where this man came from. Margie wrote a few notes.

"Maybe while we are waiting for Abdul to get home, we could see his room."

Sadiq didn't move. Margie waited. He didn't offer any objection or give permission. Margie cut her eyes toward Jones. Did his silence indicate consent? Could they go ahead and look for Abdul's room, and if Sadiq didn't object, take that as his consent to a search? Or at least to a look around at what was in plain sight? Jones grimaced, not offering her opinion one way or the other.

Margie didn't feel right about it. There was, if nothing more, a communication gap. She didn't want to get herself in trouble for an illegal search and risk having important evidence thrown out.

"Could we look at Abdul's room?" she asked more plainly.

Sadiq looked at her. At first, she thought he was going to shrug, still not understanding exactly what she wanted from him, and that shrug might be able to be taken as consent. But he didn't shrug. He shook his head.

"We can't see Abdul's room?" Jones pressed. "What are you trying to hide?"

"It is not my place to give permission for you to see his room. That is his space. He can decide when he is here."

So they waited. Margie thought of more questions about Abdul and asked them here and there, but was no closer to understanding the situation of the father and son than she had been when he answered the door. Was there a wife and mother around? There didn't seem to be. Had Abdul always been with Sadiq, or was it a recent development?

"Where did you come here from?"

Sadiq considered, not answering immediately. Was he worried they would judge him? Eventually, he decided to answer.

"We are from the Sudan."

And then Abdul was there. Margie hadn't even heard the door open and close, and Abdul was standing just a few feet away from her, the black hood pulled up over his head just as it had been when he had walked through the park. Maybe the permanent state of affairs. He had on a black bandana mask, pulled up high, so that when she looked into the depths of the hood, all she could see was the glitter of his eyes.

"Abdul." Margie got to her feet, and the boy took a couple of quick steps back. "No, it's okay. We just wanted to talk to you."

He looked at his father and then back at Margie again. He pulled the bandana down to his neck, revealing fine features, midway between child and adult. Vulnerable and not yet the man's face he would grow into. But no longer quite a child, either.

"You are po-lice?" he asked in a soft voice, still high in pitch.

Margie tried to make her nod as reassuring as possible. She didn't want him running away. Kids tended to be anxious around the police even if they hadn't done anything against the law. It was part of the mindset at that age.

"Yes, we are both police detectives." She was glad she had brought Jones instead of one of the male detectives. They would not be as threatening to Abdul. "My name is Detective Patenaude and this is

Detective Jones. We wanted to ask you about your walk in the park the other day."

He studied Jones and then looked back at Margie. "What day? I walk in park many days."

"Three days ago. In the evening. You were there almost until closing time. Ten o'clock."

He nodded.

"Do you remember?"

A small shrug. A look around at his surroundings for confirmation that he was still safe in his own home. He sat down on the arm of Sadiq's chair. He pulled back his hood, revealing short-cropped curly black hair. There were scars on his face. Not abuse, she didn't think. Maybe a childhood accident. "I remember."

"I want you to think about whether you saw or heard anything unusual that night. Maybe... shouting or an argument? Somebody that you hadn't seen at the park before or who scared you. Anything... that we might be interested in."

"What is this about?" Sadiq asked, his pronunciation overly precise. She was surprised that he hadn't asked before. The police showed up at the door asking for his son and he didn't even ask why?

Margie didn't answer him, but pulled out her tablet and selected a picture of Robinson. Not a picture of his body, but the one from his driver's license. She held it up for Abdul. "Did you see this man?"

Abdul looked at it. He reached out tentatively and Margie handed it to him. He brought it close to his eyes, studying it. Was he supposed to wear glasses? When had he last had his vision checked? Maybe never. They were immigrants; maybe they hadn't availed themselves of the province's health services.

After a while, Abdul handed the tablet back. "I have seen this man before. Other days."

"But not three days ago?"

His shoulders lifted and fell. "I do not remember. That day?" He shook his head. "Maybe and maybe not. I know the face."

"Do you know his name? Have you ever stopped to talk to him?"

Abdul's eyes skittered away. "No," he said in a low voice. "Why would I talk to him? What reason would he have to talk to me?"

"The other day, when I was out in a park near my house walking my dog, another man who was walking his dog commented to me what a beautiful sunset it was. We talked for a few minutes, just about the sky and the park and what it was like to live in the neighborhood." She let him think about that for a minute. "Maybe you had a conversation like that with Mr. Robinson."

"No. He never stops me to tell me it is a beautiful day."

Put like that, it did seem a little silly. A man and a woman of similar age might stop to chat, but a white man and a Black teenager?

"You have a dog?" Abdul asked, showing interest in something for the first time.

"Yes." Margie smiled at him. "Would you like to see a picture?" She pulled out her phone, selected the photos app, and found one of Stella, mouth wide in a panting doggie grin as if she had been posing for the picture. She handed it over to Abdul.

A little smile formed on his face. He touched the screen lightly as if he could introduce himself to Stella that way or reach through the screen to pet her. He swiped, looking at other photos. "Is this your daughter?"

"Yes. She must be about your age. Are you fifteen? Sixteen?"

"Fourteen," he corrected. "I am very tall."

"Yes. You are tall for fourteen. Christina is fifteen." Margie reached over and took the phone out of his hands. He didn't need to be looking through the rest of her pictures. It wasn't like she had taken pictures of anything private or inappropriate. Or had crime scene photos on it. She just didn't think he needed to be looking at pictures of her life. They were there to talk about him. His life, and how Jerry Robinson's life had ended.

Abdul's hands fell to his lap and stayed there. He didn't fidget. He just watched them. Margie couldn't imagine this frail-looking fourteen-year-old having a fight with Robinson. Physical or verbal. He was shy and uncertain. He wouldn't have a reason to approach Robinson. He said they had never talked.

He didn't appear to have any concern about talking about being in the park that night. He probably hadn't even heard that there had been a death. If Sadiq had read about it in the paper or online, maybe he had hidden it from Abdul, deciding that he didn't need to be upset by it. But Margie suspected Sadiq didn't even read the news. It wouldn't be relaxing for him to read it in a language other than his native tongue.

"The reason that we're asking questions is that man I showed you died that night."

Abdul's eyes got wide. "He died?"

"Yes. He was killed."

Abdul looked at her for a moment as if trying to translate what she had said. Maybe he was. Perhaps the shades of meaning between *he died* and *he was killed* hadn't occurred to him before and needed some thought.

"Somebody killed him?" Abdul asked. "He not just..." He clutched at his chest, miming before he found the words. "Heart attack?"

"That's right. Somebody killed him."

"Was he shot?" Sadiq asked.

Margie shook her head. She looked at Abdul, waiting for his reaction. Watching for any recollection in his eyes of something that had happened that day. He looked at his father, considering his words, and then back at Margie again.

"That is very bad," he said. "But I do not know who hurt him."

He looked directly at her with his wide, brown eyes, and Margie did not sense any deception.

CHAPTER NINE

*B*ack at the office, Margie and Jones huddled with the other detectives who were there.

"I don't think it's the kid," Margie said. She looked at Jones. "Do you concur?"

Jones nodded slowly. "He didn't strike me as being guilty or evasive. Shy, yes, and feeling his way through things. He's clearly a recent immigrant, still learning the language and the culture."

"Is he in a gang?" Cruz asked. "That black hoodie has me wondering. Just what is he trying to hide? You know that one of the reasons bangers wear loose clothing is to hide weapons. And the hoods hide people's faces, make it harder for them to identify. You're sure that's not what's going on here? Sometimes immigrants band together for safety."

"He's probably cold," Jones said. "If he came here from an African country, then he's probably freezing, even when we would consider it warm. And at nightfall, it gets quite chilly. Under ten. I don't like to go out without a hoodie at that time."

"He was wearing a face mask," Margie said. "And that could indicate that he's trying to hide his identity… or just that he's following the rules for when he is at school or on the bus. He did take it off when we introduced ourselves."

"No suspicious behavior?" Cruz challenged. "You know that these kids can be pretty glib. They've always got a story, a disarming smile. They don't necessarily act like the hoods you see on TV."

"Not my first rodeo," Margie sighed. "I've dealt with plenty of gang kids in Manitoba. I don't think they're that different here. I didn't see any sign that he was affiliated with a gang or might have any sort of freelance drug business."

"And the father? It could be the parents. They need something to stay solvent. They get the kids to traffic, but it's really the parents who are the problem."

"No. Nothing that gave me any clue that there were illegal drugs. Or fencing or any other kind of illegal or quasi-legal side hustle I can think of. They appear to be new immigrants, just trying to start a new life for themselves."

Cruz nodded slowly. "Okay. So you're pretty sure that the kid didn't have anything to do with it. Too bad, I liked the dark hooded suspect. So it's back to the drawing board. We still have a few people we haven't been able to identify. A couple of cyclists. They would be able to get away from the scene more quickly. They could have gotten there from another part of the city, farther afield. Who else is on your suspicious persons list?"

"We have more people still on it than have been eliminated," Margie admitted. "I'll spend some time tomorrow trying to establish any connections between them and Robinson."

"Sounds like a plan," Mac contributed. He had remained silent up until that point. "I think we have as much from the video as we are going to get right now. We might have to review some footage down the line, but we only have a limited number of suspects. Like one of those closed-room mysteries. It shouldn't be too hard to figure out who had a grudge against Robinson."

"In those mysteries, everyone has a grudge," Margie said. "There is always a secret lover, an illegitimate baby, an angry business partner, a spy..."

"Then we'd better get to it," MacDonald said. "Or Inspector Poirot will beat us to it." He looked at his watch. "Tomorrow. Get a good sleep tonight and start fresh."

❧

"Can we check out that park today?" Christina asked as Margie slid on her shoes to take Stella out for a walk. "You know, the one with the pond," Christina reminded her, when Margie just looked at her blankly, trying to figure out if Christina meant she wanted to go to Fish Creek Park. "The one that Grouch guy told us about?"

"Oh!" Recollection started to return. "You mean… Oscar. The one with the dog, Milo."

"Yeah, Oscar." Christina giggled at her mistake. "That's what I meant. He said there was a park over there, by the viewing platform. Across the street."

"Okay. Sure. We can check it out. We don't have a lot of time before it gets dark, though, so we won't be able to stay and explore for long."

"Yay!" Christina slid on a pair of sandals. "I didn't know there was a waterpark so close. That will be nice when it's hot out."

Margie nodded her agreement and snapped the leash onto Stella's collar. "Okay, girl! Let's go! Let's go walkie."

Margie was cautiously optimistic. Christina seemed to be in better spirits today. Margie didn't ask whether Christina had had a good day at school or whether she had made some new friends. Questions like that just seemed to irritate the girl and remind her that she was supposed to be sullen and angry about the move. So they just walked, laughed at Stella's antics, looked at the houses and the other people enjoying the pathway, and talked about other things. When Christina was ready to talk about her classes or her friends, she would.

At the viewing platform, they turned and used the crosswalk across to the other side, to what a chiseled-rock sign declared to be Valleyview Park. They walked to the top of a little hill, looked down at the pond, at the playground enclosed in a fence, and the field and sand courts beyond it.

"I was expecting… like, waterslides." Christina's disappointment was evident. "Not just a little kids' splash park."

"I'm sorry. I had no idea what it would be like. I guess this is what passes for a waterpark in the hood," Margie said, hoping to raise a smile.

Christina rolled her eyes. "Well… let's at least walk around the pond."

There were soccer goals in the open field next to the pond. "This would be a good place to throw the ball around," Margie observed. "I don't want to do it over by the ditch, for fear Stella would run right off of the edge and hurt herself. But lots of space over there and away from any traffic."

"It would be good for balls or Frisbee," Christina agreed. She scratched Stella's ears. "Next time, we'll play here for a while."

They nodded and smiled at other people walking around the pond or sitting on the benches nearby. There were walkers, kids on tiny bikes, and an old man on an electric scooter who smiled and talked to everyone who approached him. Margie was enjoying the friendliness of Calgary. She was glad that she had taken the job there.

As they walked back home, Margie talked about Abdul. Not by name, of course, and not in connection with the Fish Creek Park murder. Just casually as a boy that she had talked to that day. She folded her arms, cuddling her sweatshirt closer, remembering how Jones had suggested Abdul was probably always cold after coming from a warmer climate.

"It would be a lot worse coming from Sudan than from Winnipeg," Christina admitted, staring off at the city skyline as they walked the path along Twenty-sixth Street toward home. "I mean… I'm looking forward to the Chinooks. To the winters being a lot easier than in Manitoba. And it would be like… a totally different culture. I might not have any friends here yet, but at least I know how things work, and what to expect at school and all that. Could he even read when he came here?"

"I have no idea. They didn't say he was in any special program at school, but I didn't ask, either. It was clear that English was not his native language."

"Ugh. I can't imagine having to learn a whole new language. Thanks for not moving to… Germany or something like that. Or Norway. It's cold there, right?"

"Yes, it gets cold there."

"I'm glad we stayed in Canada. Having to deal with all of that other stuff… that would be a lot harder."

Margie was glad to see that Christina could see she hadn't had it as bad as some people did. She really was a good girl. It was just hard to stay focused on everything she had to be grateful for.

They walked along in silence for a few minutes.

"Hey, there's the guy again. Milo and…?"

"Oscar." Margie waved as they got closer. "Hi, Oscar."

The dogs sniffed each other and pranced around. "Enjoying the weather?" Oscar asked.

"May as well enjoy it while we can. It's not going to last forever." Even though Margie was a little chilly in just a hoodie, she knew better than to complain about it. A few more weeks, and there would be snow on the ground and much lower temperatures.

"Yeah, you're right," Oscar agreed. "There's no keeping winter from coming."

And would business slow down with the cold weather? Margie knew that it wouldn't. Cold weather didn't stop people from killing each other. It might help with hiding bodies until the next melt, but people who were forced to live inside at close quarters tended to get on each other's nerves. And when they got into the pre-Christmas season, then not only would the murder rate go up due to the stress and other crazy stuff that happened around the holidays, but so would the suicide rate. And suicides were investigated by the homicide department. It would be a busy time—Christmas, New Year, and then the long, cold, interminable nights of February. Margie couldn't suppress a little shudder. Christina looked at her but didn't say anything.

They talked for a few more minutes with Oscar and Milo before returning home.

CHAPTER TEN

Margie would be glad to get home after a long day in front of her computer. Her time had been broken up with various phone calls and emails to follow up on possible leads, ask some more questions, and to establish either alibis for Robinson's murder or connections with him. Computer databases, web searches, talking to neighbors, Robinson's coworkers, and anyone who might be identified as friends. He seemed to have lived a pretty solitary life, and finding even tentative connections was a slog.

By the end of it, she felt like her brain had been wrung out. Her nerves and her emotions were raw. She needed to get home to her daughter and Stella, to spend some time outside in the fresh air and to move around and get some exercise. She had known that there would be a lot of desk work associated with homicide work. That just went with the territory.

As she put her office tools away into the drawers, she tried to mentally do the same with the day's stresses and worries. A ceremonial laying aside of her work life. She would try not to take any burdens home with her, but to go home lighter and happier.

She plugged her phone into the car stereo and tapped a few times to bring up her de-stress playlist. A broadly-ranging combination of

Métis fiddlers, classic rock, and rap to help exorcise the demons of the office.

The rest of the week, she had managed to get home before Christina, but this time the front door was unlocked and she knew she had worked too late. She glanced at her watch before entering.

"Hi, honey. Sorry to be so long today. How was school?"

There was no answer. Christina wasn't in the living room or kitchen. Margie went down the hallway to peek in Christina's door to see if she was doing her homework with her headphones on.

Christina wasn't in her bedroom. Margie's stomach clenched. She looked back toward the front door. She was sure she had locked it that morning. Christina was home. She wouldn't still be at school or on the bus that late. Christina had arrived home and had unlocked the door.

Margie continued down the hall to the bathroom, but the door stood ajar and it was clear that Christina was not there either.

"Christina? Are you here?"

Margie exited the hall into the kitchen.

"Christina?"

She heard a volley of barks from Stella in the backyard and blew out her breath in a sigh of relief. Of course, Christina had just taken Stella outside.

Then there was a shrill shriek of fear or alarm. Margie ran to the back door and out into the yard.

"Christina? What is it?"

Christina ran to her, colliding on the step and putting her arms around Margie.

"What is it? What's wrong?"

Christina made a sobbing, choking noise. Margie looked for Stella, worried that she had run out of the yard and been hit by a car in the back lane. But Stella was standing in the middle of the back yard, looking happy and relaxed, not understanding why her young master was upset. Margie didn't get it either. She pushed Christina away from her to look at her face.

"Christina! Talk to me!"

Christina shook her head. "No, it's okay," she said, even though her expression was still distressed. She seemed unable to say anything else to explain herself.

Margie hugged her, pulling her close again and holding Christina firmly to try to convey strength and calm to her. Christina sniffled a few times and then pulled back.

"It's fine. I'm okay. Everything is fine," she again reassured Margie.

"Okay. Take a deep breath and then tell me what happened."

"Come." Christina stepped back and gave Margie's arm a little tug to encourage her to follow. She walked across the yard toward Stella. Stella started to bound around excitedly, wanting to play or show off about something. Christina pointed to a clump of leaves on the grass.

Margie took a closer look and saw that it wasn't a clump of sod and dead brown grass, but the body of a dead squirrel.

"Oh." Margie sighed. "It's okay. I'll just get rid of it."

Christina made a face. "I thought it was just some twigs. I was going to pick up a stick to throw for Stella, and then I realized…" She gagged. "Ugh. I almost picked it up!"

And that had given her quite a start.

"Try not to keep visualizing it," Margie advised. "If you can distract yourself with other things, it won't be saved as such a vivid memory. The less you think about it, the faster it will fade."

Christina ran her hands over her face as if trying to wipe it away. "Will you…?" She made a motion toward the squirrel.

"I'll take care of it. Why don't you get started on some dinner? Just let me grab some paper towel first so that I won't be in your way."

They went back into the house. Margie called Stella in. She didn't want the dog to get in the way while she was trying to deal with the squirrel. Especially if Stella thought it was some new game for her and tried to take the squirrel back away from her.

"You stay in here," she told Stella sternly. "Go lie down. I'll get you a treat when I come back in."

"Mom?"

Margie looked at Christina.

"You don't think… Stella didn't kill it, did she?"

"No, I'm sure she didn't," Margie assured her. "She likes to chase squirrels, but she's never caught one. I don't think she'd have any idea what to do with it if she did."

"Yeah." Christina's face relaxed, her relief clear. "Yeah, you're right."

She turned to the cupboard to look for something to make for supper. Margie went back outside with her handful of paper towels. She approached the squirrel's corpse with trepidation.

Which was pretty funny, considering what she did for a living. Why should she be anxious about a dead squirrel? She, who dealt with dead people all day long? A dead squirrel wasn't even going to hold a candle to the horrors of murdered men, women, and children that she had seen and would yet see in the future.

She picked it up in the paper towel. She had planned to just throw it straight into the green bin without looking at it, but she heard Christina's question in her mind and had to make sure that Stella could not have killed it. If she had, they would have to make sure that she was not allowed outside on her own. She would always have to be supervised until they were sure that she wasn't a squirrel-killer.

The body was stiff. Not a fresh kill. Margie squinted at it, looking for bite marks. Looking for the injury that had killed it. There were many ways a squirrel could die. It could have eaten poisoned mouse bait. It could have been electrocuted running on one of the power lines. It could have been hit by a car, killed by a cat or another dog. How it got into her yard was another story. But an animal could have dragged it there. A person walking down the back lane could have picked it up and thrown it over the fence. Why, she didn't quite know, but it was possible. People were highly unpredictable.

There was dried blood on the torso. It looked like a clean edge, not a bite mark. Not any of the accidents that she had thought might befall an unwary squirrel. But there could be other things. Something sharp... on the ground... or a barbed -wire fence... maybe a tin can that the squirrel had crawled into, looking for nuts or something that had smelled good. What looked like a knife edge could have been a dozen other things. She wasn't a medical examiner. She wasn't performing a necropsy and trying to analyze who or what had killed the squirrel. She just wanted to make sure that it hadn't been Stella, and it hadn't been.

Margie walked briskly to the back gate and out into the alley to toss the body into the green bin. She made sure it was well-wrapped and then threw more paper towels down on top of it, so that she would never have to see it again.

Rest in peace, little squirrel.

Margie went back into the house to help Christina prepare supper.

CHAPTER ELEVEN

The next morning as they prepared for the day ahead, Christina asked, "Mom, could we go see Moushoom again? Maybe after school today?"

Margie considered her workload and schedule for the day and nodded. "I'll try to get home around the same time as you do, and we'll go over. The staff said he could eat what he wanted, so we could take him food this time."

"Burgers?" Christina suggested.

"If that's what you want, sure. I'm sure he would like that."

"Do you think he would like something else better? Could we make him something traditional? Something he hasn't had for a long time and that you can't buy in the restaurants?"

Margie blinked. "What a great idea. I'm sure he would just love that. I don't have a lot of time and energy after work, though, I don't think we can make anything too ambitious."

"Maybe we could just make bannock this time, but we could plan something else next time. When we have more time to shop and prepare."

"Perfect. Great idea. You don't need many ingredients for bannock, so I think I can manage that without a shopping trip. Somebody said it's harder to bake in Calgary because of the altitude, so it might not turn out quite the way we expect. We might have to try a few different times before we get it just right. It's just a matter of learning how to cook in a new environment."

"How does the altitude affect baking?"

"I'm not sure. I'll have to look it up. I know that water doesn't boil at the same temperature."

Christina looked at her like she was crazy. "Water always boils at the same temperature. One hundred degrees."

"One hundred degrees at sea level."

Christina shook her head, still not believing it. She wedged more books into her bag and looked across the room out to the street.

"There's the bus! I gotta run!"

Margie wasn't even sure if Christina heard her 'goodbye' as she belted out of the house. There was certainly not going to be any hug and kiss and sage motherly advice that morning. It would have to wait until their visit with Moushoom.

❧

SHE WAS glad after work that they were going to visit Moushoom. She needed something to help take her head out of her work, and her de-stress playlist had not done it. She and Christina put their heads together in the kitchen to make a batch of bannock, which had turned out fine despite Margie's misgivings. Maybe bannock was just one of those recipes that was impossible to screw up. They wrapped it up so it would still be warm from the stove when they got to Moushoom's apartment.

When they reached Moushoom's room, they again found him parked in front of the TV. Moushoom beamed at them and waved his hand at the TV. "You can shut that off. The nurses are always turning on the TV's to keep people quiet. And after trying to ignore it for a while… you kind of get dragged into it. But I don't want it on while my granddaughters are here to see me!"

Margie moved a TV table over Moushoom's knees and put down her bundle. "Wait until you see what we brought for you. This was Christina's idea."

Christina ducked her head and looked shy, but also excited and proud. "We made it together."

"Bannock!" Moushoom exclaimed in delight. "I don't remember when the last time I had bannock was!" He immediately broke off a piece and popped it into his mouth. "This is the best thing you could have brought me. It takes me right back to my childhood; sitting in my mother's kitchen, eating the bannock hot from the stove. Even in hard times, there was still bannock to fill hungry tummies."

He closed his eyes, savoring it. He opened them again.

"Come on, come on. Bring chairs over. You come have some too. We'll have a proper little feast here. Like we were away at school, sneaking food after lights out."

Margie and Christina did as he instructed. Margie laid out the butter and jam that she had brought along. She thought about what it had been like for Moushoom, back in the days of residential school, when the white man was so intent on beating the Indian out of the children. Anything that reminded them of their own culture had been banned. The Indigenous languages, spiritual beliefs, clothing, food, and ceremonies. They cut off their hair like the Philistines in the Christian Bible, trying to take away Samson's strength.

"Eat, eat," Moushoom encouraged, bringing Margie back to the present. She smiled at him and broke a piece off, eating while smiling at him. The white man had failed. They had not been able to steal Moushoom's culture away from him. They had not been able to stamp out all of the Indigenous cultures, though they had tried their best.

They sat down, lowering their masks to eat. Margie hoped that they were far enough apart to prevent an infection. She didn't want Moushoom getting sick. Sharing food and the knife for the butter was not a good idea, but they had both sanitized their hands before taking the elevator up.

"It must have been awful for you, going away to school," Margie said.

Moushoom's smile dimmed. He closed his eyes for a moment against the unwelcome memories, then shook it off and looked at her with a confident smile. "We learned far more than the brothers ever intended to teach us. They thought that they could crush us. Could squash the Métis out of us. We were like prisoners of war. But we were warriors. They could not overcome us."

He nibbled at some more bannock.

"Not all of us," he admitted. "Many of my brothers and sisters never came home." He looked at Christina and shook his head. "You seem so young to me now, but you are as old as I was when I left that place, a full-grown man, expected to fend for myself. A fully-educated man, looking and acting like a white man. You wouldn't believe it if you saw pictures of me then. But I went back to my people, grew my hair out, put on my sash, and I never let my culture go. Even when I came west and settled here, I didn't pretend to be white. I am Métis. I will always be Métis."

Christina nodded. She lifted her chin a little. "I am too. I'm still going to school. I want to get my education, but not so that I can be like them."

"There is nothing wrong with being educated. As long as you don't let them write their stories on your heart."

"I won't."

"Good girl."

Margie let her eyes drift around the room as she buttered and ate small pieces of the bannock, making it last as long as she could. Like Abdul's house, it was starkly furnished. Moushoom had not been able to bring many of his possessions there. But there were still decorations intended to remind him of his heritage. And he wore as much traditional clothing as he could.

There were certain parallels between Moushoom and the immigrants. Even though they represented opposite ends of the spectrum, one preserving his old traditions and the immigrants trying to adapt to an entirely new culture, they were similar to each other, out-of-step with the mainstream. Outsiders.

At least Abdul did not have to experience what Moushoom had. He went to public school with other children of all different races and traditions, and there was no one telling him that he could not keep his own name, no one shaving his head or beating him if he spoke his own language or didn't answer a question the way that they wanted him to. There were still rules, but they were not brutal and were not designed to erase who he was.

"What are you thinking of?" Moushoom asked.

"A boy I interviewed recently. He is from the Sudan, in Africa. Very far away and very different from the children here. I was talking to Christina the other day about how hard it must be for him to adjust to a new language and culture. Like you did."

Moushoom nodded his understanding. His dark eyes shone with interest and intelligence. There had been stories before Margie had moved to Calgary, suggesting that he was growing senile, that he didn't understand what was going on around him and easily forgot things. But so far, she had not seen it.

There was a crash out in the hallway or one of the nearby apartments, followed by shouting and swearing.

Despite his advanced years, Moushoom was immediately on his feet, his eyes wild, looking toward the disturbance. In his hand was the knife that only moments before had been on the TV table for them to spread butter and jam on the bannock.

"Moushoom!" Christina looked frightened by his reaction and rose as well, crashing into the TV table and nearly knocking it over.

Moushoom turned toward her, the knife held up in a defensive stance. Margie steadied the table.

"Sit down, Christina," she said quietly.

"But—" Christina looked at her Moushoom and then toward the noise in the hall. She looked terrified.

"Just sit down. You're safe. But you're frightening him more."

Christina looked at her mother for a minute, black brows drawn down in confusion. Then she obeyed, lowering herself slowly to her seat.

Moushoom wavered. He looked at Christina, then at Margie. His eyes, though still quick, were different from the way they had been. He was separated from them by time. How far in the past he was, she didn't know, but she would give him however long he needed to calm down and make his way back to them.

"You are safe," she told Moushoom. "I don't know what is going on out there, but I don't think it is any danger to you."

Moushoom's stance gradually relaxed. He put the knife back down with the bannock with a self-deprecating laugh. "Who wants some jam?" He sat down again in his chair with a deep sigh, as if at the end of a long, physically arduous day.

"Did it scare you?" Christina said tentatively.

Margie wouldn't have tried to question Moushoom about his reaction, but she didn't stop Christina. If Moushoom didn't want to talk about it, he could say so; Margie didn't want to stop Christina and imply that it was a forbidden topic or that Moushoom was not free to share whatever he pleased.

"I am an old man. Old men scare easily."

"Why did it scare you?" Christina's eyes were on the knife. Old men might scare easily but, in Christina's experience, they didn't take up weapons to defend themselves.

"You do not know all the things that happened when I was a boy," Moushoom said slowly. "We don't talk about it." He looked at Margie. "Not all of it. We don't want to relive those years." He was silent for a few moments. "But make no mistake... we were at war with our captors. It was a silent war. But we were still warriors."

CHAPTER TWELVE

Margie's sleep was restless, interrupted by dreams that were fleeting, sliding away from her as soon as she tried to remember and analyze them. She tossed and turned, got up and had a drink of milk in the hopes that it would help her to settle down, and lay down to sleep again.

The alarm rang too early in the morning. Margie forced herself to swing her feet over the edge of the bed and to get up and get moving. Once she had been up for a little while, once she had showered and had a cup of coffee, it would be easier. Even if she were short on sleep, she would still be able to function and make it through the day.

She listened to make sure that Christina got up when her alarm rang. She let Christina choose her own wake-up time and routine, as long as it got her to school on time. Christina was old enough to be responsible for those details herself. And she had shown herself to be responsible. Most of the time. They had both found it difficult to settle down after the long visit with Moushoom. Margie's brain had been busy with all of the things they had talked about.

"I'm up," Christina croaked from her room. She knew that Margie would be close by, checking in.

"Do you want me to put bread in the toaster for you?"

"Um… yeah," Christina agreed. They both knew that food was one of the things that was sure to get her out of bed.

Their morning preparations were slow and involved their bumping into each other and into other things a lot that day. But despite their fatigue, neither was grumpy and irritable. It was just kind of a slow-motion morning. Margie saw Christina off to the bus and hopped in her car.

&

A LOT of the high schools only had a half day on Friday. Christina would be arriving home by one o'clock, and Margie wasn't sure what she would be doing in the time until Margie returned home. Doing her homework early so that she wouldn't have to worry about it all weekend? Margie suppressed a smile. Doubtful.

She wondered if Abdul, too, would only have a half day. His father had been home when they had visited before. Margie wasn't sure what kind of a job he had, whether it required him to work on shift, or whether he could work remotely from home. Would Sadiq be watching for Abdul to come home? He didn't seem like the kind of father who supervised his son closely. He came from a culture where the children were probably allowed to run around the village barefoot all day, as long as they didn't have to be at school, work, or doing chores. Of course, that was just what Margie thought after seeing commercials about giving aid to emergency relief in the African countries. Or the occasional telethon or news report on happenings around the world from them. She didn't really know anything about the Sudan personally.

She took a break from the mind-numbing work of eliminating or prioritizing each suspect to do a quick Google search of the Sudan to learn what she should probably already know about their culture and history.

CHAPTER THIRTEEN

argie sat with her eyes closed for a long time.

She didn't want to believe it.

She sat there, thinking things through, going through all of the variables in her mind, putting the pieces together. The picture they formed was complete, but it wasn't what she wanted to see.

She looked around the squad room to see who else was there. She'd been working with her head down for so long that she had missed the comings and goings of the other detectives. Cruz was leaning back in his chair, rubbing the back of his neck. Clearly, he had been working too long at his computer as well.

"Detective Cruz, do you want to go for a ride?"

He nodded, rolling his shoulders and continuing to rub his neck. "Yeah. Anything to get away from this desk. What do you need?"

"I think… I need to talk to Abdul James again."

He studied her face. "Abdul. I thought you had decided he wasn't a suspect. Too young and shy. Wouldn't have any motive."

"I know. I had decided that. He didn't seem like a danger. And yet…" She thought about Moushoom the night before, grabbing the table knife. Nobody would expect a frail old man to be a danger either. But he had reacted in an instant, ready to defend himself.

"You think he might be the doer, or you think he knows something?"

She wasn't ready to float her theory yet. It was too soon. She wanted some verification first. She needed more information. "Let's go over there. See if we can find anything else."

He nodded his acceptance of this plan and didn't insist that she tell him all of her thoughts. Margie agreed to go in Cruz's car. He knew his way around the city better and she wouldn't have to demonstrate her complete lack of a sense of direction. They put on their masks before sliding into the enclosed space. Cruz didn't even use his GPS when she gave him the address, but pulled out into traffic and headed toward the community.

Margie watched out the windshield, trying to memorize everything she could about the layout of the city. "Have you lived in Calgary long?"

"Fifteen years now. Four with homicide."

She was not surprised he had been there so long. He seemed to be comfortable with the culture in Calgary. He didn't sound or act like a new immigrant. And he obviously had to have the years behind him in a Canadian police force to have earned the position of detective. He couldn't do that straight off the plane.

"Do you like it?"

"Calgary or homicide?"

"I meant Calgary, but either."

"It suits me. Other than the weather. I still find it cold. The summers are nice, but they are short."

"Yes. Same with Winnipeg."

"How long did you live in Winnipeg?"

"I've been in Manitoba my whole life. Winnipeg… since high school."

"And before that?"

"A Métis community you've probably never heard of. But I wanted to get an education. There wasn't much available if I stayed home. I always figured I would go back after I finished school, but then… there's the problem of finding a suitable job. And I wouldn't have been able to find something there. Not in law enforcement."

"Have you always wanted to be in law enforcement?"

"No, not really. I kind of gravitated toward it during college. I thought I might have an aptitude for it."

He nodded and didn't express his opinion one way or the other. She hadn't worked with him long enough for him to have an opinion anyway. As long as she didn't think she was a bad detective, that was fine.

"What made you take another look at the kid?"

"Something that happened last night… and then… I couldn't stop thinking about it. I did a bit more research and thought that… I really didn't take a hard enough look the first time. I didn't get the full picture."

"You think he had motive?"

"Not exactly."

"We're going to need motive."

"Maybe."

Cruz found the street without directions. Margie wondered if he had looked it up before. Maybe he had suspected the kid and had wanted to know where he lived. How feasible it was that he had walked to the park regularly. Maybe looking for gang associations in the area.

Margie led the way to the door. She again rapped hard, demanding attention. Sadiq might not be so happy to see her again. He might want to just ignore the knock at the door and pretend he didn't hear it. Margie was impatient. "Mr. Paul!" She hammered on the door again. "I want to talk with you."

Sadiq opened the door. His dark eyes took her in, then went to Cruz, standing casually behind her, one hand in his pocket.

"What is it? I thought we were finished."

"I need to talk to you and Abdul again. Is he home?"

"No."

"Will he be home soon?"

He looked around, frowning. "Yes. It is Friday. He will be home very soon."

"We'd like to come in to talk to you."

He reluctantly opened the door and ushered them in again.

Margie looked around, experiencing again the starkness of the room, the warmth of the traditional objects that made it a home, however bare it was.

"You said that you and Abdul are from the Sudan."

"Yes."

"Are you his father? His biological father?"

"No."

Margie looked at Cruz. It meant nothing to him yet, but it would.

"How did you come to be Abdul's guardian?"

Sadiq sat down on one of the chairs. "Things in my country are very bad. Terrible things happen there."

"There is a lot of war and unrest."

"Yes."

"And Abdul was orphaned?"

There was another hesitation. "Yes. Perhaps. It is hard to be sure. People disappear or are relocated. Families are broken up. They don't always know what happened to each other. Abdul lost his parents."

"How did he lose them?"

"Families get separated. His mother and sister were killed. His father... I don't know. He fought. He could not stay in his village."

Cruz turned his head suddenly and Margie realized that, once again, Abdul had slipped into the room and was standing there silently, without her even being aware of his entrance.

"Abdul. Come in. Sit down with your... guardian. We were just talking about you. About what happened in the Sudan."

He pulled down his bandana but not his hood, looking at each of them anxiously. He moved around them to sit down with Sadiq, looking only slightly comforted by being close to someone familiar.

"When your mother was killed and your father was fighting, what did you do? Who took care of you?"

Abdul didn't answer immediately. He stared straight ahead, unmoving. He didn't fidget. He just sat there like a statue.

"I had no one," he said finally. "Many children die. They sleep in the streets. Forage. No one takes care of them."

Margie nodded encouragingly. "Is that what you did?"

"At first. I didn't know where to go or what to do. But then I found out about the battalion. The Children's Battalion."

Margie's heart beat harder. It was awful to think of what had happened to Abdul. Even though she didn't know the whole story yet, her heart went out to him. She imagined Christina or another of the many children in her extended family orphaned in a war zone.

"In the Children's Battalion, they would feed you," Abdul explained. "Three times a day! As much food as you needed. We had bunks in the barracks while they were training us. We had clothing."

"How old were you when you joined them?"

"I was ten. Not old enough to fight yet. I carried messages, acted as a spy. We had a network passing the information back to our commanders."

Margie looked at Sadiq. He had made no attempt to stop Abdul from talking about what had happened.

"How did you come to be Abdul's guardian?"

"Abdul was rescued by UNICEF and the UN. They put him through reeducation. Counseling. And they brought him and some of the other... refugees here. I wanted to help. I said I would take a child."

"Were you a child soldier as well?"

Sadiq shook his head slowly. "My mother was. She was abducted and became one of their wives. She was fifteen when I was born, and escaped. She tried to return to her village, but she was shunned as a spy and a used woman. I grew up on the streets and in orphanages until someone sponsored me to come here."

Margie swallowed. The story was told without emotion. Not something Sadiq was outraged about. Just the story of his life. How he had come to be there.

It was a fact of life in the Sudan. He and Abdul had both suffered loss and privation at an early age. It had affected them, caused changes to their brains. Maybe long-lasting. Maybe permanent.

She looked back at Abdul.

"You said that at ten, you were too young to fight. Did you become a fighter before you were rescued?"

Abdul stared down at his hands. "Yes."

"You were forced to fight?" She thought of the pictures she had seen on the internet. Children cradling submachine guns. Empty eyes. Blank faces.

"They did not force me," Abdul disagreed. "It was… what we were there to do. We had to defend our country. Our honor. It was our duty. We were glad to do it."

"You killed people."

"In a war, people die," he said flatly.

"I know… but in most wars, children are not recruited to do the killing."

He shrugged. "That is the way it was where I come from."

Margie moved on. Abdul was not responsible for what he had done in the Sudan. They put a gun in his hands and trained him to use it. Even if he had joined the battalion voluntarily, he was not the one who was responsible for those deaths. The adults who recruited and trained him were the ones at fault.

"Do you like it here in Canada?"

He smiled, showing teeth. "Oh, yes. It is a beautiful country. And no war."

"You like school?"

"Yes."

Margie looked at Sadiq. She wondered if he would stop her. It didn't seem like he would. He didn't know what the laws were in Canada or how to react like a typical Canadian parent.

"Do you get scared?" she asked Abdul.

Abdul considered the question. He nodded slowly, looking down at his hands. "Sometimes."

"I was with my grandfather yesterday. When there was a big bang and people yelling, he grabbed a knife from the table. When he was a child, he was often beaten. I don't know what else happened to him. But he was afraid. He grabbed the closest thing he could use as a weapon to protect himself."

"That is good," Abdul said with a nod. "You must protect yourself. Even an old man."

"Or a child?"

"Yes."

"Do you carry a knife to protect yourself?"

"Yes."

He turned his head, looking at her with those guileless, open eyes. Why would he feel guilty for carrying a knife? Why would he think it was wrong? He had been trained. He knew he had to protect himself. For most of his life, no one else had protected him.

"Can I see it, please?"

Abdul reached into the large pocket of his hoodie and drew it out. Not just a jackknife like she might find at a department store or Scout shop. It caught the light as he held it out to her.

A folding combat knife.

Just like a soldier would carry.

CHAPTER FOURTEEN

Margie quickly pulled a glove on over her hand and took the knife from Abdul. She didn't open it. She already knew everything she needed to. It fit the description of the kind of blade that had killed Robinson. Even if he had cleaned it well, it might still have microscopic spots of blood left on it, perhaps in the hinge. Cruz provided an evidence bag and Margie slid the knife into it.

"How did Mr. Robinson scare you?" she asked Abdul softly.

"I was walking in the trees. It helps me, walking where there are lots of trees. Alone, away from all of the people. I like Calgary, where I can live close to the park."

Margie made an encouraging noise.

"He grabbed me and yelled at me. I didn't know what he was going to do, why he was attacking me. I was just walking in the trees." Abdul blinked a few times, thinking back. Replaying it in his mind. "I don't know what happened. He did not have a weapon. I thought he would have a gun." He shook his head, trying to make sense of it. "But he died. He fell on the ground."

"Did you try to help him? To stop the bleeding?"

"No."

"Did you try to talk to anyone else? To get the police or ambulance here to help him?"

"No."

"You should have."

"I didn't want them to find me. I didn't know if there were others —soldiers who had guns. I went back home. No one followed me. I went to bed."

"Did you tell Sadiq what had happened?"

"No."

Sadiq shook his head to confirm the point. "I did not know."

"Did you know he carried a knife?"

"No."

"Abdul, you're going to need to come with us."

Abdul looked down at the floor, sighing. "Am I going to prison?"

Margie's eyes were hot, and there was a lump in her throat as she helped Abdul to his feet and closed cuffs over his stick-thin wrists. "I don't know what's going to happen, Abdul. We're going to tell the authorities what happened. If it was up to me..." Margie trailed off.

What would she do if it were up to her?

What was the appropriate consequence for what Abdul had done?

How could they do him justice and still protect others from him?

CHAPTER FIFTEEN

Margie and Cruz relayed the developments to the rest of the team, gathered together in the briefing room.

"Robinson was probably telling him to stay on the pathway or to follow some other real or assumed park rule," Margie suggested. "Abdul doesn't even know what he said. Just that Robinson grabbed him and was yelling at him for something. I guess… he had a flashback or reacted instinctively, and before he knew what he had done, Robinson was dead on the ground."

"He's got to be a psychopath," Jones said, shaking her head. "I was there when you talked to him the first time. I heard him say that nothing out of the ordinary happened at the park that night. I saw his eyes… there were no tells. Nothing to indicate that he was lying or avoiding anything."

"I think… he didn't act guilty because he doesn't feel guilty about it," Margie said uncomfortably. "Not because he's a psychopath, but because that's how he's been trained and conditioned. He lived in an environment where he had to kill or be killed. Sadiq said he went through retraining, but clearly he hasn't made the transition. Whether he ever can or not, I don't know, but he doesn't live in our world. A world where you expect to get through the day without any violence, without someone attacking or trying to kill you. Robinson attacked, he defended himself, and he survived. That makes it a good day."

"He's not going to get off of murder charges because he has a troubled past," Cruz said. "He's going to go away, and they're not going to let him out for a long time."

Margie knew Canada's laws, though. At fourteen, it was highly unlikely Abdul would be sentenced as an adult. Especially not without any kind of connection to Robinson or evidence of premeditation. For a young person, the maximum sentence for first-degree murder was ten years, and for manslaughter was likely to be far less. The judge would recommend a rehabilitation program before he would be reintegrated into his community.

That was humane and wasn't designed to punish him, but to help him. But he had already been through a rehabilitation program when he had been rescued from the Children's Battalion. Would Canada's efforts be any more effective in helping him to become a normal, contributing member of society and no longer a threat to others?

All too soon, he would be back at school with other children, walking free on the streets and trails again. Was there hope that he would understand the seriousness of taking a life in Canadian society and no longer be a threat to anyone else?

She closed her eyes and said a prayer in her head for Abdul. And for those he would touch in the future.

EPILOGUE

Over coffee, he read the article in the online paper one more time, studying Detective Marguerite Patenaude's picture in the paper and rereading the few sentences that described the homicide Detective Pat was credited with solving. There were few details because of the involvement of a young offender who, of course, could not be named or identified. But there was enough there for him to understand what had happened.

Within days of moving into Calgary, Detective Pat had already solved her first murder. She thought she was so smart. She thought that she, as an affirmative action hire, could just waltz in and show everybody up.

He put his mug in the sink and filled it with water. Then he got into his car and drove to the house where Detective Pat lived with her teenage daughter. He parked across the street and gazed at the house. She had no idea what it was like to be him. She thought she lived in his world now, but she didn't. She could turn around and go right back where she had come from.

He had plans for their Detective Pat.

He would see how she handled the next case.

FISH CREEK PROVINCIAL PARK

Fish Creek Provincial Park was established in the Fish Creek valley in southern Calgary in 1975 and is the second largest urban park in Canada, featuring over 100 km of trails for walking, running, and biking.

It offers Sikome lake, a man-made lake, for swimming. Boating and fishing is permitted on the Bow River and Fish Creek. There is an environmental learning center, a visitor center, aquatic center, and day use picnicking areas.

Most of the park remains in its natural forested state.

The Friends of Fish Creek Provincial Park Society is a non-profit, volunteer-run organization which helps to provide visitor services and many essential functions around the park.

AUTHOR NOTE

The last residential school in Canada closed its doors in 1996. The effects of the abuses perpetrated in these prisons impacted thousands and continues to affect the Indigenous community today.

On May 27, 2021, the Tk'emlups te Secwepemc First Nation announced the discovery of unmarked graves containing 215 children who had been residents of the Kamloops Indian Residential School using ground-penetrating radar. This was not an isolated incident, but part of a larger genocide that took place all across Canada. Other discoveries have been made and the tragic histories of the 139 residential schools that operated in Canada need to be exposed.

The Truth and Reconciliation Commission's final report in 2012 made specific calls to action with regard to missing children and burial information which have not been honored.

How the government of Canada responds to this discovery and makes good on their many promises made to Indigenous peoples remains to be seen.

I have been concerned for a number of years about the intergenerational trauma caused by residential schools, living conditions on reservations, and discrimination faced by the Indigenous peoples in this land, and have written about some of these issues previously in *Questing for a Dream.* It is my hope that my writing can raise awareness and educate readers on both the history and the current conditions of those who have lived these experiences.

If you are also concerned about these harms, I would encourage you to write to your MP (if you are Canadian), encouraging the federal government to follow through on the calls to action made by the Truth and Reconciliation Commission and the promises they have previously made with regard to such things as clean water, medical care, and keeping Indigenous families together.

You can also make a donation to a charity that benefits residential school survivors, such as the Indian Residential School Survivors Society.

In the Sudan and many other countries in the world, children are recruited to fight in wars and rebellions. UNICEF, United Nations, and others are working hard to put an end to these practices and to rescue and re-educate children who have been harmed by this practice. Many children have been rehabilitated and live happy, productive lives away from the wars.

For a first-person account of what it is like to be a child soldier, I recommend reading *A Long Way Gone,* the account of Ishmael Beah's experience in Sierra Leone.

LONG CLIMB TO THE TOP

PARKS PAT MYSTERIES #2

*To those who are
leaving legacies*

CHAPTER ONE

argie Patenaude didn't need to be a detective to know who had left the dirty dishes in the sink.

"Christina!"

"Gotta go, Mom," Christina said, rushing into the room. She swept her long black hair out of the way as she shouldered her backpack so that it would not get caught under the strap. "The bus will be here any second. I'll see you after school." She headed toward the front door. "Oh, and you remember what I told you, right, about the Métis Club meeting after school today? So I'll be late. Don't expect me right after school."

"You left dishes in the sink—"

"I have to go. If I stop and do them now, I'll miss the bus, and then you'll need to drive me to school." Christina had the door open and was halfway out. "Sorry. I'll load the dishwasher tonight. Okay? Bye!"

Margie watched her fifteen-year-old race across the street to the bus stop. And she was right, of course; the bus was making its way down the street, and if she had taken an extra ten seconds to have a conversation or rinse off the dishes, she would have missed it. But that was no excuse for Christina to leave them in the sink in the first place, when she knew she was supposed to rinse them and put them directly into the dishwasher.

She sighed and did it herself. She had to drive into work, and the other homicide detectives and Sergeant MacDonald wouldn't know whether she had left five minutes later because of her daughter or if she had just hit the lights wrong or run into a traffic snarl on Blackfoot Trail. She checked the table and counter for any other orphaned dishes and didn't find any. In another minute, she had the dishwasher running, Stella was settled for the day, and Margie was walking at a quick clip out to her car. It was a cool, crisp morning.

"Oh, Detective Pat!" called Mrs. Rose, a sweet little old lady who was the first and only owner of the 1960s bungalow next to Margie's.

Margie stopped, anxious to get on her way but not willing to be rude or pretend that she hadn't heard Mrs. Rose's call. She took a couple of steps toward her neighbor, but stopped the prescribed two meters away. "Yes, Mrs. Rose? What can I do for you?"

"I just wanted to make sure that you had heard that the 55+ Society is open again."

Margie's expression must have betrayed her consternation at this announcement. Mrs. Rose smiled her sweet, pink-lipstick smile. "The 55+ Society. It's over there on Twenty-Sixth Avenue, where your grandfather lives."

"Oh, yes…?"

"And it's been closed since the whole pandemic thing. But they've opened up again. And they have lots of programs for the seniors in the area. You should take a look at the activities and clubs that they run, see if there is anything that your grandfather would like to go to."

"Oh! Okay, I will," Margie agreed. She would see if there were anything that might interest Moushoom. "Thank you for letting me know."

"They probably have flyers in the lobby of the building he lives in. But if they don't, the 55+ Society is just about a block away. You can stop in there any time they are open and get their program guide. And they can give you a tour. They're very helpful over there."

"That's great. I'm glad you let me know." Margie gave Mrs. Rose a firm nod, then turned back toward her car. "Have a wonderful day."

"I will, dear. You too."

❦

THE WORKDAY PASSED QUICKLY. The homicide team was working on a number of open cases, but none of them was burning hot. It was a matter of chasing down leads one at a time. Doing background checks on persons of interest, interviewing them, looking for connections or alibis. The day-to-day work of a homicide department.

She found it easier to move from one case to another than to stay focused on one all day, so she gathered shorter tasks from the primary investigator on each of the cases, read the file to bring herself up to speed, and worked on her assignment. Then she would jump to the next case.

No one on the team seemed to mind her ADHD approach. They were happy to have some of the less-desirable tasks taken off of their hands. Margie was eyeing the clock, trying to decide whether she would have time to review one more case before leaving for the day when Sergeant MacDonald—Mac—walked up to her desk. He was a tall man, towering over her when she was sitting down. His hair was almost entirely silver and he had lines of 'experience' around his mouth. He readjusted his thin-rimmed glasses.

"Yes, sir?" Margie immediately tried to think of what she might have done to attract his attention. Good or bad, she didn't want to be under the sergeant's scrutiny too often. Too much praise from him and the rest of the team would resent her, and too much criticism... well, any criticism was likely to keep Margie up half the night with anxiety over her mistake and how to avoid making it again in the future. No one liked being criticized, and Margie felt that she was particularly thin-skinned about it. She criticized herself for not accepting criticism well. How was that for a fault?

"I've got a case for you. I know you like to be home when your daughter gets home from school, but this one is going to need your immediate attention."

The duty room was still as everyone else listened in. Margie had just solved the Fish Creek Park murder case. The next case should have gone to someone else. Although everyone else already had active files and Margie did not, so maybe that was why he had picked her.

"Uh, yes sir. She's going to be later today and, of course, when it's urgent, I can take the time I need to get started on it. She's old enough to be on her own for a few hours if I'm needed elsewhere."

She didn't ask him what he had for her but, of course, that was the question on the minds of everyone in the room.

Mac nodded his appreciation. He ran his fingers through his short gray hair and leaned on her desk. "Here's the thing. It's the same MO as the Fish Creek Park murder."

Margie's eyes went wide. She stared at him in surprise. "The same MO?"

Robinson had been killed with a single stab wound. Margie had caught the killer. So they knew that it wasn't the same killer. Just because another person was killed by a stab wound, that didn't make it the same killer or the same case.

"The same MO," MacDonald agreed. "It's another provincial park. Male victim. Single stab wound with a single-edged blade. Bled out. No apparent provocation, no one heard yelling or was aware that anything was wrong. Body discovered by a family walking the trail with a toddler in a stroller."

Not a dog-walker this time. But Margie was sure there were probably a number of dog-walkers close by. That one difference didn't make the case different from the Fish Creek murder.

She hoped that the toddler hadn't seen anything and wasn't old enough to remember it later. Hopefully, she had been sleeping peacefully in the stroller at the time. It was a good time for an afternoon nap.

"Okay. I'll look up this park and go see," Margie agreed. "Is it near Fish Creek Park?"

"No. Halfway to Cochrane. It's actually outside of Calgary city limits, but we are heading it up because of the connection to the Fish Creek case. Since it looks like the same killer."

"It's not, though," Margie pointed out.

"There's always the possibility that we got the wrong person for the Fish Creek murder."

"But he admitted to it. We didn't get the wrong person."

"I don't think so either. But innocent people do confess. It's also possible that he was released on bail or under his foster father's supervision and is no longer in custody."

"But if this other park isn't close to his home… how would he get there? He couldn't walk there like he did to Fish Creek. Is there a bus that goes all the way out there?"

"No, I don't think there's any bus service out there. Tours maybe. I'm sure it's not related. But because of the similarity in the cases and the sites of the homicide, it's your case."

"Okay. Give me the details." Margie looked at her watch. If she remembered correctly, Cochrane was west, toward the mountains. Margie's home was in the east, on the opposite side of the city. She was going to be more than an hour or two late getting home for Christina. Just the travel time would add an extra hour, forget any investigative work and waiting for someone from the medical examiner's office.

"Glenbow Ranch Provincial Park," Sergeant MacDonald told her. He spelled it out for her. "Do you want directions?"

"Will it be on my GPS? If it's outside of the city, it might not be…"

"Should be. It opened in 2011, so it's been there long enough".

CHAPTER TWO

argie hit the road, driving west down Crowchild Trail. Rush hour appeared to have already hit and both Memorial Drive and Crowchild Trail were heavy with traffic. Progress was slow, which meant she would be all that much later getting home to Christina. She couldn't rush things at the murder scene. It would take time to process the scene. That was just the way it was. She used her Bluetooth to send a message to Christina, giving her an update and asking her to let Margie know when she was home.

There were several C-Train stations down the middle of Crowchild, and the trains ran past her every few minutes. They were packed with people. Despite the pandemic and all of the new protocols to follow, a lot of people were back to working downtown, and they all needed to get home to the outlying areas. She glanced as another train went by. Most people were masked, in compliance with the by-law recently put into place mandating masks in public places and the transit system in particular. Infection numbers were down, and she hoped that they stayed low despite the reopening of the schools.

Over to her right, there was a big white temple spire with a gold figure on top. The speed of the traffic was picking up, so she couldn't gawk at it for long, but it was pretty. A surprise to see something like that at the edge of the city. In another minute, she had reached city limits and Crowchild Trail had turned into Highway 1A.

There were rolling hills, but not a lot of trees like she had expected to see. She remembered how thickly Fish Creek Park had been treed and had expected the same type of scenery. There were fields and farmyards and small stands of trees here and there.

After a while, the GPS warned her to get into the left lane, and Margie obeyed, though she couldn't see any sign of the park. It seemed strange to have a park all the way out there. They wouldn't get foot traffic like Fish Creek Park did. A road sign announced that Glenbow Park was three kilometers away, but the GPS urged her to turn immediately. She watched for a break in the oncoming traffic and turned left onto a gravel road. Once on the gravel road, there were a few houses off to the left and thick trees to the right. The gravel road was on an incline, down into a valley. Margie slowed down and took the gravel and the curves in the road carefully.

Zipping down them like it was an emergency wouldn't do her any good. She couldn't save the man who was already dead, and if she ended up with her car in the ditch, it was just going to take that much longer to get done. Not to mention the reputation she would get. Detectives often ended up with nicknames within the department, and she did not want to be "Ditch" Patenaude.

It was farther than she would have expected. There was a public parking area, but Margie saw a gray-shirted officer standing up by a locked gate, watching the incoming traffic. She drove up to him. He bent down to talk through her window. He wasn't wearing a mask, and Margie pulled back, a little irritated that he would get so close to her.

"Are you the detective?" he asked. "Uh, Detective Pat?"

"Patenaude," Margie agreed. "That's me."

"Come on through, and drive down to the parking area beside the house." He pointed in the direction of a big ranch house. "I'll walk down to you after I lock up here."

Margie waited while he swung the big gate open, then drove down to the lot he had pointed to. The house had perhaps been someone's home before the creation of the park. It had the feel of a family home rather than a conference or education center built by the government.

Margie put on her mask and got out and stretched, looking around. After the golden brown grass on the fields and hills up above, she had expected a stark setting. But down in the valley, there was lush green growth—lots of trees, long grass, and wildflowers. Bees buzzed around her and orange butterflies fluttered here and there. Despite being the site of a murder, everything seemed peaceful and pleasant.

The Conservation Officer who had let her in the gate walked down to her. "Is this your first time in the park?"

"Yes. I'm just new to Calgary. So I've seen Fish Creek Park, but that's about it. I guess you heard about that."

"Yeah. It was in the news and as soon as we came across the body here… well, it was just too similar to ignore. We called the RCMP; it's their jurisdiction, but they looped your department in right away. You're the one with the deep knowledge on the Fish Creek case, so you get control."

"Is the RCMP already here?"

"They sent a couple of guys out. Our Conservation Officers controlled the scene. Just waiting on you."

"How about the forensic team and the medical examiner? Have they been notified?"

"Notified, but not here yet. It takes a while to get out here, as I'm sure you found." He looked at his watch. "An hour since we called you. And it's rush hour."

Margie nodded. "Okay, thanks. So, where is your body? I gather it's not in the house?" She tilted her head toward it.

"No. We all manage to get along pretty well in the Park Office." He gave her a roguish grin. "No murders there yet."

Margie smiled.

"I'm CO Richardson." He put out his hand to shake.

Margie shook her head. "Sorry, no unnecessary contact," she apologized. He should have known that. The police force, by the nature of their contact with the public at large, were already at higher risk of infection. She didn't want to be out of work due to a virus or quarantine, or to inadvertently pass something on to Moushoom, who was vulnerable due to his age.

Richardson rolled his eyes and lowered his hand. "If you'll come with me, I will take you to the scene."

Margie nodded. She got out of the car. "How far is it? I can walk a ways…"

At Fish Creek Park, the murder site had been too far from the parking lot for her to comfortably walk there to investigate. She hoped that the distance would be shorter at Glenbow.

"We have almost forty kilometers of trails. The body is only a couple of clicks away, but if you want to get home to your family tonight…" He looked at his watch. Margie was sure he wanted to get back to his regular duties as well, or to sign off at the end of his day. A murder scene might be an exciting novelty, but preserving the scene and dealing with curious visitors would be a pain. And it got dark early this late in the year. Everyone would want to have the scene cleared before it was too dark to see.

"Lead the way," Margie sighed. "One of these days, I'm going to have to come explore some of these parks for recreation instead of a murder investigation."

"You like to walk?"

"Yes, I do. I'd like to do more. There are some multi-use trails near my house, but so far, all I've been able to do is walk the dog on the closest ones."

"Where do you live?"

"In the southeast." Margie knew enough now not to mention that it was close to Forest Lawn or part of Greater Forest Lawn. She didn't think that the area warranted the reputation it seemed to have all over the city. "Near Pearce Estate Park, if you know where that one is?"

"Oh, sure. Harvie Passage is over there. Where the weir used to be."

Margie shrugged, not sure of any of this. Richardson correctly interpreted her reaction.

"The weir was there for a lot of years. People would go boating or fishing over there, or swim or fall in, and they would get killed in the weir, because of the way that the water going over the weir would create a circular flow." He twirled a finger horizontally to demonstrate. "Getting caught in it would just keep spinning you over and over, like being stuck in a washing machine."

"Oh."

"So eventually, they built out a series of rapids to replace the weir. They take rafters down the river in a series of steps so it is not so dangerous. It took a few tries to get it right, but it's all in place now, much better than it was. It's named the Harvie Passage, after the same family as used to live here," he pointed to the ranch house as he led her to the garage, "the same family as donated the lands for the park."

"Wow. A pretty philanthropic family."

"They are," he agreed. "There are a lot of things named after them and after Glenbow in and around Calgary. You'll come across a lot of them. The Glenbow Museum. The Dorothy Harvie Gardens. The Glenbow Park Ranch Foundation was set up by the family and shares this building with Alberta Parks. The foundation runs the Visitor Center, other park education and programming, and various other projects."

He used a keypad to let himself into the garage and directed Margie to one of the golf carts waiting there. "We'll drive over in this."

In a few minutes, they were driving slowly down the pathway, working their way past the walkers, runners, and cyclists enjoying an afternoon at the park. It was a more open area with little shade, and she could see the rolling vistas. She could see mountains on the horizon, under bright blue sky and washboard clouds. She turned her head to look back toward the city. She could see the downtown skyline in the other direction.

"Do you like the water?" Richardson asked.

"Water?"

"Just wondered if you would be interested in rafting down the Harvie Passage. Since you live close to it. People often don't take advantage of the facilities that are closest to them."

"Me... no, I'm not really interested in boating or watersports. I know the Canoe Club is close too, just off of the trails where I walk Stella. But I don't think I'll be taking any lessons."

He gave her a look, then nodded and continued to navigate around the many park walkers. It had been a cool day, and Margie was surprised that there were so many people out in the park. But apparently, they knew enough to dress in layers and be prepared for changes in the weather. Calgary was notorious for its changeable weather. Margie thought she had seen flakes of snow that morning when she took Stella out. It seemed awfully early in the year for snow, and she hoped that winter would hold off for another month or two.

She could see the pale blue river off to her left as they drove through the hills. Margie thought they were traveling roughly west.

"That's the Bow," Richardson said, nodding to the river. "Same river as goes past Pearce Estate Park. And Fish Creek Park, for that matter."

Margie imagined boating all the way from Glenbow Ranch Park, though the city, out to Fish Creek Park. It made her a little queasy thinking about it. All of that water rushing downstream. The picture that Richardson had put into her mind of a body tumbling over and over at the old weir. Her throat felt like it would close up just thinking of all of that water over her head.

"You don't think this murder is related to the body out at Fish Creek Park, do you?" Richardson inquired.

"No. We caught the killer in that case. I don't think it's related in any way, other than the fact that the body was discovered in a park."

"And he was stabbed."

"Right. But that's not particularly unique. Lots of people get stabbed."

He nodded in agreement. "True."

They started going uphill again, into an area more heavily treed. The pathway was narrower and gravel rather than paved. "This is part of Tiger Lily Loop. A short loop. Nice for families. You avoid the steep hill that you need to use to get to the rest of the park."

It was still pretty hilly. Margie studied the landforms and vegetation with interest and looked up to the sky to watch birds wheeling around them.

"If you're lucky, you could see our osprey. It's quite something to see them diving into the water for fish."

"Wow, yes. What other kinds of animals do you have out here?"

She was glad that the dead body was, as far as anyone had said, a fresh kill, and had not been subject to predation. There must be some large predators in the park, considering its size.

"Plenty of different birds and insects. There are bee and bird counting programs. Ground squirrels—you know, gophers. Badgers. Coyotes. Porcupines. Mule deer. You'll see the cattle; they still graze the park lands as part of the vegetation management program. There is an occasional bear sighting and we are on the lookout for cougar. But there haven't ever been any attacks on humans. The animals will do their best to avoid people and dogs."

Margie hung on as the cart climbed a steeper part of the trail. They were into the shadows of the trees and there were fewer hikers around.

Then they reached the yellow tape. Richardson hit the brakes and parked the cart. "Here we go."

Margie climbed out. There were a couple of conservation officers and RCMP uniforms. Margie nodded at the nearest RCMP officer. He was wearing a gray shirt similar to the conservation officers', with a tactical vest.

"Detective Pat?"

"Yes."

"Good to see you. I'm Sergeant Shack. You've been briefed?"

"I don't know much, other than the fact that there was a stabbing victim, similar to the Fish Creek murder that we just put away."

He nodded. "Not many details to give you at this point. You want to come have a look?"

"That's what I'm here for."

She stopped to put on protective gear to keep her from contaminating the crime scene, and they worked their way around the perimeter of the tape rather than through the middle. Margie took each step carefully, eyes alert for anything that might be evidence, even outside the tape. Then they ducked under the tape and moved toward the center of the cordoned-off area.

"Male, mid to late thirties," Shack said. "Doesn't appear to be robbery. No sign of a fight, no one has come forward who witnessed an argument or violence between the victim and someone else."

Margie nodded. Similar to the Fish Creek murder. She studied the body. The man was on his back so she could see the location of the stab wound. "I might be wrong, but I think the point of entry is a bit higher than the one in Fish Creek," she said. She leaned closer to get a better look at the body without touching it or compromising anything else at the scene. "Hard to judge his height and the angle of entry from this position."

"Your suspect in the Fish Creek case…"

She raised her brows at Shack. "Yes?"

"It was a juvenile offender?"

"Yeah. Tall for a fourteen-year-old, but still not an adult. How long ago, do you think?" Margie had nitrile gloves on. She touched the man's wrist to gauge his temperature. She couldn't feel any warmth through the thin layer of protection. It hadn't just happened. But she knew it had been over an hour since the Calgary police had been called in. Presumably, it had taken some time to sort out who should be involved in the investigation, and the family with the toddler had not reported seeing or hearing any violence, so the body had probably been lying there for some time before they saw him.

"Medical examiner will give us a better idea," Shack said. "I'm not sure yet. There's no predation or significant insect activity, so probably not long. It's close enough to the trail that you would think someone would have noticed him within a couple of hours."

"Definitely today."

"Oh yeah. Maybe early morning, but I'd be more inclined to think that it happened while the park was open. The conservation officers are pretty good at keeping people off of the park until it opens. You can't catch everybody, of course, but there's only one public lot, and not many people hike in."

Margie looked back in the direction of Calgary. "That would be quite a hike."

"Pretty impossible to come in from Calgary, actually. You need to take the highway, because there's no trail access through Haskayne Park yet. Eventually, there will be, but for the moment, Glenbow is cut off from the Calgary trail system." He pointed the other direction. "Cochrane, on the other hand, is only a couple of clicks away, and there are some pathways into the park from there."

Margie pulled out her notebook and made a couple of notes. "And those pathways would not be patrolled."

"Not likely. Checked now and then, but the CO's are going to be focusing on the public parking area."

Margie looked around. "How many people come through this trail during the day?" It seemed unlikely that a murder had been committed while people walked by on the trail. It would take a pretty bold murderer.

"You'll have to get those details from the CO's. They might have some video footage too. But it's not busy. You can often walk this area and only see a few other visitors. It's relatively remote."

"The family that found him, are they still around?"

"They had a kid. Couldn't stay around for long, but they left their information. You can call or go see them."

Shack pulled out his notebook and relayed the contact information he had taken down from the witnesses. Margie wrote it in her own book.

"Did the child see…?"

"No. I don't think so. Didn't seem to be upset about anything except having to sit around while the grown-ups talked instead of exploring."

"Good. You always worry about trauma."

"If she saw him, she probably didn't understand what was going on. Just that someone was sleeping in the grass." Shack looked at the body. "I mean, it's not horrific."

"No. You're right." Margie could make out the hole that the knife had made and the darker areas of the shirt where blood had soaked into it. No pools of red blood or gore.

They could hear a vehicle approaching and all turned to look for it. In a few moments, a white van came into view.

"Medical Examiner's office," Margie observed. "Hopefully, they'll have a few answers for us."

CHAPTER THREE

Suited up and masked, Dr. Kahn from the Medical Examiner's office took a cursory look at the body, then looked at Sergeant Shack and Margie.

"Whose scene is it?"

"Calgary's," Margie said. "That's me."

"Okay. Nobody's touched the body?"

"I touched his wrist. Gloves on. Conservation officers and RCMP were here before me."

Shack took a few minutes to run through the steps since the body had been discovered with Dr. Kahn to establish the integrity of the scene. Kahn went through the motions of checking the body for any vital signs.

"Body is in rigor," he observed. "No pulse or respiration. Cool to the touch. I'll take ambient and liver temps. Looks like he's been here for a few hours."

Margie nodded. They would narrow it down more once the medical examiner had run through all of the usual protocols. And perhaps there would be video, like there had been at Fish Creek Park, to establish the time that the victim had arrived on the trail.

"Is there any identification on the body?"

Dr. Kahn took a brief look at the stab wound before moving the man's clothing and feeling for a wallet. It was there in a zipped jacket pocket. Kahn passed it across to Margie. She examined it closely before opening it, looking for any trace that they needed to preserve. Then she opened it, keeping her gloved fingers on the very edges.

"David Smith."

"Well, great," Shack grumbled. "There are only a few hundred of those in Alberta."

"He's got a driver's license, so we have his address and date of birth." Viewing the card through the display window, Margie calculated the date in her head. "Age thirty-eight." She looked at the edges of the cards that peeked above the card slots. "Looks like Visa, Air Miles, Bank of Montreal access card, and AMA."

She displayed them to Shack, and he nodded his agreement. Margie didn't pull any of them out, and didn't pull out the plastic card accordion file she could see tucked into the next section. The forensic team would want to handle those, check for fingerprints and any other trace evidence.

Margie thumbed the cash section open to see a couple of bills. Blue and purple. "Fifteen dollars in cash."

She took an evidence bag from her shoulder bag and put the wallet into it. "Anything else in his pockets? Keys? Business cards? A list of people who might want to kill him?"

Shack snorted in amusement. Dr. Kahn didn't crack a smile. "Keys. Water bottle. Phone."

"Is there phone service coverage out here?"

"From my experience, yes, most of the park has coverage," Shack advised. "The exception being a blind spot as you get to the top of Glenbow Road. That's the gravel road you drove in on. Right at the top where you'd expect the coverage to be the strongest, it completely cuts out."

"Weird. Just today, or all the time?"

"As long as I've been coming here."

"Do you come here a lot?"

"Yeah. A couple of times a month, usually. I like to walk, take pictures."

"That's nice. You must live close."

He didn't answer at first, but when Margie kept looking at him, eyebrows raised, he realized that she expected an answer and it hadn't just been rhetorical. "Uh, yes. I'm just over in Tuscany."

"I'm new to Alberta. Is that in Cochrane or Calgary?"

"Calgary. West side. Did you see the Mormon temple as you drove out? White spire with an angel on top."

"Yes."

"When that's on your right, Tuscany is on your left."

"Oh, okay. That is nice and close. I'm not sure, but I'm thinking it's going to take me an hour to get home from here."

"I probably wouldn't be coming every week or two if I was that far away. Especially city driving." He gave a shudder. "I'm a country boy at heart. Southern Alberta farmland."

"Is that like this? Or prairie?"

"Prairie. Definitely. You can grow some crops around here. You'll see a couple of fields across the river growing canola or other crops. But it's hilly, so mostly this is ranching country—cows—rather than food crops."

"I'm from Manitoba."

"Ah, so you're used to flat. Yeah. Southern Alberta is more like that. Glenbow is mostly riparian. River and foothills."

❧

THE SUN WAS GETTING low in the sky by the time David Smith's body was loaded into the medical examiner's van and the forensic tech had finished going over the ground with a fine-toothed comb looking for any possible evidence in the case.

"There isn't a lot to find," a technician named Joe said apologetically. "Looks pretty clean. The ground hasn't been trampled. There isn't any litter. It's a stab wound rather than a gun, so there aren't any shell casings to look for. No sign of the weapon here. The killer must have taken it with him."

Margie remembered Abdul, the killer in the Fish Creek case, casually pulling a hunting knife out of his hoodie pocket when asked about it. It had been cleaned and well-maintained, but they had been able to find traces of blood in the hinges and in the hoodie itself. No matter what anyone said, she knew that Abdul could not have been David Smith's killer, and that he had been Jerry Robinson's killer. There hadn't been a DNA match on the blood evidence yet, but there was blood on the knife. Abdul had not just confessed to murder for attention. The confession had not been coerced. He reacted as he'd been trained to, killing the man who had confronted him in the park. He thought it a perfectly natural reaction and the only way to protect himself from possible violence.

Darkness started to gather, the chill in the air deepening. The medical examiner's van was gone. The forensics team was gone. She and Shack and the others who were still there removed the yellow tape perimeter, looking one last time for anything that might have been missed. None of them found anything.

"You'll check for video evidence and send it on to me?" Margie asked Richardson, continuing the conversation they'd been having while the forensic experts were combing the ground for any other evidence. "Parking lot, trail cams, wildlife cams, whatever you've got. You never know how it might be helpful."

"Sure," Richardson agreed. "We'll go through it in the morning, make sure you get a copy."

Margie kept her mouth shut and didn't tell him that he needed to get it to her that night, and not wait until morning. But what did it matter? She wasn't going to look at it until morning anyway. As long as he got it to her, she didn't have anything to complain about.

He gave her an amused look, and Margie suspected that her irritation had been clear even with her face mask. Sometimes her emotions were too transparent.

CHAPTER FOUR

Margie's estimate that it would take her an hour to get home from Glenbow Park had not been far off. She followed her GPS directions, which seemed to take her all the way around the north end of the city. But the speed limit was mostly one hundred and there was no significant traffic, so she really couldn't complain about the route it had selected.

She paused for a moment before unlocking the front door. She did her best to mentally push the homicide aside, walling off all of her questions and theories. Tomorrow would come soon enough and she didn't want to be crabby with Christina or to bring her down with her own mood. She took a couple of controlled breaths, then turned the key in the lock and opened the door.

"I'm home!"

There was a thunder of running feet, and Margie braced herself for the full weight of her dog, excited about seeing her after a long day apart.

"Who's a good girl? Were you a good girl? Were you good for Christina?" Margie scratched Stella's soft brown ears and kissed the top of her head, trying to calm the excited animal. "Such a good girl. Yes, you are."

Christina was at the kitchen table with her school books spread out around her, but she was on her phone rather than working studiously on her textbook and computer. She waved at Margie, but made no sign that she intended to break off the call.

Margie took another deep breath, reminding herself not to be impatient with her teenager. She petted and scratched Stella some more, then went to the fridge. She'd had a granola bar in the car, but otherwise had not had any supper. Not that there was very much in the fridge. She hadn't gotten into the habit of cooking. Things had been too disrupted since moving to Calgary. Getting everything unpacked and in order, registering Christina for school, visiting with Moushoom, solving the Fish Creek murder. It hadn't left much time to stock the fridge.

Christina shoved her books around on the table looking for something and came up with a half-package of fries from A&W, which she handed to Margie.

They were cold, but maybe they would give Margie the energy she needed to open a can of something. Margie smiled her thanks at Christina, pulling her mask off to make sure that Christina could see that her gift was appreciated. She squirted some ketchup on top of the fries and stood leaning against the counter. She nibbled the fries, checked her email using her phone, and waited for Christina to get off of her call. It sounded like she was talking to a school friend, but not about the homework scattered over the table.

That was okay. With the amount that Christina had complained about having to move to Calgary, and then how bad she had said things were at school, Margie would happily accept her daughter being distracted by a friendship for a bit.

After finishing the fries, she checked the fridge again, and then the freezer. There was ice cream. Fries and ice cream were not a healthy dinner, and she would never have let Christina get away with a meal like that, but she really didn't have the energy to make much else. She sliced a slightly-soft banana into a bowl—that was fruit, and fries were a vegetable serving—and then added a small scoop of ice cream. Dairy. And there was nothing wrong with a moderate amount of sugar. At least it wouldn't keep her up at night when she needed to sleep.

Christina finally got off of her call. She looked at Margie, brows raised. "Ice cream is not dinner."

"Do you want some?"

Christina laughed. "I already had some."

"I hope you at least had a burger to go with it."

"Veggie burger. Yeah."

"I'll be sure to take Stella out for a long walk. Burn off the extra calories."

"I already took her out. And it's dark; you said not to go out after dark."

Margie looked for an excuse why it was okay for her to do, but not for Christina. "Well… I don't know; it will still be dark in the morning if I take her out before work."

"Safer early in the morning than late at night."

"It's not that late yet."

Christina gazed at her.

"Fine," Margie sighed. "But I'm the one who's supposed to be parenting you, remember?"

"Grover says hi."

"Grover?"

"Whatever his name is. Oscar."

"Oh, Oscar." Oscar was a man in the neighborhood who often walked his dog Milo on the pathway when Margie and Christina walked Stella. "Well, hi back, the next time you see him."

CHAPTER FIVE

The video from the park wasn't in yet the next morning, so Margie checked the server to see what other evidence might have been processed by the medical examiner's office or forensics department. She would need to give a briefing on the Glenbow Park murder to the homicide team that morning, and so far there wasn't much to tell them. It might be a look-alike to the killing in Fish Creek, but the parallels were very general and could simply be a coincidence. How many people were normally stabbed in and around Calgary in a month?

Pictures of the contents of the wallet and the man's pockets had been posted to the workspace for the David Smith murder. She paged through them one at a time, looking at each of the cards and bits of paper in the wallet. It all seemed pretty routine. The usual bank and credit cards and customer loyalty cards. The cash that she had noted, a five and a ten. A scrap piece of paper with a woman's name and number on it. A photo of what looked like a high school, with kids in the distance. Maybe he had a kid in school. A club membership card and a rec club card. No sign of anything illegal or alarming.

The contents of his pockets were not much more enlightening. House and car keys. Loose change. Cough drops. Parking ticket stubs. The same type of stuff as she would expect anyone to have in their pockets.

She reviewed the pictures of the crime scene carefully, looking for anything that she hadn't noticed while she was there. There was no medical examiner's report yet, but she hadn't expected there to be. The body had been logged in, that was all.

Margie sighed. She went through her notes and thought through the various angles. They would need confirmation that it could not have been the same killer as the Fish Creek murder. She looked up the number for the Young Offender Center and gave them a call. Identifying herself as a law enforcement officer, she explained that she needed to know whether Abdul James was still in custody.

"Just a moment," the phone receptionist said politely. Margie could hear computer keys tapping rapidly, and then a pause while she waited for the results to display. "And the answer is… yes. Abdul James is still in custody."

"And you're sure he couldn't have been released or… wandered off. Sorry to be such a stickler about it, but sometimes these things do happen, and I need to reassure my investigative team that there is no way he could have been involved in this incident yesterday. No day release?"

The receptionist spent some more time looking through the records, tapping her keys briefly now and then. "No. I don't see anything. He's definitely still here and hasn't had any kind of day pass or work release. He hasn't even been out for court or medical care. Nothing that would have taken him out of the building."

"Good. That's very helpful, thank you."

By the time she got off the phone, she could see the others gathering in the briefing room for their morning "stand-up" meeting. Margie took her notes with her and joined them. Using the computer in the boardroom, she displayed a couple of pictures of the scene and the evidence on the big screen.

"How are things going?" asked Kaitlyn Jones, a blond, round-faced detective. "Were you very late getting home yesterday?"

"Later than I would have liked. But that's gonna happen when you have a murder. Couldn't very well leave it until today. Some coyote might have dragged off the body."

Jones's eyes widened. "Really?"

Margie laughed. "No, I think it would take several of them together, or a bear, to drag away a full-grown man. More likely they would just… eat in rather than take out."

Jones made a face. "Gross, Patenaude."

Margie knew that Jones had seen plenty of murder scenes, many of them more gruesome than an outdoor scene with animal scavenging. But she was still sensitive enough to be disgusted by Margie's suggestion. Or at least to pretend to be disgusted.

"So, anything helpful at the site?" Jones looked at the pictures on the screen.

"We'll go over that in a few minutes. But… not really. Nothing yet. And it was a pretty straightforward stabbing; I don't think they're going to find anything on the post."

Staff Sergeant MacDonald entered the room and everyone straightened up and stopped their conversations. Mac, a tall, gray-haired man with a military bearing, looked around to make sure that everyone expected was present.

"Good morning, all. Detective Patenaude, why don't you brief us on the new case?"

Margie nodded. She outlined the basics and indicated the pictures on the screen. There was little to tell them. "And I have checked with the Young Offender Center about Abdul James. He was definitely in custody all day yesterday and could not have been at Glenbow Park." She shrugged. "Not that I thought he had anything to do with this from the beginning."

"No," MacDonald agreed. "I don't think any of us did, but it is a little disconcerting to have two such similar cases so close together. Where do you plan to go next?"

"I'm waiting for video surveillance and the postmortem. Maybe those will help to narrow the investigation for us. We have his driver's license; I will start to track down his friends and family. Ask questions. See if he was dealing with someone in his life who might have done something like this."

MacDonald nodded. "I doubt that this was a random thing. It will be someone that he had regular contact with. An ex or his ex's new boyfriend. A family member. No sign of drugs or gang membership?"

"No. everything seems clean. And he has no record."

Margie looked around at the team for any other suggestions. But it was a reasonably straightforward stabbing. All she could do was go through the usual police work. Chances were, family and friends would have some idea of directions to look.

They went on to discuss other cases.

DAVID SMITH'S GIRLFRIEND—ACTUALLY his fiancée—was absolutely baffled by the suggestion that he might have been killed by someone he knew. She dabbed at her eyes and blew her nose repeatedly, trying to stay in control of her emotions as she answered Margie's questions. Cathy Lin was an Asian woman with delicate features, several years Smith's junior, with short hair that framed her face. Margie sat on the other side of the conference room table, as far away as she could and still feel like they were having an intimate conversation rather than shouting across the room at each other. She would have to disinfect everything before interviewing anyone else, with all of the tears and mucus…

"I don't know anyone who would want to hurt David." Cathy sniffled. "He didn't have any ongoing arguments with anyone. He didn't have an enemy or an unhappy ex. He was just… David. He was quiet, got along with people. He wasn't involved in drugs or gambling. None of that makes any sense."

"Please don't think that we're accusing him of anything," Margie said. "We're just exploring all of the possibilities. It is very rare that someone does something like this randomly. The victim is almost always known."

"But it still does happen randomly." Cathy sniffled. "There are still… mentally ill people who hear voices telling them to stab someone. It doesn't have to make sense."

"Of course it is possible, but most killers do not have diagnosed mental illness. Hallucinations commanding people to hurt others are very rare. That's why you hear so much about them when they do occur. Because they are novel. Something that doesn't happen every day. Of course we will be looking into the possibility. But it is more productive for us to look at David's life and figure out if someone targeted him. I know it's a shock, and I'm sorry that we have to talk to you about it right now, when your grief is so fresh."

"It's okay. I don't mind. It's just that… I can't think of anything that would help you. I can give you the names or numbers of his friends and family, but there is no way any of them had anything to do with this."

"Did David walk in the park a lot?"

"Yes, he liked the outdoors. He likes to walk and be in nature. Liked. It's calming. He would relax at the end of the day or get out there in the early morning."

"Did you ever go with him? Did he have any walking partners?"

"Sometimes I would go with him on a Sunday, when I had more time, but not usually during the week. I couldn't get out of bed that early, and I don't like walking while it is dark."

"Did he have other people he went with?"

"No. Sometimes when I would go with him, he would see people that he knew. You know, he would wave and say 'that's Ken' or whatever. They were regulars that he saw other times. Some people were in the park all the time, walking or volunteering, and they got to know each other by name. But they were just acquaintances. Not anyone that he brought home for dinner or went out for a beer with."

Margie nodded. She took a minute to make some random notes before pursuing her next question so that it wouldn't sound like an accusation. "He drank?"

"No. Not a lot. He would go out for a beer now and then. He wasn't an alcoholic. He never got drunk."

"And he never said anything to you about getting into a fight at the bar. An argument. Losing a darts game and someone got upset. Something that seemed overblown or that he was worried about."

Cathy took longer to think about it, really considering the question. Maybe she hoped to find an explanation that was simple and wouldn't point to anyone she knew. Something that made sense.

But she shook her head and dabbed at her eyes. "No. I don't remember him ever saying anything like that."

"Okay. If you think of anything, please let me know." Margie pressed one of her business cards into Cathy's thin, moist hand. "I'm so sorry for your loss."

CHAPTER SIX

*M*argie had dealt with enough grieving family members and friends for one day. She needed a break. Everyone had said the same thing anyway; they couldn't think of anyone that David Smith ever had a problem with. He was shy and kept to himself and was a genuinely nice guy. He enjoyed walking in the park and was recognized by many of the regular walkers there. No one knew of anyone he'd had an argument with, cut off in traffic, or beat out for a promotion at work. He hadn't stolen or slept with anyone's girlfriend. He didn't have a load of money put away that his next of kin would like to get their hands on.

They were all just grief-stricken and Margie really couldn't deal with it anymore.

She decided to learn more about the setting. Maybe what had happened to David Smith had to do with something that had occurred in the park. Perhaps Smith and his killer preferred their own company but had the same favorite place to sit and reflect. Maybe Smith had a memorial there for a family member and someone had disrespected it, or vice versa. People sometimes became possessive about places or about a certain set of rules being followed, even if it didn't make sense to an outsider.

She pulled up the Alberta Parks website and read through the details about how the park had been established by the Harvie family, following through on the legacy their father left, protecting his favorite place from encroachment by the city. There were facts on the names of the trails, the elevations, the hours of the Visitor Center.

Margie switched to a broader internet search to see what other information was available and found the Glenbow Ranch Park Foundation's site. There were a number of educational programs and opportunities being run. A review of the social media sites and image searches showed a wide variety of flora, fauna, landforms, and old buildings and equipment that could be found in the park. There was a book on the history of the land, *Grass, Hills, and History*. Margie thought it might be a good idea to get a copy for herself to see what the history of the place was.

There was always the possibility of a land dispute. Someone who thought that the land should belong to him. Or maybe Siksiká lands or sacred sites that had been taken away from them.

She looked through the pictures of the old houses, school, and other buildings that had once graced Glenbow in its glory days. There had been a thriving village, a sandstone quarry, and many other services at one time. Now it was all gone.

Margie read it all with interest. She saved some of the files to the case workspace to refer back to later. While there was the possibility of a land dispute, why would someone kill David Smith over it? He didn't have any claim over the park or the land. He wasn't misusing it, just taking walks out there. If someone had a dispute, it would be more logical to aim it at the provincial government or the Foundation, or even the Harvie family members. Not a random park visitor.

Unless David himself had a bone to pick with someone about it. But from what his family and friends had said, she didn't think that was very likely.

She came across a treasure hunters site which claimed there were Indigenous artifacts still in the park, that there was something of value from the old quarry, or that one of the old residents of "Millionaire Hill" had buried money somewhere on the grounds to keep it safe. Margie read the remainder of the page. Maybe somebody had thought that there was something of value there. It wasn't very likely, but people loved to believe unlikely stories. Especially when finding treasure was a possibility.

Had David Smith found something? Or said that he knew where some priceless artifact was? If he was always walking the park, then who was more likely to have an idea of the location of a treasure or artifact?

She jotted down some notes. It probably wasn't anything, but it was a nice diversion from talking to the grieving family and friends.

After consideration, she called the number of the Visitor Center. It was answered by a cheerful female voice offering to help.

"I don't know if you can help me." Margie identified herself. "I am working on the investigation of the… death out your direction. I was just reading some information online about the possibility of artifacts or treasures in the park. I don't suppose you would have any information on that, do you?"

"Well…" the voice on the other end of the phone was hesitant. "We consider the natural features of the park to be its treasures. The plants and animals, the landforms and viewscapes… it's all very important to us and brings joy to our visitors. You can't put a price on that."

"Of course." Margie couldn't help smiling. "But you know that's not what I'm talking about. Nobody killed David Smith over a viewpoint. Are there other artifacts in the park? Things of monetary value?"

She didn't suppose there was any point in asking. If there were something known to be of value, then it would have been removed, not left in place.

"I suppose there are," the receptionist said. "We don't make public any of the archaeological sites where there may still be artifacts present, but we are aware of several sites with archaeological importance. There was a study done before the park was even formed, and there have been a number of follow-up studies since then by various organizations or students."

"What kind of sites?"

"I really can't discuss them. They are not disclosed to the public so that they won't be overrun. People wouldn't leave them alone if they knew where they were. We have taken our lessons from other parks."

"Indigenous artifacts?" Margie questioned. "Money or treasures from the old ranchers or townspeople? Something still in the quarry?"

"The only thing that was ever in the quarry was sandstone," the woman replied with a laugh. "And not even the highest quality sandstone, at that. It was used to build several of the buildings in downtown Calgary and the Legislature in Edmonton, but they found better quality sandstone elsewhere, and the quarry was turned to a brickworks. But then it too went under. There wasn't any way for Glenbow Village to survive without industry, and gradually people moved out until it was a ghost town."

Margie made a couple of notes in her notepad. The helpful visitor information lady had not answered whether there were any Indigenous artifacts or treasures from the old ranchers. What had they discovered on archaeological digs in the past? It was frustrating that they wouldn't release the information to her. She didn't have enough evidence that it was relevant to get a subpoena to demand copies of the archaeological studies. There might be some of the information she needed in the Glenbow history book, but she suspected that if it was not fit for public consumption when someone called the information line, it would have been kept out of the book too. Still… it might be worth looking and finding out some more information about the park's history. Then she would have a better idea of whether there were anything worth pursuing.

"So is Glenbow considered a ghost town?" Margie asked. "I didn't realize that any of it was still standing. Do you have people exploring there?"

"The ruins of Glenbow are out of bounds. Visitors are not supposed to be on or in those ruins. We don't want anyone stepping on a rusty nail or having some other accident out there. It isn't safe. It's in our best interests to just keep people away from the townsite."

"How much of it can you still see?" Margie was still tapping in computer searches and paging through the various image results. On typing in 'Glenbow Village ruins,' she was presented with pictures of a house with a sagging roof and several chimneys or other brick or sandstone structures that remained of houses long since gone. "Hmm. Not very much, I guess."

"No. We only have one house still standing, and no one is allowed to go inside. That would be very dangerous. And we don't want any vandalism." Her voice lowered to a serious tone. "People have very little respect for historical sites."

"I'm not surprised to hear that." Margie remembered being a patrol officer, and the amount of graffiti and destruction they'd had to deal with in Winnipeg. It was sickening how little people cared about historical sites or even just the spaces they lived in. A lot of hard work went into building communities, and their appearance and reputation could be destroyed in a few minutes with a can of spray paint or a few bullets or kicks.

"Do you get a lot of vandals in the park?"

"Luckily, not a lot. We are far enough away from the city that people don't happen onto the park by accident. They have to plan to come out here and have transportation. And we have Conservation Officers patrolling the park and trying to keep any... unwelcome parties out of the park."

"Yes, I've met a few of your CO's. They seem to be very diligent and dedicated to the parks they patrol."

"Our CO's are some of our greatest fans. We have some of them out here even on their days off, just because they want more time to walk the park and just relax and recharge."

Margie felt a sense of longing to be home with her daughter and to take Stella out to the park for a walk. Even just that little strip of green space along the ridge of the irrigation canal meant something to her. She could see how the Conservation Officers would fall in love with the parks they spent so much time protecting.

"Do your CO's use the golf carts all the time, or do they do foot patrols?"

"They walk, use carts or trucks, or ride horses. Whatever is the best way to get to where they want to go."

"They ride horses?"

"Yes, we have a few horses in the park that they can take out as needed."

"That's awesome." Margie had only ridden horseback a couple of times, and she had loved it. She didn't know if it was in her blood, because of her ancestry, or if she just happened to enjoy it, but she wished that she lived somewhere she could ride occasionally. When she had some spare time. But so far, spare time was just about as rare in Margie's life as a horse to ride.

"If I was to come to the park tomorrow, do you think someone could give me a short tour?" she suggested. "I'd like to get a better sense of the scope of the park, and whether these archaeological sites might have anything to do with David Smith."

"Of course, someone would be glad to help you out. Let me just look at the schedule for tomorrow and make sure that we will have someone available with a cart." There was silence for a few minutes, then the woman was back. "Yes. I'll make a note of it here. If you will come by the Visitor Center in the morning, we can have someone help you out."

What were the chances that Margie was going to find anything related to David Smith's death on her little guided tour? Margie put them at slim to none. But she would at least get a ride around a beautiful park, and that was almost like taking a holiday.

CHAPTER SEVEN

Margie had not planned on just vegging out in front of the TV when she got home. She had lots of plans. After taking Stella for a walk, she and Christina would take some time to unpack the few boxes that were left. They would wash the windows, vacuum, and maybe she would make some of the phone calls that were way down on her list that she just hadn't been able to summon up the energy to make.

But she was wiped out at the end of the day, and a person had to take a break now and then to just rest and regenerate, didn't they?

"Mom? Mom!" It took several calls before Margie was roused from her deep meditation in front of the silver screen.

"Christina! I'm awake. What was that?"

"Mom, did you see the way Stella is acting? I think there might be someone in the back yard."

"What?" Margie blinked herself awake, shaking away the cobwebs with a quick twitch of her head. She looked across the kitchen to where Stella slunk at the back door, sniffing the crack on the bottom edge with great concentration. "Stella? What is it? Is there someone there?"

Stella looked up for a moment, regarded her, and then put her nose to the floor again to sniff the air coming in under the door.

"Can you see anyone out there?" Margie went into Christina's bedroom, which looked into the back yard. She held her face against the window, staring out into the darkness. She could see little more than darkness. But looking out the window with the light of the kitchen and living room glowing behind her, she was probably very visible to anyone who happened to be in the yard.

"Is there anyone there?" Christina asked in a hushed voice.

"Not that I can see. She might have just smelled a skunk. There are a lot of them around."

"Yeah." Christina giggled. "Every time I look at the community page, somebody is complaining about their dog getting sprayed by a skunk. So probably *not* the best time to let Stella out into the yard."

"Probably not," Margie agreed.

As she pulled back from the window, she thought she saw a movement. Just her own reflected image in the glass? Or had there been something else out there? Something or someone who waited until she had pulled back from the window and couldn't see out anymore?

Margie shook her head. She was tired, and if she let her imagination get away from her, she wouldn't be able to get any sleep. Every noise the house made would sound like someone breaking in.

They were in a safe place. Nothing was going to happen to them there. Stella would be barking if there were some sort of threat outside the door. She would go nuts if there were an intruder and she thought she needed to protect her pack.

"I don't think it's anything to be concerned about, hon," she told Christina in a calm voice.

Christina nodded and took it in stride, not doubting Margie's words. Margie went to the freezer, wondering if there were any ice cream left.

MAYBE BECAUSE SHE had been worrying about not being able to sleep, Margie ended up tossing and turning. It seemed impossible to find a comfortable position in her bed. She usually slept well. She worked hard, and she had a walk with Stella after she got home, and after unwinding for a while in front of the TV, she was able to get to sleep quickly after tucking herself in.

But it was different this time. She closed her eyes and then, a few minutes later, opened them, wondering why she had bothered to close them in the first place if she was not tired. She had so much to do. It was going to be a busy day the next day if she were going to make her way all the way back out to Glenbow Park for another look around and a golf cart tour.

Margie was wide awake. It wasn't like those super frustrating nights when she was so overtired that she couldn't find sleep. She felt perfectly awake. She had no desire to sleep or sense of sleepiness at all.

She got up quietly and checked to make sure that Christina was in bed with the light off and all of her devices tucked away for the night. She walked around and checked the locks on the door, even though she had done that as part of her regular get-ready-for-bed routine. Stella noticed that she was up and padded after her, sniffing at each of the doors studiously, gathering whatever information her prodigious nose could sniff out. Stella looked up at Margie and whined.

"I know," Margie said. "There's nothing to worry about. I just couldn't get to sleep. I know there isn't anything out there. I just needed… to be sure."

Stella made a noise halfway between a huff and a sneeze. Margie wiped off her wet ankle. "Gee, thanks. Do you think you could slobber on your own feet?"

Stella pushed her nose into Margie's hand, demanding pets and scratches. Margie scratched her ears. "Yes, you're a good girl. You're a good dog. Even if you do sneeze and drool on me."

Margie warmed up a glass of milk in the microwave. Not the way her grandmother would have made it but, hopefully, it would still do the trick. She and Stella took one last circuit around the house, looking out each window and making sure that everything was secure.

SHE WAS sure that would be the end of it. Just one of those nights when things seemed disrupted. When she woke up in the morning, everything would be just like normal and all of the unease of the previous night would have disappeared. But instead, Margie felt worse than ever when she forced herself to slide out of bed and get started on her day. There was a tension in her belly, a tightness like a knot. Margie looked in on Christina and was relieved to see her in her bed sleeping peacefully. She'd dealt with too many parents in the past who had put their children to bed at night, and when they got up in the morning, they were gone. Teenagers, usually, but sometimes younger schoolchildren or even toddlers. They wandered off sleep-walking or were abducted by spouses. They ran away or left to go to a party and never returned. The parents had to live with the guilt that went along with letting their child wander off in those few hours they were blissfully unconsciousness.

A person couldn't be vigilant all day. Margie couldn't protect her child from all evil influences. There were things she could never protect Christina from, no matter how hard she tried.

Margie started the coffee brewing. While she was trying to cut back and not have coffee every morning before breakfast—or *for* breakfast—she knew that she couldn't do without it after a night like that. She was going to need the caffeine to get her motor running.

Of course, caffeine didn't help with anxiety. In fact, it amplified it. She reminded herself as she breathed in the smell of the coffee as it brewed that she would probably feel worse in the afternoon. She would get an initial kick from the coffee, but she would have a mid-afternoon crash. Being so tired and anxious, it would probably be a doozy, and she needed to keep in mind that it was just because of the caffeine. It didn't mean that anything was really wrong with the world or that anyone was out to get her.

Stella was scratching at the back door to get out. Margie let her into the yard. She went into Christina's room, where she could see through the window that the back gate was still shut and latched.

"Hey, sleepyhead. Time to start getting up."

"Not yet," Christina groaned.

Margie was going to protest that Christina needed to get up and moving if she were going to catch the bus and get to school on time.

"You said I can choose what time to get up," Christina mumbled. "You said as long as I was getting to school, you wouldn't bother me."

She was right, of course. Margie was trying to allow her daughter the space to learn to be a responsible adult, and that meant that if she didn't choose to get up until ten minutes before the bus and ended up having to eat on the run and fly out the door in a panic, that was the natural consequence of her choice. As long as Margie didn't get reports from the school that Christina was late to or missing classes, Margie wouldn't enforce a specific bedtime or wake-up time.

"Okay. I just wanted to check the back gate. If you want to get a few more minutes sleeping, you can."

"'Night." Christina's long, even breaths resumed. Margie was impressed with Christina's ability to go back to sleep once she'd been awakened. She herself probably would have found it impossible to get back to sleep again and would have had to get up, whether she liked it or not. Margie went back to the kitchen to start on her coffee, then to the bathroom for a quick wake-up shower. If she got hers in early, she wouldn't have to fight Christina for it later when there was no longer time for both of them to use it.

By the time she got back to her coffee , she could hear Christina stirring. She got up and used the bathroom. When she came into the kitchen, she ran her fingers through her tangled hair, blinking in the sunlight.

"Hi." Her voice was rough and sleepy still.

"Morning. Did you have a good rest?"

"Yeah, it was fine." Christina helped herself to a cup of coffee.

Margie bit her tongue and didn't say anything about it. She couldn't very well criticize Christina for drinking coffee when she herself did. Allowing Christina some privileges of adulthood helped Margie enforce more important rules, such as no alcohol. At least, Margie hoped it would work that way.

Christina took a few swallows of her coffee. She went to open the door when Stella barked to be let in.

"Mom!"

Margie moved quickly at Christina's cry of alarm. She saw Stella on the back step, mouth open in a pant, her muzzle bloody.

"Is she hurt?" Margie crouched down in front of Stella for a closer look. She pushed back Stella's lips to look at her teeth and gums and examined her nose and face for any sign of an injury. She'd heard of people tossing meat spiked with sewing needles into back yards to injure pets. She couldn't see any sign of injury on Stella. She looked around, scanning the yard for the source of the blood. If it didn't come from Stella, then…?

"There's something over there," Christina motioned to a dark mound Margie could just barely see.

Margie slid on a pair of garden clogs—one day, she was going to start gardening—and strode through the cold, wet grass to see what it was.

It took a minute for her to be able to recognize the lump of fur stippled with dark blood as a rabbit. She stared, trying to process it. Stella surely hadn't killed the rabbit. She chased rabbits sometimes when they were out for a walk, and Margie knew that she was hope-less at it. The rabbits always zig-zagged away, leaving her in the dust. Maybe if one were already sick or injured…

Her stomach was tied in knots. She knew there were city by-laws about vicious animals, including animals that had killed other animals, but she didn't know all of the details. She might have to look them up.

Margie looked more closely. She was a homicide detective; it didn't bother her to look at the dead body of a rabbit. Except it did. Just as looking at a human body always stirred deep emotions despite her need to remain impassive and to compartmentalize those feelings. She tried to look past the areas where Stella had worried at the body. Stella had not been hungry, but curious. Margie tried to figure out how the animal had died. Maybe it had been hit by a car and crawled into their yard. Or another animal had killed it.

But she saw a wound with straight edges.

That didn't make any sense. She remembered the squirrel they had found in the yard. Also dead. Also cut with something with a straight edge. Margie had explained it away to herself that time. The squirrel could have caught itself on something sharp. Animals did get hurt in the wild. Maybe there was a sharp can or a piece of abandoned equipment that she wasn't aware of. A lawnmower blade someone had put aside to clean and sharpen and then never followed up on.

But two dead animals in her yard with injuries caused by a straight edge was hard to explain. The first time she had picked up the body and discarded it in her compost bin. This time it was a bigger animal. Harder to ignore. Harder to explain away how a second dead animal came to be in her yard. It would be one thing if an animal had mauled them. Everyone would assume Stella had killed them. But Stella didn't carry a switchblade in her pocket.

"Mom? What is it?"

"It's just a rabbit, Christina."

"Did Stella—kill it?"

"No. I don't think so."

Christina stood on the back step, looking at her, waiting for her to explain further. But Margie didn't want to clarify unless Christina asked for more details. It was better if she didn't know. Christina didn't ask for more. Maybe she knew better from Margie's silence or her body language.

"Are you going to clean it up?"

"I'll do it a bit later. You'd better finish getting ready for school."

Christina looked down at Stella, still by her side. "What about Stella? Will you clean her up?"

Stella would probably eventually lick everything off. But it would be better if Margie wiped her muzzle and face with a towel so they didn't have to look at it or worry about Stella getting flecks of blood inside the house.

"Yes. Would you get me a towel?"

Christina nodded and went to get one.

CHAPTER EIGHT

Once Christina was on the bus, Margie placed a call to her own department. MacDonald was in and was able to take her call.

"Detective Patenaude. How can I help you?"

"This is a personal matter, sir, but I wonder if you could help me out and tell me who to call. And to let you know that I won't be in until later today."

"What's up?"

Margie explained about the rabbit in her yard, and he wasn't too concerned about it until she described how both it and the previously discovered dead squirrel appeared to have been killed by a blade or sharp piece of metal and left dead or dying in her yard.

"You're sure they weren't killed by your dog."

"We've never had anything like this happen before. Of course she chases squirrels and rabbits, but she never catches them. I'm not a pathologist, but I don't see how a dog could leave marks like that. A clean incision. It's possible that once, it could just be some weird acci-dent. I thought maybe a tin can or piece of sharp trash. But twice? Left dead in my yard both times? It wasn't the dog and it couldn't be a coincidence."

"Have you had any threats? Anyone been hanging around your

yard? Any contact from someone you didn't want to have anything to do with?"

"No." Margie cast her thoughts back, trying to identify any threats she might have received, any anger that seemed inappropriate or weird behavior from anyone she'd arrested or had anything to do with since she got to Calgary. It wasn't very hard. She hadn't really had contact with that many people since arriving in Calgary. And the only person she had arrested was Abdul. She had talked to other people. But Abdul was the only one who she had taken into custody.

She remembered Abdul asking about her dog and looking at Stella's picture on her phone. Flipping through the pictures without asking, seeing Christina's photo too. A girl about his own age.

But Abdul was in custody. That had already been established.

"There's… Abdul's foster father. But he never made any threats or said anything inappropriate. He didn't even seem that upset, he just sort of took it in stride."

"He could have been masking deeper emotions. Sometimes it's the quiet ones who feel things the most. Do you want us to pick him up?"

Margie resisted. "No. I don't think it could be anything to do with him."

"Would he know about your dog? Where you live?"

"Well… it's a possibility. He was there when Abdul and I talked about Stella." She was embarrassed and tried to explain further. "I was trying to establish a relationship with him. To talk about how he might have come to be talking with Robinson. You know, two people out walking dogs start talking to each other about the dogs, the view, and so on. Maybe Abdul and Robinson might have struck up a casual conversation about the weather or the view or the fact that they had seen each other there a few times before."

"Are your phone number or address listed anywhere? Somewhere searchable? Do you find them if you Google search yourself?"

"I've been careful; I don't think so. I'll check."

"Did you talk about what area you live in? What it's close to?"

She tried to remember what else she might have revealed around

Abdul or his foster father, Sadiq. "I don't think so, but I don't remember every word I said around them."

"It might be a good idea to check in on him, ask a few questions."

"Yeah. I'll think about that. Who should I call about this rabbit? Is there someone who will come and have a look and not just brush me off as a hysterical woman? I have a daughter. If one of us is being stalked…"

"Let me get you a name. I'll text it to you."

"Thanks. And I'll be late getting in today. Actually, I was thinking of going back to Glenbow Park today for a tour and another look around. Maybe I'll just go out there once I finish here? If I'm going to miss the stand-up meeting anyway, it's a lot faster to take Stoney Trail than to go through downtown rush hour traffic."

"Sure. I'll let everyone know that's where you are. And they can call you if they have questions or information you'll want to hear?"

"Yes. I'll be available on the phone. One of the guys I talked to at the park said there's only one place that has spotty reception; my phone should be working the rest of the time."

*

THANKFULLY, the officer who came out to have a look at the dead rabbit and talk to her about what had happened was serious and engaged and didn't act like Margie was crazy for thinking that someone might be trying to send her a message. Constable Evans nodded and made notes and looked at the body of the rabbit, with flies starting to buzz around it. He pulled down his mask to speak to her, standing well back.

"I'm going to take this with me, if you don't mind. I agree that it doesn't look like it was killed by an animal or an accident, so we'll want to follow up and see if this is something to be concerned about. If we have some sicko out there killing animals then, even if he isn't specifically targeting you, there is still reason to be concerned."

Margie nodded. Everyone knew that killing or torturing animals could be the beginning steps of someone who would later turn to killing or torturing his fellow human beings. If they could catch him before he moved on to people…

She squirmed, anxious and sick to her stomach. She had just arrived in Calgary. She wanted her daughter to be safe. She didn't want to have to worry about some sicko who wanted to terrorize them or was just really enjoying his brutal hobby.

"Do you think…?"

"I think you were meant to find it," Evans said slowly. "If he was just randomly killing animals and throwing them over fences, then I wouldn't expect him to throw them into your yard twice in such a short period of time. If your neighbors were all finding dead animals in their yards, I think you would hear about it pretty quickly."

"Yes. We don't know everybody, but we do… say hello, talk over the fence, stuff like that. And there is a community Facebook page. If there were a lot of animals being killed, I'm sure it would have been mentioned there. Unless it just started."

"Maybe he'll move on to another area to avoid being caught, and this is all that you'll see."

"I hope so. I have a daughter. I don't want to keep finding things like this in the yard. She's here alone sometimes after school or if I have to go out to a crime scene. I want her to be safe being here alone."

"Of course. We'll look into it and see what we can find out. See if there are any similar reports anywhere else in the city, especially in this area. Have the lab examine the rabbit and see what they can tell us about it."

"I'm sorry I already got rid of the squirrel. I expect the bins have been emptied since then. And even if they haven't, it will be buried in there under everything else. I don't imagine the lab techs would be able to tell much about it in that state."

"Maybe if this was an episode of *Bones* and I was from the Smithsonian…" he teased. "But I'm not," he added seriously. "I wish I could tell you that the body is bound to give us the answer as to who is doing this, but I can't do that. Maybe it will tell us something, maybe nothing."

They grimaced at each other. Evans pulled out a business card.

"You can call me directly if anything else happens. Even if you just have an insight or a random thought about who could be doing something like this. Call, text, or email."

Margie took the card. "Thanks."

He nodded. "I'll let you get on to work now. Good luck with your case."

CHAPTER NINE

The young man who met Margie at the Visitor Center introduced himself as Ian. Margie was surprised at how young he was. She had expected that, like at a lot of the museums and conservation areas she had gone to, the docents would be retired folks. People who still wanted to keep their hand on a pet project even when they were no longer able to work there.

"Ian. Nice to meet you. How long have you been working here?"

"A couple of years. Don't worry; I know all of the important stuff. If you have any questions I can't answer, we'll look them up when we get back or I'll find out the answer from someone who knows."

He opened the garage, and Margie saw several golf carts that hadn't been there when she had last seen it. Big carts for a lot of tourists, with a canopy sunshade overhead.

"Oh, I wasn't judging, just surprised that someone so young would be working here."

"We get a lot of kids. University students who are working on their thesises, looking for a summer job, wanting to do a particular study in the park. We have older guides as well, our park stewards in particular, but today you get me."

"And I'm sure you'll do a great job. This is a fascinating place. I was doing some research on the internet about it. There's really a rich history."

"There is," Ian agreed, climbing into one of the smaller golf carts and motioning for Margie to take the seat next to him. Margie sat down. He backed up, turned around, and off they went. He didn't take the same trail as Margie had taken the day of the murder, west to Tiger Lily Loop, but went the other way and, in a few seconds, they were nosing down a long, steep hill.

Margie hung on to the side of the cart and leaned back, but she didn't need to worry that it was too steep for the golf cart. Of course, Ian was used to driving up and down it all the time, and he didn't have any trouble controlling the cart or weaving slowly between various small groups of walkers, cyclists, and mobility scooters.

He smiled at her. "Downhill is easy. The hard part is always making sure you've got enough electricity to get back up the hill again."

"What do you do if you don't?"

"Walk. Or everybody walks except for the driver and, hopefully, he has enough electricity to get it up the hill without the extra weight of passengers. Otherwise, you're going to need to get a tow or a lift in the back of the truck, and that's pretty embarrassing. They'll call you 'Juice' to the end of your days because you ran out of juice."

Margie laughed. "That's cute. Is that your nickname?"

"Not mine." He crossed his fingers and looked heavenward. "Hopefully, it won't ever be."

After the hill, they traveled over a long, level trail out in the sun. It would be a challenging walk on a thirty-degree day.

"Is there running water in the park?"

"No. The washrooms are outhouses. And there are no water foun-tains. If you need water, you have to carry it in with you. There is bottled water available at the Visitor Center when it is open, but it isn't always open. If you've been here once, you generally remember after that."

"I guess so!"

She was silent, looking at the brilliant azure sky with barely a cloud in it. The trees in the direction of the river were starting to change into their autumn colors, pretty yellows dappled among the green. She watched the birds, butterflies, and bees flying among the flowers and bush beside the trail.

"There was frost this morning. I wasn't expecting such a warm day."

"September in these parts is very changeable. You can have frost overnight and twenty-eight or nine during the day. I don't think we'll see any more thirty-degree days this year, but you never know. We still could. What they used to call an Indian summer, before it became politically incorrect."

"Not that anyone in your generation ever called it that."

"No."

He pointed out several different topographical features for her and talked about the bee homes and bird and bat houses built to help preserve various species in the park. The special fescue grasses that were important in the sequestration of carbon. What people had done there when the village was still populated. He mentioned the cattle kept on the property that helped to keep the long grasses cropped down so that they wouldn't be a fire hazard.

There was a growing noise behind them. Margie searched the trees for the origin of the loud rumble. Ian slowed the cart to look, and pointed out the train that Margie could just see through the trees. "You'll be able to see it better in a minute. The CPR line runs through the park and is still quite active. We are part of the shipping route between the coast and Eastern Canada. The CPR line runs from coast to coast."

Margie knew some of the stories of the building of the railway. It had been an important development for Canada, helping to build a unified country. But it had been built on the backs of migrant workers under terrible work conditions, with four Chinese workers being killed for every mile of the railway line through the Fraser Valley. Immigrant labor had just been a commodity, and the big corporations didn't particularly care how many lives were lost in building the railway, just as long as there were plenty more available. Building the railway had also meant moving Métis populations, which had led to the Red River Rebellion.

"What can you tell me about the Indigenous peoples who lived here and any artifacts left by them or the villagers?"

Ian looked at her sideways. "Are you…?"

Margie raised her eyebrows, waiting.

"Are you Native? I mean, you look a little like it…"

Margie chuckled. She patted at her bun, which kept her long, black hair coiled neatly away. Her face would rarely be mistaken for anything but Indigenous Canadian. Maybe Asian or mixed race if you squinted, but her Cree heritage showed.

"I am Métis."

"Oh, okay." He looked relieved that he hadn't put his foot in his mouth by thinking she was something she was not. "Do you come from around here?"

"Was this a Métis settlement?"

"Well, no. The people here are mostly Nakoda. There are other tribes as well, but it was the Nakoda who mostly settled along the Bow River here."

"No, I don't come from this area. I come from Manitoba."

"The Red River Rebellions and all that?"

"Yes. All that."

He nodded wisely. "Well, to answer your question, of course there were Native peoples on this land thousands of years before the white man. It is Treaty 7 land, and the Tsuut'ina Nation is just to the south. We have a good relationship with our neighbors, and they sometimes join us for special park programs and observances."

"So what kinds of things could you find around the park? Teepee rings? Arrowheads? Graveyards?"

"They can answer some of those questions at the Visitor Center. But we can't say too much about what archaeological sites there are in the park or where they are located, so that we don't have treasure hunters ripping stuff up and destroying it. We study what we can. In a very respectful way, following proper archaeological procedures."

"Do you get a lot of people who ask? Or people who wander around here on their own looking for treasures? Have you had much vandalism because of it?"

"We field questions about it pretty regularly," he agreed. "But we do what we can to discourage people from trying to find artifacts. It is destructive."

Margie watched as the vegetation and topography transformed around them again. Every few minutes, they went from one kind of tree dominating the landscape to another; the trail went out to the water and wound away from it again. The shaded areas were cool and the open areas made her break out into a sweat. It was such a varied landscape; she could see how walkers and bikers would want to see it again and again, exploring all of its different facets.

"Tell me some more about Glenbow Village."

He had pointed out the ruins that they had passed, but it was all too quick, and Margie wanted to get a better sense of it. She knew, in the back of her mind, that it really didn't have anything to do with her investigation, and she should finish up her tour of the park and get back to the office where she could continue her desk work. But it was nice just being out in nature, even if it was zipping by a little too fast.

Ian told her some more stories about the village as they continued, pointing out various pieces of their life that the former residents had left behind. Wagon wheels and the shell of a motor car. The old quarry and brickworks. He talked about the school and how it had been moved and preserved.

"This is as far as we are going to go," he told her as they approached the Narrows. "I'll just get turned around, and we'll head back."

"And the trails don't continue through to Calgary?"

"Not yet. But someday soon…"

"Is there a projected date?"

"There are plenty of projected dates. They are doing work on the Haskayne Park access right now. So hopefully *soon*…"

Margie nodded. She knew how city projects could drag on for years. Building and developments promised, infrastructure that had been projected for years and still wasn't anywhere in sight. They couldn't be prepared for all of the changes in the economy. For a downturn in development due to red tape. For the pandemic. Who could ever have predicted the way 2020 alone would unfold?

She recognized the trail as they got close to the steep access hill. "Can I get back to Tiger Lily Loop from here?"

"Yes." He looked at his watch. "But I can't take you there. I have to be back for a scheduled tour."

"That's okay. If you can just point me in the right direction, I can get there. I'd just like to take another look around and to… walk the victim's footsteps, if you know what I mean. Maybe something will occur to me that hasn't before."

"Well, of course you're welcome to walk around and have every right to be investigating up there, so have at it. Just take this trail." He pointed. "Watch for a branch to the right, take that trail, and then you'll be on Tiger Lily Loop. You can go either direction and it will get you back up to the top where the access to the parking lot is. There is a map, so you can stop and look and orient yourself if you're not sure. Or ask someone else who looks like they know where they are going. We have a lot of visitors who come back multiple times and know their way around the park very well. Okay?"

"Yes, that sounds good." Margie looked along the trail but couldn't see where it branched off. But it sounded very straightforward. "Thanks very much for the tour and all of the information. I don't know that it will help at all with the case, but it has certainly made me want to come back for another visit, and to bring my daughter with me next time. Maybe my dog too."

There had been lots of dogs amongst the walkers that she had seen. She knew that there was a leash rule, which was fine with her. Stella was happy to be on a leash, and it would ensure that she didn't chase after any of the ground squirrels or the cattle or a moose or something else that could do her harm.

Ian waved goodbye and turned up the steep pathway to the top.

Margie started out along the trail.

It was afternoon and she hadn't had lunch. She'd barely had breakfast. She had only walked about a kilometer when she realized that she should not have started out without a bottle of water. No food in her system and no water with her, the sun beating down on her on a trail that had minimal tree cover. Not a very good idea if she wanted to complete her walk quickly and still get back to the homicide department to do more work there before the end of the day. All in all, she was afraid it was going to be a wasted day, having gotten no closer to tracking down David Smith's killer.

She shook her head and kept walking, but at a reduced pace. She didn't want to overheat and overstress her body trying to get the walk finished too quickly. One step at a time at a steady, leisurely pace, and she would eventually come out on top and wouldn't be too much worse for wear.

Bicyclists whizzed by her in both directions. She saw walkers of all shapes, ages, and descriptions, from fit-looking oldsters with neatly pressed clothing and wide-brimmed hats to young people in skimpy outfits showing off brilliantly tattooed bodies. Mothers with little children, retirees and amputees on electric scooters; it seemed like everybody had chosen that day to be out enjoying one of the last hot days of the year in the park.

Margie wiped her sweaty forehead and neck and kept going. She hadn't even thought to bring a hat with her. She hardly ever needed a hat; she was never out in the sun long on her walks with Stella and, with the shortening days, the sun was usually too low in the sky both in the morning and the evening to worry about exposure.

She stopped and looked back behind her and then ahead of her. She didn't see any sign of a branching trail. Had she somehow missed it? She didn't see how she could have. She had stopped at a map and looked over it but, to her shame, Margie was terrible at the spatial planning and memory needed to read a map and keep it in her head as she walked. She tried turning on her phone and looking at Google Maps, but the paths were not well marked and were not labeled, so she couldn't be sure if she were on the correct route or not.

She reached a lookout and stood there for a few minutes, looking at the mountains in the distance, the trees beside the river, and a stone chimney jutting up toward the sky. It was not the same view as she had been able to see from Tiger Lily Loop. She was pretty sure she had missed her turn. She didn't know if the trail she was on would eventually loop around and return her to the place she had started with Ian. Even if it did, she was pretty sure she had covered about three kilometers already, and she really didn't want to guess how much farther it would be. She swore under her breath. She turned around and retraced her steps, trying to remember what the turnoff Ian had taken had looked like so she wouldn't go too far back again, but could get up the steep hill and to her car in the parking lot and not keep wandering into the middle of the park, where she might eventually have to call to have someone rescue her.

Ian had told her to watch for the branching trail to her right so, having turned around, it would be on her left. She mentally reviewed both hands and clenched the left so she wouldn't get confused as to which side the branch would be on.

Margie was relieved when she found the trail that broke off to her left. The tension in her shoulders and abdominal muscles relaxed, and she felt like she was in control again. She enjoyed the view, smiled and nodded at other walkers, and stepped forward with confidence. She would check out the loop, satisfy herself that she hadn't missed anything—or alternatively, gain some insight that they had not had before—and she would still have some time to go back to the office to review any other evidence or leads that had come in during her absence. She might be a little late getting home, but Christina would be fine on her own for a couple of hours.

Margie's stomach tightened again when she remembered the squirrel and the rabbit and the possibility that someone was stalking and threatening her. She didn't want to be late getting home. She didn't want Christina taking Stella out for a walk alone. A dog was good defense, and people wouldn't usually attack someone accompanied by a large dog. But it didn't always hold. There was still the possibility that someone would recognize Stella's true wuss nature and not be worried about her reaction. Or they would bring a knife or a gun and be ready to take her out. Or a piece of meat spiked with poison or sewing needles.

She picked up her pace. She shouldn't be wasting so much time walking around the park. Her tour hadn't given her any insight into whether the killer or Smith might have been some kind of treasure hunter, maybe rivals in hunting artifacts. It had been a long shot, but she had hoped that being there would provide the key piece of information that she needed to solve the case.

Nothing on the pathway looked familiar. But Margie had come onto it a different way than she had previously. Or was it the same route as she had taken when Richardson brought her in on the golf cart, and it was just her perspective or speed that made it seem foreign? Margie scanned the scenery, not seeing the beauty anymore, just desperately looking for something that resonated with her. Something familiar that would reassure her that she was on the right path. She had taken her first left, so it should have been the Tiger Lily Loop. She'd missed it the first time but, when she had reversed, coming back from the tall, ominous-looking chimney, she had taken the correct turn. She was sure of it. Ian had said to take the right, and she had reversed direction and taken the left.

For a long time, she didn't see anyone else. The trail dipped down when she had expected it to continue to rise. The trees didn't look right. Nothing looked right. A couple of cyclists whizzed by her, too fast for her to flag them down or ask any questions. Finally, she saw a woman neatly dressed in khakis and a white hat coming toward her, a trekking pole in each hand.

"Excuse me…" Margie stopped her.

"Yes?"

"Is this Tiger Lily Loop?"

"Oh, no, dear. This is the Badger Bowl. Tiger Lily Loop is that way." She gestured back behind Margie.

"Are you sure? I was following the directions that the young man from the Visitor Center gave me…"

"Yes, I'm sure. The trail heads are quite close together; it's easy to mistake them."

Margie turned and looked back the direction she had come, heart sinking. She kept taking the wrong turns. She was going to have walked a half-marathon by the time she got back to the parking lot. On an empty stomach and no water.

"Are you okay, dear? The Badger Bowl is still a nice walk. I'm sure you'll enjoy it."

"I need to be on the Tiger Lily Loop. That's where… I'm a police detective, and that's the one I'm supposed to be checking out."

"Oh, I thought the police were finished with all of that. Didn't you get everything you needed earlier?"

"We gathered all of the evidence. I'm just looking for… inspiration, I guess."

The woman smiled, her wrinkles curving gently upward. "Well… you'll get out of the Bowl faster if you go back the way you came than if you continue around the loop. If you don't mind walking with me, I can show you which way."

"That would be really helpful, actually. I'm so turned around. I don't know the park, and I thought it would be simple to get from one place to another, but I'm not good with directions."

"Not everyone is," she agreed placidly. "My name is Joanne. I'm not fast, but I know my way around. So if you just stick with me, I'll get you to where you need to go."

"I really appreciate that."

They started walking, Margie turning around to go back the way she had come. She sighed. "It really is a beautiful place. I wish I was here for a reason other than the investigation, so I could enjoy it."

"You'll have to come back sometime when you can just relax and take it all in. Or take one of the cart tours. The park is pretty big, but the cart tours can get you from one end to the other so you can get a better idea of the scope."

"I took a quick tour today. It is pretty impressive."

"There's a lot to see."

"Do you know of any artifacts or anything valuable in the park?"

Joanne considered. "Its value is its history and all of the diverse species in the park. Not in anything of monetary value. The park land itself is worth millions. But you can't put it in your pocket and sell it on the street."

"No." Margie made a face that Joanne couldn't see behind her mask. She was puffing a little as she went up the hill again. Joanne seemed to be breathing just fine, keeping a steady rhythm with her trekking poles. Margie was probably just breathing hard because of her anxiety and the feeling that she had to get to the Tiger Lily Loop quickly, even though she didn't expect to find anything there.

"I was so sad to hear about David Smith," Joanne said. "You're investigating the stabbing?"

"Yes. Did you know him?"

"Not well. Just to say hello when we passed each other in the park. He seemed like a nice man. He cared about the park and his health. Like most of us here. We are all doing what we can to stay active, to take care of ourselves and the environment. Getting time in nature is very important. You can't sit in front of electronic screens all day without negative effects. I like my Netflix as well as the next person, but you need to take a break regularly to get your dose of nature and fresh air."

Margie nodded. She felt guilty that she hadn't been able to exercise very much lately, but she was just settling in with a new job. She would find more time. She was walking Stella every day or twice a day. Not long walks, maybe, but it was something.

"I guess I don't need to tell you about the benefits of nature," Joanne said, giving a little laugh. Margie looked at her.

"What do you mean? I mean—I do try to get out, but I'm not sure why…"

"Because you're Indian, I mean. Or whatever the politically correct term is these days. You are, aren't you? I'm glad to see that someone like you is able to get onto the police force. You always hear about racism and how people like you can't get into anything but physical labor."

"Oh. Yes, thank you. And you're right; I was raised to love and respect nature. I don't spend as much time as I should, but I love to be out here." Margie made a motion to include all of the plant and animal life around her.

She thought of Moushoom. She needed to go see him too. Maybe she could take him from his little apartment over to the pathway along Twenty-Sixth Street where she walked Stella. He would probably really like that. She was sure he needed the exposure to nature too. Probably more so than she did. He had grown up in a much more traditional lifestyle, where he had been much more in touch with nature than she had. Maybe that was why he had a much better sense of direction than she did.

Or maybe that was just something about the brain she was born with. While her Cree progenitors probably had an excellent sense of direction, who knew about the early explorers? How many of them had just happened to stumble upon their discoveries because they had no idea where they were going?

She realized that she and Joanne had stopped talking and were just walking in silence. She felt suddenly awkward. "Sorry. Did you ask something?"

"No. Just enjoying the quiet."

"Oh. Okay. Me too. I don't do this very often."

She relaxed as they walked, listening to the rhythm of their feet. They would get there when they got there; there was no point in her getting all wound up about getting back to the office at a specific time. If there were anything urgent, someone on the team would call her. She pulled out her phone to make sure that she still had power and coverage. Both appeared to be strong. They could get her if they needed her.

Eventually, they reached the trailhead.

Joanne pointed. "This is the one you need to follow," she said, indicating the gravel pathway and tracing its directions in the air in front of them. "You can go either way, it's a loop and they will both get you to the parking lot eventually. You're about halfway, so you can take the one you want."

Margie tried to remember which she had taken with the conservation officer to get to the murder scene. She thought it was the left.

"Thank you so much for your help. Who knows how long I would have been wandering if it wasn't for you."

"Oh, someone else would have helped you. You only have to ask. Chances are, the person you ask will know the way. If they don't, just ask the next one. Most of the visitors come regularly."

"I appreciate it. Thanks."

Margie started up the left leg of the trail. "And I can't get lost from here, right? There's no way I'm going to end up in the Badger Bowl again?"

"No. You'll either end up in the parking lot or back here again. Those are the two connection points. And it's pretty hard to miss the parking lot. There's a big sign." Her eyes crinkled as she smiled. "A whole bunch of parked cars."

Margie laughed. "Thank you. Have a great day."

"I will. You too."

Margie breathed a sigh of relief as she started up the trail again. She was going to be just fine. A short walk through the loop. Richardson had told her it was only a few kilometers, and she could walk that far. Then she could stop somewhere in Calgary for a couple of bottles of water and something to eat, and she'd be back at the office again.

CHAPTER ELEVEN

Margie was dragging her feet, but she started to recognize some of the landmarks that showed she was at or near the murder scene. She couldn't remember enough to locate it precisely. It was a lot steeper than she remembered. She wandered off of the path, looking down at the ground for some sign of where Smith's body had been. The vegetation should be crushed—if not by his body, then by the various law enforcement officers and techs gathering forensic evidence and the vehicles that had been parked nearby. There would be some sign that they had been there.

Margie walked back to the trail, went a little farther, and veered off again. It felt closer. But she still wasn't sure.

As she looked around for some sign of where the vehicles had been parked and the yellow tape tied, she suddenly felt as if she were being watched. She stopped and listened. There was no sound of anything but the birds singing and the wind in the trees.

A twig snapped off in the distance somewhere.

An animal? Someone watching her? Someone exploring on their own?

Was someone else looking for the murder scene? Maybe the killer realized he had dropped something? Or was there a treasure he had been afraid David Smith was going to discover first?

She looked around, trying to pick out a figure in the trees. She couldn't see anyone, but couldn't shake the feeling that she was not alone. Why had Smith been killed there? Was there any significance to the place? Or was it just by chance? A random stranger? As much as she had emphasized to Cathy Lin that most murderers were not random crazies, there were a few. Every now and then, it did happen.

Another twig snapped, from a different direction this time. Margie turned slowly, aware of her peripheral vision, paying attention to whether someone was trailing or flanking her, trying to avoid being seen.

"Excuse me! You're supposed to stay on the pathways!"

The loud male voice made her jump, and Margie whirled around to confront the speaker. For a split-second, she was afraid. The man was closer than she had expected. Big, well-built, not someone whom she was going to be able to beat easily in a physical confrontation, if it came to that. But within a couple of seconds, she recognized him as the RCMP officer who was involved in the investigation.

"Constable Shack."

"Detective Pat." He rolled his eyes and blew out his breath. "It's you. I'm sorry, I didn't recognize you when your back was to me. Figured you were some curiosity-seeker, or maybe our doer, returned to the scene of the crime."

Margie wasn't sure whether she should be insulted that he had identified her as a potential suspect. But there was nothing to say that the killer hadn't been a woman. A sharp blade skillfully handled didn't require the upper body strength of a man to be effective. She wondered whether there was anything in her mailbox from the medical examiner's office yet. They should have had the time to do the postmortem—at least the preliminary results.

"You startled me."

"Sorry about that," he apologized again. "Force of habit. And I have a naturally loud voice. My wife is always getting after me for shouting when as far as I know, I was just using a conversational tone."

"Am I in the right place? Is this where he was?"

"Just a little farther up the trail." He pointed the way and then led her on. "Are you looking for anything in particular?"

It was strange that he had been drawn back there too. Was it because they had so little to go on? They had both returned, hoping to find a little something more to make sense of the situation?

"No. I just needed to see it again. Get it firmly in my mind. See if I could connect up anything… anything that might have been motive. I don't like the idea of a killing without a connection to the killer. There had to be some kind of motive. If it wasn't robbery or drugs or something personal like jealousy or rage, then what was it? What made him kill Smith?"

Shack nodded his agreement.

They went a little farther up the trail, and then Smith indicated the area. "Right over here."

They walked through it silently, separating and casting about on their own. Margie was becoming more and more anxious about Shack being there. She had wanted to be there alone. She had wanted to connect with the murder scene somehow, and having him there was blocking her. She felt like she had to watch him and be aware of him the whole time.

Eventually, they both stopped and looked at each other. "Nothing?" Shack asked.

"No. Nothing."

"Me neither."

She looked carefully at his hands and then his face. He had stooped down a couple of times to examine the ground; she had watched him out of the corner of her eye. But he didn't appear to have picked anything up. If he had, then he was skilled at sleight of hand.

Margie took out her phone to record the GPS coordinates. If she came back again, she would be able to find it on her own. And she might search the GPS coordinates on some treasure hunter sites, just to see if anything popped up. It was far from the village or any artifacts as far as she knew, but it would be worth checking out, just to be sure.

"Calling someone?" Shack inquired.

"No. Just making a note."

He waited, she thought, for an explanation, but she didn't give him anything more. Their departments were cooperating, but that didn't mean that she needed to float all of her ideas past him. They would share evidence and information that had been verified, but she didn't have to tell him everything she was thinking.

She remembered the medical examiner. "Do we have the post results yet?" she asked Shack. "I have been busy with other things and haven't seen it."

"Yeah, about an hour ago. Nothing unexpected. No drugs or poison or tattoos of secret societies." There was a smile in his voice at this joke. Margie didn't smile in return.

"So, nothing of interest."

"Nothing that jumped out at me. But of course, you might see something. I haven't read it in detail yet either, just skimmed through for any red flags."

"Okay. I'll look at it when I get back to the office." Even so, she wanted to make sure that she had received it, so she unlocked her phone and navigated to her mail, running her eye down the list of email subject lines. She tapped to open the email and then the attachment.

One thing she wanted to check just to confirm to herself… she found the description of the stab wound and what the medical examiner had been able to deduce about the blade used and the attacker.

"It was a downward stroke," she pointed out, demonstrating stabbing down into someone.

"Yes," Shack agreed.

"The Fish Creek murder was not. It was lower, and an upward stroke. Someone shorter than the victim. Going up under the ribs instead of trying to stab down through them." Abdul had been trained to kill. He knew a knife went in more easily under the ribs.

"What are the comparative heights of the victims?"

"They were both a shade over six feet."

"And the Fish Creek murder fits with the guy that you arrested. A kid. Someone shorter than him."

"But not this one. For a downward stroke to hit him in the chest where it did at that angle, you're looking for an attacker who is taller than Abdul. Someone closer to six feet tall himself."

"Good to know. But you already checked that it couldn't be the boy anyway, didn't you?"

"Yeah. I just want to eliminate him as a possible suspect in as many ways as possible. He didn't do it. There's no point in speculating that it could have been him."

Shack nodded. "Okay. The kid is off the table. At least there's one thing we know, in a whole lot of nothing."

Margie sighed. "Yeah."

"Can I walk you to your car? You know where it is?"

"Oh, no. I'm fine. I just follow this trail until I get to the parking lot."

He nodded. Margie went back to the pathway and started walking.

"Uh, Detective Pat?"

"What?"

"Other way. Unless you want to take the long way around."

She squinted at the sun, which was too far overhead for her to tell directions by it. She didn't think she was walking back the direction she had come. But she wasn't sure enough to argue with him.

"Oh. Right. Thanks."

She turned around and walked the other direction. She could tell that Shack was watching her all the way until she was out of sight. Even then, she couldn't relax. She couldn't shake the feeling that she was still being watched.

CHAPTER TWELVE

By the time she reached the parking lot, she was exhausted, hungry, thirsty, needed to use the washroom, and was irritated with herself and everyone else for the long hike. It was supposed to be an easy walk. Just a quick zip around the loop. It had ended up being a lot more than that, and she was still jumping out of her skin every time she heard a voice, a dog bark, or a twig snap.

Luckily, there was a washroom just off the parking lot. Only an outhouse, as Ian had told her, but it was better than nothing. That took care of one problem. She then climbed into her car, turned it on, and blasted the air conditioning. She didn't have any water in the car. Maybe she should keep it stocked if she were going to go on unplanned walks in the park.

She pulled back onto Glenbow Road and pointed her car uphill to get back to the highway. She hit her Bluetooth button and called the office. Detective Jones picked up on the third or fourth ring.

"Well, hello, stranger. Long time no see."

"Sorry I've been MIA today. I spent longer at the park than I expected to."

"I hope that means it was a productive trip and you found something."

"No, it was pretty much a bust."

"Pretty much?"

"I ran into Constable Shack out there."

"Really?" Jones's voice was curious. "What was he doing there? You're the primary. I would think that he would let you know if he was chasing anything down."

"Me too. I don't know that he had anything, though. I guess he was just doing the same thing as I was, looking for some clue as to why the killer attacked Smith. There had to be a motive for killing him."

"But you didn't find anything."

"No. Neither of us found anything. Or if he found anything, he didn't tell me about it."

"But you were there together, so he couldn't have found anything."

"I don't think so. It kind of creeped me out, Shack being there at the same time as I was. He had no way of knowing that I would be there. I didn't even know that I was going to be there at just that time."

"So, he wasn't there to meet you."

"No."

"It was just luck that you both ended up there at the same time."

"Exactly." Margie pondered on it. "I felt like I was being watched. Both before I ran into him and after."

"And you think..." Jones trailed off, waiting for Margie to jump in and complete the thought.

"I don't know. Was he watching me? Following me? He offered to walk me to my car. Why? Did he want to make sure that I was really leaving? Or was he being polite? Or did he think that I could be in danger?"

"He's an RCMP constable. I'm sure he was just being polite," Jones said firmly.

Margie wished she could believe it, but her imagination was running overtime. She hated the wired, anxious feeling. She looked in her rear-view mirror. There was a car behind her, but she couldn't see the face of the occupant through the glare on the windshield.

"I saw that the postmortem results came in. I'll have a look at them when I get back. Was there anything else?"

"Nothing that seemed to lead anywhere. An inventory of the items collected at the scene. What has been processed for prints. Pictures. It's kind of weird—"

Suddenly, Jones was gone.

CHAPTER THIRTEEN

Margie looked at her display and saw that the call had dropped. She looked in her mirror again at the car that was following her, as if it might somehow be his fault.

What did she think? That he was jamming her signal to keep her from talking to her office? That it was Shack, making sure that she couldn't get some vital piece of information on a piece of evidence that had been processed?

She pulled quickly onto the highway, spraying gravel behind her as if Shack were pursuing her, and she had to get away before he could ram her or force her off the road. The car behind her didn't pull out at such a reckless pace, but smoothly pulled into traffic and hung a few cars back from her. She watched to see if it would stay behind her. It did. But more than likely, he was going back to Calgary just as she was. There was only one way to go to get there. He stayed behind her because she had pulled out quickly and was staying just over the speed limit. He wouldn't pass her unless he broke the speed limit.

She kept an eye on the car, but started to relax. Shack or Dr. Kahn had told her there was a spot where the cell signal dropped, right at the top of the hill where she had been cut off from Jones. That was all it was. Right where you expected the signal to be the best, there was a blind spot and the call would drop. And he had been right.

Feeling silly about her panic, Margie called Jones back. "Sorry, I lost you there. Bad cell signal. What were you saying?"

She still kept an eye out for the car that had followed her off of the park, but tried to push away the anxiety.

"Just that I was hoping you would go through the items that he had on him. Something doesn't feel right."

"What?"

"I don't know. I can't put my finger on it. There's that woman's name and number…?"

"Right, I remember that. Nothing weird about someone writing down a phone number."

"Except today, who writes it on a piece of paper and puts it in his wallet. You'd put it in your phone, wouldn't you?"

"Well, I would, but some people are not big on technology. My mother wouldn't."

"And it's not a phone number."

Margie frowned. "It isn't?"

"Not unless he wrote it down wrong. It's only six digits. I think it is something else. Like a serial number."

Even though Canada had required ten-digit numbers for several years, Margie still often only wrote down the seven digits after the area code, unless it was a different area code from what she expected. Calgary had long been area code 403, and people still left it off when giving their phone numbers or writing them down. Margie hadn't even noticed that the number on the slip of paper was only six digits long.

"Hmm. I guess it could be something else. Maybe… he reported a theft?" Her mood lifted a little. Maybe it was a break in the case. "Maybe… if there was a theft, could it have been related to his murder?"

"I don't know," Jones's tone was doubtful. "That doesn't really… make much sense. How would a serial number lead the police to a burglar? How would killing Smith keep them from finding out?"

"Maybe he hadn't made the report yet, but he was going to.

Maybe the killer knew, and he knew that if the report was made, it would lead him to a pawnshop claim ticket or a Kijiji ad. Maybe…?"

"Maybe. But it doesn't feel right."

"Okay. Well, I'll look at it when I get there. Maybe something will come to me. I'm a little muddled right now."

"You'll be here in half an hour or so?"

"Bit longer. I'm going to grab a bite to eat. I haven't had anything today, and I've been walking forever."

"I thought you were going on one of those golf carts?"

"I did for the first part, but then I wanted to walk the Tiger Lily Loop, and I ended up in Badger Bowl…"

Jones giggled. "Are those really the trail names? I like Badger Bowl."

"Yeah, those are really their names. I didn't see any badgers, though."

"Luckily. I understand they're pretty vicious."

"Are you going into Cochrane to eat?"

"Into Cochrane? Why would I? That's the opposite direction."

Margie automatically checked the road sign coming up to confirm that she was driving toward Calgary, not Cochrane.

"Ice cream."

"Ice cream?"

"Yeah, MacKay's. They are the best place in the region to go for ice cream. You have to go there."

"Well… not today. What makes them so good?"

"They make all kinds of cool flavors. They're an institution. They've been there since I was a kid. Since my parents were kids."

"I'll have to take Christina there one day. Make it a mother-daughter date."

"Yeah, you have to do it," Jones said, sounding envious. "I should have told you before you went out there today. I forget that you're not from around here, so you wouldn't know about MacKay's."

❧

HER BLOOD SUGAR back on an even keel and one bottle of water under her belt, Margie was feeling a lot better when she got back to the squad room. She laughed at herself for being so paranoid about somebody following her or being anxious with Shack being there at the same time as she was. She should be happy to know that he was investigating as well. She needed all of the help she could get.

She said hello to the various team members who were working away busily on their cases, staring at computers, talking on the phone, and making notes on the files. Jones greeted her cheerily. Margie sat down at her computer to look at the evidence again. Everything that had been in Smith's pockets had seemed normal at the time, but she might have overlooked something. Like the woman's phone number not being a phone number.

She brought up the photograph of the piece of paper and studied it.

Stella.

Like her dog. It was always funny to run into familiar names in other places. She didn't think she had ever met a person named Stella. That didn't mean that there weren't any, just that it wasn't a very common name anymore. People associated it with that scene in *A Streetcar Named Desire*. If she went by Jones's instinct that it might be a serial number, then Stella might be a brand name. Margie did a quick internet search.

A fashion company. A new Calgary condo development. Lager. She followed a link to the Stella condos and clicked through a few pages. Maybe Smith had been planning to move. The number could be a real estate listing. A phone number that he'd copied down wrong. Maybe some kind of land titles reference number. She would call around and see if she could find out.

While she was at it, she figured it was time to look at the other items that had been on the body again. Pictures of his phone had been posted, but none of the content. Maybe they hadn't gotten to it yet, or maybe there was nothing on it. Or they were still trying to get it unlocked. Those things could take time. There was a photo that had been in his wallet. His cards.

Margie cracked open her second bottle of water as she leaned forward to study the screen. She had a headache at the back of her head that she thought was from dehydration or the sun, so she needed to drink more. She enlarged the photo on the screen.

Having met Cathy Lin, she expected to find the young woman in the picture somewhere, but she was not there as far as Margie could see. She was too old to be a high school student, if that's what the building in the picture was, but she could be a teacher. She didn't remember asking Lin what her profession was. The picture didn't seem to focus on anyone in particular. Like it was a stock photo of a school, very generic. A day in the life. Apparently, nothing to be found there.

Cards in the wallet. Driver's license, credit cards, bank card, Canoe Club, Calgary Co-op membership, Community Natural Foods membership, Optimum points, library membership. Just a regular guy doing normal, everyday things. No firearms permit. No radical or religious groups. No cards in names other than that of David Smith.

She rubbed the back of her head and neck, hoping the pain and fatigue would go away. She had another sip of water and went back to the workspace for the case to check for further information.

CHAPTER FOURTEEN

Margie made sure to get off of work in good time. She could do some more work on the case later in the evening while Christina was working on her homework. But she didn't want Christina to be alone in the house after she got home from school. It was important to make sure she was safe.

Margie wasn't sure what to tell her about the rabbit and her suspicion that someone might be stalking or trying to scare her. Christina knew, of course, that since Margie was a police officer, she could be hurt in the line of duty. They both knew there were risks, though Margie wasn't sure whether Christina understood them as well as someone older and more experienced. Teenagers tended to have a strange relationship with mortality, not understanding how frail human life was and that they and those around them were only on the earth temporarily. They took risks. They acted as if they didn't know the consequences of the things they chose to do. Or as if the rules wouldn't apply to them.

So she didn't know whether Christina would take the news of a stalker in stride, or whether she would overreact to it, or if she would have another reaction that Margie hadn't even foreseen. She had come to accept that Christina was different from her. A separate and independent person with her own headspace. It was sometimes difficult as a parent to understand that this person who had come from her didn't think and react the same way as she did.

So she didn't say anything to start with. She would see if Christina brought it up herself. Then play it by ear.

"Shall we take Stella out for her walk?" Margie asked.

Christina had barely gotten home and might well complain that she needed some time to relax before having to go out again. But instead, Christina seemed relieved by the suggestion. "Yeah. Let's go out. Walkies, Stella!"

Stella went excitedly to the peg her leash hung on and panted happily as she waited for one of them to hook her up. "I think she's ready," Christina laughed.

"Sure looks like it. She's such a good girl!"

Stella's tail swept back and forth, appreciating the praise. Christina attached her lead and they left the house, headed for the pathway along Twenty-Sixth Street. They had to stop every couple of minutes for Stella to sniff at lamp posts and rocks and bugs crawling across the sidewalk and whatever scent signatures the other dogs in the neighborhood had left in the grass and on the trunks of trees. But it was relaxing. A nice, unhurried journey.

"How was school today?"

"It was okay." Christina's shoulders lifted and fell.

"Has it been as bad as you thought it would be?"

Margie knew what answer she wanted to hear. She wanted Christina to tell her that it was fine, that she was adjusting quickly and making friends, and it wasn't as bad as it had seemed the first day when she'd practically had a meltdown over having to go to a new school.

Christina didn't answer at first. They walked along, letting Stella set the pace, breathing the cooling air scented with car exhaust fumes, freshly-cut grass, and a hearty garlic scent from someone's supper cooking in a house they walked past.

"It's been better and worse," Christina said finally.

Margie didn't press for more details, just waited.

"The classes aren't bad, and I think the teachers are ten times better. A lot of stuff is the same wherever you go. Riding on the bus sucks, especially in the middle of a pandemic. School lunches." She rolled her eyes and shook her head. Margie wasn't sure whether she disliked taking lunch to school or buying lunch at the school cafeteria. She had a choice. Maybe she disliked both equally.

"And what's worse?" she prompted eventually, when it seemed that Christina wasn't going to explain any further.

"I didn't think it would be so hard to make friends. I didn't realize how few Métis there would be. And we had lots of racism in Manitoba, but at least there were a lot of us, so we could band together and just shrug it off. But here, it's more subtle, and I don't know who will have my back. There are kids who are not white but have white friends, and there are groups that will only hang out with other kids who are the same race. And there are others that… I just don't know. I'm kind of afraid to get to know the white kids, especially if they're popular, but I know they're not all bad." She shrugged. "I hate being in the youngest grade at the school. It's good because everyone is making new friends with kids who went to different schools than they did, but I don't like being… so vulnerable." Christina sighed and shook her head. "I just wish I didn't have to be there."

"Do you want me to look at other schools? Or do you want to do online? A lot of kids are right now because of the pandemic. No one would think you were weird."

"No," Christina used that long-suffering teenage voice that asked her why Margie was so intent on ruining her life. "I don't want to do that."

"Is there anything I can do?"

"We could go back to Winnipeg." After she said it, she looked at Margie. "I know we can't. You've got a job here…"

"Would you really want to? Go back to the way things were before? Leave Moushoom here by himself?"

Christina scowled, staring down at the pathway as they walked. "I don't know."

"I thought we should bring him out here one day. Do you think he would like that?"

Christina brightened, as she always did when they were talking about her grandfather. "He would like that," she agreed. "But could he? I don't think he can walk very far."

"We could use a wheelchair."

"I think that would be great. He's always so sad, stuck inside like that. He should be out where he can commune with Mother Earth."

"Good. We'll do it, then. Maybe this weekend."

Christina nodded, smiling at the opportunity to do something for Moushoom. They got to the block where they usually turned off to go home. Christina pointed farther down the pathway, where there was a branch off to a steep downhill road.

"What's over there?"

Margie looked for a moment, knowing she had been down that far before when she checked out the route to the bicycle overpass and downtown.

"Oh. The Canoe Club. They put their canoes into the irrigation canal down there."

Christina nodded. "We should try that sometime. Do they do lessons?"

"I don't know. We could find out."

Christina knew that Margie didn't like watersports, so Margie didn't see the need to point it out. If Christina wanted to take some canoe lessons, Margie was sure it could be arranged. She would just be watching with her feet firmly planted on the bank. She was willing to spring for anything that would help Christina to feel like she belonged there.

Or almost anything.

***

Something had been niggling at the back of Margie's mind since she had returned from her walk with Stella and Christina. She felt uncomfortable and anxious without knowing why. She kept an eye on the windows as it started to get darker, not liking it that she couldn't see out. She turned on the outside lights so that she would know if someone were in the yard again. Christina was doing her homework at the kitchen table with her headphones on, and if she thought this was strange behavior, she didn't bother to say anything about it. Margie wondered how much money it would take to get a good alarm system installed. Or maybe just motion-detecting lights and a webcam, so that they could get a picture of whoever entered the yard.

She sat down at her computer to review the postmortem report on David Smith. She was finding it difficult to focus, but the report didn't say anything she didn't already know. She looked again at the various personal items that they had recovered. Still no more information on the contents of his phone.

Stella

Membership to the Canoe Club

A picture of a high school

Margie sucked in her breath so suddenly that it made her cough and choke. Christina pulled one of the earbuds away from her ear, looking at her. "Are you okay?"

"No!"

Christina looked startled. She got up quickly and went to the sink to run a glass of water for Margie. Margie took it with shaky hands. She took a few sips, trying to calm the racking coughs.

"What happened?" Christina asked. She patted Margie on the back. "Are you choking?"

Margie shook her head and put her hand over her mouth to try to stifle the cough. With her other hand, she pointed at her screen. Stella and a reference number. Christina peered at it and shook her head.

"Stella's license number? What about it?"

Tears running down her face, Margie patted her leg to call Stella to her. She looked at the number on the tag attached to Stella's collar. Christina was right. It was Stella's license number. She forced more of the water down.

"The Canoe Club," she choked out.

"The Canoe Club? Yeah? What about it? Mom, you're being weird. It's like we're playing charades, but I don't even know what the theme is."

Margie scratched Stella's ears and bent down to kiss her on the top of the head, trying to calm the coughing.

"Make sure—the doors—locked."

Christina didn't ask why this time. She just took a few steps to the front door, made sure that the bolt was turned, and then jogged through the kitchen to the back door and checked that one.

"They're locked," she reported back. "Now tell me. What's going on?"

"I just think… something is wrong. I have to call Constable Evans. And Sergeant MacDonald. I think…" Margie cut herself off and shook her head. She couldn't finish the thought. It was like saying what she was thinking was the last line to complete a spell, and if she said it out loud, he might materialize in front of her.

When Constable Evans had come to take her report on the dead rabbit, she had put his business card in her pocket and had not yet entered it into her phone. Margie felt her pockets and eventually came up with the card.

She cleared her throat a few times and seemed to be able to talk without more coughing, though her voice was weak and rough. She grasped Christina's hand before placing the call.

"It's going to be okay, Christina."

"What's okay? I'm scared, Mom."

"I know." Margie looked at the windows again. She still couldn't see anyone outside. Once it was dark, people didn't walk around the neighborhood anymore. Not much. They might drive to the grocery store or to do what other errands they needed to, but they wouldn't be out taking a stroll. There wouldn't be any reason for anyone to be walking down her back alley or peeking into the yard.

She tapped Evans's digits into her phone and waited for it to connect. Of course, she probably wouldn't be able to get him until the next day, when he was back on shift again. If he was even on shift. He might have the day off.

"Evans."

"I'm sorry to be calling you after hours, Constable," Margie apologized. "It's Margie Patenaude, from this morning. The rabbit."

"Yes, I remember you. I'm afraid I don't have anything back on the case yet. These things take a few days. But rest assured, we are taking it seriously."

"There's more. I'm worried… he may be dangerous."

"Has he been back? Do you know who it is?"

"I don't think so. And I'm not sure exactly, but… he may be connected to another case I'm working."

Evans knew that Margie was in Homicide. Christina did too, but she didn't seem to put it together, at least not as quickly as Evans did.

"Oh. I see." His voice was serious. "We'll put a rush on it, then. Are you in danger? You should have called 9-1-1 if it is an emergency."

"I haven't seen him, though, so I don't know that it is. I just… do you think you could send a couple of patrols by tonight? Just to be sure everything is okay?"

"Yes. I'll get on that. Do you have any evidence that ties the two cases together?"

"Can you tell me… how someone would get my dog's license number?"

Evans was silent for a moment. When he spoke, it was in a tone that suggested that Margie might be completely off her rocker. "How would someone get your dog's license number? From you, I guess. Or if they were right there to look at the number on her tag. Or maybe someone who worked in the licensing department."

"Somebody had it."

"Who?"

"Somebody had her name and the license number written down."

"Who?" Evans repeated urgently.

"The Glenbow Park victim. It was in his wallet."

"Oh." He was taken aback, but also calmer upon hearing this. "Well then… if he's dead, he isn't going to do you any harm."

"He was dead before the rabbit. He died… between the squirrel and the rabbit."

"That doesn't make much sense."

"It does… if the killer put it in his wallet."

CHAPTER FIFTEEN

om... I'm freaking out," Christina said. "I don't get what you're saying here. What do you mean the killer put Stella's number in the dead guy's wallet? Why would he do that?"

"To taunt me." Margie tapped Sergeant MacDonald's number into her phone. "He copied everything he could from the Fish Creek murder so that I would be called in on the Glenbow Park murder too. And then he planted things on the body to taunt me. To tell me that he was close to me, and I didn't even see him there."

She swallowed and held tightly to Christina's hand. Christina squeezed back. Neither let go.

Margie's phone was in speaker mode so that she didn't have to pick it up and could continue to hold Christina's hand and to work her mouse at the same time.

"Patenaude?" MacDonald said sharply.

"Sir. I'm sorry to call you at home. I may have a break on the case. And… I might need some help."

"Of course. What have you got?"

"You remember the name Stella and the number on the paper in his wallet?"

"Yes."

"That's the name and license number of my dog."

She gave him a moment to process that. It didn't take him long.

"He knows you."

"He must. He couldn't get that number from anywhere else. Unless he works in the licensing department. He could only get it from me or by looking at Stella's collar tags. And I didn't give it to anyone. He wanted me to know… that he's been close to me."

"It's an assumption, but let's go with it. Was there anything else on Smith's body that was suspicious?"

"His address is close to Glenbow."

"Yes. Makes sense, that's why he's able to walk there frequently."

"But he had a membership card for the Canoe Club."

"They must canoe on the Bow over there. Put out on the water in Cochrane, maybe."

"Do you know where the Canoe Club is?"

"No."

"It's two blocks from my house."

"And you're not in the northwest."

"I'm about as far from there as you can get."

"You're in Forest Lawn, aren't you?"

"Almost. Greater Forest Lawn."

"It still might make sense. He could be a member of the Canoe Club and still canoe over by the park. It's a possibility."

"Yes."

"Anything else?"

Margie gave Christina's hand a tug, encouraging her to sit down on the couch beside her. Christina sat down and put her arm around Margie.

"Sir, you're on speaker and my daughter is here." She probably should have told him that at the beginning of the conversation.

"Christina, right? How are you, Christina? Hanging in there?"

"Yes," Christina said in a small voice.

Margie clicked through images on her computer. "Christina. Can you look at this picture?"

Christina leaned in toward the screen. She nodded.

"Where is this picture taken? Do you know?" Margie asked.

"Yeah. That's my school. Forest Lawn High."

"Are you sure?"

"Yes."

"Sir, that picture found on Smith—" Margie started to tell MacDonald.

Christina put her finger directly onto Margie's computer screen. "You see… there I am. Right there."

Margie wouldn't have recognized the back view of her daughter. The sliver of her caught in the photograph was too small. But she realized that the shirt and pants could have been Christina's, and the girl in the picture had long black hair. Margie took another swallow of her water, trying to wash down the lump that was suddenly stuck in her throat.

"Christina, are you saying you're in the picture that was found at the homicide scene?" MacDonald demanded.

"If that's where this picture is from. Yes."

"It is," Margie agreed.

"I don't like this," MacDonald said. "I want someone there with you. Especially considering—the other thing we discussed this morning."

"Christina knows about the squirrel and the rabbit," Margie told him. "And I already called Constable Evans to ask him if they would send patrols by the house."

"This guy clearly knows a lot about you, including where you live and where Christina goes to school. He's planted clues to let you know he's out there watching. You don't know who he is?"

Margie drew in a long breath and let it out slowly, trying to clear her mind. Who had been close enough to them to see Stella's dog tags? Had he been in the yard? Maybe Stella had run up to greet him when he had planted the squirrel. She was a gentle creature and would have considered a stranger who brought her a dead squirrel her new best friend.

Had he been following them? Or was it someone they knew?

"We don't have the parking lot video yet?" Margie asked.

"Not yet. I'll light a fire under someone. And I don't know if the phone will hold any clues… it is possible that he took a picture of the view and managed to catch the killer in the frame at some point. I doubt we would be so lucky, but I'll push to get that phone cracked too. I'd like someone there with you tonight, just in case… Do you have any preferences?"

"Well… two single gals here… I'd rather it was a woman, so we don't have to be worried about walking around in our PJ's."

"Jones, then?"

"Yes."

"I'll see if she's available. If I can't get her, you'll take someone else on the team?"

"Yes. Of course."

"Okay. Expect one of the team on your doorstep within a couple of hours. Don't open the door without verifying who it is first."

"I won't."

He hung up the call without saying goodbye. Christina leaned her head down onto Margie's shoulder and stayed cuddled there, like she was a little girl again, and not a couple of inches taller than Margie.

"Are you okay?" Margie asked.

"Yes."

"It's scary."

"Yeah."

"But you're okay?"

"I'm here with you."

"Is it all right with you if I get my gun out?"

Christina nodded.

While Margie's duty weapon stayed in her locker at work when she returned home at the end of the day, she did have a personal weapon at home. She left Christina sitting on the couch and went to her bedroom closet, retrieving the gun and ammunition from the gun safe on the shelf. She had never needed it for personal protection before. She kept it oiled and took it to the range every couple of months, but she had never before felt like she needed it. She returned to her seat beside Christina and lay the gun down within reach on the side table.

Christina didn't return to her homework, cuddling up to Margie once more. Margie turned on the TV to provide a distraction. Neither of them paid it as much attention as they normally would have, aware of every noise that Stella or the house made as they sat there waiting for something to happen.

Morning came too soon for Margie. She hadn't slept more than a couple of hours, and what little sleep she'd gotten had been restless and plagued by nightmares. She peeked in on Christina and found that she was still asleep. Detective Jones was still sitting in the living room, prowling occasionally to each of the windows to check for any intruders.

"Hi," Margie greeted softly. "No trouble?"

"No. Quiet neighborhood. Some neighbors heading out to work already, a few walkers, but nothing suspicious."

Stella whined at Margie and took a few steps toward the door, wanting to be let out. Margie ducked into Christina's room to look out the window. It was still dark but, with the outside lights on, the yard was fairly well illuminated, and she couldn't see anything suspicious.

"I'm just going to check out the yard before I let Stella out," she told Jones. "Make sure we don't have any more little surprises."

"Take your gun with you."

Margie wanted to argue that it wasn't necessary, but she didn't. She retrieved her weapon and went outside, preventing Stella from following her out until she could clear the yard. Stella barked and yipped in protest.

Margie took a quick turn around the yard, but didn't find any dead animals this time. She heard footsteps crunching down the alley and followed them with her eyes, waiting for the walker to come into view. She relaxed when she saw it was Oscar. He smiled and waved at her

"Hello, Oscar. Hi, Milo." She couldn't see Milo walking beside him, but could hear him panting and his chain jingling.

"Looks like it's going to be a nice day," Oscar observed. Margie agreed. He kept walking, disappearing from her view a few houses down. Margie went back to the door and let Stella out. She stood in the doorway with Jones, watching Stella race around the yard and then check out each of her scent posts one at a time.

"That was one of your neighbors?" Jones asked.

"Yes. And no."

Jones raised her brows in query.

"I know him from walking the dogs. He walks Milo and we walk Stella. We run into each other on the pathway. Stop and talk for a minute sometimes."

They were both silent.

"He's a nice guy," Margie said.

"Nothing suspicious there, then?"

"No."

Margie gave Stella a couple more minutes and then called her back in. She got herself a cup of coffee. Christina came out of her room, blinking owlishly.

"Hi," Margie greeted, and pulled Christina close to kiss her on the forehead. "How are you this morning?"

"I didn't think he lived over here," Christina said, and it was an instant before Margie connected that Christina was talking about Oscar. She must have heard her talking with Jones or seen her wave at Oscar. "I thought he was in Dover. Just... not here. I've never seen him in the neighborhood before. Only on the pathway."

Margie nodded.

She looked at Jones, who was standing nearby listening. "She's right."

CHAPTER SEVENTEEN

Margie was reluctant to let Christina get on the bus to go to school. Christina told her with forced cheerfulness that everything would be fine and gave her a hug and a kiss on the cheek, then ran to catch the bus just in time. Margie watched until the bus was out of sight. There didn't appear to be anyone following it, friend or stranger.

In a few minutes, Margie was on her way back to Glenbow Park. It would take her nearly an hour. She couldn't help being nervous about what the day would bring. She tried deep breathing when she got out to the ring road. She tried chanting. She tried putting her de-stress music list on the radio.

None of it helped very much. Margie was still just as anxious when she got to the Glenbow Road turnoff from the highway. She looked behind her as she slowed down to make the turn, but couldn't see anyone tailing her.

The Alberta Parks guy that MacDonald had talked to told her the gate would be unlocked for her; she just had to get out of her car to swing it open. Then she could drive down to the Park Office. There she would meet with someone who would have the various surveillance videos for her.

She had known that the gate would be a pinch point. She could feel eyes on her as she got out of her car to open it. She brushed her fingers over her gun in its holster. As she walked to the gate, another car drove down Glenbow Road and pulled to the side. A tall figure got out. Margie watched with a sense of disbelief as his dog jumped out to join him. Man and his dog. Doing everything together.

"Margie!" Oscar smiled pleasantly. "Fancy running into you here! I thought you would be at work by now."

It was, of course, no coincidence that he was there. Despite Margie not being able to see him behind her on the way over, one of the tail cars had picked him up and informed Margie of the fact.

"You're very smart, aren't you?" she asked Oscar blandly. "You had everyone fooled."

His eyes narrowed a little. "I don't know about that," he said. "The news never reported any connection between the two murders."

"No one ever thought they were the same killer. They were just similar enough to get me over here to investigate."

He nodded. "That was all I wanted."

She could tell that he was bursting with pride. Excited to tell her how smart he had been. How he had planted every clue and watched her trying to break the case, laughing at her when they would meet on their evening walks.

She could see him in her mind, making a fuss over Stella, scratching her ears and telling her what a good dog she was. Cuddling her close to his face. Close enough to see her license number.

"You took longer than I thought to figure out the clues. I thought you would get *Stella* right away."

"And when I figured that out, was I supposed to know that it was you?"

"No." He laughed. "I could tell you were suspicious this morning. But that didn't stop you from coming back here. Why did you need to come back here again when you were here so long yesterday?"

So he *had* been watching her. It hadn't just been an overactive imagination.

Oscar was walking toward her. Just inching forward every now and then, like if he did it slowly enough she wouldn't know he was within striking distance until it was too late. It was difficult for Margie not to pull her gun immediately to protect herself.

"I came for the surveillance tapes. To see if I could find you on any of them."

He nodded. "Well, you're not going to get the chance, I'm afraid."

His hand was in his pocket. Holding an open knife, if she weren't mistaken.

"Why would you do all of this? Go to all this risk? Kill a man you didn't even know just to get my attention?" Her voice was getting higher and louder, though she tried to keep it under control.

"*Detective* Patenaude," he said slowly, sounding each syllable out distinctly. "You didn't tell me you were a cop when we first met. Or any time after that."

"It didn't come up. We just talked about the dogs and the weather."

"You thought you were smarter than me, but you weren't."

He took another step toward her, closing in quickly, pulling his hand with the knife in it out of his pocket and raising it to stab downward into her chest, as he had with David Smith. But Margie had her gun clear of the holster, and there were shouts from half a dozen other police officers who had been watching and listening from their vantage points, now visible with guns raised and shouting at him to freeze.

Oscar looked around at them, stunned. "How…?" He dropped his knife and raised his hands, giving them no reason to shoot him. He blinked, baffled.

Margie secured him in handcuffs and patted him down before answering. "It was a good idea you had, using Stella's license number."

He shook his head. "What?"

"I didn't know your last name or where you lived. So we looked up Milo. There aren't very many dogs named Milo licensed in the southeast. Actually, just one in the Greater Forest Lawn area."

"But you didn't know I was coming here! You didn't know I was following you again."

"I didn't see you. You're pretty good. But the cars a kilometer back were able to spot your vehicle, when they knew what to look for. And *I* knew where I was going, even if you didn't. So that officers closer to the scene could get here ahead of us."

His usual wide, white smile was gone. His face was red with fury. She waited for him to shout at her that it was not fair, that she had cheated. And maybe she had. She hadn't let him play out the game the way he had wanted to.

But he said nothing more.

CHAPTER EIGHTEEN

"I don't get it." Margie sighed as she worked her way through the reports that had to be filed to document all the evidence that had pointed to Oscar as a suspect, and his capture and arrest in the park. "What would make a person do something like this? So random and… so bizarre. He didn't even know Smith. He did it all just so he could feed me clues and watch me work the case?"

Detective Cruz was leaning against Detective Jones's desk nearby, giving her a hand in getting everything filled out properly and offering his own commentary on the case.

"Not much in his background that explains it. No prior arrests. No restraining orders. He seems to be a law-abiding citizen, right down to properly licensing his dog."

"And picking up after him," Margie contributed. "He was always very diligent. Never 'forgot' his bags at home or pretended not to notice a mess."

"I did find one thing," Jones offered, catching a stray curl of blond hair and smoothing it away as she stared at her computer screen.

Margie waited for more information. Cruz leaned toward Jones to look at her computer screen. "What?"

"He washed out of the police academy."

Margie stopped typing. Other keyboards and discussions all went silent at the same time. The room was still, everybody listening in.

"He was a cop?" Margie demanded, flabbergasted.

"He wanted to be. Did fine at the written test and initial screening." Jones's fingers tapped the keys lightly, the key-clicks loud in the silent bullpen. "But during training… something happened. He dropped out. Resigned or was asked to leave; there aren't really any details here. You would have to talk to his trainer." A few clicks of the mouse to drill deeper for the information. "Christensen." Jones paused. "Elizabeth Christensen."

Margie's mind went back to Oscar's words. *You didn't tell me you were a cop…. You thought you were smarter than me.* The anger in his tone. Accusation.

"He had problems training under a woman," she guessed. "Doesn't think we should be cops. Much less to be successful at something. Like at being a homicide detective."

Cruz and Jones were both nodding.

"And not just a woman," Cruz pointed out, "but a Native woman. You've heard, haven't you, about how all these ethnics are pushing out the qualified white men?" His sarcastic tone dispelled any thought that he gave such an attitude any credence.

"You'd better watch out," Margie warned. "They'll be coming after your job next."

"I'm not a white ma—" Cruz caught the glimmer in Margie's eyes and cut himself off. He shook his head, letting out a puff of breath. "You almost had me there, Detective Pat. Almost."

Margie winked at Jones.

It hadn't been *almost* at all.

۶ﻮ

MARGIE HAD one more trip to make to Glenbow Ranch Provincial Park. It wasn't exactly on her way home, and it was hard for her to take that time away from her family, but she believed that community policing in Calgary meant more than just catching the bad guy and going on to the next file.

Justice and healing required more than an arrest.

After she parked her car in the staff parking area, a woman came out to meet her. Long, brown hair, fine wrinkles around her eyes, and a light step as she approached Margie and offered her hand to shake.

"Alice," she offered, as Margie squeezed her thin, dry hand. "I'm glad to meet you in person, Detective Pat."

"Thank you. You're sure this is okay? I don't want to do anything that would get you in trouble or reflect badly on the police department if someone complained."

"Oh, no," Alice proclaimed. "We acknowledge this is Treaty 7 land. Our First Nations have been allowed to perform ceremonies here. It's never been a problem."

Margie had run into many people who mouthed treaty acknowledgments as they were expected to when they clearly didn't mean or understand them, but Alice seemed to be sincere.

"Even though I'm not part of that treaty?" Margie asked, making sure there could be no misunderstanding.

"Of course not. We know you're Métis. But it isn't like you're some blond-haired thirteen-year-old making excuses for starting a grass fire."

"Okay. Thank you."

Margie had made the decision not to go all the way down to where David Smith had been murdered. She didn't want to get lost or spend that much more time away from her family. She walked instead into a stand of trees a short distance away, the closest wilderness space, and prepared herself.

Despite Alice's words, she watched Margie from a distance, eyes sharp to make sure that there were not any sparks or embers that might start the dry grasses on fire. Margie ignored her. She unfastened her braid that had been coiled into a bun and let it hang down her back.

Margie took several items out of her shoulder bag. She draped the sash that had been given to her by her band before leaving Winnipeg around her shoulders.

She unwrapped the bundle of sacred herbs and placed them in the smudge bowl. She lit them with a match and blew gently to make them smoke. Smudging was not actually a traditional part of Métis culture, but her people were open to new rituals and traditions, and many had adopted smudging as part of their spiritual practice.

Thinking about Smith, she offered the bowl in each of the four directions. The smudge smoke drifted down the hill. Margie started a low chant, praying for healing for Smith's girlfriend and family, for the family who had discovered his body and the other park users who had been troubled by it. For the police and professionals who had all helped to gather the evidence to address the wrong that had been committed.

And for Oscar, a man whose soul had been so hurt that he had struck out in violence against someone he didn't even know, and someone he thought he did.

She prayed for peace and healing for them all.

When the herbs stopped smoking, Margie picked up a hand bell and tolled out nine chimes. The low ringing of the bell stretched out over the landscape and faded like the smoke.

Margie packed her things and left the park without looking back.

CHAPTER NINETEEN

Christina wanted a turn pushing the wheelchair, so Margie let her take over. As the sun started to set, there was a chilly wind setting in. She bent down to tuck the extra blanket around Moushoom to make sure that he was comfortable.

"How is that? Are you nice and toasty?"

"This is wonderful," he said comfortably. "It has been so long since I was able to get out."

Margie smiled, pleased that her idea had been a good one. Moushoom wrapped his hands around his Tim's hot chocolate and raised it to his mouth for a sip. "It is nice to have family around me, and to be able to get out into the fresh air and make contact with nature again."

It wasn't exactly like he was in the wilds. Maybe one day, she would take him to Glenbow Park for a cart tour. Then he could really get out somewhere that he could connect with Mother Earth. But for now, he was happy being out on the pathway, with the long, yellowing grass beside him, trees growing in little bunches putting on their autumn colors, and people out for a stroll or to walk their dogs. Stella waited patiently for them to start walking again, her tongue hanging out of her mouth.

"I'm glad we could all get out together too. I like that we live close and can come by for a visit whenever we want. I'm sorry it's been a few days, I've been tied up with work."

He nodded and had another sip of hot chocolate. "Remind me again what it is that you do."

Others in the extended family had whispered about the possibility of senility, but to Margie, Moushoom had seemed sharp and aware in the times they had seen him so far. This was the first time that he appeared to have forgotten something she had told him. But he couldn't be expected to remember every piece of information, could he?

They started walking again, Margie staying beside Moushoom, where he could still hear and see her.

"I'm a police detective," she reminded him. "I work on the homicide squad."

"Homicide." Moushoom shook his head slowly. "That must be very hard on you."

"Well, it's not easy. But our solve rate is eighty percent. We do good work."

"I didn't mean that it was hard to solve them," he said, as if that should have been obvious. "I mean, it is hard on your mind and your spirit."

"Oh. Yes, I guess so." She didn't know how long it would take her to get over the nightmares or to stop jumping at every little sound in the house, to stop herself from checking on poor Christina every fifteen minutes.

And even though she had known that they needed to take Stella out for a walk and she wanted to take Moushoom out, it had been hard to make herself put her plan into action.

She felt vulnerable walking on the pathway as the sunlight began to fade, and they were left in twilight, and then in darkness. She scrutinized every face as people walked by them, looked at every dog. She knew logically that it had only been one man; only one dog walker had been dangerous. But that didn't stop her brain from checking every single face and dog to make sure that it wasn't Oscar and Milo, or someone else who might have bad feelings toward her.

As safe as the pathway seemed, she wasn't sure she would ever feel one hundred percent safe again.

GLENBOW RANCH PROVINCIAL PARK

In 2006, the children of Alberta rancher Neil Harvie sold 3,246 acres of land to the Government of Alberta to conserve the land, fulfilling the vision of their father. At that time, the author was working as a legal assistant with Andy Crooks, the family's lawyer, and had an insider's view as plans for the park rolled out. She was involved in and present at the park opening in 2011.

Workman has worked closely with the Glenbow Ranch Park Foundation (a non-profit organization that handles many of the visitor services for the park) on a number of levels and like many of the stewards and Calgary west/Cochrane residents, considers it "her park."

As indicated in the title and storyline, the park features some challenging hills. It is a dry park, so when you visit, be sure to bring your water bottle!

DARK WATER UNDER THE BRIDGE

PARKS PAT MYSTERIES #3

*That all fears may
be overcome*

CHAPTER ONE

The sun was still low in the sky, orange light filtering into the kitchen. Margie "Detective Pat" Patenaude was sipping her morning coffee and staring into the depths of her fridge, trying to decide whether to make herself a bag lunch to take to the police station with her, or whether she would take a break and go find something over lunch. She hadn't explored many restaurants near the office, so she wasn't sure what was available. Not that she was that picky.

"The same things are in there as the last time you opened the door," Christina teased, echoing the same words Margie used when her daughter stood staring vacantly into the fridge. "Nothing new is going to materialize while you stand there with the door open."

"You're a smart aleck," Margie told her.

But Christina was right. Margie already knew what was in the fridge, and inspiration wasn't going to strike just because she was standing there with the door open, letting all of the cold air spill to the floor and raising the energy bill. She sighed and closed it.

"I don't know what I want today."

"We need to go shopping. Get something good."

"I think you're right," Margie agreed. They could go to the Co-op, or the No Frills down Seventeenth Avenue, and stock up on some easy to prepare meals. Margie never seemed to have the time or energy to make much when she got home from work.

The phone rang. Margie looked at it, hoping it would just be some telemarketer so she could ignore it. She didn't want to have to deal with a real phone call so soon. She didn't even have one cup of coffee down yet. But it was Detective Cruz, a Filipino-born cop on her team.

"Patenaude," she answered briskly.

"Is this Detective 'Parks' Pat?" There was a note of amusement in Cruz's voice.

"Parks Pat?" That was a new one. Margie understood where the nickname came from, of course. Since she had moved to Calgary, she had been primary on a murder in Fish Creek Park first, and then a similar one in Glenbow Ranch Provincial Park. They had not been related, except by circumstances, but both had been reported in the news, and it would seem that she had now earned her homicide team nickname. Parks Pat.

"That's what they're calling you," Cruz acknowledged.

"Well, okay. It could be worse. What did you need?"

"Have you ever been to Ralph Klein Park?"

Margie let out a puff of breath. "Ralph Klein Park. No, I haven't even heard about that one. Is it out there near Glenbow?"

"No, actually this one is close to you. That's why I figured you might have been there. It's new. Just opened in 2011."

Margie thought about the little park she had visited while taking Stella out on a walk with Christina. It had a little pond and a splash park for young children. She couldn't remember the name off the top of her head, but was sure it wasn't the one that Cruz was talking about. "Another provincial park?"

"City of Calgary park, this one. Though it might be out of city limits, I'm not clear on that. It's right on the eastern edge of the city, anyway. Think you could get out there?"

"Yes, of course. What... am I going to find there?"

"We've got another body. Sorry."

Well, that was to be expected when she worked homicide. "Another body in another park? But we know it isn't either of the same killers, because we already caught them both. They're locked up where they can't do any more harm. Was it the same cause of death?"

"You'll have to get more information when you get out there, but preliminary indications are that it is not. No visible stab wounds on this one."

"Good. I think if it was the same cause, I might have been a little freaked out."

"We're all a little on edge. I'm going to head out there before long too; I'll back you up."

Margie wondered why he hadn't gone to investigate first. If he was the one who had taken the call. "I'm primary on this one? Why?"

He chuckled. "Because they asked for you in particular."

"Me?"

"Parks Pat. They figured if it's in a park, you should be the one in charge."

"That's just—"

"I know. And don't worry, I'm sure that sooner or later you'll get a body that wasn't found in a park. But for now, that's your assignment. Go to the park, make nice, find out what you can about our newest victim."

CHAPTER TWO

Christina assured Margie that she would be ready to get on the bus when it arrived and wouldn't be late for school. She was grown up enough to deal with her own transportation. And Margie knew the fifteen-year-old could handle it. She had been going to the high school via bus since the first day, when the body at Fish Creek Park had been discovered. Margie had promised to drive her that day, but it had not worked out. As a teenager, Christina was as independent as Margie would let her be. Margie figured she should be thankful that she wasn't getting constant requests to be driven here and there all over the city. Calgary sprawled over a huge area, and it could be challenging to get from one end to the other. So far, Christina had been content just riding the bus between the house and the school.

So Margie left Christina to finish getting ready and climbed into her car. She put the park's name into the GPS. She quickly braided her long black hair and coiled it into a bun and waited for the GPS to start receiving coordinates from the satellite and plotting a course. She should be happy that she was being assigned to parks. She enjoyed being outside, connecting with nature. She liked to walk and hike and might even take Stella out there with her one day. For sure she was going to take the whole family out to Glenbow Ranch. When she was off and could arrange it around Christina's school schedule. She would schedule a golf cart tour so that they could take Moushoom, Margie's grandfather, with them. He would like it there. Sometimes, the Nakoda out that direction participated in ceremonies in the park. Moushoom would really love that. They didn't speak the same language or come from exactly the same culture, but Moushoom would understand the symbols and the ceremonies.

The GPS beeped and the robotic voice directed Margie what direction to drive. She put all other considerations aside and focused on following the GPS instructions. Despite her Métis heritage, she had a terrible sense of direction and, if she made a wrong turn, it could take another twenty minutes to get back on track again. Not just because it was sometimes difficult to get turned around if you ended up going the wrong way on a highway or main thoroughfare, but also because she was totally capable of then getting back on the exact same road headed the wrong direction a second time. Or getting flustered and taking another wrong turn.

So she kept an eye on the GPS screen previewing the curves and intersections ahead so that she would not miss any exits or turn the wrong direction. She was glad that Cruz had mentioned it was on the edge of or just outside the city, or she might have started to panic when she ended up driving alongside golden brown fields in an area that felt too remote to bother with a park. But she remembered how Glenbow Park was down in the valley below the highway so, even with its vast size, it had been invisible until she had driven down the last road.

There were a couple of signs, and then she could see a few people walking or cycling to the left of the highway. She turned onto the access road into a grouping of trees. The road curved toward a building that looked like it was built with children's blocks. The medical examiner's van and the forensic team were there, pulled up onto the sidewalk. Rather than parking beside them, Margie followed the road past the building to a public parking lot. It probably filled up on a weekend, but early in the morning on a weekday, it was quiet. A few scattered vehicles. Unlike at the provincial parks, there were no Conservation Officers in gray shirts waiting to drive her in an electric golf cart to the scene of the crime. She had seen a small group of people gathered past the playground, so she knew where the body was and it wasn't too far to walk.

Margie got out and strode towards the big education center. She walked through a small plot of short apple trees that declared itself The Orchard. The apples were turning from green to a rusty red. Some were scattered on the ground with two or three small bites out of them. Not the work of squirrels, by the size of the bite marks.

She stopped when she got to a railing and looked down. What Cruz had not bothered to mention to her was that Ralph Klein Park was a wetland. She stared down at water, which was nearly black and seemed bottomless. The education center jutted out over the water, walkways around it in two tiers up above the water. She swallowed and looked around to focus her mind somewhere else.

She circled the education center around the land side. There was an unusual playground like a pile of sticks, a zip line stretching away from it toward a pond or canal where the rest of the crime scene investigators were. Margie picked up her pace and strode toward them.

Bodies in the water could be ugly. Bloated up with gases, swollen and unrecognizable features, skin starting to separate from the flesh. Predator and insect activity.

But she would stay calm and keep things moving forwards. She would be strong and professional and there would be no issues.

One of the figures by the water waved at her. Margie nodded and joined them just outside the yellow tape perimeter. The group parted so that she could see the woman's body. She was wearing a white blouse and dark blue or black pants. She was face-down in the water, close enough to the shore that they would be able to pull her out without hip waders.

"You're Detective Pat?" a man in a Calgary Police Services uniform and black mask asked.

"Detective Margie Patenaude, yes," she agreed. "Who discovered the body?"

"Early morning jogger. Over there." He nodded to a young man in tights and a jacket sitting some distance away from the scene. "I've got a brief outline from him, but you can take his statement."

"And this is where she was? He didn't move her?"

"He says he didn't touch her."

"Okay, good. Do you think he did?"

The constable considered her question seriously. She took the moment of silence to read his name bar. Archambault. "I don't think he did. It's natural to reach out to someone like this, check to make sure they're really dead and that it's not just a mannequin. But his shoes were relatively dry." Archambault looked down at his own shoes. His shoes and pant cuffs were covered in mud.

Margie raised her brows. "So, you did touch her?"

"Just did what I'm supposed to. Made sure she was good and dead, then came back here and called your team. Preserved the scene."

There was a large area cordoned off with yellow tape. Margie would have made it bigger, but it was a judgment call.

"You checked for a pulse?"

"Just radial. It was obvious touching her that she was dead."

"Rigor?"

"Yes. And… sodden. She's been in there a few hours."

Margie didn't feel the need to touch the body herself to verify this. She felt sorry for Constable Archambault. But she'd had enough opportunities to check for life signs herself. It was one of the less enjoyable parts of being a law enforcement officer.

"Thank you." She nodded to him.

He nodded back his thanks. Margie looked at the body again. A sweeping glance. She was trying not to commit more to long-term memory than she could help. "Did she have a purse? Wallet? Anything to identify her? There's no missing person report?"

Everyone there shook their heads. Margie looked around. "Let's protect any nearby garbage cans or bins. Extend the perimeter up and down the stream another… twenty-five meters. Watch for footprints. She didn't fly into that water. Someone killed her here or dumped her here. We want to find out all that we can about that. Surveillance video in the parking lot?"

"We're waiting for someone from the education center to get here.

Apparently, they will have access to the security video," one of the forensic guys advised.

"Okay." Margie hoped that there was good video. They wouldn't have been able to identify the killer in the Fish Creek case if they hadn't had good video footage. Multiple pathways, several cameras in the parking lot, and even wildlife cams had enabled them to establish the people who had been in and out of the area the victim was killed in. That made it a lot more practicable to find the killer.

"I'll let you guys work out the best way to get her out of the water and collect any evidence," she told the forensic team and the doctor from the medical examiner's office, whose nametag identified him as Adrian Galt.

They seemed to be happy that she wasn't telling them how to do their job. Margie was sure they would be much better at working out the best procedure than she would. And she wouldn't have to get any closer to the water herself.

CHAPTER THREE

It was a while before someone from the education center came out and met Margie a short distance from where the forensic team was erecting screens. Margie was afraid it would be a teacher or docent who didn't have any authority or in-depth knowledge of the park, but the tall, thin man who introduced himself as Arby Finkle seemed to be in charge of operations there. He wore a suit and tie, which seemed excessively formal.

He was literally wringing his hands, his expression deeply distressed. Margie was glad Finkle couldn't see the body past the screens. He might have had a complete breakdown.

"I'll need you to tell me everything you can about the security here and…" Margie tried to focus, "about the water system. Some of this is man-made." She motioned to the deep pool she had first seen adjacent to the parking lot. "I just need as much background as you can give me. Whether or not you think it would be relevant."

"Of course, of course." Finkle wrung his hands more. He looked at her with great intensity, eyes glittering with emotion. Becoming aware of his hand-wringing, he tried to hold still, but he just ended up squeezing the blood out of both hands until they were as white as the woman's corpse. "I can't believe that something like this could happen here. Why would anyone…" He shook his head, not even able to finish the sentence. Margie waited, hoping to hear whether he said 'kill someone here' or 'dump someone here.' Which did he think it was?

But he didn't finish; he just shook his head, sobbing in a low thrum Margie could barely hear.

"We will need the security video," she prompted, trying to get him started.

"Yes. Of course. I'll get you whatever I can."

"Whatever you can? Don't you have a fully operating system?"

"Well… yes, most of it is functional. What we have."

"I don't like the sound of that," Margie warned.

"Yes… well, we've had some vandalism over time, and it takes the city time to get around to fixing it. Our little park isn't exactly high on their priorities list. There are probably buildings downtown they are more interested in. City Hall. The new library. You know, they'll get *their* security fixed a lot faster than us."

"How long has it been out of service?"

"Well… a while," he admitted, unwilling to put a time estimate on it.

"Get me what you can." However much that was. She was gathering from his reluctance that there wasn't going to be very much at all. Would they at least have something showing who had been in the parking lot during the hours before the woman's body was found?

"I am sorry," Finkle apologized. "There is more coverage inside the education center. We have some very valuable displays, so we want to keep them protected…"

"Yeah. That makes sense," Margie said flatly. Not because she was feeling gracious. She could see that they had not prioritized the security of the park itself. The indoor footage was not likely to help them much unless the woman and her killer had been in the education center before she had been killed, which Margie thought was unlikely.

She pulled out her phone and thumbed through the photos, including the ones that Dr. Galt had texted to her just a few minutes earlier. The victim was wearing a semiformal blouse and slacks, not a t-shirt or other casual wear. She suspected it might be the uniform worn by the education center staff. The ones who didn't dress quite as formally as Finkle.

"I'd like you to see if you can identify the victim for me," she said slowly. "Do you think you're up to looking at a picture?"

"Yes, of course."

Margie didn't show it to him. "You need to be prepared. I am going to show you a picture of the dead woman's face."

He nodded impatiently. The two hands with the death grip on each other stayed intertwined, and he leaned forward, waiting for Margie to show him the picture.

"You need to understand what the water does to bodies," Margie warned. "There hasn't been a lot of animal or insect predation yet, but her face will seem quite swollen. It may be difficult to recognize her."

"I want to help in any way I can."

Margie waited for a few seconds longer, then finally turned the phone around to show it to Finkle. He stared at it without expression for a long few seconds. Margie expected him to shake his head and tell her that no, he didn't have a clue who it was.

Finkle turned away from her and, for a moment, Margie thought he was going to unlock one of the doors to the education center and take her inside. But that wasn't why he was turning away from her.

He staggered a couple of feet away and threw up. Margie took a couple of small, discreet steps back. It was a few minutes before Finkle regained control of himself. He wiped his mouth on his sleeve and turned back to her, looking miserable.

"I don't know who that is."

"Okay. Thank you for giving it a try." Margie hesitated. "Why don't you go on in, get yourself together and have a glass of water or cup of coffee and, when you're ready for me, let me know." She handed him one of her business cards. "Just give me a quick call or shoot me a text when you're ready."

"I'm sorry…"

Margie waved the apology away. "No. It's a shock, and you weren't prepared to see that. You're certainly not the first guy to react that way."

"It's not like it is on TV, or seeing a picture in the paper."

"No, it's not."

He nodded and wiped his mouth again. "I'll just be a few minutes, then," he said, and walked away from her, heading for the education center.

❧

MARGIE DIDN'T NEED to supervise the technicians as they gathered their evidence for Dr. Galt as he prepared the body for transport. She was the most senior law enforcement officer on the scene, but they had much more training than she did in handling evidence and they knew what they were doing. After the medical examiner's van drove away, Margie stood watching the forensic team searching through the garbage cans. The whole process included taking pictures of the garbage cans before they were touched and laying everything out on a plastic sheet. Harvesting one layer of trash from the can at a time as if it were an archaeological dig. They needed to be able to say exactly which layer anything suspicious had come from.

Detective Cruz arrived. Margie gave him a brief update. They stayed outside the yellow tape at the bank of the creek and around the garbage cans. As far as Margie knew, they hadn't found any footprints that would be helpful.

Of course not. That would have been too easy.

"No ID yet?" Cruz asked.

"No. Hopefully, they'll find her wallet or purse in one of the garbages, or drag this part of the stream to see if it was dumped here with her."

Cruz looked up and down the waterway at the area that had been taped off, and seemed satisfied with it.

"What have you found out about the water system?" he asked. "Was she killed here? Dumped here? Or was she dumped somewhere else and the water carried her downstream?"

Margie breathed shallowly.

"I assume she was just dumped here. The water doesn't seem to have much of a current. I guess we'll hear more from the medical examiner. I'm waiting for this guy," she motioned to the education center, "to pull himself together so he can answer some questions about how she got there, what else we need to know about all of this… water."

Looking upstream, she saw a floating dock, where several children sat examining the contents of buckets of water scooped out of the stream. Her stomach turned over queasily.

Cruz looked at her, then at the children. "What's wrong? You think they're going to dip something out of the water that's evidence in the case? The woman's wallet or fingers or something?"

"She still had her fingers," Margie protested.

"Well, the way you were looking at them…"

"I just… I'm worried about them being out there. It doesn't look safe."

Cruz looked at them again.

Margie tried to keep her tone casual. "They're kneeling on the edge. The adults are several meters away. If one of the kids went in…"

"It would probably scare them. But as you say, there isn't any noticeable current. And there is a lifesaver right there that their dad could throw to them and one of those rescue hooks to pull them in."

"Oh, is there?" Margie pretended that made it okay. "I didn't see that. Right."

He gave her a quizzical look but didn't pursue it. "So… what's with the monument on top of the hill? Is that some kind of memorial?"

"I didn't go to the top yet, but I guess it's some kind of art installation. There are actually three monoliths and some berms. I'm afraid it's a bit highbrow for me. I don't really *get* it."

"Doubt if there's anything to get. I'm not much of a modern art guy myself." Cruz looked at the garbage can the forensic techs were currently going through, and the screens still up at the water's edge. "Tell you what, why don't we go up for a look?"

Margie agreed. She didn't want to get in the way of the investigation. They wouldn't think much of her if she ended up messing with any of the evidence.

She and Cruz walked down a gravel path along the river, then up the small hill to gaze at the art installation. Tall grasses and wild-flowers grew beside the trail.

"Well… I still don't get it," Cruz admitted, staring up at the monoliths.

"Me neither."

They looked down at the crime scene. Margie realized that from their elevated position, she could see over the screens. They should have used a tent. At least it had still been early morning and there hadn't been a bunch of kids or their mothers at the top of the hill, hysterical because they had seen the dead, drowned body of a woman on the other side of the screens.

CHAPTER FOUR

"Whoops," Margie murmured, looking at the screens. There was nothing to see anymore, so it was too late to do anything about it. But the next time, she would remember to look up at possible vantage points.

Cruz chuckled through his mask. "Glad we didn't end up in trouble over that. Let's go down to the dock."

The 'we' was generous, since Margie had been the one in charge of the scene and Cruz hadn't even been there when the screens were set up. Margie walked down the hill with him, and then along the path to where the children were dipping minnows out of the stream into their buckets. Cruz stepped confidently from the land onto the gray plastic cells that formed the little dock. Margie stayed back on the path. Cruz walked up to the edge where the children were and started a conversation with them. The father stood close to Margie, a tall, sandy-haired man. He looked at Margie.

"You're police?"

"Yes. Detective Patenaude. My partner there is Detective Cruz."

"What's going on here?"

Margie knew he would find out eventually anyway. And he wasn't likely to be calling any reporters.

"There's been a death."

"A murder?" he asked immediately.

"That hasn't yet been determined."

The man looked toward the screens. "I don't think too many people just come out here and die of natural causes. It isn't like it's a swimming hole or the ocean."

Margie shrugged and didn't agree or disagree. "How long ago did you and the kids get here?"

"Oh, about twenty minutes ago. We're homeschoolers," he explained, "this is a really good hands-on activity. They like the education center, but the best part is getting out here and playing in the water."

"Sounds like fun." Margie smiled, but she didn't go out on the dock. She let Cruz talk to the children. He seemed to be enjoying himself. Her queasiness returned when he leaned out over the edge to look into the dark water. "So you didn't see anything unusual when you arrived today? Anything that seems different or out of place?"

"Just you guys. Normally it's pretty quiet this early in the morning. A few people out getting exercise. Walking, running, biking. Sometimes we see other homeschoolers out here, but most families don't get out until later in the day."

Margie looked around, her eyes sharp for anything in the area that didn't belong or might have been dropped by the killer. It was pretty clean, no garbage blowing around. But the water was murky. She couldn't see down into it. It was impossible to tell how deep it might be out at the edge of the dock where the children were or what might be under the water.

"Are they safe over there? Should they be wearing life jackets?"

"No, they're here all the time," he told her with a tolerant smile. One of those parents who thought she was overprotective and nothing bad would ever happen to his kids. But he hadn't seen the things that she had. "They know what they're doing, and I'm here if anything happens. Which it won't."

But before she and Cruz had approached, he'd been looking down at his phone. Reading his email? A text from his wife? Facebook? His eyes had not been on the children, even though he should have been showing more caution than usual with his awareness of the police presence.

"You haven't had anything unusual happen around here the last few days? People around who you don't know and who don't look like they belong? Arguments? Smells or sounds that were out of place?"

"No." His brows came down in a frown. "You don't mean that a dead body has been here for a few days, do you? I would think that someone would have noticed that."

"We're still in the very preliminary stages of investigation. We can't make any assumptions."

"Well... no, I haven't seen anything unusual. It's just been normal."

"Thanks. Can I get your contact information in case I think of something else I need to ask you?"

He was hesitant. "I said I don't know anything. I don't know why you would need to ask me any other questions."

"You never know when I might need the insights of someone familiar with the park. You can't beat the knowledge and insights of someone who has boots on the ground." Margie laid it on as thickly as she dared.

The man looked pleased. "Yes, of course. I guess that makes sense. And we really know our way around here. If you have any questions about the wetlands, my kids probably know more than the teachers in the education center, they've been here so much."

CHAPTER FIVE

Margie waited until Cruz was finished talking to the children, and looked toward the education center to let him know that she wanted to go there next. He walked back over the dock, making the floats bounce up and down in the water as he moved over it. The kids laughed in delight.

"Find anything out from the dad?" he asked once they were a distance away.

"No. Got his information just in case, but I don't think he knows anything helpful. How about the kids?"

"Good kids. Really into the wetlands thing. They could tell you all kinds of things about how these different features filter stormwater naturally. But anything about how a body got in the creek? No."

"As long as it's not their mom."

"I think someone might have mentioned if they were missing her." Cruz agreed dryly.

"I want to see if the head guy here, Finkle, is ready to talk to us yet. He was a little bit… wobbly after seeing a picture of the dead woman."

"Yes, I can see how he might be. You thought it was a good idea to show it to him?"

"I thought it might be someone who worked here. Went out for lunch and never came back… something like that."

"And did he know her?"

"Didn't recognize her. But drowning victims bloat up so much…"

He nodded. "Still could have been an employee."

"Hopefully, he's settled down enough to talk now. I want to get security video from him, and any information he can provide on how things work around here. Whether she was dumped there or washed down from somewhere else…" Margie trailed off. She started walking around the building.

Cruz held out his hand to stop her. "We don't have to go all the way around the far side of the building. We can get to the front doors from this side. Just over the catwalks. They go all the way around."

Margie looked at the catwalks over the deep, dark water. "I think I'd rather go around the other way."

"This is more convenient, and we've already seen the other side. Come on." Cruz strode toward the nearest walkway. He paused to look back after a minute. "Come on, Patenaude. You afraid of heights?"

"No."

"Let's go, then."

Margie looked for a reasonable excuse. She wanted to check on the techs out by the creek again. She thought they might have missed a garbage can in the corner of the building. She wanted to check under the unusual playground equipment to make sure nothing had been dumped there. But they would all have sounded like fake excuses. Which they were.

She dragged her feet after Cruz. He made it look so easy. He was very casual as he stepped from the gravel path to a small grillwork bridge. To Margie, it was nearly as bad as the pictures she had seen of the glass lookout over the Grand Canyon. Why couldn't it at least have been concrete? Why did it have to be something with holes in it?

She forced herself to walk over the bridge and followed him onto one of the boardwalks that hugged the building. They weren't actually boards, but were fully concrete and shouldn't have been a problem for her like the grillwork. However, the railing along the side was an open mesh or grill that she could see through to the still, dark, bottomless water. She grasped the top rail, and it was all she could do to keep from gripping it like a drowning man. She just steadied herself, tried to keep vertigo from kicking in and making her stumble or fall. It was like her worst nightmare, the thought of falling into the dark water in the pool beneath her.

Cruz looked back a couple of times, but kept going, not stopping to help or harass her. They climbed a metal flight of stairs to go up to the second level. Farther from the water, but a longer distance to fall if she went over the edge. She didn't know if it was better or worse. Finally, Margie managed to make it around the walkway to the building's front entrance where Cruz was waiting. He raised his brows. Margie couldn't see his mouth under the mask, but it didn't look like he was laughing at her.

"You *are* afraid of heights."

"No." She looked down at the black glassy surface. "Water."

"You're afraid of water?"

Margie tried to shrug it off. "Everyone is afraid of something. That just happens to be mine."

"You were really struggling to get over there."

"Yes." She waited for him to laugh and tease her about it.

"Good for you. You kept going and you did it."

Margie stared at him, surprised at the response. She hadn't expected any kind of understanding. He was a tough cop. And he came from the Philippines. An island. Surrounded by water. He had probably been in the water every day of his life before immigrating to Canada. It was as natural for him as breathing.

"I have kids," Cruz said, turning toward the doors and pressing a call button. "My youngest, Alejandro, he has anxiety. He's afraid of a lot of things. The doctor says that the only way for him to get over the fears is to push through them. Willingly expose himself to them and push through. Like climbing a hill." He gestured at the hill with the monoliths on top of it. "Eventually, the anxiety peaks, and your body will start to relax and recover."

"Yeah. That's what they say. Avoidance just makes it worse. But avoidance sounds much more attractive."

His eyes crinkled at the corners. "I'm sure it does. But you were brave and went ahead and did it anyway. And you survived."

Margie smiled back at him, her face warm. "Thank you."

The door opened and Finkle stood there. He seemed a little better than he had been when Margie saw him last. A bit more color in his cheeks. He still wrung his hands, though it was less obvious.

"Detective Pat. And…" He looked at Cruz. "Detective…?"

"This is Detective Cruz. He's helping me out today. We've taken a look around, and I wonder if you're up to answering some questions now."

He nodded and escorted them into the building. He took them to a lobby where there was some seating. They all sat down in a close grouping.

"Are you feeling a bit better?" Margie asked Finkle.

"Yes, a bit, thank you."

"Have you had a chance to pull your security footage yet?"

"I'm working on it."

She wondered whether they were ever going to see any footage. When he said that a lot of the cameras didn't work, what did that mean? Did it mean there was *no* outdoor footage? Or nothing beyond a view or two in the parking lot? And if so, how many people knew that? Had the killer known that none of his movements would be recorded?

"I told Detective Cruz that you were not able to identify the individual in the picture I showed you," Margie said. "I wonder, though, whether it might have been an employee that you don't know well, or that the water might have distorted her features enough that you just didn't recognize her."

He looked nervous. Probably afraid that she would make him look at it again to make sure that he couldn't identify the victim.

"She was a young woman," Margie said. "Mid to late twenties or early thirties. Blond, shoulder-length hair. No obvious scars, tattoos, or distinguishing features."

He considered this. "There are a few employees who could meet that description."

"Do you think you could give me their names and maybe call to make sure they are okay? You can say that there was a computer problem and you wanted to check when their next shift was. You don't need to say it's anything to do with the murdered woman or our investigation. We would just like to know that all of your employees are accounted for. The ones who could meet that description."

"Uh… okay." Finkle nodded. "I can do that." He looked at them for a minute uncertainly. "Right now?"

"You said there were just a few employees who meet that description. It wouldn't take long to check in with each one, would it?"

"No. I guess not. I thought you would have other questions, though. Then I'll call once we're done."

"Okay. Have you had anything strange happen in the last week or two? It doesn't need to be anything violent. Just whether there were any unusual occurrences. Arguments. Flower deliveries. Phone hang-ups."

"No, I can't think of anything. The education center was closed until school started again, so it's only been a couple of weeks. Everything… has seemed pretty normal. I mean, as normal as anything during the pandemic. It's a bit different with masks, social distancing, and sanitizing anything that the kids might touch during a tour. It's more work. But we're doing everything we can to keep the students safe."

"Of course. Have any of the employees taken unexpected vacations? Called in sick? Just not been available when you thought they would be?"

"No."

"Anyone sick at all?"

"Of course we've had a few people sick. But not the virus. Everyone was tested."

"No, I didn't mean that. It's more about whether everything has just been routine or there have been unusual scheduling changes."

"I can't think of anything. When you work with young people, there are always some changes. They decide they have to go away with friends for the weekend, and if you say no, then they call in sick at the last minute." He rolled his eyes. "And you know very well that they aren't really sick, they just wanted to make it to that party or wedding."

Margie nodded. "*Millennials*," she offered.

"Exactly. It isn't the way we were raised, I'll tell you. The work ethic just isn't the same."

"And you didn't have anyone do that the last couple of weeks? Since you reopened after the summer?"

"No, I don't think so. We haven't been back for long enough."

"And everyone has been working together well? Nothing unexpected? No personality changes since you were last operational?"

"Personality changes." His brows came down like he didn't like her choice of words.

"Sometimes, when people are stressed about something or have had big changes in their lives, it shows up as changes in personality or behavior. Someone very patient before is suddenly blowing their top unexpectedly. A sloppy employee suddenly seems OCD or vice versa. Someone is jumpy. Has unusual fears." She didn't look at Cruz as she said this.

Water was not an unusual fear. Well, maybe it wasn't common, but people did drown. It was dangerous, even for people who didn't think it was.

Finkle thought about this. His hands slowly stopped their wringing motions, and he smoothed his fingernails with the pad of his thumb. "Well... there was Patty."

Margie nodded, waiting. She pulled her notebook out and worked the pencil free of the coil where she had stashed it.

"She seemed overly emotional. I thought... maybe she was pregnant. Or she could just have PMS. I don't know. It isn't like you can ask a young woman these things. She just seemed like that. Hormonal."

"What is Patty's physical description?"

"She's... medium height and build. Thirty or so."

"Blond?"

"Yes, I suppose so. Light brown or dark blond."

"Do you have her number?"

He shifted uncomfortably. "In my office."

"You don't have it on your cell phone? Employees never call when you are away from the office, or you don't need to phone them to line up substitutes if someone calls you after hours to say they can't make it the next morning?"

Finkle hesitated. Margie was beginning to get impatient with him. She wasn't sure why he didn't want to call any of his employees, but he needed to get with the program. They needed to identify the woman out in the water. Patty? Another employee? Someone not associated with the park at all?

"Mr. Finkle. I want her number. Give it to me now, or go to your office and get it. Now."

He started to flush red. Not angry. A lot of men would have been furious to be spoken to like that by a woman. Or a cop. But Finkle wasn't the aggressive type. He was embarrassed or scared. He ducked his head, reminding her of a turkey.

Finkle pulled his phone out of his pocket. An older model, small screen, not one of the modern oversize ones. He tinkered with it for a moment, presumably finding the contacts app and then filtering down to Patty's name and checking her contact information.

"Do you want me to call her? Or do you want to?"

At this point, she was worried that he would completely screw it up if she let him make the call. For whatever reason, he didn't want to call his employee in front of Margie. Were they having an affair? Had he made up the part about her being moody or hormonal?

"Just give me the number, please."

He read it out to her. Margie wrote it down. "Okay. Give me a minute." She got up from her seat and walked away from Cruz and Finkle, turning her back on them. She walked far enough away that it would be difficult, if not impossible, for Finkle to hear what she was saying in a normal tone of voice. She dialed the number into her keypad and took a deep breath, unsure what she would say if Patty answered the phone. Apologize and say it was a wrong number? Explain that she was with the police and just doing a welfare check? Say that something had happened at work and she didn't want Patty to come in without knowing that there was something wrong?

The first three rings went unanswered. Most people, if they were going to answer, would do so within three rings. But sometimes the phone was across the house, or they were already on a call with someone else, or the phone started ringing on Margie's end before a connection was made. She had no idea what the cell coverage was like at the education center. She pulled the phone away from her ear for a moment to check the bars. Weak, but still connected. She put it back to her ear and waited. The tone continued to ring, and ring, and ring.

Patty wasn't there. Or she wasn't someone who answered unidentified phone numbers. Plenty of people screened by the Caller ID and wouldn't chance talking to a stranger. Especially Millennials.

Eventually, the call clicked through to voicemail. Patty hadn't recorded a message of her own, but let the default automated message answer. Margie hung up. She could try again later when they had identified the victim. Or when they hadn't.

She walked back to Finkle and Cruz. "No answer. Does she usually answer her phone?"

Finkle thought about it. He nodded slowly, hesitantly. "Yes. I think she was pretty good about it. It's hard to remember, you know."

"Yes. I'm sure you have a lot of people to keep track of. Can you give me the names and numbers of the other women who might answer the general description I gave you? Patty and who else?"

He worked through a few names, spelling them out for her and digging their numbers out of his phone.

CHAPTER SIX

When they left Finkle, Margie tried Patty's number once more. She looked at Cruz while she waited for an answer she didn't expect to come.

"What did you think of Finkle?"

"Nervous guy."

"Definitely. Very anxious."

"But… at the same time, not the type I would expect to be involved in a homicide. I don't think he's anxious because he did something. Just because he's a naturally anxious type and doesn't know how to react to a police investigation."

Margie nodded. She hadn't picked up on a lot of deception flags from him. A few, but not a lot. More hesitant and unsure of how he was supposed to act than lying or being evasive.

The call went through to voicemail again. This time, Margie left a message. Very generic, giving her name and asking Patty to call her back. No mention of police or an investigation. It could be anything from a telemarketer to a bank manager or a schoolteacher wanting more information about booking a class program. She hung up.

They were walking in the direction of the forensic techs to see if they had found anything or needed any additional assistance or direction. Which Margie was sure they didn't need. Instead, she called

Detective Jones, who she hoped would be at her desk with the computer in front of her.

Kaitlyn Jones answered, her tone cheerful but not too bouncy. "Detective Pat?"

"Hi, I wonder if you can check for me and see whether there is a missing person report filed on Patty Roscoe."

"Sure, hold one minute."

They continued to walk as Jones looked it up. She was back a couple of minutes later. "Yes. Entered just this morning."

Margie looked at Cruz. "Bingo."

"You think this is our victim?" Jones asked.

"I think it is. She's an employee at the education center out here who might have been under some additional stress lately. Fits the description of the deceased. We couldn't reach her on the phone; I took a chance it might be her."

"I'll follow up on this end. Get as much information as I can."

"Get whatever pictures you can, any background, criminal history, social networks. Who reported Patty missing?"

"Husband."

"He just reported it this morning?"

"Yes."

"Where was he last night?"

There was silence from Jones as, Margie assumed, she read through the highlights of the report that had been filed. "He figured he couldn't report it until she'd been gone for twenty-four hours. Then he decided he couldn't wait that long and made a call."

"Hmm." Margie knew that many people still thought that they had to wait twenty-four or forty-eight hours before they could report someone missing. But they usually started the process early anyway. Or started making calls to hospitals and were told by them to make a police report. "Okay. Well, start gathering what you can. Have someone bring the husband in for an interview. We'll get there as soon as we can."

"Will do," Jones agreed.

Margie hung up. She looked at Cruz. "How long would you take before you started making calls about your missing wife?"

He considered. "I'd probably be calling the last place she was supposed to be once she was an hour late. Then calling her friends, colleagues, anyone who might have known what her plans were. By the time it was a couple of hours, I'd be pretty worried. Of course, my wife doesn't go out a lot. If she was someone who was routinely unreachable for hours at a time, or who had a history of disappearing for a night here and there, then I might not call until the next day."

Margie made a mental note of these details. It was always good to see it from someone else's perspective. There were people that you would start worrying about if they were twenty minutes late for an appointment, and there were people you wouldn't start *really* worrying about for a day or two. It depended on the person. But the way that Finkle had talked about Patty, he had made it seem as if she was a usually dependable employee who had only started having problems recently.

They reached the tape perimeter, and Margie and Cruz stood outside of it, waiting for the opportunity to talk to someone. The tech who seemed to be in charge, Mitchell, according to his name badge, drifted over to them. He had a clear face shield, so Margie wasn't concerned when he lowered his mask to speak with them.

"How is it coming, detectives?"

"We've probably done about as much as we can here. How are things going with you?"

"Going to be a while yet. Calls in to see how long it would take to get equipment here to pump out some of this water and drag for any larger foreign objects. May not be feasible, but we'll see."

Margie indicated the hill with the monoliths on it and pointed out about the screens not being enough to keep prying eyes from the body, if it had still been there when visitors had started to arrive on the site. Mitchell looked up at the hill, chewing on his lower lip, and nodded.

"Hadn't even thought about that. But it was early. They got her out of here before there was a lot of foot traffic."

"That's not always the case, though. I'm just as much to blame; I never thought to look up there and see what the sightlines were."

"Next time, we'll both be wiser."

Margie nodded. "Yeah. We may have a name. It probably won't make any difference to your work, because you're not going to throw anything away that has another name on it, but our victim may be Patty Roscoe."

"Patty. Okay." He did a rapid mental review of whatever they had found thus far. "I don't think I've seen that name or any P initials on anything we've pulled today."

Margie's surprise must have shown.

"You'd be surprised at how much stuff gets thrown out in these garbages. School assignments, employee shift schedules, coffee cups and lunches with names or initials on them. But I don't think we got any Pattys."

CHAPTER SEVEN

One of the tragedies of murdered or missing cases was that the people who were closest to the victims, those who ended up reporting their friend's absence or death, were the people who were most suspect in any violence against them. Spouses and significant others, parents, children, best friends. They all worried about their loved ones, called the police to try to get some help, and ended up under the microscope themselves.

So while Margie always went into an interview with the knowledge that they might be talking to a murderer, she also kept in mind that they might be completely innocent, genuinely grieving the loss of a loved one. And, of course, many people were both the culprit and the chief mourner. They weren't exclusive.

At the police station, Scott Warner had been welcomed, given a bottle of cold water, and settled into an interview room pending Margie's return. She looked in on him before entering the room. He looked around the room restlessly, not distracted by his phone, and also not crying or banging the table, insisting that someone deal with his missing persons report. There was no outrage over being left alone in the room while they looked into his report. No obviously guilty behavior.

"I'm just going to freshen up for a minute," Margie said. "Then we'll see what he has to say."

She took a quick washroom break, splashed water on her face, and chugged a mug of coffee before re-masking and entering the room to speak with her suspect.

"Mr. Warner. I'm sorry for keeping you waiting. We have been investigating. My name is Detective Patenaude. May I…?" She gestured to the chair opposite him as if she needed his permission to sit down. Put him in a position of power. Make him feel like he had control over the interview.

"Yes, please. Have you found anything out? I called the hospitals, but they won't say anything over the phone. And I worried about what if she was brought in unconscious or had amnesia, how would they even know who she was then? Have you checked?"

"If she was taken to the hospital, she would have had her ID, wouldn't she?" Margie countered. "They would be able to figure out who she was."

He looked confused for a moment, then nodded. "Yes. Right. Of course. They would know. But they wouldn't necessarily talk to me. More and more patient rights these days, they won't tell you anything without the patient's permission, and if she is unconscious and can't give it, then what?"

"We haven't heard anything back from the hospitals yet. You'll have to wait a bit longer."

Warner sighed and nodded. He looked down at his phone, thumbing it on, looking at it, waiting for it to ring. Maybe Patty would call him to tell him her car had broken down. Or that she'd been hit on the head, but was okay. Something that would mean she wasn't gone from him forever.

"Why don't you tell me about your wife?" Margie said. "I know you've already made an official report. Filling out all of those routine questions. But that doesn't give me a real taste for the person that she is. There is so much more to a person than just the physical description and what their last movements were."

Warner nodded. "Yeah. That's so true. Patty is… a wife and mother first and foremost. We have two young children…"

"Was she a stay-at-home mom?" Margie asked, already knowing the answer was negative.

"No. But not because she didn't want to be. If we'd been able to afford it, then of course we would have. But they have a good daycare, and Patty is really good at her job. She loves teaching at the education center. She was thrilled to be able to put her degree to good use. She was passionate about the environment."

"She sounds like a really special woman. Tell me about her movements? When did you see her last?"

"When she went to work yesterday morning. I picked up the kids from the daycare after I got off work, like I usually do. She gets home after me... then we have supper, put the girls to bed..."

"But you became concerned when..."

"She didn't get back from work when she normally would. I called her cell phone a few times, but she wasn't answering. I know she doesn't answer if she has a class or tour, or if she is in a meeting with her boss. But when it got to be a couple of hours... well, she's never done that before. She's always at home, never more than an hour late. And even if she was running a few minutes late, she would have called to let me know that she was late, and when she expected to be home. She was very good about that. Better than me." His voice cracked a little.

And he was the one who was supposed to be picking up the kids. Margie didn't imagine it went over very well if he were running late and forgot to inform either the daycare or Patty.

"No calls at all? Had you talked to her during the workday?"

"Yes. Once or twice. I don't remember specifics. You know, we just check in with each other now and then. Ask the other person how it's going or call to vent about our jobs." He rolled his eyes. "Even if you love your job, there are still those days when nothing goes right."

"Of course. So, you don't know what times you talked to her?" Margie nodded to Warner's phone. "You can check your call log...?"

"Oh... I would have called her from my work phone. Not this one."

Margie let that sit for a minute before going on. "Okay. So maybe a couple of times during the day. Have you called anyone at her work? To ask what time they saw her last or when she left?"

"No. I don't know her coworkers. I know first names, of course; she talks about different people she is teaching with, or who she likes or doesn't like. In a superficial way. She didn't hate anyone, of course. Some people would just rub her the wrong way, get on her nerves."

"How about her boss?"

"Uh…" He looked blank. "I really can't tell you. I know her supervisor… that's… Sally something. And of course, the director, that guy." Warner shook his head, blinking and trying to recall. "Fink? Barney?"

"Arby Finkle."

"Yes. Him."

"Did they get along? Or did she have problems with him?"

"I think they got along okay. I know that she and some of the other workers… well, they made fun of him a little. Behind his back, not to his face." He shrugged. "Not mean-spirited or anything. Just like you do at an office. Blow off some steam talking about the stupid things your boss does."

"Sure," Margie agreed in a neutral tone.

"I guess he was kind of… I don't know. Fussy. Maybe a little…" He gave a limp-wrist gesture. "You know."

Margie looked at him, head cocked to the side slightly. "What?"

"I don't think that he was, but they talked about him a bit. About maybe he was… closet gay. Like… *Tinkerbell-Finklebell*." Again he tried to shrug it off. "Just all in fun. Not serious."

"I see." Margie didn't write anything in her notebook, but continued to look at him, waiting for more.

"I don't know. She got along with everybody okay. And she liked the job. It was important to her."

"You weren't able to contact anyone from her work. So what did you think had happened? Did you think that she was still at work, or that something had happened to her on the way home? Or just that she was out running errands and might have stopped in to see friends?"

"I thought… maybe an accident on the way home. That's why I

was calling hospitals." He rubbed at the corners of his eyes. Margie couldn't see any tears, but that didn't mean that there weren't any threatening. Or that he wasn't grieving just as much as the spouses who came in weeping like fountains.

Margie nodded. "She wouldn't normally have been anywhere else between work and home? Stopping at the grocery store? Gas station? Did she ever go out with friends for a drink or coffee?"

"No. She came home. We did errands at other times. She would come home to help with the kids. Making dinner and putting them to bed."

"Who made dinner?"

He looked at her like she was crazy. "What?"

"Did you make dinner or did she?"

"Yesterday?" he asked blankly.

The night before, he had obviously been the one to make the evening meal, if he were telling them the truth.

"Normally. Did you alternate? Did you make it because she got home later than you? Did you agree on certain days?"

"Well, no, Patty was usually the one who made dinner. I was so tired at the end of the day, you know, and I brought them home from daycare, so when she came home from work, it was her turn. I just wanted to relax in front of the TV for a while."

Margie nodded. "So she usually made dinner arrangements. Or maybe if she knew she was running late, she would tell you to go ahead or would pick something up on the way home?"

He shrugged. "Yeah. Maybe."

"So, you had to make the dinner instead last night."

He nodded.

"How did that make you feel?"

His eyes widened. "How did it make me feel?" He demanded, his voice startlingly loud. "I was sick with worry! I made the kids some KD and gave them a cookie when they were done, but I couldn't eat a bite. I was just... I could barely function. I didn't know what to do. Who to call. I was alone there, just the kids and me, and I didn't know what to do."

"That must have been difficult."

"It was! You have no idea what it's like just to have someone... not come home one day."

Margie nodded slowly and made a few notes in her notebook. "We would like to talk to the kids. Where are they?"

"They're... I took them to daycare. I didn't want them around here. I knew I would be waiting around and they would be bored. And I don't want them... wondering what's going on."

"What do they think happened to their mother?"

"They don't know."

"I mean, what did you tell them? What explanation did you give them?"

"I just told them that she would be home later. They wanted her to get home, but they didn't really ask about what she was doing. Just when she was coming home."

"And when did you tell them she was coming home?"

"Soon. I didn't want to say anything specific."

"We would still like to talk to them. How old are they?"

"Two and four." He shook his head, scowling behind his mask. "They're too young to be able to tell you anything. All they know is that Mommy didn't come home last night. You talking to them... it's just going to traumatize them."

"We'll be very careful. I'll have Detective Cruz help out. He has young children at home."

In truth, Margie didn't know how old Cruz's children were. But she imagined they were young. Either way, he was a dad. He was understanding of his son's anxiety rather than being impatient and macho about it. He was clearly good with kids. He would treat Warner's children kindly.

"No." Warner shook his head. "I don't give you permission to talk to my kids. I don't have to, right? You can't talk to them without my permission."

"It depends on the circumstances." Margie made a note in her notepad. "We'll do what we can without them, but I'd like to be able to discuss this with them too."

"They're too young. They don't know anything, and you'll just confuse and upset them. I've heard of how police can plant false memories." He stared at her accusingly, as if she had already told his children that it was his fault their mother was missing. "I don't want anything like that to happen."

"I understand that. Of course we'll be very careful not to traumatize them or to plant any suggestions—"

"No. I already told you no. No way. There's no way you're talking to my kids."

His expression was fierce. Margie remembered the homeschooling dad at the park and how casual he had been about protecting his kids near the water. On the other hand, this father was not taking any chances on exposing his children to something that might be harmful to them.

She nodded and went on. "You've given a description of your wife's car in your report?"

"Yes, of course."

"Have you had any car trouble lately, anything that might make you more concerned about a traffic accident? Or maybe a stall beside the road, leaving her stranded?"

"Just the usual. You know how it is with cars. Something always needs to be fixed."

"How was your wife's mental state lately?"

"I don't know…" He thought about it. "Okay, I guess? I mean, everyone has stress in their lives…"

"She hadn't had any unusual stresses lately? Any signs of depression? Drug or alcohol use?"

"Why? What does that have to do with anything?"

"Is it possible that your wife could have harmed herself?"

"No. I don't think so." His answer was certain at first, then less so. He stared off into the distance, thinking about it. "She had her down days, like anyone else. But she wasn't *always* down. She didn't talk about killing herself."

"Not everyone does. Has she been moody lately? More impatient? Wanting to be by herself?"

"Maybe."

"Do you have contact information for some of her friends? Her family? People who she might have talked to? Maybe even a doctor?"

"She was estranged from her family. Doctors… I don't think she even has a GP. She just uses a walk-in clinic if she needs to get something checked out for herself. She has a pediatrician for the girls, but it's so hard to get a good family doctor these days…"

"Friends? She must have had someone she talked to."

"I'll see if I can get into her computer. I honestly don't even know last names, let alone phone numbers."

"You didn't do anything with them? Double dates or group things?"

"Sometimes, but Patty was always the one calling them. I'd call a couple of my friends if she wanted a bigger group, but she was the… social director in the family."

"Don't try to get onto her computer. Bring it in here. Along with any other devices she might have. Tablets, cameras, sports watch, anything that will help us to build a picture of where she was going and what she was doing. Do not try to get onto them. Leave that to us."

He was reluctant, but nodded his agreement. "Okay."

"You don't know what kind of security measures she might have. Some of these devices will wipe if you enter the wrong information too many times."

"She wasn't that security conscious. Her password is probably one of the girls' names,"

"If you could write down their names, birthdates, any important birthdays or anniversaries, her parents' and siblings' names, your phone numbers, anything like that." Margie pushed a pad of paper and a pen across the table to him. They would probably be able to access her various accounts by subpoenaing them from the service providers, but she was interested in seeing what he would write down. How much did he know? Was he the kind of person who kept track of important dates and bits of information or not? She already suspected not. Patty was the one who had managed their social lives; he didn't even bother to know the names of her friends.

She watched him puzzle over the information.

"Was Patty having problems with anyone? Any arguments? Threats? Phone hang-ups?" she asked.

"No, I don't think so. Not that she mentioned."

"You say she was estranged from her family. Why is that?"

"She…" he looked for a way to answer the question politely. "They didn't approve of all of her choices."

Margie considered. The woman's body had not had any tattoos, significant scars, or multiple piercings. Patty had married and had two children. She had a good education and was working in a good, respectable position that utilized her strengths. Any parent she could think of would have been delighted with her choices. She was not a free-spirited rebel.

"Does that mean they didn't like you?" she asked baldly.

Warner turned white. He looked at her and tried to decide how big his lie would be.

"They didn't, did they?" Margie pressed. "For whatever reason, they took a dislike to you. We're going to talk to them. And that's what they're going to say. So you may as well be truthful about it. Lying will only make it look worse."

"Okay, yes. You're right. They didn't approve of me and of her marrying me. They didn't think I had much going for me. But I've always been devoted to her and the girls. I've always worked to help support the family. I'm not some kind of deadbeat."

"Sometimes, people just rub each other the wrong way. Maybe they liked the guy she dated before you, so they were disappointed that she dumped him. People are emotional creatures more than logical."

He nodded along with her, the tension around his eyes relaxing. "I wish there was something I could do to make them like me better. But they don't, and Patty didn't want to do anything with them because of it. So we never really had a chance to make it up."

He twisted the wedding ring on his finger.

And it was too late now, whether he knew that or not.

CHAPTER EIGHT

Margie met with the rest of the team after she was finished her interrogation with Warner. They did not tell him that they knew Patty was dead. She hadn't been properly identified yet. She might not be who they thought. Once they had confirmation that it was her, and had everything they could get willingly through Warner, they would let him know and see how he responded. She suspected that he knew she was dead already. Even if he hadn't had anything to do with her death, he knew when she didn't come home that night. She had either walked out on him and the children or something bad had happened to her.

"It sounds like there might have been some issues at work," Cruz suggested, leaning forward on the conference room table. "He can say all he likes that making fun of Finkle and telling stories on him behind his back is good fun, but the fact is, Finkle probably knew about it. A guy like that might not look dangerous," he raised one brow at Margie to solicit her opinion, "but if you push him too far and he blows…"

Margie nodded slowly. "It has, unfortunately, been my experience that everybody has a breaking point. You can drive anyone to violence if you push them hard enough. And Finkle was pretty distressed today. I thought at the time that it was just the discovery of a body in 'his' park and then seeing her picture. But it could also be due to a guilty conscience."

"We should dig a little deeper there. Maybe get him in for an interview. Check out his background, social media," Siever suggested. Margie had found his suggestions and careful documentation of their evidence to have been very helpful in the other cases she had worked on. He was a serious man, not as inclined as the others to joke and make sarcastic remarks. The kind of guy who tended to keep to himself most of the time, but was always watching and cataloging everything.

"Yeah. Definitely. Where are we on getting Patty's phone records? I'd like to start talking to some of her friends. And this should help us track down her family." She pushed the page of possible password details she'd had Warner write down into the middle of the table where others could see it. He might have denied knowing her friends' last names, but he had written down her parents' full names. No birth dates, but it was enough to get them started.

"We need to get a positive identification," Jones advised. "We're tracking down dental records. Without much help from Mr. Warner, I have to say. If we can get her electronics from him, she probably has her dentist in her contact list. He's probably right about her using one of the kids' names for her password. It's pretty common."

"Do you want to make arrangements to stop by the house and get them? I'm afraid if we wait for him, he's not going to move on it. Or he'll try to crack them at home and we'll lose important information."

"Sure," Jones agreed with a brisk nod. "No problem. I'll get over there right away."

"Okay, well…" Margie looked at the list of items to follow up on in her notepad. "We've got a lot to do, so we'll just keep moving things forward."

⁂

It didn't feel like they had accomplished much at the end of the day, but Margie knew that she had been working hard on it ever since she'd received the call early that morning. It felt like she had been working for three days straight, so when MacDonald prompted her to go home and get some sleep so she'd be able to be productive on the case the next day, she admitted she was too exhausted to do anything else on it and packed things away.

Christina had beaten her home and had already eaten supper by the time Margie got there.

"I'm sorry," Margie apologized. "It's been a bear of a day."

Christina rolled her eyes but didn't complain about how that always seemed to happen and maybe it had something to do with Margie's choice to join the Calgary homicide department. Maybe things would have been quieter if she'd taken a different position, or moved to a small town instead of somewhere busier.

"I know. I'm saying that too often. Did you have something good for dinner? Was there enough in the fridge?" Margie opened the fridge and then the freezer, hoping to be inspired about what to make for her own dinner. The only thing that looked appetizing was the ice cream, and she had to be the adult and not be a bad example for her daughter. Eating ice cream for dinner was the wrong standard to set.

Christina grunted. "This and that. There was some leftover pizza."

Margie looked in the fridge. Christina had finished it off. Which was probably a good thing. Margie should eat something that was good for her. Lots of fruits and veggies. A salad, maybe. She shut the doors of the fridge again.

"There's pasta in the cupboard," Christina suggested. "Or, you could have a sandwich."

Probably the same things that Margie would have suggested to Christina. Kids were good at reflecting back what they heard from their parents at inopportune times. Margie opened the cupboards and eventually settled on a bowl of raisin bran. Christina watched as she poured a bowl and added milk.

"That's breakfast, not dinner."

"Today, it's dinner. Give me a break this one time."

Christina was silent, looking back down at her homework.

"How's it coming along?" Margie asked. "What are you working on?"

"Just… English… math…"

"You need any help?"

"No."

"Okay."

Christina didn't look up as she scratched out some math equations. "Are you going to tell me about the new case?"

"I can't really say much about it. A body was found at Ralph Klein Park."

"Is that near one of the other ones?"

"No. It's not far from here, actually. Driving, that is. Walking, it would be too far."

"Yeah? What's it like?"

"Wetlands. Lots of ponds and water catchments and canals or streams. There is a playground with a zip line and an education center to teach kids about the wetlands."

"Cool. We could take Stella there. She'd think it was great!"

Margie thought about Stella jumping into the big basin around the education center and shuddered. She wouldn't be able to jump in to pull Stella out if something happened to her.

"There were signs up that there aren't any dogs allowed in Ralph Klein Park. We'll take her to Glenbow one of these days. And go into Cochrane for ice cream." Margie glanced at the closed freezer door. She was definitely hung up on ice cream tonight.

"Yeah! I want to do that. I was talking to Stacey about Cochrane, and she says MacKay's is awesome. They have ice cream flavors like you never even thought of there, and it's always changing, so you can try new things."

"It sounds really cool. I want to see it too."

"*Cool*," Christina repeated with a grimace, picking up on the unintended pun.

Margie laughed. She continued to munch on her raisin bran.

"So, what else?" Christina asked.

"What else?"

"About your case. It was at Ralph Klein Park. Closer to us this time. But not anyone we know, right?" she asked lightly.

"No one we know involved in this case," Margie assured her quickly.

They didn't need more nightmares.

"Was it… like the others? Another stabbing?"

"No. I didn't see any marks on the body. The medical examiner will have to do the postmortem and report back, but it was probably a drowning."

Nothing that Christina wouldn't read in the news in the morning. If it hadn't already been reported.

"Do you know who did it?"

"No. We have some suspects. First, we need to conclusively identify the victim. We think we know who it is, but it takes some time to be absolutely sure. In the meantime, we're investigating all leads."

"You'll find him?"

"Calgary homicide has a very good solve rate. We'll find him."

"At least you didn't have to go in the water." Christina looked up from her notebook. "Right?"

"No. Not in the water." Margie couldn't suppress a shudder. "Just… close. And… over bridges." She didn't describe the walkways around the education center. She didn't want to picture them or remember them in any detail. She tried to block as much of that experience out as she could. Maybe, as Cruz said, the only way for her to get over her anxieties was through exposure to them, but that didn't mean she was going to dwell on them any more than she already had to.

"You went over a bridge?" Christina asked.

"Yes."

"In the car or on foot?"

"On foot. Actually, I had to go over one in the car too. But that was easier."

"Wow. Good for you." While Christina would laugh and tease Margie about her unreasonable fear of the water at other times, she always encouraged Margie to be brave and face her fears and try new things. Margie tried to do the same with Christina, encouraging her to do the things she was afraid of.

It was always easier to tell someone else to face their own fears than it was to face her own.

CHAPTER NINE

The next day Margie had a report from the medical examiner's office on her desk indicating that their victim had not had water in her lungs. She had not been drowned in the stream out at Ralph Klein Park.

Margie took a few deep breaths, her heart racing and stomach feeling queasy. Even though the medical examiner said that the woman had *not* died of drowning, she still couldn't help but imagine that cold, dark water flowing over her face, sealing off her mouth and nose, blinding her. She imagined sinking farther and farther down into the muck at the bottom of the stream, trying sluggishly to move, but being trapped like in a nightmare. Frozen, too afraid to even fight back against the water.

"Detective Pat…? Margie?"

Margie tried to break free of the vision. She wasn't drowning. The victim hadn't drowned. There wasn't any point to imagining it. She didn't want to see it, so why was she?

"Margie." There was a hand on her arm.

Margie opened her eyes and looked into Detective Jones's concerned blue eyes. She drew a deep breath. She could breathe just fine. She wasn't drowning. No one was drowning.

"It's okay. I'm okay."

"Are you sure? You were kind of… wheezing. Are you asthmatic? Do you need an inhaler?"

"No. I'm okay. I was just…" Margie trailed off, not wanting to have to explain it. "I'll tell you about it later. It's just… a distraction."

"You got the ME's report?" Jones nodded to it.

"Yes. Not drowning." Margie studied it for more details. "Several blows to the head. Subdural hematoma." She shook her head. "A fight… someone really got angry with her."

Jones sighed and shook her head, eyes closed. Margie thought about Finkle. Could he have snuck up on Patty? Approached her when she had been deep in thought or busy with something. Maybe not something quiet, like Margie had been picturing, but something noisy. The noise would distract her, cover up Finkle's footsteps. And then…

She couldn't see him sneaking up and bludgeoning her. That didn't make any sense. She tried again. An argument? A disagreement over something that had resulted in Patty throwing one of her insults in Finkle's face? Not behind his back, this time, but face-to-face, so that he couldn't deny it. Couldn't pretend that his staff respected him.

A slur or insult that had pricked him to act. It was too much, and he had just picked up the nearest possible weapon and slugged her with it. Repeatedly. Or he had knocked her down and continued to beat her.

In those scenarios, Patty would have to have been the last one there with him at the end of the day. So that no one else had seen or heard what had happened, or observed him disposing of the body.

Would Finkle have disposed of the body in the waterways of his beloved park? Would he have thought it fitting to return her to nature and to bury her in the water that she too had been so passionate about? Or would he think that was polluting the waters that they were trying to purify by running through the natural filters of the wetlands?

"They were both passionate about nature," Margie mused aloud. "What could they have fought about?"

"Who?"

"Patty and Finkle." Margie closed her eyes, thinking about it for a minute. It wouldn't have been because Finkle had propositioned Patty, something that happened in many workplaces. If she and the others thought that he was in the closet, then he clearly wasn't sexually harassing the women who worked under him. Unless it was to overcompensate. To make them think that he was just as big a pig as any other man who had ever abused them.

"Did we get the ID?"

"Dental clinic near her house. They're sending over x-rays. ME should have a positive ID by the end of the day."

"Good." Margie was relieved about that. She didn't want Patty's family and friends to be wondering any longer than necessary about what had happened to her. They deserved to have a little peace, knowing that she was not suffering. Knowing was better.

"Multiple blows," Jones mused, skimming the ME's report over Margie's shoulder. "Torn nails and defensive bruises on her hands. Broken finger. It was a fight. She didn't just go down with one blow."

"No." Margie pictured Finkle. Had he had any scratches or bruises on his hands? He'd been constantly wringing them. Margie had spent a lot of time looking at them, winding and squeezing each other. She was pretty sure she would have noticed if he'd had any bruising on his hands.

But then, if he'd used some kind of an object as a bludgeon, he wouldn't have bruised his hands.

There could have been someone else at work, someone who had propositioned her, or someone she had been having an affair with. Someone bigger and more explosive than Finkle.

"We need to talk to her family and friends. See if she and Warner had marital issues. See if they knew about the situation at work. Or if she'd been under more stress lately. Finkle said that she had been moody. Why?"

She remembered what else Finkle had said. He'd thought that maybe she was hormonal. Maybe pregnant. She flipped through the pages of the ME's report, scanning the rest of the information. She shook her head. No pregnancy. That was something, at least. It would have been worse—or at least, felt worse—if Patty had been pregnant when she was killed.

"I'm going to make some calls," she told Jones. "I know we don't have a confirmed ID yet, but I want to start talking to others before they know too much. People start to make things up. They start to imagine the reasons things happened the way they did. I don't want confabulation. I want the facts."

"Sure. Do you want me to make some calls?"

"We'll start with Mom and Dad. They can let us know who else we should be talking to."

"All right. The contact details we were able to pull are in the workspace. Interview room is yours as long as you want it."

Margie appreciated Detective Jones taking care of these little details and smoothing the way for Margie's investigation.

"You want to sit in with me?"

"Sure, if you want. That won't be too many people?"

"No, I don't think so. I think they'll feel better if they feel like more people are involved in seeing that justice is served."

CHAPTER TEN

ecause Patty was estranged from her parents, they hadn't known she was missing before Margie's call. Margie invited them to talk to her, telling them as little as possible. Certainly not that she was with the homicide department. Let them think, at least for a little while, that Patty had just not gone home for one night. There could be a perfectly reasonable explanation for that.

Their eyes were wide and frightened when Margie met them in the reception area. She took them to the interview room. Nothing between the lobby and the interview room indicated to the couple that they were dealing with homicide rather than with missing persons. They were both housed in the same building and on the same floor. Only the room numbers gave it away to those who knew those little details.

"Mr. and Mrs. Roscoe, thank you for coming in. I'm sorry to have to involve you in this."

Mrs. Roscoe was wiping her nose with a well-used tissue. Face masks were not an option when people were crying. Margie gave them a box of tissues and a garbage can and sat at the other side of the table, her own mask firmly in place.

"Is she really missing?" Mrs. Roscoe asked. "My baby!"

"I know it must be a shock to you. This is something that no parent ever wants to hear."

"No," she agreed. Mr. Roscoe shook his head, blinking his eyes rapidly.

"When was the last time you saw or talked to your daughter?"

"Well… it's been a long time, actually. I don't know if anyone told you…" Mrs. Roscoe looked down at the table, her face pink with shame. "We were not talking with each other. Things were not good between us." Tears escaped her eyes and flooded down her cheeks. "Why couldn't we have made up before now? I don't even know when the last time we talked to each other was."

"Did you have any communication at all? Texts or emails?"

"No. I still saw her social media posts sometimes. But… well, I didn't respond to them."

"I understand. What was it the two of you fell out over?"

"Her husband. That Scott. Scott Warner. I suppose he told you all about it."

"No, he didn't have much to say about it. I think he would have preferred not to have talked about it at all. But I told him I would be talking with you, so he might as well fill me in because I was going to hear it from you anyway."

She nodded. "What did he tell you? About how unreasonable and judging we are, I suppose. That we never gave him a chance."

"Why don't you tell me in your own words?"

The couple exchanged glances. Mrs. Roscoe was the one who was more comfortable talking, but maybe she felt that her husband would sound more reasonable. Logical rather than emotional like she was.

"Just take your time," Margie urged. "I'm listening."

Mrs. Roscoe turned back to her and began reluctantly. "He just wasn't any good. I knew from the start that he wasn't going to amount to anything. I can't for the life of me imagine what she saw in the man. It wasn't even like he was good looking, so she couldn't say that it was his looks or love at first sight."

But she wasn't judging Warner.

"What made you think that he wasn't good for your daughter? They didn't have shared interests?"

"He's a bum. Patty is the one who has had to support that family from the start."

"He has a job, from what I understood."

"Yes. A job. But no education. Patty is the one who has always made the lion's share of the family's income. He should have just stayed home with the kids; then they wouldn't have had to pour money into daycare. But no, he couldn't do that either. He had to have a career. He had to show everyone that he could amount to something."

Margie made a couple of notes. "So, your concerns were mostly financial?"

"No, not just that. He wasn't a nice person. Isn't. I'm sure that hasn't changed. I didn't want him anywhere near Patty. Or my grandchildren."

"In what way wasn't he nice?" Margie didn't want to suggest that they had argued or that there had been any violence in the family. She didn't want to feed them anything. Let them offer it on their own.

"He was always talking down to her. Like he was the one who had the university education rather than her. He acted like she was... inferior. He was more intelligent, understood politics and the world economy better than she did. He thought he was naturally smart; he didn't need book learning. In fact, he was better without it. Less tainted."

"Really. A know-it-all. They can be very annoying."

"Yes. No one else ever knows anything. If you do, then you're wrong. He has to correct everything you say, and make sure everyone knows that he is the one who gets it all, that he's somehow... an advanced species over everyone else around him."

Margie nodded.

"That might be an exaggeration," Mr. Roscoe temporized. His wife gave him a withering glare. "I don't think it was that bad," Mr. Roscoe said. "At least... not that obvious. The two of them usually seemed to get along pretty well. She allowed him to express his opinions and didn't try to correct him and make him feel bad about the stuff he got wrong. She was very patient with him."

"A wife shouldn't have to be patient with her husband. Not like that. She shouldn't always have to tiptoe around his ego and make him think he's better than she is. That's just wrong."

"It seemed to work okay for them. They didn't fight a lot. Not around us."

"They were never around us," Mrs. Roscoe said. "I saw him for what he was in the beginning, and I said I wouldn't be around them."

Mr. Roscoe gave a nod and shrug. He clearly didn't find Warner quite as objectionable as his wife did. Maybe because he was a man and felt a certain kinship to him in his situation that his wife couldn't feel. Perhaps he could see how Warner might feel in a marriage with a stronger, more outspoken woman. Or maybe his wife was just better at picking up on the subtleties of Patty's and Warner's relationship.

"You must have seen her sometimes. Did you go to her wedding? See the children when they were born or at other times?"

"They had a civil ceremony and didn't see fit to invite us to that," Mrs. Roscoe said stiffly. Another problem that she had with Warner. "When the children were born... Yes, I did go by the hospital to see them when that man was not there. But the rest of the time..." She closed her eyes and shook her head slowly. "I didn't see them. Didn't babysit for them or have family dinners together." She swallowed and dabbed at tears. "I should have made up with her when I had the chance. Now... it's too late. She's gone. Thinking I didn't care."

"She knew you cared," Mr. Roscoe told her, putting his hand over hers. "She knew that the reason you didn't want her with Scott was that you did love her and wanted her to be happy."

But it had probably not made her happy to have to choose between the two of them. Or not to have her mother in her life.

"So if you haven't seen them lately, and didn't have anything to do with them regularly, then I don't suppose there is anything you can tell me about their relationship. Or whether she was under any new stresses the last little while."

"No... we just weren't a part of her life anymore," Mrs. Roscoe said. "I was... waiting for her to see the light and to leave him."

Margie sincerely hoped that wasn't what had resulted in Patty's death.

"How long had she worked at the park?" she tried. "Do you know anything about how she enjoyed that? Whether she got along with everybody she worked with?"

"She's been working there since she got out of school. She liked it. At least, she did back then. I don't know if she's had any problems since then. I guess if she's still there, she must like it. Otherwise, she would have left by now."

"Do you remember anything about her coworkers? I know it has been a few years since you would have heard anything about them, but is there anything you remember?"

"No… not really. There were always other students or recent graduates working there. Lots of young people her age. So it was comfortable for her, lots of people she could relate to."

"And her bosses or supervisors? They must have been older than her."

"She talked about them sometimes… everybody has frustrations with supervisors at work. Policies and procedures. Getting to work late. Trying to get a raise after a positive performance review. You know how it is."

"Of course," Margie agreed. "Was she not advancing as fast as she had hoped?"

"I think all kids think they're going to change the world. She thought she could walk in there and make a difference. Teach them all of the things she had learned in school. But you can't just walk into a place as the newest employee and update all of their procedures, implement all of the latest science. It takes time and experience."

Margie nodded. "After five years, or however long she has worked there, hopefully she was able to put some of her ideas into action. I guess you wouldn't know…"

The two of them shook their heads. There was a lot of sadness in Mrs. Roscoe's face. Not just grief over whatever had happened to her daughter, but the realization that she had missed out on her daughter's life the last few years when she didn't have to. If it had been Margie, she would also be wondering what would happen to the children and whether she would ever see them again. If something had happened to Patty—as they had to guess it had—then what were the chances that Warner would allow them to be a part of the grandchildren's lives?

❧

MRS. ROSCOE HAD BEEN able to provide some of the names of Patty's friends, at least the ones she had spent time with before getting married. And she had Patty's email address, even though they didn't still correspond with each other. Assuming Patty was still using the same email address, it gave them not only a chance to get into her email, but also her cloud storage and syncing. If they couldn't guess her password on the first few tries, they could get a subpoena for the service provider once the identification was verified.

"Do we have confirmation on the dental records yet?" she asked the team in general as she returned to the duty room after finishing with the Roscoes.

"Dr. Galt says it is a match," Siever confirmed. "He'll get us his official report later today."

"Yes!" Margie had harbored the secret worry that they were going in completely the wrong direction and they would find, on comparing the dental records, that it wasn't Patty Roscoe at all. "I mean, that's terrible, but at least we have a name now. Did we get the devices?" She looked over at Jones.

"We did." Jones pulled down her face mask for a moment and grimaced. "Hubby claimed not to know the unlock password on the tablet, but it looks to me like it's been sanitized. I'll send it over to the lab to have them see if they can recover anything. It's possible that she was just using it as an e-reader, but most people will at least put their email on the thing."

"She might have just used it as an entertainment device for the kids too," Cruz offered. "That's mostly what my wife's gets used for. Electronic babysitter when she has to stand in line for something. If the kids are going to be playing on it, you don't want them to have access to your email or schedule or anything else that they could end up messing around with."

"That's a possibility," Jones admitted. "It does have Netflix Kids and Disney+ on it."

Cruz nodded. Jones swore under her breath, not happy about this. "I've got her laptop as well. Hopefully, it has better security and he didn't guess her password before I got it from him. I don't trust the guy."

"I have a few friends to run down," Margie said, looking down at her notepad. "I'm hoping some of them were still in close touch with Patty. And then I might have another talk with Finkle. I have a feeling he wasn't totally honest with us."

CHAPTER ELEVEN

The calls with Patty's friends did not go as well as she had hoped. They were old friends, but had not had a lot to do with Patty during the last few years. They had gone different directions, had different friends, and most were still single or childless. One woman who did have a child only had a baby, none close to Patty's children's ages. So they hadn't spent much time together recently.

They expressed the appropriate shock that Patty was missing and something might have happened to her. Margie tried to gently broach the possibility that her husband might have had something to do with it with each of them, but didn't have much success.

"Do you know her husband, Scott Warner?" she asked Mindy, the one with a baby.

"Oh, we've met. I don't know him well, but he seems like a nice guy."

"You didn't ever think that he and Patty might be having problems?"

"We didn't see much of each other," Mindy reminded her. "I didn't see them together a lot. But she didn't complain about him that I heard. And when they were together, or I could hear him in the background, I never thought he was being an—well, I thought he seemed like a nice enough guy. They didn't fight or snipe at each other in front of me. He didn't tell her she was stupid or push her around."

"You didn't find him critical or argumentative?" Margie asked, thinking of what Mrs. Roscoe had said.

"Well, he was a man. Of course he was argumentative. Wanted to make sure you heard his side of the story and knew that he was the expert on everything. But that's kind of par for the course with guys like him."

"Like him?"

"Well…" Mindy looked for a word. "Kind of… guys who think they're smart? Have all of the answers, even if they change from one day to the next."

"A know-it-all?"

"Yeah. Like that. But not… I wasn't scared of him. He wasn't threatening or the kind that would get all hot and bang the table if you disagreed with him. Just… he wanted you to know how smart he was."

Margie thought about Oscar. He had wanted her to know how smart he was, too. Couldn't stand the thought that a woman might be more intelligent than he was.

❧

MARGIE LOOKED DOWN at her phone. She wanted to get some more work done, but she'd been on the phone for hours. Her ear was hot and sore. Christina would soon be arriving home from school, and Margie didn't want her to be on her own for too long. She could continue her investigation from home. There were other people she could call or email, some research and background she needed to do. She still hadn't talked to Finkle again, but she suspected that he would be leaving the park soon if he hadn't gone home already, and she hadn't asked him for his personal number. With a sigh, she started to put her things away.

"Heading out?" MacDonald asked, startling Margie as he came up from behind her somewhere.

Margie caught her breath and pressed her hand over her racing heart. "Yes. I'll do some more from home, but I want to see my daughter—"

"Don't take your work home with you. Go home and relax and spend time with your family. Come fresh in the morning. You'll be more productive if you balance it out and take breaks than if you try to push through. You can't keep up that pace every day. We'll run this guy down, but it's going to be slow and steady, not a race. We'll eliminate suspects, process evidence, dig into the history. It's not all going to happen in a day."

Margie paused and considered his words. "I *have* been putting in a lot of hours on this."

"And you need to take care of yourself. You've had three back-to-back leads since you arrived here. You're going to burn out if you don't give yourself recovery time."

"Okay." Margie nodded. "All right. I'll take tonight off. I won't do anything. Just take some time with my family."

Mac nodded. "Good. We'll see you tomorrow morning, bright-eyed and ready to get back to it."

It was like physically training for a race or building muscle. Margie needed the rest days and breaks in between to be alert enough to see what was in front of her.

CHRISTINA WAS LYING on her bed, chatting on her phone when Margie got home. She rolled over and looked at her mother, eyebrows raised.

"Just a minute," she said to her friend, and covered the phone. "What are you doing home?"

"I wanted to spend some time with you. I know I've been working too late the last couple of nights."

"Nice."

"I didn't even bring anything home with me. I have a free night. I can cook while you're doing your homework, and then we can do what we want. Take Stella out for a long walk. Run some errands—"

"Go visit Moushoom?"

"Sure, of course. I'm sure he'd be happy to see us again."

Christina nodded. She returned to her phone call. "My mom is home," she said in an exasperated voice. "I have to do homework."

Margie was taken aback for a moment at this change in attitude. Then she laughed to herself. Christina just didn't want whoever she was talking with to think that she was uncool, wanting to spend time with her mother and Moushoom. Teenagers weren't supposed to care about that. They were supposed to be all about gaming and streaming video and social media. Margie went into the kitchen and looked through the fridge, this time with an eye to actually cooking something rather than just feeding a craving for sugar at the end of a stressful day. Salad, maybe a stir fry and rice. Maybe Christina would want some tofu or one of the various vegetarian meats they had purchased to try out.

If she had enough vegetables for dinner, maybe she wouldn't feel like dessert afterward. Her belt was starting to feel just a touch tight, and she didn't want to let her weight get away from her. She might not be a beat cop anymore, but that didn't mean she didn't have to keep up her fitness level. She never knew when she might have to run or get a combative suspect under control.

Christina came into the kitchen. She gave Margie a sideways hug, also gazing into the fridge. "Some noodles too?" she suggested. "We can make lo mein?"

"Okay, sure."

They busied themselves getting the ingredients out and fell into a rhythm chopping vegetables.

"How was school?"

"Oh, you know. It sucked. And then it was over."

Margie chuckled. "Who was on the phone? I don't know about any of your new friends."

"Tracy."

"Tracy. Is she the one who was telling you about MacKay's?"

"No, that was Stacey."

"Oh. Who is Tracy? What is she like?"

"He."

"What?" Margie looked up at her. "He? Tracy?"

"Yes."

"The poor guy. Who names their son Tracy in this day and age?"

"I guess there used to be a lot of guys named Tracy. Before it became a girl name. Seems like people are always giving their girls boy names, but then all of the guys with that name end up being judged as being feminine."

"Yes, it was used more a couple of generations ago. But now… I didn't think anyone would pick it for a boy name."

"Well…" Christina popped the end of a carrot in her mouth. "He's Chinese, actually, and his family adopted English names to make them fit in better. So they let the kids pick their own names. And he didn't know then that it was kind of a girly name now. He just picked it out of a book or off of a website of boy names."

"Well… it's nice he was allowed to pick his own name, but maybe they could let him pick a new one now. He doesn't have to make it his legal name if he doesn't want to, just something else for people to call him."

"I think he'll probably just go back to his Chinese name. Plenty of the Chinese kids around here go by their Chinese names and never adopted an English name."

Margie held her cutting board over the wok and slid the chopped vegetables into it. They immediately started to sizzle. "That's good. I don't think people should have to pick another name because they're from another culture. Canada isn't supposed to be a melting pot like the States. It's supposed to be a cultural mosaic. So why not keep your cultural name?"

Christina nodded her agreement. "Is that why you never changed Marguerite to Margaret?"

"It's a very common Métis name. It's not hard to remember or pronounce, so I don't see any reason to change it."

"Do people give you a lot of hassle about Patenaude?"

"I get a lot of 'Detective Pat.' It's easier for people, and I don't mind. They don't make fun of it." Margie stopped to read the instructions on the faux meat package that Christina had taken out of the fridge. "Do you get hassled for it at school?"

"No. People ask how to pronounce it or spell it, but a lot of the names are weirder than Patenaude. The Asian ones with too many consonants that we would put vowels between. It isn't like I have a name that's ten syllables long."

Margie was relieved that Christina wasn't being bullied over her name. She had been worried, going from Winnipeg to Calgary, with such different demographics, that their Métis culture would cause friction. And there would still be a few people who were jerks about it. That went without saying. But it wasn't like Christina was the only dark-skinned girl in a sea of white. The school was full of kids with all different shades of skin, from redheads with starkly white skin or freckles to ebony black with a blue sheen that she had rarely ever seen in Manitoba. Margie had been pleased with the diversity.

<h1 style="text-align:center">CHAPTER TWELVE</h1>

It was still light enough when they got to Moushoom's apartment to ask him if he wanted to go out for a walk with them. He loved to get out into the fresh air and nature whenever they could take him. The old Métis man always looked like a painting to Margie. He dressed in a mix of traditional clothes, including buckskins and a sash, and store-bought clothing like the long-sleeved boldly-colored dress shirts and dark sunglasses that he loved. Despite a long life full of tragedies and sorrow, his deep wrinkles seemed to always point up in a smile. She could have stared at him for hours and wished she had the skill to draw or paint him how he appeared to her.

"I want kisses from my two favorite girls," Moushoom declared, making them lean down to embrace him and kissing them on both cheeks, despite the pandemic. "I'm so glad that you came to live in Calgary."

"Me too," Margie told him. "It's wonderful to be so close to you."

"Do you want to go out?" Christina asked, looking through the clothes in Moushoom's closet. "You will need a jacket."

"Yes, let's go out," he agreed. He patted Margie's arm. "She is getting so big."

"Isn't she? I can't believe it sometimes. It seems like she was a little baby just yesterday."

"She is a woman now."

Christina found a jacket that she deemed suitable for their outing. It was blue with contrasting white stitching and beadwork. "This is beautiful." She helped Moushoom to get it on, then took charge of the wheelchair, releasing his brakes and pointing the chair toward the door. Moushoom folded his hands in his lap and smiled.

A few years ago, he would have insisted on getting around under his own power. He would have walked, no matter how much it cost him later. It gave Margie a little pang of pain to realize how he'd had to accept his physical limitations. He had been such a strong and active person for so many years. Now he was shrinking and becoming more dependent. That was the way of life, but she didn't like seeing him getting weaker.

She pasted a smile on her face and didn't show what she was thinking. There was nothing to be done about advancing age. All they could do was enjoy the time that they had together the best they could.

Moushoom took a deep breath when they got outside. "It was warm today," he observed. "You never know at this time of year whether it will be warm or cold."

"We had frost last week," Margie said. "And it was rainy and smoky the beginning of the week, but today was warm."

"And sometimes we have a foot of snow mid-September." Moushoom shrugged. "It has been nice so far this year."

"It has," Margie agreed.

"Where did you go this week?" Moushoom asked.

"Where did I go?" Margie wasn't sure what he meant. "Umm... I've just been here in Calgary. I went to work."

"No park this week? You were telling me all about that big park last time."

"Oh. No, I haven't been out to Glenbow Park again yet. I want to take you and Christina and Stella out there soon. When it's a nice day. We can take a tour. They have golf cart tours, so you don't have to walk and we don't have to push your wheelchair up the hill."

"I'm light."

"It's a big hill!"

"Who is Stella?" Moushoom studied her. "You only have one daughter."

"Stella is our dog."

"Oh, yes," Moushoom nodded and chuckled. "She is the dog. You didn't bring her?"

"Not today. I wasn't sure if we were allowed to bring her into the building or if you would want to go out today."

"You can bring her into the building. Some of the people there have dogs of their own."

"Great! We'll bring her next time, then."

They walked for a few minutes in silence.

"I did go to a different park this week," Margie offered. "Have you ever heard of Ralph Klein Park?"

He shook his head. "Another new one? I remember Ralph Klein. He's dead, isn't he?"

"Yes. That's probably why they named a park after him. They don't usually do it while the person is still alive."

"Is it a good park?"

"Umm... I didn't get to explore it much. It's not big, like Glenbow or Fish Creek."

"It has water," Christina offered. "Mom was saying that it is a wetlands park, so it has a bunch of ponds and streams."

"Wetlands are good," Moushoom said, licking his lips. "The white man destroyed too many of them. Why they think it's a good idea to wipe out the natural habitat and replace it with concrete, I'll never understand." He motioned to the development around them. In a minute, they would be onto the pathway beside the irrigation canal, and he would be much happier. Even though it was only a narrow strip of land, it was better than being surrounded by concrete and buildings. And on a good day, they could look out past the city to the mountains. There was too much smoke in the air for them to see anything today. But hopefully, it would dissipate in the next few days.

"One of the girls is afraid of water," Moushoom said. "Which girl is that?" He turned his head to look at Christina, pushing his chair. "Is it you?"

"No." Christina smiled at him. "It's Mom."

"You?" Moushoom looked at Margie. "Is it you? I couldn't remember."

"Yes," Margie admitted. Her face got warm, but between her complexion and the dimming light, she didn't think he would be able to tell she was embarrassed. "It's me. I know it's silly, but it's not by choice."

"We don't get to choose what we fear," Moushoom agreed. "We can choose how to behave in the face of our fears, but we do not get to pick our fears."

Margie nodded.

"You are not limited by your fears," Moushoom went on. "You live a full life."

Was it an observation or a command? Was he pleased that she didn't let her fear limit her, or was he telling her not to?

"I try to," she told him.

"Good." He reached out to pat her hand, then looked on ahead toward the green space, his expression softening, mouth going slightly slack. She didn't try to draw him into conversation, letting him think about whatever it was he was remembering or imagining.

CHAPTER THIRTEEN

Margie felt relaxed and clearheaded the next morning as she drove in to work. She was glad she had listened to Mac and put her work aside for the night. The time with Christina and Moushoom, and later on her own without any agenda, had helped. She had slept well and woke up feeling like a new person.

She listened to a classic rock station on the way downtown, enjoying the music and ignoring the DJs' chatter. Other days, when she was stressed, she couldn't stand to hear their drivel.

Margie was energized by her morning coffee and dove into her work, quickly reviewing her notes from the day before and any new information that had been uploaded into the workspace for the case. Not a lot had been done since the time she had left, which was probably good because overworking the lab or medical examiner's office was not a good idea either. Everybody deserved to get their rest.

Her eyes were on her computer screen and she didn't look to see who was calling before answering the ringing phone.

"Detective Patenaude."

"Detective! This is Carol Roscoe." Patty's mother's voice was high-pitched. She sounded panicked.

Margie winced. If Dr. Galt had issued his official identification of Patty Roscoe, as Margie assumed that he had, then she was going to have to inform Mr. and Mrs. Roscoe that their daughter was dead, as they had feared. Or maybe Mrs. Roscoe already knew. Had someone else informed her? Or had the news been leaked, and she had found out on social media or the morning news? She was definitely not in the same place emotionally as she had been the day before.

"Mrs. Roscoe. I'm glad you called," she said, in a voice intended to soothe Mrs. Roscoe. Half of the battle was making a caller feel heard. She would find out the reason Mrs. Roscoe had called and, hopefully, leave her in a better place than she had found her.

"I got an email," Mrs. Roscoe said, her voice wild, cracking up and down like an adolescent's. "An email from Patty!"

Margie blinked, staring at the screen in front of her and trying to figure out if she had heard correctly. "I'm sorry. You got an email about Patty?"

"No, from Patty. I got an email from Patty."

"I don't think that's possible, Mrs. Roscoe."

"I did!"

"What does it say?"

"There is a video recording attached. A video of Arabella."

Arabella. It took a couple of seconds for Margie to remember that was one of Patty's daughters. The older one, if she remembered correctly.

"So did this email come from Arabella?" Margie queried. "Have you ever gotten anything from the girls before?"

"You need to listen to it. Something has happened to Patty. Something… I knew that Scott was no good. I told you. I told Patty. She always said that I was wrong and he was perfectly good to her, but I knew she wasn't telling me the truth. He was mean and manipulative. He kept her from me."

Mrs. Roscoe seemed to be forgetting the fact that she was the one who had cut off communications from Patty.

"I would be happy to listen to it. Do you want to forward it to me? I'll give you my email address."

Mrs. Roscoe covered up the phone to talk to someone else, her voice going muffled. Margie could still just make her words out. "Do you know how to forward this?"

"What's the address?" Mr. Roscoe answered.

"She's going to give it to me."

The phone was taken from her. "Detective?" Mr. Roscoe asked.

"Yes, I'm here."

"What's your email address? Am I supposed to send this to you?"

"Yes, if you could." Margie gave him her email address as slowly and clearly as she could.

"Okay, I'm sending it to you now." There was a click, and Mr. Roscoe was gone.

Margie shook her head. She pressed the Send/Receive button on her email client and waited to see if it would appear. He might have taken her address down wrong. Or pushed the wrong button and it was still sitting in his drafts folder. Or it might just be taking time to process, if it had a video attached. As much as she expected email to be instantaneous, she knew that it still took time to get from one place to another.

She clicked Send/Receive again and waited.

The third time she refreshed, a bolded message appeared in her inbox. Margie double-clicked it, and then clicked on the video attachment.

The picture was fuzzy, the little girl too close to the device and not pointing it directly at herself. She was talking to herself in a whisper. Margie turned it up, plugged in earphones, and rewound to start it over again. She leaned toward the computer as if that might make the picture and words clearer.

"Mommy said do Gramma's picture," Arabella whispered. "The red button then the Gramma button. Send a message."

Margie blinked, watching it. Did Arabella have Patty's phone? An iPod of her own? A burner phone for emergency calls? Arabella was clearly talking herself through whatever instructions her mother had given her previously.

Arabella looked up, away from the phone, listening or watching something else. Her face came into focus for a few seconds. There were tears on her face. Red blotches. Her pudgy fist wiped away some of the tear tracks. Her nose blew a snot bubble. There was background noise. Margie turned the system volume up as far as it would go. She could hear voices in the background. Two voices, a man and a woman. The TV? Scott Warner and a visitor in another room? Margie tried to make out the words, but could only catch a phrase here and there. There was a crashing noise that drowned everything else out, screaming that made the hair on the back of Margie's neck stand on end, and Arabella's hands both flew up to her face, the camera getting buried in the blankets of her bed. There was a male voice shouting, Arabella crying softly to herself, and then the video ended.

Margie stared at the end frame in confusion.

"Detective Siever?" She called across the duty room to him. He looked up from his screen.

"Uh-huh?"

"I… I…" Margie stared at her screen, trying to form the question in her mind. She shook her head. "Can you help me with something?"

He got up from his desk, exhaling noisily. His chair creaked as he pushed himself to his feet. "Yeah? What is it?" he asked as he approached her desk.

"This video… it doesn't make any sense. Is it possible that… could that be Patty Roscoe in the background?"

"I thought the ME had a positive identification on her."

"Me too. That's why… I'm not sure I understand what's going on here."

He bent over and pressed play on the video. Margie switched it from her headphones to the external speaker. The bullpen quieted around them as everybody listened. Margie was even more sure the second time. It had to be Patty and her husband in the background. Arguing, and then… was it possible they had a recording of the murder?

"Where did this come from?" Siever asked.

"It came from Patty's mother. She said she got it in an email from Patty. The little girl recorded it."

"And then she didn't send it until today," Siever said. "Or else the device didn't have a connection until today, so it was sitting in the queue waiting."

"Is there any way to tell when the video was recorded?"

Using her mouse and leaning over Margie's shoulder, the other detective clicked around, examining the email and the attached file.

"I'm going to send it to forensics and get them to look at it," he said. "But it looks like it was recorded a few days ago."

"The day of the murder?"

His eyes went to the stand-up calendar on Margie's desk, counting through the days. He nodded. "Yes."

Margie swore under her breath. "That poor girl. No wonder Warner didn't want us talking to them. Did he know that Arabella overheard them?"

"Even if he didn't, they would have known their mother had been home the night before. That his story of her never coming home was a lie. Now, a few days later, he's covered. A little girl that young isn't going to be able to tell us which day she saw her mother last. And even if she could, he could just say she was confused."

"This is enough to arrest him. I'll let MacDonald know." She looked at her watch. "Warner will be at his workplace. That's good. We can arrest him while he is away from the girls, no chance of him taking them hostage."

"Have them picked up from the daycare."

"Yes," Margie agreed. "They can go to the grandparents, at least initially. Oh, I'd better call them back. Poor Mrs. Roscoe is in a state."

"I would be too," Jones contributed from where she was sitting at her desk.

"Yeah." Margie tried not to think about the sound of Patty's scream. The more she reviewed it, the stronger it would be in her memory. She needed to stay focused on her next actions rather than what she had heard and the emotional impact. Compartmentalize and not think about how this was going to affect the Roscoe family and the little girls. "Me too."

She got up and walked over to MacDonald's office in the corner. His door was closed, and she hadn't noticed whether he was in or not. She pulled out her phone and called Mrs. Roscoe back while she tried to peer through MacDonald's blinds to see whether he was in.

"Mrs. Roscoe?"

The woman cried on the other end, not managing to get out anything coherent.

"You don't have to talk right now," Margie told her. "I'm just letting you know that I got the email and have watched the video. We're going to take action on it right away. We'll arrest Scott Warner. We're going to pick the girls up from their daycare. Are you home, and are you prepared to take them for a few days?"

Mrs. Roscoe sobbed and managed a shaky "Yes."

"Okay. We'll talk later."

CHAPTER FOURTEEN

Margie hung up and slid the phone back into her pocket. She knocked on MacDonald's door, looking into the bullpen at the other detectives. "Is he in? I wasn't paying attention earlier."

She was answered by MacDonald's voice from within. "Come in."

Margie opened the door and stuck her head in. Mac was sitting at his desk, phone in hand, muffling the receiver against his shoulder.

"Detective Patenaude. A break in the case?"

"Yes. It was the husband. We have enough for an arrest."

His eyebrows went way up. "What did you find?" They certainly hadn't been expecting to come across any evidence that would be that decisive.

"One of the little girls recorded a video the night of the murder. You can hear the parents arguing in the background. Hear a physical altercation and Patty screaming."

"That doesn't necessarily establish murder. There might have been any number of fights."

"I think… when you hear the video, you will agree. Detective Siever is forwarding it to forensics, and they'll verify the data on when it was recorded to make sure it lines up with the time of death. But even before they do that, we have enough to bring him in. It proves that, at the very least, he was physically abusive."

"If you can establish that it's him on the video. Does his face appear?"

"No. But you can hear them in the background. I recognize his voice."

MacDonald nodded. "Okay. Bring him in for questioning. We'll get the details on the video verified as soon as possible."

"Great. Will do. And we're going to have the girls picked up from the daycare; they can stay with their grandma for the time being."

But when she returned to the duty room, Jones shook her head grimly.

"They're not at the daycare. Warner didn't bring them in today."

Margie looked at her phone to verify that it wasn't the weekend. "Why didn't he take them to daycare today? That means... they're with him. He must not have work today."

The other detectives on the team gathered closer to work it through.

"He's not making funeral arrangements," Margie said, thinking aloud, "because we haven't informed him that we have an ID yet. He has to pretend he doesn't know she's dead."

"So he's taking a personal day," Cruz said. "What husband wouldn't take a day or two off when his wife goes missing? It would look suspicious if he didn't."

Margie nodded. "Then he's at home. Do you think?" She was worried about the video. What if he found out about it from Arabella? What if Mr. Roscoe decided to go over there to confront him? Now that they knew without a doubt that Warner was the killer, Margie was afraid something was going to go wrong before they could take him into custody. "Do you think he's just at home? Having a lazy day with the kids?"

The detectives looked at each other. Margie was sure they were going through scenarios in their heads, just as she was.

"Cleaning up, maybe," Siever suggested. "Going over the floor with bleach another time. Making sure that anything that got broken during the fight has been disposed of. And whatever he used as a bludgeon. He's got to know that we'll want to search the house once we have identified her."

"I'll call him," Margie decided. "I'll let him know that we've identified the body of his wife. We should be able to tell by the background noise whether he's at home or somewhere else."

No one disagreed with her suggestion. He had to be notified anyway. It wasn't going to come as a surprise, though they'd see how good an actor he was when he heard about it and faked a breakdown.

Margie sat back down at her desk and picked up her phone. She breathed a few times, slowing her respiration and distancing herself from the situation. It was just a notification. She'd done dozens of them before. She was able to separate herself from it emotionally. It was her job to figure out where he was. She needed to be able to make a snap judgment.

She hit the speakerphone button before placing the call so that the others would be able to hear too. More ears were better. Warner might be able to tell that she had him on speaker, but he was going to have to deal with that. She tapped in his number and waited for him to pick up.

All she got was a long period of ringing, followed by his voicemail.

"We'd better get over there," Margie said, hanging up. She didn't want to rush into anything, but the thought of the murderer with two young children in the house set her heart thumping at a much faster speed than usual. "Maybe he's just ignoring my call, or washing the floor like Siever says, but those children are defenseless. I have to make sure they're okay."

"You want me to go with you?" Jones offered.

"Uh, yes. But separate vehicles. If he bolts, I want to be able to stay on him. One of us."

Jones nodded. They both removed their sidearms from their lockboxes without comment and vested up. Who knew if he had an illegal weapon and would decide to do something stupid like holing up in his house and trying to shoot anyone who got too close?

"You two be careful," Cruz advised, even though it was obvious that they were taking the proper precautions.

"We will," Margie confirmed.

"At the first sign of trouble, you call for help and fall back. Don't push a confrontation."

She and Jones both nodded. Margie expected him to try to trade places with Jones to go along, but he didn't.

"Cover all exits. If it is an apartment building, call for backup."

"Yes."

Margie finished getting ready. She looked at him for any further advice. He just nodded. "Okay. You got this."

CHAPTER FIFTEEN

Margie's heart was beating so fast as she drove to Warner's address that it felt like it would burst right out of her chest. She didn't feel like she had it covered by any stretch of the imagination. So many things could go wrong.

But it could all go fine too. She might just be overreacting. Warner hadn't uttered any threats when she had interviewed him previously. He hadn't said or done anything that showed a propensity for violence. He hadn't argued, called her names, insisted that they needed to drop everything else and get on top of his wife's case. While there was an estrangement from Patty's parents that he acknowledged was due to their not liking him, Mr. and Mrs. Roscoe had not suggested that they thought him capable of violence toward her or the children. She'd left the conversation wide open for them to make whatever claims they chose to. Warner had no domestic violence charges, no previous calls to the house over noise complaints or neighbor concerns. She hadn't checked Children's Services reports.

They didn't race to his house, but drove within the speed limits and didn't use any lights or siren. No need to get him or anyone else wound up. When Margie pulled to the curb near the house, Jones pulled up beside her.

"I'll go around back. Just in case. Don't stand in front of the door when you ring the bell."

Margie nodded. "Okay. Thanks. I'll give you a couple of minutes to get situated."

She watched Jones drive around the block, and used the interim to scope out the street. There was no car in front of Warner's house, and she couldn't see a garage in the back. But there might have been a gravel pad for parking; she couldn't be sure. Or the family might not even have two cars. Patty had to drive out to the park, and if Warner worked within the city or remotely, then he could bike or take the transit to work.

She didn't see anyone cross in front of the living room window while she was sitting there, but that didn't mean anything. They could all be in different parts of the house, Warner working on something for his job, washing the floor, or making other plans. He might have additional evidence to get rid of or a girlfriend that Patty hadn't known about.

Margie startled when her phone buzzed. She took a quick glance at it. Jones was ready in the back. She closed her eyes briefly to center herself, then got out of the car and walked up to the house. Standing to the side of the door, she rang and then pounded on the door with her fist loudly enough that anyone in the house would be able to hear. She didn't shout 'police.' That was mostly for cops on TV. She waited, listening for any sound from within or any movement in the window. Jones waited in back, quiet. No one trying to escape that way.

Everything was quiet. No sound of breaking glass. No footsteps within. Margie allowed herself a glance toward the street where she had expected a car to be parked. Where was he? Where would he go with the two little girls? It wasn't like he was taking them to the grandparents. He wouldn't want them anywhere near the Roscoes. She didn't know where his family was; he'd made no mention of them during their interview.

She rang and knocked a couple more times. Sometimes, residents were in the basement or the shower, somewhere they couldn't hear very well. Warner might have earphones on, listening to music as he cleaned. He could be gaming on his computer.

Eventually, Margie walked around back to where Jones was waiting. "Looks like he's out."

"Where do you think he is? Went out to get ice cream with the kids? Visiting family? Funeral home?"

Any of those were possibilities, but none of them rang true. Margie shook her head. She looked around the back yard. There was a gravel pad for parking, but no car. So, if they had two vehicles, Warner had taken the second out.

"We'll need a motor vehicles search to find out what he's driving."

Jones nodded. "Yeah. You going to put out an APB?"

"Yes… but I'd like to figure out where he's gone first. We should be able to figure this out."

"You don't think that he'd put the kids in danger, do you?"

"No. He doesn't have any reason to harm them."

Or did he? What if he did have another girlfriend and she didn't want kids? What if he'd never bonded with them in the first place and preferred to be on his own? What if the children were afraid of him and made him feel guilty whenever he looked at them?

There were plenty of reasons that he might want them out of the way. He might want a fresh start.

"I don't think so," she amended. "Warner didn't say anything that made me think he might…"

But the words sounded hollow in her own ears.

Where would he go?

If he didn't like the Roscoes, and of course he didn't, then he wouldn't take the children to them. And he hadn't taken them to the daycare.

He was not used to being home alone with them for more than an hour or two while he waited for Patty to get home from her job each day. He would quickly find out that single fatherhood was no walk in the park.

Margie's brain caught on the phrase. *No walk in the park.*

She didn't think that he had taken them out for ice cream, but what about a walk in the park?

She walked back around the front of the house, Jones trailing her and asking something Margie didn't hear. She looked up and down the street. A neighborhood playground? No. He wouldn't need the car then. Somewhere farther away. In her memory, she saw Patty Roscoe's body in the water. She flashed on the children dipping minnows from the water from the little floating dock, their father standing back, watching them with unconcern.

They could fall into the water. Even though it wasn't deep and there was a lifesaver float right on the dock to be used if someone went into the water, something could still happen to them there.

And if a father's intentions were violent rather than just unconcerned that anything could happen to them…

There was a certain symmetry in the children drowning where their mother's body had been dumped—a way of giving them back to her.

"They've gone to the park," Margie told Jones. She was sure of it. She could feel it in her bones. "I'm going to head over there. We'll need a warrant for the house in case I'm wrong. Can you get that moving?"

"Yes, but I'm coming with you. You're not going on your own."

Margie nodded. "Yeah. Okay." She was probably right. That was just the kind of thing that a TV heroine would do—racing toward disaster, all by herself. No one to back her up.

"Do you know where it is? Have you been there before?" she asked Jones.

"Never been there before. But I studied the maps and the layout as part of the investigation. I can get out there."

"Okay. Just in case we get separated in traffic."

With a nod, the two of them separated to go back to their cars. Margie took one more look at the house for any sign that there was someone home, watching them through a window. But she didn't see any sign of life.

She checked through her GPS destinations and brought up the one for the park again. She knew where it was, but she didn't want to get it wrong. No wrong turns today.

CHAPTER SIXTEEN

Margie was impatient with the traffic lights on the way to the park, but she didn't want to use her lights and siren. They didn't know for sure that anyone's life was in danger. It was only a gut feeling that Warner was taking the children to the park. Even if they found him there, they couldn't assume that he had any intention to harm the children unless he took some action to indicate that he did. They would arrest him for his wife's murder, but that was all they could do to start with. MacDonald had said to bring him in for questioning. Hopefully, before they got very far, they would have confirmation that it was his voice on the recording and that the time record on the video put it in the window of time of Patty's death.

As she got out to the highway, she could see Jones's vehicle behind her. They were going to get there. They were going to arrest Scott Warner. They were going to take the children to their grandparents.

It would be a happy ending.

Not for Patty, but for everyone else. Her killer would be brought to justice. Her family would be reunited. They would be safe.

Margie couldn't see Warner at the creek where Patty's body had been dumped. She continued to drive around to the public parking lot but, rather than stopping, drove up over the sidewalk as close as she could to the education center, looking for Scott Warner's figure with the two little girls. She only had a vague picture of the little girls in mind, built from the blurry video of Arabella. Warner hadn't brought them with him the day he was interviewed. He hadn't shown her any family pictures. He hadn't wanted the police to have the opportunity to talk to the girls about what had happened to their mother.

Maybe he knew that Arabella knew something. Maybe he knew only that the girls knew their mother had come home, that they hadn't gone to bed waiting for her to return home.

She got out of her car, looking around. People were walking around, enjoying the mild weather—many of them stopping to look at the two vehicles driving up on the sidewalk. The cars were not marked squad cars, so people were probably pretty confused as to why the two women would drive their cars right up to the education center. Until they saw the women's vests and gun holsters. Then they'd have a pretty good idea.

Margie led the way around the education center, ignoring the queasiness and the pain in her chest as she climbed onto the walkways to go around the building. She could have told Jones to go around that side and gone around the other side of the education center on solid ground herself. But she hadn't been able to see Warner or the children in the playground on the other side of the education center. She had the little floating dock in her mind. That was where the children would be. That was what Scott Warner had in his mind. He would take them out there, show them how to dip their little nets into the water, and dump the contents into a bucket.

He would wait until they were happy and distracted. And then he would strike.

She could hardly breathe as she rushed along the walkway, up the stairs to the next level, and then out to the little bridge and pathway that would take them around the hill with the art installation and to the dock. Jones hurried behind her, asking questions that Margie couldn't hear or answer. It took everything she could to get over the grille on the bridge to where she felt safe.

CHAPTER SEVENTEEN

arner was right where Margie had expected him to be. Standing on the floating dock with the two children kneeling in front of him, just like she had pictured. She had to blink her eyes a couple of times to clear them and make sure she wasn't really seeing the homeschooler dad or another small family group. Was she only seeing what she had thought she would see?

But Jones was swearing under her breath, hurrying along behind Margie.

"I'll fall back and flank him," Jones suggested. "You engage with him, talk to him, get him distracted. Keep him looking in your direction as much as possible. I'll get in behind him, closer to the children. We'll try to cut him off from them."

Margie nodded. Her brain objected that it wouldn't work, but she had to do what she could. Without a good plan of her own, she fell back on Detective Jones's.

"Mr. Warner," she called out, projecting her voice. She had a tough, no-nonsense, don't-mess-with-me cop voice. That, combined with a glare she had perfected as the mother of a teenager, was usually enough to get a suspect's attention and make him think twice about what he was doing.

He turned toward her, away from the two blond little girls with pails. Margie kept moving, walking on the path going past the dock, making him turn his body to keep facing her. His expression was one of shock. Eyes wide, skin pale, his mouth a slash of color that stood out in stark contrast to his skin.

"What are you doing here?" he demanded in an, aggrieved tone.

"We were looking for you. You weren't at your house, so I thought maybe you were here."

"What made you think I would be here?"

She didn't point out that since that was where his wife's body had been dumped, it seemed a logical choice. She didn't want to wind him up more, escalating the fear and anger he was already feeling. He felt vulnerable. He hadn't expected them to know that he was there. He had thought he would be safe and anonymous. He could bide his time until just the right moment, when no one would see or understand what he was doing. He had counted on being unknown and able to choose his timing.

"I'm glad we found you, Scott." She used a warm tone and his name. Make him feel seen. Make him feel validated. Important. "This has been a tough week on you."

"You're not kidding!" he agreed with a bark of laughter that was anything but amused.

"How are you feeling? Is there anything we can do for you?"

"*Why* are you here?" he asked again, shaking his head slightly.

"We just want to make sure that everyone is taken care of." She had planned to mention the girls, to ask him how they were doing, but she didn't want him to focus on the girls again. She wanted him to stay looking at her, talking to her, while Jones slipped between him and the children.

"You *know*." His tone was flat. Certain.

"What do we know?" Margie cocked her head as if she were curious. As if she didn't know what he was talking about.

"I had no idea. No way of knowing that she had given Arabella a phone." He shook his head in irritation, but did not turn to look back at his daughters. "I knew she was playing with one, but I thought it was Patty's old phone that didn't work anymore."

"What did she do with the phone?"

"Don't mess with me! I know that you know. The minute I saw that email go out to Patty's mother, I knew I was sunk."

Margie took a step closer to Warner, to keep his attention as much as to get close enough to do anything. Jones was staying quiet, trying to remain invisible and not to attract Warner's attention with her movements.

"How did you know about the email?" she asked Warner.

"I monitored Patty's email so that I would know if she was contacting her mother. Her friends. Trying to keep secrets from me. I would know if she was seeing someone behind my back."

Margie nodded slowly. "So you set something up so that you would be notified or copied any time she sent out an email."

"Of course I did. Anyone in my position would have done the same. I was protecting her. Protecting my family."

"Protecting them from what?"

"That mother of hers hated me. Right from the start, for no reason at all. How is that fair? How do you start off hating the person your daughter is dating without even knowing anything about them? Nothing at all!"

"That must have been hard for you."

"I was doing everything I could to keep us together. You don't know what it was like. How exhausting it was to keep on top of everything she was doing, to make sure that she was safe. That our family was safe from any outside forces. You have no idea how hard that is."

"No." Margie took another step toward him. They were almost close enough for her to grab him now. Just a few more steps, reaching out quickly, and she would have him. She didn't see a weapon, but that didn't mean he didn't have one. If he were doing everything he could to protect his family, then she wouldn't be at all surprised if he were carrying a knife or a gun. Or both. Gun violence was less common in Canada than it was in the States, but it wasn't nonexistent. People still shot each other. With registered or unregistered weapons. Warner didn't have a firearms license, but that didn't mean he hadn't acquired a gun somewhere.

"What happened? What was it that drove a wedge between the

two of you?" she asked with as much compassion as she could muster. "Was it just her mother? Or were there other things? Money? Other pressures?"

"Her mother was a thorn in my side. She said that she wouldn't have anything to do with Patty while the two of us were together, and it was tearing Patty up. I thought that as the girls got older, it wouldn't be as much of an issue. She would establish a mother-daughter relationship with them, and her connection to her mother wouldn't matter so much. But I think the opposite was true. The older the girls got, the more she wanted to make up with her mother. I told her she couldn't. She couldn't be the one to give in first. And the only thing her mother would be happy with was the two of us getting divorced." He gave Margie a fierce look. "And we weren't getting a divorce."

Not for anything. He would kill her first.

Margie cast around for something else to ask him. But at that moment, he realized that Jones was there, working her way between them, cutting the children off from Warner.

Making a noise like an enraged bull, he threw himself at Jones. She wasn't expecting it, but she was well-trained and solidly built, and she absorbed the initial impact.

"Mr. Warner, you are under arrest for assaulting an officer of the law," she told him in a calm, clear voice, grasping his arm.

But somehow, he slipped out of her grasp. Having failed in pushing her farther away from his family, he tried the reverse. Before Margie could take one step forward to stop him, he had rushed at the girls, sweeping them out into the water. There were a couple of strangled screams of surprise and fear before they went under the surface of the dark water. Margie ran toward them, her mind a horrified blank, unable to process what had happened or what she should do about it. Warner charged her, bowling her over. The collision knocked the wind out of her, and she was left on the ground, her head spinning. She stared up at one of the towering monoliths, then forced herself to move. Roll over. Regain her feet and her balance, look around for Warner. But the babies were behind her, and what was she going to do about them?

"Go!" Jones shouted at her. "I've got the kids. Go after him!"

Margie's movements were slow, like swimming through concrete. She saw Jones pick up the lifesaver and toss it into the water. As she turned away to look for Warner, she heard a splash and knew that Jones had jumped in.

CHAPTER EIGHTEEN

arner was on the run. Margie shut everything else out and focused on gaining on him. He couldn't be allowed to get back to his car and make an escape. He had killed his wife, had intended to kill his children, and she was not going to let him get away. She didn't know if he had planned to kill himself too, but running suggested to her that his instinct to preserve his own life and liberty was still strong.

Her feet crunched through the gravel of the pathway. Warner was headed for the education center, toward the big pool and the walkways elevated over the water. Margie's mind rebelled against the idea of running toward them. The last thing she wanted was to end up plummeting into the water. But she had a job to do. She was a cop and she couldn't let her phobia control her decisions. She had been told more than once that the only way to overcome her fear was by exposing herself to it. So in reality, running toward the water at a breakneck pace was good for her.

She had a stitch in her side. She had let her running habit fall by the wayside when she had moved to Calgary. If she wanted to stay in shape, she would have to get up earlier in the morning to run, and morning was not her best time. But she was getting out of shape, and should at least consider it.

Warner entered the walkways. He slowed down, but was still moving at a pretty quick clip. Margie put on a burst of speed to catch up with him and stepped onto the walkway herself. Her heart was in her throat. She could barely breathe. Her vision was narrow so that she could only see what was in front of her. She knew the way out. She needed to keep pushing forward, and then she would, in a couple of minutes, be on solid ground again. She could tackle Warner in the parking lot. Cuff him and take him into custody. It would all work out just fine.

She was no longer running, but was pushing herself to move as quickly as she could. The walkway felt narrow and unsteady. She knew she was suspended above the water, and her brain was telling her that at any minute, she could die. She went up the stairs to the second. She listened, but could no longer hear Warner's footsteps clanging ahead of her. He must already be off of the walkways and into the parking lot. That meant that she didn't have much farther to go.

A blow hit her from the side as she turned a corner. She was stunned and thrown off balance. Where had it come from? She grabbed onto the rail to steady herself and to try to reorient herself. She could see the water below her. Just her and a thin grille topped with a railing to keep her separated from it. Whose idea had it been to put young children and the frail and infirm so close to danger? Why had they thought it such a good idea to build out on the water instead of on solid, safe land?

She caught a flash of his face in front of her—an angry, maniacal grimace. "Leave me alone! You think a woman is going to get the better of me? Never!"

Before she had a chance to anticipate what he was going to do, he slammed into her again, the weight of his body throwing her against the low barrier. His hands grasped her elbow and knee, and he lifted her off of the ground. Using their momentum, he had her up and over the railing before she could catch hold of anything.

She was airborne, arms and legs flailing frantically for something to stop her fall. Then she was in the water. It drove all of the air out of her lungs when she hit the surface and then sank beneath it. Shockingly cold. The water enveloped her. She couldn't see. She held her breath and flailed and hit bottom. She was disoriented, feeling the mucky, slimy floor of the pond bottom beneath her. Had her brain blocked out the sensation of falling through the water? It seemed as if the journey to the bottom of the pond had taken only an instant.

She tried to push herself up, her hands sinking into the mud and not propelling her toward the surface. She tried to swim up toward the surface, and her hands broke out of the water.

Margie repositioned herself feet downward, and tried to stand. The muck prevented her from doing it very gracefully, sucking her feet and ankles down, but the water was not even to her waist. Margie took in gasps of air and tried to settle her panicked body and brain. She could breathe. She wasn't drowning. But she was in the middle of the pond, sinking almost to her knees in muck.

She looked around, trying to figure out the best way to get out. The education center towered above her, and the walls were sheer rock, too steep to climb.

Someone was yelling at her. Margie blinked foul water from her eyes and tried to focus on the voice.

"...okay?" she heard from somewhere up above her. Margie tipped back her head to look at the figure standing on the edge. Finkle, his hands making anxious movements.

"I'm okay," she confirmed, still gasping.

"Can you turn around? Or are you stuck?"

Margie lifted her feet one at a time, pulling them out of the sucking mud and looking for somewhere more solid to put them down. The water was frigid. She was already shivering.

"Over to your left, you see the rock steps going down into the water?"

Margie saw a stonework of long, shallow steps. A couple of other workers stood there gaping at her.

"Just make your way over there," Finkle told her in a calm, even voice.

Margie waded through the mud, one painstaking step at a time. It would undoubtedly be faster to lie down on the surface of the water and swim across, unimpeded by the mud, except that she had never learned to swim. Even floating was an issue for Margie, especially with her face in or close to the surface of the water. When she finally got close enough to the steps, Finkle was waiting there, still encouraging her in a measured, reassuring voice. Finkle reached out a hand for her. His grip was strong. With his help, she was able to drag her feet one last time out of the mud and crawl back onto solid ground. It was an effort to break the surface tension. And then she was above the water.

Finkle patted her on the shoulder. "You're good. Keep going."

At the top, back on firm ground, someone wrapped a blanket around her.

"Ambulance is on the way. Just sit down here and stay warm."

Margie shook her head. She felt better standing. Like she was a grown-up, not a little kid. She wiped foul pond water from her face, looking around. Jones was a short distance away, mothering the two children, all three of them soaked. But they seemed to be in better shape than Margie, who was shaking like a leaf and having problems catching her breath.

"Are you okay?" Jones asked, looking over at her.

Margie cleared her throat. "I wasn't planning on going into the water."

"No," Jones gave a little laugh. "None of that was planned."

"Where did he go?" Margie looked at Finkle. "Did you see where Warner went? What direction…?"

"Back into the city. Headed north. Couldn't tell you more than that."

"They've got hawks out," Jones said.

Margie didn't understand at first. Jones pointed to a black helicopter in the sky some distance away. Helicopter Air Watch for Community Safety—HAWCS. The police services helicopter.

"Does that mean they know where he is?"

"I don't know. Need to get back to the radio in my car to touch base. I don't think either of our phones are going to work. They called 9-1-1," Jones motioned to the various education center workers who were standing around, some helping and some just watching. "And the chopper was scrambled pretty quickly. I called in the APB on

Warner's vehicles as we were driving over, so they knew what he was driving. But they'll be waiting for an update from us."

"We'd better do that, then." Margie attempted to squeeze some of the water out of her clothes and headed to the cars. At least they weren't very far away. Jones left the children under the supervision of one of the teachers and followed.

They stood outside of the vehicles, dripping everywhere, while Jones called on her radio, asking to be put in contact with the homicide department and with the HAWCS and other police on the ground. In a few minutes, they were all on the same channel, exchanging what information they could.

Margie bent her head close to listen. "He's in Erin Woods? I know where that is. That's not far from my place."

"You want to go over?" Jones asked. "I'm not sure how close we'll be able to get to the action, but you're going to have to go home to get changed anyway."

Margie nodded. "Yeah. Let's do it."

"More than likely, they'll just tell us to stay out of the way. But you can at least see HAWCS up close."

"Yes."

"You know your way around there? How to get there? Do you want to meet up in a particular place if we get separated?"

"I don't know my way at all." Margie reached into her car to grab her GPS. She tapped in Erin Woods and waited for something to come up on the screen. "Uh… the Community Center. How about that? We'll meet there, or get as close to it as we can."

CHAPTER NINETEEN

here were squad cars everywhere. The big armored rescue vehicle used by the CPS Tactical Unit was stopped in the middle of the Community Center parking lot. Both still dripping, Jones and Margie were directed to the tactical unit leader who got what details he could from them as to what had happened at Ralph Klein Park.

"So, what is your evaluation of his state of mind?" Sergeant Burns queried. "He's on the run, so you would think he was concerned with self-preservation, but if we've got a man who might be armed and who really doesn't have any reason to live, we need to know that before going in."

"Do you know where he is?" Margie asked, trying to discern from the activity around her just what the status of the pursuit was.

"He ditched his vehicle and took off on foot, so he can't have gotten far." HAWCS continued to buzz around overhead, looking for him. "We'll have scent dogs in a few minutes and they'll find him. But how he's going to behave once he's cornered, that's always a concern."

"He killed his wife. We have the proof and he knows it. He knows he's going down for it. He's looking at years of incarceration. He went to the park to drown his children. What I don't know is whether he planned to kill himself, or to disappear and start a new life somewhere else."

"So he doesn't have anything to lose when we catch up to him. Death or prison. Those are his only options."

Margie nodded. She looked at the armored Tactical Unit members. "Be careful. I don't think he's armed, but there's no way to know for sure. I don't think he's going to come easy."

Sergeant Burns nodded briefly. He'd probably already guessed that, but it was vital for him to have as much information as he could get.

"Is there any way we can help?" Margie asked.

"You don't have a relationship with this guy?"

"I've interviewed him before. He wasn't antagonistic then. But today…" She looked down at her dripping uniform. "I don't know whether he intended for me to drown, but he did throw me over a railing into the water."

"So, no," Burns said dryly. He looked at Detective Jones. "And you?" He observed her soaked uniform as well.

"No. Although I can tell him that his kids are okay. If he thinks he succeeded in drowning them, he might be more desperate. If he knows they're okay…"

Burns scribbled notes into a notepad. "Whoever tracks him down can pass that along. You're right; it might be just enough to make the difference between him being taken into custody quietly and suicide by cop."

He didn't tell them anything else they could do, so Jones and Margie stood around awkwardly, watching the rest of the officers who were involved moving from one position to another and reporting to Burns. The dog handler arrived with a German shepherd at his side and, after a few minutes, the dog was put onto the scent he was to track. Margie watched him put nose to ground and cast around. She imagined Stella trying to do the same thing. Stella sometimes thought she was a hunting dog, but she wasn't very good at it. She could track a quarry a few feet, but then she lost the scent. The shepherd with the dog handler seemed to be up to the job. In a couple of minutes, he was pulling hard on the harness, following Warner's trail from the car he had ditched. He led his handler to the far corner of the school field, which then joined with a pathway, out of their sight. Margie looked at Jones, then around at the houses close to the Community Center. There were a lot of residents looking out their windows or doors or hanging around the sidewalk. They looked up at HAWCS and took pictures of the tactical vehicle with their phones.

"The Twitterverse is buzzing," Jones observed. "Let's just hope that Warner isn't following it."

Wherever Warner was, crouched between houses or hiding under someone's car, Margie didn't imagine he was tapping on his phone, checking out all of the social media.

Would he hide? Would he try to walk out of the area? Get on a bus and escape the police net? She really wanted this guy. She wanted to make sure he was put behind bars for as long as possible.

She tried to squeeze more water out of her chilly, chafing clothes.

"You should go home and change," Jones suggested.

"I know. But I want to see how this all ends up. It won't take long, right? Just a few minutes?"

"You never know. Sometimes a standoff can go on for hours before the person finally gives up to the police."

"I'm going to stay for a while, at least. I really want to see them catch this guy."

CHAPTER TWENTY

hey heard the dog barking in the distance. They all stood as
still as statues, waiting for gunshots and explosions. Margie
could hear Sergeant Burns's radio crackling, the reports coming in
one on top of the other. He had been spotted entering the back yard
of a house across from Erin Woods Park. The Tactical Unit worked to
surround and contain him. Still no shots fired. Margie breathed shallowly, not wanting to miss anything. Over the radio, she heard the
shouted command for him to come out with his hands up. Warner
yelled back, wanting to know the status of his children and of the
police women at the park.

Margie and Jones listened to the information being relayed back
to him. Would their reassurances be enough to deescalate him? Was
he past that, too desperate to be calmed down?

No shots.

He exchanged words with them another time. And another.
Margie started to breathe normally again. He was having a conversation. He had not attacked or made threats. He hadn't said he had a
weapon and charged one of the team.

It was working. They could all breathe again. Margie would be
filling in paperwork for days, but they would have him. The children

were safe. The other people in Warner's life that might have crossed him one too many times were safe.

Eventually, a voice came over Burns's radio.

"We're clear. Suspect in custody."

❦

MARGIE FOUND she didn't care about the paperwork. She was happy to go home to change and then drive back downtown with towels on her car seat and report back to the office to be debriefed and get started on the pile of reports that would need to be filed.

"The Roscoes have the children," Cruz told Margie. "They were taken straight there. Children's Services will follow up to evaluate the home and finalize the placement, but they will be safe with family tonight, not in foster care."

"But they don't know the Roscoes. So it's still going to feel strange and foreign to them."

"Better to be with family, though. They can start settling in and getting healed, instead of being disrupted with a series of placements and maybe getting separated. And I suspect they know Grandma and Grandpa better than we think."

Margie raised her brows. "Oh? I didn't think Mrs. Roscoe was lying when she said she hadn't had any contact with them."

Cruz pointed to Margie's computer screen, where the video Mrs. Roscoe had received from her daughter's email account was still frozen in a small square in the corner of the desktop. Margie pressed the 'play' triangle, and it started from the beginning, Arabella talking herself through the instructions that her mother had given her. Tapping on the picture of Grandma.

Cruz nodded. "She knows who Grandma is. Her mother showed her pictures and talked to her at least enough to recognize the picture and know who it was. Maybe they didn't have any direct contact, but the little girl had been told who she was, and that was who she was supposed to send the recording too. She knew that Grandma would do something to help them when she received the video."

CHAPTER TWENTY-ONE

In a few days, Margie was with her own grandparent, secure in the knowledge that Warner was behind bars awaiting trial and Patty's daughters were safe. Moushoom had been quick to agree to go with them to Glenbow Ranch Provincial Park for a golf cart tour, and after that, to MacKay's for ice cream.

"You are in for a treat," he told them, eyes shining. "MacKay's is a tradition."

And traditions were important in Margie's family and community.

"I didn't think you'd know about them," she told him, glancing at him in surprise as she navigated the highway between the Park and Cochrane. Ice cream was just two kilometers away.

"I took your mother there when she was a little girl," Moushoom said. "We were just visiting then, I hadn't moved to Calgary yet, but MacKay's was there back then, and it was one of our favorite outings."

Margie's mother had always loved ice cream. Margie looked at Christina and grinned. It was a family trait.

Jones had told Margie that MacKay's had dozens of flavors, but she had still not expected the densely-written chalkboard she saw when she got there. She and Christina stared at it with their mouths open, marveling at all of the options.

"Bubblegum," Christina pointed out almost immediately.

Margie remembered blue stains on many of Christina's collars when she was a little girl, when blue bubble-gum ice cream had been her favorite treat. So sticky and messy. At least now, as a teenager, Margie wouldn't have to worry about Christina staining all of her clothes.

"What is 'barn door'?" Margie asked no one in particular.

A helpful patron described the ice cream concoction that included marshmallows, chocolate chips, chocolate chunks, Reese's peanut butter cups, fudge brownie bits, cookie dough, nuts, Oreo cookie crumbs, and coconut.

"Oh, my."

It wasn't going to be an easy choice. They had the cherry custard and cotton candy, two flavors she had enjoyed as a child when camping by the lake.

"Maple bacon," Christina murmured reverently.

"I thought you were vegetarian now."

Christina opened her mouth, considering. "I don't think maple bacon ice cream counts," she said finally, without bothering to give an argument as to why that was.

"I know what I am having," Moushoom announced.

Margie looked at him. She was expecting to have to read the board to him. But either his eyes or his memory was better than she had expected.

"What are you having, Moushoom?"

"Nanaimo bar."

"Oh…" That was tempting. But if Moushoom was getting it, then she was sure he would allow her to taste a bit of his custard and chocolate concoction. Sharing ice cream during a pandemic might not be such a good idea. She'd get a spoon and have a taste before he started it. That way, neither was contaminating the other.

They were getting to the front of the line, and Margie still hadn't made up her mind. She skimmed over the board once more.

"What is 'shark attack'?"

"Blue raspberry ice cream with red raspberry jam ripples," the young woman at the counter advised. She didn't have to check. She probably told ten people an hour all day long. Behind her face shield, forehead and temples glistened with sweat despite working with frozen desserts all day.

Margie's mind went back to Warner attacking her at the park and throwing her into the water, thinking she wouldn't make it out alive.

No, it wouldn't be shark attack. Not this time.

RALPH KLEIN PARK

The Ralph Klein Park is much smaller than the previous two parks in the series, but this little place packs a punch with manmade wetland features, public art installations, a community orchard of apple and pear trees, a unique playground with a zip line, and an education center.

Ralph Klein Park is on the east side of Calgary, and like Glenbow Ranch Provincial Park, opened in 2011.

It is named after former Calgary mayor and Alberta premier Ralph Klein, who lived to witness its opening and passed away in 2013.

IMMERSED IN THE VIEW

A PARKS PAT MYSTERY #4

To the survivors

CHAPTER ONE

Margie was puffing by the time she got to the park. She was getting into better shape. She could go farther than she had been able to when she started, but she was still in pretty sad shape compared to what she had been as a beat cop, getting plenty of exercise walking the streets. Sitting at a desk was not good for her, and she had not been getting as much exercise as she had thought she would once she arrived in Calgary.

She still hadn't started cycling in to work, using the new pathway over Deerfoot and under Blackfoot, then through Pearce Estate Park and continuing downtown. She had followed it a couple of times on Google Maps to make sure she knew the way, but hadn't yet tried it in real life. She was working her way up to it and wanted to make sure she knew the route really well before she tried it, not wanting to get turned around and lost.

She had promised herself that once she reached Valleyview Park, she would give herself a break. Walk around the pond, have a drink of water, take a few pictures, and get her breath back before returning home. The whole route was only about three kilometers and, once she was comfortable with that, she intended to increase the distance by adding a loop through the pathways by the Max Bell Arena. Calgary had a lot of green space and pathways; she might as well make use of them.

Margie slowed to a walk. It was a clear morning, the sun shining brightly and the greens of the trees and blue of the pond looked like a painted picture. Despite the early hour, it was already 18 degrees Celsius. Actually, it hadn't gotten below 18 the night before. The last few days had had 36-38 degree highs, almost unheard of in Calgary. Most homes—the ones in Margie's neighborhood, anyway—did not have central air conditioning. She had been lucky enough to find a window AC unit a month before when the first heat wave had hit at the beginning of June. It was *never* 30 above the first week in June, she was told. There had been a few flakes of snow on Victoria Day, just a week before that. Calgary didn't normally hit 30 until August.

With the AC unit in Margie's bedroom, they could at least sleep. Christina had said at first that she would be fine in her own room, she didn't need to come sleep with Margie like a little kid who'd had a bad dream. But that didn't even last a full night. With the house heating up and holding on to the heat, Margie's bedroom and the unfinished basement were the only tolerable spaces.

Now it was already Canada Day. July first. Margie didn't have to go in to work, and Christina was out of school, so they had stayed up a bit late the night before to watch a movie while they waited for the house to cool. But Margie had promised herself she would still go for a run, and knew that she would need to head out by six if she wanted to beat the heat. She was glad that she had.

She nodded and said good morning to an elderly man walking around the pond with a cane. She had seen him there before. And she could see a couple with a pair of dogs approaching that she recognized as well. A lot of people wanted to get out and enjoy a bit of fresh air before it got too hot.

Margie sipped her water, then put it back into the holder on her running belt and took out her phone for a few pictures. She walked by the little waterfall, bubbling happily away. Even just this little slice of nature, listening to the trickle of the water and the whistles of the red-winged blackbirds, helped to restore her peace and serenity after all the recent news. Down below that, there was a marshy area with cattails and some scum and plant matter floating on top of the water.

There was something in there. She had seen a muskrat a couple of times in the pond and figured that was probably what it was. He was remarkably brave about all the people and dogs who walked around the pond. Most of the time, he just ignored them unless they got right to the edge of the water, and then he would dive, disappearing below the surface.

But as she got closer, she could see that whatever was in the water was much larger than that. It was obscured by the weeds, but it looked as though someone had dumped a dark blue suitcase into the water. A short distance away, she could see the bottom of a shoe floating on the surface of the pond, which confirmed to her that it must be luggage. Why would somebody throw that into the water?

Margie left the pathway to get close to the water's edge where she would be able to see better. The closer she got, the more clearly she could see that it was not a suitcase and random assortment of clothing that had been dumped into the water.

What she had initially taken for the fabric side of a suitcase was the broad back of a man in a denim shirt. The shoe she could see floating a few feet away was still on the foot of its owner.

CHAPTER TWO

ey! Some help over here!" Margie shouted to the man and the woman walking their dogs.

She scrambled out onto the large sandstone rocks at the edge of the pond and tried to reach the man. Facedown in the water. Not a good sign. Floating just a little too far away for her to grab his shoulder or shirt. She shuffled toward his feet, her knees protesting at the hardness of the rocks. She would end up with bruises just from kneeling there. Margie reached out again, overbalanced, and nearly toppled into the water.

She drew back, breathing hard, her heart racing. She hated the water. She couldn't swim. She couldn't even wade, not without going into full-blown panic mode. But she forced herself to try again. She was a police detective. She had a responsibility to the public. She was a first responder, and it didn't matter whether the emergency was on land in the water; she was expected to take action.

There were concerned questions from the dog walkers as they approached, not yet sure what was going on.

Margie caught the corner of a pant-leg. She hooked her fingers around it to pull it tightly into her palm, then tugged the entire leg toward her. The body was heavier than it looked, dragging on something as she tried to pull it to the edge.

The man handed his girlfriend the second dog's leash and hurried to Margie.

"What happened? Did you see?"

Margie shook her head. "No. I just got here. Saw him." She continued to tug the body closer, wondering whether she would be able to break the water tension and get it out of the water. The victim was not a small man.

The dog walker knelt down at her side, closer to the head. Because Margie had already pulled the body closer to shore, it was easily within the man's reach. He grabbed an arm and the cloth of the denim shirt and pulled hard, bringing the body to the shore and partially out of the water. Margie got her hands around both of the legs and hauled on them, trying to bring them up onto the rocks she knelt on.

"Let's try it together," her helper suggested. "One, two, three!"

On three, they both tried again, and managed to pull the body out of the water and drag it up onto the rocks. Margie was out of breath—not from running anymore, but the exertion and the adrenaline rush.

"What do we do?" the man asked. "Is he breathing?" He called over to his girlfriend. "Did you call 9-1-1?"

The woman nodded impatiently, still talking to the dispatcher on her phone, answering the series of questions that Margie knew the operator would be asking her. *Name? Location? Phone number? Nature of the emergency? Are there any weapons present? Is everyone safe?*

Margie looked down at the bloated face turned to the side and knew that it was way too late to be attempting any lifesaving measures. She shook her head at the dog walker. "He's dead."

"We should do something. Should we do CPR?" her helper asked.

"No. It's too late."

"Sometimes you can't tell," he objected. "On TV, sometimes they think someone is dead, but they can be revived. If we keep his blood pumping until they can shock him…"

"No," Margie told him again. "I'm a police detective. I'm an experienced first responder. It's too late."

He looked around. "Where is your police car? Don't you carry those v-fib machines?"

"I was just out for a run." Margie went through the motions of checking for pulse and respiration, in order to reassure him that they were doing everything they could, even though she knew it was far too late.

A siren whooped. The fire station was only a few blocks away. First responders must have been dispatched from there. With just a few blares of the horn, the firetruck came into view. It pulled into the parking lot and a couple of firefighters climbed out.

Margie stayed where she was. The man looked around, not sure what he should do. He stood up as the firefighters with black masks approached, giving them room to get in and see to the victim.

"Sorry," Margie told them. "Too late to do anything for him. I'm Detective Patenaude." She repeated it, pronouncing it clearly for them, "PAT-en-ode. I came upon the body by chance. I will take control of the scene until it is assigned to someone."

"Parks Pat?" one of the firefighters asked, the skin beside his eyes crinkling in a smile. So the name had spread further than just the homicide department.

"Yes, that's me," she agreed, her face warm.

"Well, lucky us." The firefighter also checked for any signs of life but, like Margie, he knew there was no point in it. "Have you called it in?"

"Not yet. The young lady called 9-1-1. I was busy getting him out of the water."

Becoming suddenly more aware of the water, Margie backed away from the edge of the pond, her throat constricting.

"You need a radio?" the second firefighter, a redhead, offered, indicating his shoulder mike.

"No, I've got my phone and I know the numbers." Margie got to her feet and stepped back from the body. "There's nothing we can do until the crime scene techs and medical examiner's office get here. Let's make sure there is no more contamination of the scene."

The two firefighters agreed and also took several steps back. Margie had nothing with her but her running belt. No yellow tape.

She didn't even have her police ID. Luckily, everyone had taken her at her word that she was in law enforcement.

"Thank you," Margie told the man who had helped pull the body out of the water. She nodded to his girlfriend, standing farther away. The young woman looked both anxious and excited, her skin very pale in the bright morning sun. Margie pulled out her phone and dialed Staff Sergeant MacDonald.

"Detective Pat," Mac greeted. "You're off duty today. I thought you were going to be spending the day with your daughter. Get off the phone and go enjoy your holiday."

It wasn't actually a day of celebration for Margie and her daughter, but it wasn't the right time to point this out. "Actually, I was out for a run this morning… and I found… a body in the pond." She was aware that her voice squeaked up slightly at the end of her statement, making it sound like a question.

There was silence from MacDonald for a few seconds. Margie pictured him running his fingers through his silver hair, eyebrows raised, trying to process what she had just told him.

"You *found* a body," he repeated.

"Yes, sir."

"Is this some kind of a joke?"

"No, sir. Sorry."

"Well, that's going above and beyond, don't you think?"

Margie chuckled. "Yes, sir. It wasn't exactly planned."

"Where exactly is this body? Am I your first call?"

"A bystander called 9-1-1. We have first responders on the scene. We're all in agreement that there is nothing we can do for him. You're my first call."

"You're supposed to be off today, but I'm going to make you primary since you're already there. There isn't any point in calling someone else to take over. Are you able to handle the preliminaries?" He sounded suddenly uncertain. "Your daughter isn't there with you, is she?"

She appreciated his concern. "No. She's still at home asleep. I just went out for a quick run. The body is in Valleyview Park. I can get things started on this end. I can't spend all day, but I've got a couple of hours. I don't think there will be much for the forensic team to do. The scene is pretty small."

"Any sign of violence? Cause of death?"

"I haven't made any kind of examination of the body. No blood or trauma that I can see."

"Okay. Valleyview... I think we had a drowning there a few years ago. Is this a drowning?"

Margie looked back toward the body. "A definite possibility. I don't imagine it will take the medical examiner long to find out."

"Give them a call."

"Yes, sir. Will do. Can you send me a couple of units? I was just out on foot, so I don't have crime scene tape or anything. We'll need a little crowd control and to canvass the houses around here to see if we can narrow down time of death and if anyone saw or heard anything last night or this morning."

"I'll send you some backup. Could the body have been there longer? A few days? Sometimes it's hard to be sure. If the body sank or was hidden...?"

"No, I don't think so. It's a very small park. Nothing like Fish Creek or Glenbow. Just a little pond with a pathway around it. And lots of foot traffic. Runners, walkers, dog people. I don't think it could have been here any longer than last night or early this morning."

CHAPTER THREE

couple of police units rolled up within a few minutes. Margie was more relaxed once they could cordon off the pond and the pathway that looped around it to prevent anyone from getting too close to the scene. They covered the body until they could get screens up to shield it from view.

At that point, it became a waiting game. Margie supposed she should have guessed that there would be only a skeleton crew on in the forensics department and medical examiner's office due to the statutory holiday. There were people on call, but it would take time for them to get out to the scene, especially if they had been planning to spend the day with family, as Margie had.

She stood watching the various walkers rubbernecking to see what was going on, gathering in little clumps to speculate with each other. She didn't see anyone who looked concerned, as if they might be missing a family member and worried about some misadventure. At least she didn't have to deal with trying to keep a mother, brother, or best friend away from the body.

The crows were cawing loudly and the magpies screaming, drowning out the sounds of the blackbirds she had been listening to earlier. Margie had noticed that the magpies had become much more vocal since their babies had left the nest, frequently calling warnings of predators or other perceived dangers. The black and white magpie fledglings were so large that it was hard to tell them apart from the parents, other than by the fluffiness of their baby feathers or their behavior if she watched them for long enough.

"There they are," one of the constables commented.

Margie blinked her eyes and looked around, realizing that she had zoned out listening to the birds. Not a good idea. As a detective, she needed to have her head on a swivel, always looking around for possible dangers, clues, people she needed to talk to, behaviors that might give people away. It wouldn't do to let herself be distracted.

The medical examiner's van and the forensic techs both rolled up, nudging their way into the now-crowded parking lot, then rolling through the opening for the pathway to drive over the grass and stop beside the body. No point in trying to carry a body and the equipment back and forth to the parking lot. Much more efficient to have everything right at hand.

Margie nodded to each of the techs. She recognized them from earlier cases but wasn't sure enough of names to address them with certainty.

"What's this I hear?" one of them asked, a tall fellow with a goofy grin that he covered with a mask as he approached, "You're providing your own bodies now?"

Margie's smile felt stretched thin, like her emotions over the past few weeks. It was taut and uncomfortable. But he didn't know how she was feeling. The nature of their business often led to morbid humor.

"I didn't plan it that way, believe me. I was supposed to have the day off."

He chuckled and went to work, scouting around the area, getting equipment out of the truck, working in tandem with his partner. Margie recognized the death investigator who got out of the medical examiner's van.

"Dr. Galt. Nice to see you again."

Dr. Galt nodded. He had white hair and a small white beard and appeared to have missed a spot shaving that morning. He probably had not been planning to go out anywhere and had shaven quickly when he got the call. But he was calm and unhurried in his approach. Everyone worked together to set up privacy screens so that they could uncover the body again without spectators. Dr. Galt looked the man over very slowly, not touching him.

"Who discovered the body?"

"That was me."

By his lack of reaction, she suspected he already knew that and was simply asking as a matter of course. "In the water or out?"

"In. Face down. I could see his back and one shoe, to start with."

Dr. Galt nodded. He gave the techs various instructions, making sure that all visible evidence was retrieved. They stretched a white body bag out next to him and then, together, turned him over, setting him into it, so that for the first time Margie was viewing his chest instead of his back. She saw his long black hair, brown skin, and the Indigenous cast apparent in his features, even with how bloated his face was. Margie sighed.

"Does he have any identification on him?"

They looked in her direction, but ignored the question, going over the body in their own methodical procedure. It was a few minutes before they pulled out a slim wallet protruding from his pocket.

"Bruce Hungry Bear, according to his identification."

"Thirsty Bear, more likely," one of the techs intoned. The other, the tall one, punched him in the shoulder.

"Hey! What was that for?"

"Shut up. Look at her."

The tech who had commented turned and looked at Margie not-so-surreptitiously. It was a moment before everything apparently clicked into place and he realized his mistake. Making racist remarks about a victim in front of an Indigenous detective was not a particularly smart thing to do.

"Sorry," he muttered. "Didn't see you."

Margie was counting off each intake and exhale of breath, trying to keep herself from breaking into a tirade. He was going to make *drunk Indian* jokes about a victim? In the current political climate?

Hundreds of unmarked graves had been revealed at residential schools in the last six weeks. The entire Indigenous population of the country was in mourning, many calling for the cancellation of Canada Day celebrations altogether, and he thought it was appropriate to voice his racist biases out loud? In front of Margie?

There were going to be fireworks all right, and they wouldn't be the ones that would be going off at midnight.

"What is your name?" she demanded.

The man swallowed and pretended to be occupied with carefully rechecking all the evidence that had been bagged so far. He looked away from Margie, out at the glass-smooth surface of the pond. There might be more evidence out there. Might have to drain the pond to check.

"Your name," Margie repeated. "Now."

"Oliver Symons. But it was just a joke. I didn't mean anything by it. Just trying to lighten the mood. Morgue humor."

Margie didn't have her duty notepad on her, but she had her phone. She woke it up, tapped out his name below the notes she had already made about the investigation, and slid it back into her running belt. "Your comment was not funny," she told him flatly.

She could see it was a struggle for him not to respond. He wanted to justify himself. Maybe to call *her* a few choice names. But he'd already dug himself deep enough, and he was clearly fighting the urge not to dig himself any deeper. He pressed his lips together and continued to work the scene. There were no more comments about the race of their victim.

Margie stayed out of the way, fielding inquiries on her phone from MacDonald and the constables who were canvassing the nearby houses. They each had a job to do there and, while she was the primary and was there to supervise the gathering of forensic evidence, she believed that, as a rule, the techs were better when left to do the job the way they had been trained than for her to micromanage the process.

"Detective Pat!"

Margie turned at the familiar voice. It was Detective Cruz, one of the other detectives on the homicide squad. A good cop and a good man. Filipino. Her smile of greeting was not as plastic as the others had been.

"Cruz. You didn't need to come out."

"You aren't even supposed to be on today. I am."

"I can take care of this. Didn't you want to take the day off with your kids?"

He was older than Margie, near the age when she expected him to retire from homicide, but his children were younger than Christina. Margie wasn't sure how many kids he had. She had seen them at the department Christmas party, but they had all looked so much alike that she had lost track of how many there were and which was which.

"No. We are going to wait until the heat breaks, and then take them out for some fun. In this weather… about all they want to do is paddle in the wading pool. The heat doesn't bother me so much. But they were all born here in Canada and they are not used to it."

"So maybe Saturday you can do something with them."

Cruz nodded. "And until then, I'm at your service. Where do you need me?"

Margie removed her hat and wiped the sweat collecting along her forehead. The day had warmed very quickly, and everyone was moving slowly and looking uncomfortable. "You know what? I need to move around a bit. I ran here, and then I've been standing around and my legs are seizing up. I'm going to scout a wider perimeter, just to make sure that there's nothing we've missed, then I'm going to run home, shower off, and come back in my car."

"You're that close?"

"Just about a kilometer from here." Margie swallowed a couple of gulps of water to replace what she had already sweated out. "So I'll be back in a few minutes. Probably before the techs are done."

She looked back toward the men around the body. When she looked back at Cruz, he gave her a puzzled look. "What's going on?"

"What?"

"You're looking kinda ticked off, there. Is it just the heat?"

"Symons there… making racist comments."

Cruz's brows went up. "Really? That doesn't sound right. Never heard anything from him before."

"Maybe he's okay with Filipinos."

"But not you? You're about as Canadian as they get."

"Too Canadian. Doesn't have much respect for Indigenous peoples, I guess."

"Do you want me to say something to him?"

Margie laughed. "No. I'll make a report. Let his department deal with it. I was here and saw and heard what he had to say. You didn't."

"You just say the word, and I'll take him in the back alley," Cruz teased. "Or we could do it right here. I could help him look under the water to see whether there's any evidence to be gathered there."

"Don't beat anyone up before I get back."

He grinned and nodded.

CHAPTER FOUR

argie made a large loop around the park, crossing over Twenty-Sixth Street to the hill overlooking the irrigation canal and Deerfoot Trail. There was a lookout point there that she and Christina often stopped at when they were taking Stella out for a walk. Margie looked for anything that was out of place. There was no litter, and there were no breaks in the foliage or tracks through the grass that she could see. Nothing out of the ordinary. It was a high-traffic area, lots of people through there with their dogs, plenty of wildlife, including foxes and coyotes right there in the middle of the city. And skunks, of course. Stella had recently had a close encounter with one of the little black and white stinkers.

She returned through the parking lot where the police vehicles were parked, along the longer loop that got closer to the houses, looking into the back yards for anything that might have been thrown over the fence in an attempt to get rid of evidence. Bystanders watched her curiously, but didn't approach to ask any questions. When she reached Twenty-Eighth Street on the other side of the splash park and volleyball courts, Margie stopped and gazed at the chain link fence by West Dover School. Someone had tied orange ribbons through the links.

There were no signs explaining the memorial, but Margie didn't need one. Orange ribbons for the children who had died at the residential schools. Currently at the forefront of the minds of the public because ground-penetrating radar was being used at some of the old residential school properties to seek out the Indigenous children who had been buried there, victims of abuse, neglect, and disease, their resting places and identities obscured during the intervening years.

Her chest was tight. She had listened to the stories. She could imagine having Christina ripped from her arms to be sent away to a school designed to "beat the Indian out of her." Having her stolen away, knowing full well that she was going to be abused and might never return home.

Margie breathed deeply, trying to loosen the tension in her shoulders. She crossed the street to touch a couple of the ribbons. She took a few pictures from her phone and then put it back away.

She completed her circuit around the park, back past the church with the cross on top, through the playground, and to the parking lot again. She called Cruz's number as she crossed Twenty-Sixth Street again to run the pathway home.

"Detective Cruz," he answered.

"Pat here. There are a number of garbage cans and bins in the area. The school, the church, the playgrounds, and the park itself. We'll want to at least have a cursory look to see whether anything was thrown away."

"On it. See you after your shower."

&

MARGIE WAS REALLY SWEATING. The weather pattern was extreme compared to what she had been accustomed to in Winnipeg, and she wasn't used to running in the heat. She slowed to a walk for the last block and chugged the rest of her water.

Stella barked excitedly and ran around when Margie walked in the door, clearly wanting to be taken out herself. Margie glanced around, not expecting Christina to be awake.

But Christina was in the kitchen, leaning against the counter, eyes partially closed, waiting for the coffee maker to finish its duties.

"Hi, Mom." Christina yawned and rubbed her eyes. "What time did you get up? I thought you would be up really early for your run. You said you wanted to beat the heat." She looked Margie over accusingly. "You'll get heatstroke."

"I'm fine, thanks." Margie laughed. Christina had taken on the role of mother lately, repeating back all the things that Margie had taught her about eating properly, cleaning up after herself, getting enough sleep, and all of the other things that Margie had assumed Christina hadn't been listening to over the years. "I'm going to have a quick shower and then I'll tell you about it."

Christina was still in the kitchen when Margie got out, sitting in one of the kitchen chairs with her feet on the seat and her knees to her chest while she sipped her coffee. Too hot for a day that was so warm. Margie was craving one of the cold cans of Coke in the fridge but didn't want a lecture on healthy eating from Christina too. She got herself a cold bottle of water instead.

"So, something happened?" Christina asked, trailing her fingers through Stella's thick fur.

Stella had been spending most of the week sprawled out on the floor, using as little energy as possible. But she did have occasional bursts of activity when she was hungry or wanted outside.

"Yes... something happened in the park today."

"In the park? What?"

"In Valleyview, where we go to play Frisbee and they have that splash park?" Margie suggested, not sure Christina knew which park she was talking about.

"Yeah?"

"There was... something in the water when I went by it today."

"Did you see the muskrat? Or the ducklings?"

"Well... I'm sure they were there. But there was actually... a man died there today."

Christina's eyes widened. "What? Were you there when it happened? I saw on the internet that lots of people are dying from the heat. Old people."

"He didn't die in front of me. His body was in the water when I got there. Maybe drowned, we'll have to wait for the autopsy."

"I can't believe it." Christina shook her head. "Parks Pat strikes again. Detective Patenaude investigating another park murder."

"I wasn't *trying* to find a body. And I certainly didn't have anything to do with it being there."

"That's crazy." Christina ran her fingers through her long, black hair. "It wasn't anyone we know, was it?"

"No. No one we know." Margie decided to pour herself a little bit of coffee. It smelled so good. She took a sip, looking down into the depths of her cup with sadness welling up inside. "One of our brothers. A Siksiká man, I think. But not one I've ever met before."

"Oh." Christina too dropped her eyes, considering. It had been a difficult month for everyone in the Indigenous communities, opening old wounds and bringing fresh trauma. "That's sad."

Margie nodded her agreement. "I have to go back. I just came home to shower and change. Will you take Stella out for a bit? Not for too long, I don't want either of you to get overheated…"

Christina nodded. "Sure. We'll go for a walk."

"Thanks, sweetie." Margie leaned forward and kissed Christina on the forehead and scratched Stella's ears. "*Maarsii.*"

৯৯

WHEN MARGIE GOT BACK to the park, things had quieted considerably. Most of the police vehicles were gone. The forensic techs and Dr. Galt were gone. Which of course meant that the body had been removed. Margie took a deep breath in and blew it out again. She joined Detective Cruz once more.

"Looks like things are moving along."

Cruz nodded. "There is nothing suspicious, probably just an accident. We'll have the scene cleared pretty soon."

"Good. Run into any trouble?" Margie didn't specify whether she was talking about more comments by the tech, bystanders, or any one of a hundred other things that could go wrong at a scene. Let him interpret it as he saw fit.

"No. Everything has been quiet. We'll check the rest of the

garbages," Cruz took a quick look around. "Then, I think we'll be done."

"All right."

Cruz pulled his phone out to look at the screen. "We have the address from his driver's license. Are you up for a death notification?"

Not Margie's favorite part of the job. Not any homicide detective's favorite part of the job. "Yes. Of course. Is it close by?"

"He lived in the neighborhood."

"Do we know who he lived with?"

"Jones ran down the address. Looks like friends or roommates. She'll check social media too, and we'll get a look at his personal effects, talk to the friends, see whether he had family who need to be notified."

CHAPTER FIVE

et's take my car," Cruz suggested. "Yours can stay here for now. I'll drop you back here when we're done. No point in wasting gas taking two vehicles."

Margie was just fine with that. It meant that she wouldn't have to use her GPS or follow Cruz. Her sense of direction was bad enough to make her ancestors turn over in their graves.

Cruz didn't even bother looking up the address on his phone, he just drove directly to it. Calgary was a big city and it amazed Margie how well he knew his way around. Hungry Bear's house was only a few blocks away, but it wasn't Cruz's neighborhood. Maybe he had looked it up on his phone map before Margie's return. But even then, he'd been able to remember what he had seen on the map and to translate it to real life in order to find the house without any wrong turns, which, in Margie's mind, was still pretty impressive.

Cruz checked the time as he called in to let the team know where they were. "Should be late enough for people to be up, don't you think?"

"My teenager was up, if that's any indication. And I don't know how anyone could sleep once it's this hot out."

"If they have an air conditioner or basement room. Teens, young adults, night shift workers, plenty of people *could* still be asleep now.

But I'm going to assume that they're up. If not… I guess we're their wake-up call today."

Margie was on board with that. They got out of the car and walked up to the door of the bungalow. No children's toys on the lawn or sidewalk. Grass that had been mown at least once during June and was now burning in the summer sun. No gardens. Some shrubbery around the front door and windows, which really wasn't a good idea if they wanted to prevent a burglary. The cars on the street in front of the house were a combination of nondescript leases and older vehicles that were probably paid for. She didn't hear any voices from inside the house as they approached. Windows were open and box fans were running as the residents tried to keep the house cool.

Cruz rang the doorbell and knocked hard on the door. They both stood slightly to the side, always watching for anything that might be off. Anything that might indicate that they were about to walk into a meth house or a domestic situation or anything else that could be dangerous for them.

A few minutes passed with no answer. Cruz knocked again, hard, his knock undoubtedly echoing through the house and audible to all the residents. Unless they were downstairs. Or wearing headphones. Or asleep.

This time, Margie could make out voices. Complaining, arguing over who was going to get the door, tired and frustrated.

Cruz knocked again.

A minute later, the door was opened by a skinny blond woman, her hair stringy and tangled. She was swearing before she even opened the door all the way.

"What's your problem? People are trying to sleep!"

"Calgary Police, ma'am," Cruz cut her off. "Can we come in?"

"Police?" She stopped complaining and just stood there scowling at him.

"Yes, ma'am. If we could have a few minutes with you…"

She pushed a hank of hair back behind her ear. "What's this about?" She looked out the door, craning her neck to see around them. "Did someone hit my car? Or steal it?" She could apparently see it sitting there unharmed and withdrew back into the house again. "What is this?"

Cruz stepped toward the door, turning his shoulder as if to push his way past her. She stepped back and let him in. Margie followed. They all walked into the small living room, hot and still, sealed windows preventing any air from circulating through the room. It had to be almost 40 degrees. Margie took a deep breath. Hopefully, they wouldn't be there for too long. Cruz invited the woman to sit down.

"What did you say your name is, ma'am?"

"Samantha." She looked toward the hallway. "Jonathan? Come out here."

There was grumbling and groaning from a nearby bedroom and, eventually, the padding of bare feet as the owner of the grumbles made his way in their direction.

Jonathan was a tall man with a full bushy beard, a painful-looking red sunburn around white skin in the shape of the tank top he had been wearing when he'd apparently fallen asleep in the sun. He rubbed his eyes and looked at them, surprised to find visitors in his living room. He hitched up his Sponge Bob boxers and leaned an elbow against the wall.

"What's this, then?"

"Police," Samantha said.

"About what?"

"They were just gonna tell me." She sounded aggrieved, as if he had done something wrong instead of just coming out when she'd asked him to.

"Would you like to sit down?" Cruz suggested to Jonathan.

"No, I'd like to stand. What's up?"

"Do you have a roommate in the house, a Bruce Hungry Bear?"

"Is that who you're looking for? Bruce!" Jonathan went into the kitchen, calling down to the basement. "Bruce! The cops are here!" He returned to the living room, shaking his head in amusement. "That should bring him up here."

Margie and Cruz looked at each other.

"Actually, I don't think it will," Margie said in a soft, measured voice. "We're here *about* Bruce, not to see him."

"Oh." The roommates looked at each other. "Is he in some kind of trouble? Did he get arrested?"

Samantha blinked, looking around, reaching back into her memory. "They were talking about setting off some fireworks. I told them they're not supposed to do it within city limits, you know, 'cause of the by-laws. And it's so dry with all of this heat. But I didn't think you'd arrest someone for something like that…"

"Bruce hasn't been arrested, ma'am," Cruz said gently. "I'm afraid that this morning, his body was discovered in a nearby pond. He was dead."

Cruz had done enough notifications to know not to leave any doubt in the recipient's mind that the person was actually dead. Not gone away. Not hurt or sick in hospital. Unequivocally dead. Leaving room for misunderstanding was not a kindness.

"Dead?" Jonathan swore. "Are you kidding me?"

"No, sir. I'm afraid not. Were you and Bruce close?"

"We were friendly… I mean, we didn't know each other before we rented the house together. But we got along. All of us were… pretty chill with each other. Let everybody do their own thing. You know."

Cruz and Margie nodded. "Do you know if he has any family or friends in the city?" Margie asked.

"Yeah, his folks are here," Samantha offered. She ran her fingers through her long, blond hair and looked at the man as if expecting him to contribute something.

He just shrugged. "I guess."

"Do you know their names? Where they live?"

The two shook their heads. "Maybe… the northwest some-where?" the woman suggested.

"Could we see Bruce's room? He might have something that will help us to find them."

"They would be on his phone," Samantha said doubtfully. "It's not like anyone these days has an actual address book." She gazed at Cruz as if he were ancient.

"His phone was in the water. I don't know if we'll be able to retrieve anything from it," Margie advised them. Of course, they would be able to get his phone logs and see who he had been in contact with, but that might take a few days. It was better if they could contact his parents the first day, not wait until they had heard it from someone else or come to the police to report him as a missing person.

"I don't know. Yeah, I guess you can. You're the cops." She still seemed hesitant. "You don't need, like, a warrant or something?"

"Not if you let us in."

Neither of them got up to show Cruz and Margie to Bruce's room. Margie exchanged a look with Cruz. He gave her a slight nod, encouraging her to take point. While Cruz generally came across as pleasant and non-threatening, a woman was less intimidating.

"Is there something you're worried we're going to find?" Margie suggested. "We understand that you're not responsible for whatever we find in his room."

"Well… I don't know what he could have. None of us are big partiers or anything, but what people do behind closed doors…" The woman gave a one-shouldered shrug. "Well, you just don't know."

"Understood. Like I said, we won't blame you for anything we find there. You're just helping us out by giving us access to the room so that we can find Bruce's parents and let them know. You wouldn't want them to be wondering what happened to him." Margie saw an opening. "Or calling you or coming here looking for him. You don't want to be the one having to break it to them."

Samantha's eyes got big. No way she wanted to do that. She pushed herself to her feet. "Yeah, I guess it's okay. He would want his parents to know."

She led them through the kitchen to the stairs. The man didn't follow them, and Margie could hear water running and the toilet flushing while they were partway down the stairs. She hoped he wasn't flushing whatever stash he had. They weren't going to search his possessions, and flushing pharmaceuticals was just bad for the water system.

Samantha led them down a hall. There were several closed doors.

She stopped at one and looked at them, fist closed as if she had been planning to knock.

"Do you have a key?" Cruz suggested.

"It's… not locked. We all had keys to the house, but none of us bothered to lock the individual doors."

A pretty trusting group. Cruz nodded and angled to reach past her and open the door. She stepped back and gave him room. Cruz turned the handle and pushed the door open, he and Margie standing just to the side of the door. As far as they knew, the room was vacant, but way too many police incident reports started with, *The residence was believed to be unoccupied.*

They waited for a moment, then Cruz reached around the door frame and felt for a light switch. He found it and flipped it up. They looked around. No one there. There were places they couldn't see— under the bed, in the closet, against the wall that the door was on— but no one obviously lying in wait and no one sleeping in Bruce's bed waiting for him to get home. No pit bull or psychotic cat.

Cruz gave Margie a nod and they moved into the room. "Thank you," he told Samantha, and closed the door behind them.

The two of them quickly checked the various blind spots to clear the room and ensure that they were alone. There was no desk. There was a laptop computer on the bed. Cruz pressed a button to wake it up. Miraculously, there was no lock screen. No need to enter a password or provide a fingerprint. Cruz clicked and tapped for a few moments.

"There we go. Mom's phone numbers are in his contact list. Two of them, one will be a landline traceable to an address. Only an email address and single phone number for Dad."

"Sounded from the roommates like they still live together."

"Sounded that way. If not, I'm sure Mom will have Dad's information. Maybe she'll even want to be the one to inform him."

Not likely. Margie looked around the room. "Give it a quick once-over?"

Cruz nodded. "If you want to take a look around, I'm going to spend a minute in his email. See what's been going on in his life."

Margie shook her head as she started looking through the man's drawers. "Twenty-somethings don't use email," she told Cruz. "Try Snapchat, IM's, Discord."

She could feel Cruz rolling his eyes at her. It was the second time in ten minutes he'd basically been told that he was old. "Kids these days," he quavered in a grandpa voice.

Margie chuckled. She pulled a couple of plastic bags out of Hungry Bear's bottom drawer and tossed them on top of the dresser. There were a few pill bottles in his top drawer, but none of them were prescription. Just over-the-counter stuff. Tylenol, cold pills, caffeine.

Cruz looked at the packages of herbs. "Weed?"

"No, I don't think so." Margie continued her search, checking the backs and bottoms of drawers for any stashes. The closet, including the pockets of jackets and toes of the shoes littering the bottom of the closet. It all seemed pretty innocuous. As Samantha had said, he wasn't a partier.

Cruz closed the lid of the computer and walked over to the dresser to take a look at the packages. Margie returned to look at them with him. Cruz frowned, rubbing his thumb over the contents of one of the bags to shift the contents around. He didn't open the package to smell it. That's what a cop on TV would have done. Cops in real life didn't taste unknown white powders or smell-test baggies of dry green leaves. There were labs to do proper tests.

"What are they, then?" Cruz asked.

"Tobacco," Margie informed him, pointing to one. "Sage," pointing to the other. She'd seen and handled both of them enough to easily recognize them on sight.

"So… he uses snuff and cooks turkey?" Cruz asked, giving her a puzzled look.

"No. They're sacred herbs. For ceremonies."

"Oh. Indian—*Aboriginal* stuff. Would he smoke them?"

"More likely smudge. But he could."

Cruz looked around the room. "Nothing else? No alcohol?"

Of course, Margie might have found alcohol but not drawn his attention to it as she had the herbs. There was no reason he shouldn't have alcohol in his own room.

Margie might have taken offense at the question, accusing him of assuming, like the forensic tech, that Hungry Bear was a drunk just because of his heritage. But she didn't. She understood where the answer would lead them.

If Hungry Bear had not been drunk or high, then how had he ended up stumbling into the Valleyview pond?

CHAPTER SIX

*B*ack in Cruz's car, they didn't discuss the question, both of them content to just ponder on it for a while themselves. Margie would put the question in the back of her mind and let her subconscious chew over it for a while. See what her brain came up with.

"You want to go to the northwest to talk to the parents?" Cruz asked. "I can drop you at your car if you want to go home and spend the rest of the day with Christina."

"Uh… let me talk to her first. You can find out if there is an address tied to that landline."

They each took out their phones to make their inquiries. Margie tapped Christina's name in her favorites.

"Hi, Mom." Christina answered before the third ring. "I took Stella out for a walk, and we're back home. When are you going to be done?"

"Well, that's why I'm calling you. We need to make a death notification, and it's over in the northwest. It will be at least twenty minutes' drive each way, plus however long it takes to talk to the parents. If I go, I'll be at least another hour."

"You should go."

"I'm supposed to be off today. So I *can* bow out and just let Detective Cruz take care of it."

"No, Mom," Christina said immediately. "You need to be the one."

Margie was bemused. "Because I was the one to find the body and pull him out?"

"No." There were a few beats of silence before Christina explained. "Because… you said he is Siksiká, right?"

"Yes."

"Then… you should be the one to tell them. So they have a friendly face. Someone who looks like them, not some white dude."

"Detective Cruz is not a white dude." Margie laughed. But Christina made a good point. Hopefully, Hungry Bear's parents would feel better knowing that their son's death was being handled respectfully by someone who had at least a basic understanding of their culture. Someone who would not immediately jump to conclusions or make judgments.

"Hispanic, then," Christina said impatiently. "Whatever. But he's not Indigenous."

"Filipino," Margie informed her. "And you're absolutely right. I think I should too. You don't mind? You'll be okay for another hour or two on your own?"

"Time without you looking over my shoulder telling me I should get off the computer and get out for some fresh air?" Christina countered. "Yeah, I think I can handle it."

"Okay. Love you, sweetie."

"You too."

Margie terminated the call and slid her phone away.

"A white dude?" Cruz asked, obviously having heard part of the conversation.

Margie laughed. "Sorry. Kid's not always politically correct."

"Well, thank you for setting her straight. I wouldn't want anyone going around thinking I am a white dude." A fan of wrinkles appeared around his eyes as he smiled. "So are you going with me?"

"I am."

Cruz chuckled. "Teenagers don't mind being left home alone for a while."

"No," Margie agreed. "That didn't seem to be a problem." She adjusted to a more serious tone. "She's a good kid. We had plans for today, but she wants to make sure that I'm the one doing the notification. So that they get it from… someone like them."

"Not some white dude."

"Yeah. I don't think she has anything against white dudes or Filipinos. She just knows… well, the racism that this family faces."

He nodded his agreement. He shifted the car into drive.

"You got the address?" Margie asked. "That didn't take long."

"Got it."

"Did you put it into your phone GPS?"

He tapped the side of his head. "This one here."

"You really know the city well. How can you know all of the little crescents and cul-de-sacs? They can be so confusing."

"I've had longer to learn than you have. You're still pretty new."

"Yeah, but I'm crap at directions. By the time I've been here five years, I might be able to get to a few places from memory. But I'm not going to remember every place I've ever been."

"I don't remember every place I've ever been. Most, maybe, but not quite all of them." His voice was teasing.

Margie sat back in her seat and tried to relax and not think about the duty she was facing.

❧

CRUZ WAS able to get to the parents' house pretty quickly, much faster than Margie would have liked. She took a deep breath and hoped that the lump in her stomach would go away once she did the notification. There was no way to fully prepare for these things. It was like ripping off a Band-Aid. She could completely psych herself out worrying about how bad it was going to be, or she could just pull it off and cry about it when it was done.

"Ready?"

Margie nodded. "Yes. It's not going to get any easier."

"Nope."

They got out of the car and approached the door. Cruz didn't knock as loudly as he had at Hungry Bear's house. Margie wasn't sure if it was because they were not as likely to still be asleep, or that he was showing respect and didn't want to scare them. They stood to the side slightly until the door was opened by a tiny Siksiká woman, bent over, hair almost completely white.

"*Oki*, Grandmother," Margie said, lowering her head and bending down slightly to get closer to the woman's face. "We are from the Calgary Police. May we come in?"

"Yes, come in, come in," the woman agreed, backing up a few paces to make space for them. Margie looked at Cruz. She hadn't been expecting this. She hoped that the old woman was not the only one who was home.

They followed her into the house and she motioned for them to sit down in the couch and easy chair. She sat down on another chair, maybe a dining room chair, with a straight back, but cushioned. She leaned forward to study them, her eyes quick.

"Is there someone here with you?" Margie asked. "Or are you the only one at home?"

"Alice is here. And her husband, Michael. No work today." She gazed away from them. "Canada Day," she said flatly. "A day to show pride in your country."

Margie leaned as close to the old woman as she could manage, but there was still too much distance between them for Margie to place a hand on her arm or her shoulder.

"I am proud of my family," she said. "And proud of my community. This has been a very hard time for all of us, and they have been very strong. I can tell that you are a strong woman. Like my Moushoom, you are a survivor."

"We had to be strong to survive. It was that… or die."

Margie said nothing. They both allowed some time to pass. Eventually, Cruz spoke up, uncomfortable with the silence.

"Do you think we could get Alice and Michael in here. So that we can talk to you all together at the same time? That way we don't have to repeat ourselves."

The old woman studied Cruz openly. "Where is your family from? Are you a brother?"

"I am from the Philippines." Cruz hesitated. "I hope I am a brother."

She nodded. "Your people and my people knew each other many, many moons ago."

Margie had heard of trade between the Pacific islands and the North American tribes, but didn't know whether it was true or not. Sometimes stories were just stories. Scientists believed there was a relationship between the Siberian tribes and the Alaskan Aleuts, but it seemed to be easier for them to believe that those peoples had crossed on the ice or a land bridge than to believe they could have built boats and sailed across the ocean. As if no one but Europeans could build seaworthy boats.

Cruz was willing to accept this. He nodded to the old woman and waited.

"Alice," the old woman called eventually, directing a remarkably loud and clear voice toward the back of the house. "Come out to speak to the company. And bring your husband."

There was a bit of chatter back and forth between them, too fast for Margie to follow the Siksiká words. Then a woman in her fifties or sixties, with a warm, round face joined them.

"It is so hot. We should sit outside."

No one made any move to get up. Alice sat down with the older woman, who Margie assumed was her mother or grandmother. A few seconds of silence passed, and then her husband came into the room as well. His face had sharper planes, not soft and round like Alice's, but narrow and angular as if he had been chiseled from stone. Despite his severe appearance, he gave Margie a smile, showing off several missing teeth.

With all of them assembled, it was time for Margie to make the notification. She looked at Alice and Michael.

"I assume that you are Bruce Hungry Bear's parents?"

They exchanged looks of anxiety with each other, then looked at Margie and nodded. They didn't ask what had happened. But they knew it was something bad.

"Bruce's body was discovered early this morning," she told them, as quickly and compassionately as she could. "We believe he died sometime late last night or early this morning, but will need to wait for the Medical Examiner's report before we can tell you more. I'm so sorry."

Alice let out a high-pitched keening, wailing for her son. Margie wanted to take her hands and to hold her and give her comfort. But Alice turned away from Margie, into her mother, head lowered into her chest.

"I'm so sorry," Margie repeated. She looked at the father. His face was stoic, but his shoulders collapsed inward, holding in grief and pain.

For a long time, there was no conversation, only Alice's wailing and a chanted song from her mother. They hugged and held each other, pulling Michael into their circle as well. A tiny family, lost in themselves.

The room was unbearably hot. Margie tugged at her collar and tried not to look as uncomfortable as she was. Sweat was dripping down all their faces, mixing with tears.

Eventually, the family was able to turn outward again, looking to Margie to give them more details, to make it all make sense to them.

"How? What happened?" Michael asked.

"We don't know yet. We will let you know what we find out. When was the last time you saw him?"

They looked at each other. "Yesterday. He was just here," Alice said, as if Margie must have gotten her facts wrong. He couldn't be dead if she had just seen him the day before.

"What time was that?"

"Supper... then he went home. He said he was meeting with friends later."

"Do you know who?"

"I... no. He had a lot of friends. I don't know who he was going to see."

"What were they going to do?"

"I don't know. Getting together to talk. Play games."

"Would there have been drinking?" Cruz asked.

"He was clean," Alice told him firmly. "No alcohol, no drugs. He wasn't into any of that."

"Had he been?"

"Why? Because he was an Indian?"

Cruz shook his head. "Because of your choice of words. Clean. And that he didn't use any alcohol or drugs. Most people will have a social drink. Those that don't, it is often because they have had addiction problems in the past."

Alice didn't answer right away, maybe not believing him, thinking that he was already prejudiced against her son. "Yes. He'd had a problem with alcohol." Alice looked at Margie, then glared at Cruz. "Many of our people have. How can we have strong families and communities when our children are taken away from us? Over and over again, generation after generation. Not just the residential schools. Not just the Sixties Scoop. *Now.*"

Margie nodded. Cruz looked over at her and wisely kept his mouth closed. He probably didn't see it in the city. It wasn't as bad in Calgary as it was in Manitoba. Over and over again, in trying to deal with the violence of the streets, she had seen them. Displaced children who had been unable to establish bonds. Brothers and sisters who were so *lost* by the time they reached adulthood.

"He wouldn't have been drinking," Alice repeated. "He was through that. He was back on his feet. He was clean."

CHAPTER SEVEN

Margie was quiet in the car, thinking about the devastated family. She knew that she should take the opportunity to talk it through with Cruz, but she needed time to ponder and think things through on her own first.

If Alice were right and Bruce Hungry Bear had not been under the influence of alcohol or drugs, then how had he ended up in the pond? Mac had remembered a previous death there, determined to have been an accidental death, no foul play involved. Someone who had been so intoxicated that he had apparently wandered into the pond at night and gotten turned around or passed out, eventually drowning. Tragic, but at least not violent.

If that was what had happened to Bruce, then at least his family would know that it had just been an accident. That might be some solace to them. But if that was not what had happened, then what?

"Did Dr. Galt point out any injuries?" she asked Cruz. "After I had gone?"

"Some bruises, but not anything that he could clearly identify. Maybe a fall. Not stabbed or shot. Not that he could see on his initial inspection."

"Face? Head? Hands?"

"Head. He'll know more once he's had a chance to examine the body fully. Can't tell if there are any bruises on the torso or knees until he's got the clothes off. He'll do x-rays, tox screen."

Margie kept her face frozen, willing herself not to grimace or make any sign at his reference to a tox screen. Of course Dr. Galt would have to check whether Hungry Bear had been intoxicated or under the influence of some drug at the time of his death. That was routine. They couldn't just take his parents' word for it that he wouldn't have had anything to drink. Parents were often the last to know. Since he was an adult and didn't even live with them, he could be drinking a lot without their knowing. Kids told parents stories to keep them happy. Margie had done it. She was sure that Christina did it. They liked their parents to think the best of them. It was uncomfortable to disappoint them.

❧

CRUZ RETURNED Margie to the parking lot at Valleyview to pick up her car and go home. There was one other car in the parking lot, a lone dog walker, probably. Margie glanced over the park but didn't see anyone walking. They might have parked at Valleyview and then taken the Twenty-Sixth Street pathway rather than staying in Valleyview. Or they might just be around the bend where she couldn't see them. Maybe behind the trees that had initially screened Hungry Bear's body from her view.

"You okay?" Cruz asked.

"Yes. Long, hot day. That's all." Margie looked at the time on the dashboard clock. It was still only mid afternoon. Hot, but not the end of the day. "Looks like I still have some time to spend with Christina. If we can stand the heat."

"Go to the mall. Cooler there. Or a movie if the theaters are open. I heard that some of them have reopened, but I haven't checked them out."

Margie shrugged. "Not really in the mood for a movie." Though they might watch something on the computer, stretched out on Margie's bed under the air conditioner. Margie just didn't feel like going out and being around people who were celebrating the day.

While she was happy about all the restrictions other than masking in public places being terminated, there weren't many other reasons for her to celebrate Canada Day. "Maybe we'll go to see my grandfather."

It had been a couple of days since they had seen him last. It would be too hot for them to take him out. He would need to stay in the cool of his apartment. But they could have a nice visit there. When the weather cooled off, they could make him some more bannock. Until then, she wasn't using anything other than the microwave to heat their meals.

"It's nice to have a grandfather in town!" Cruz's voice held a smile. "I would have to take my kids back to the Philippines to see their grandparents. Not something we can afford to do very often."

"Can they Skype?"

"When my brother goes to my parents' house, he takes his iPad so that they can talk to the kids. My wife's parents don't have anyone to help them out with technology, so we don't see them very often. Sometimes if they have to go into the city, there is a room in the library where they can connect." He shook his head. "Not the same as having someone in town that you can talk to face to face."

"He lives just a few blocks from us so we can go see him often."

"Nice. I bet he really looks forward to seeing you."

Margie's car's air conditioner was just starting to blow cold air when she got back to the house. She sat there for a moment in the parked car, just enjoying the cool air. But then she turned it off. She didn't want to overheat the engine, and she didn't want to get used to a colder temperature and then deal with being hotter again. She went into the house.

"I'm home!"

Stella, usually exuberant when one of her people returned home, let out a couple of barks but didn't get up from where she was lying in Margie's room.

"Hi, Mom. We're in here."

Margie found Christina lying on the bed just where Margie had imagined her, in shorts and a halter top. Her black hair, which she sometimes wore loose, was braided to keep it off her neck and back.

"Sorry to be away so long." Margie petted Stella and scratched her ears. "How are you guys managing?"

"It's hot."

"No kidding."

"It's *really* hot."

"I know, honey. I wondered if you wanted to go visit Moushoom."

Christina perked up. "Yes! It's way cooler there than it is here. And I want to see him. That's not second, it just came out in that order."

"Okay, why don't you go get ready, and we'll pop over there?"

"I just need to get some sandals on."

Margie looked at Christina, carefully considering her response.

"What?" Christina demanded. She sat up and looked down at herself. "I'm dressed. I'm clean. Hair done. I'm ready to go."

"Maybe something more appropriate for visiting your grandfather?"

Christina stared back at her. "What is not appropriate?"

"I'm just thinking of something that covers a little more skin."

"That will be too hot."

"It's up to you…" Margie didn't want a fight over it. She knew that Moushoom wouldn't criticize Christina for the way she was dressed, no matter what he thought of it. "It just might make everyone more comfortable."

Christina looked down at her cleavage and shrugged. "I don't see what's wrong with it." She got off the bed and used both hands to pull the hem of her shorts down an inch, but they still showed off much more of her long, brown legs than Margie was comfortable with. But what of it? They covered more than a bikini would have.

Margie just smiled and nodded at Christina, not making a big deal of it. "Okay, find your sandals, then, and we'll head out. Are you hydrated?"

The teen rolled her eyes. "Yes, Mom. I've had plenty to drink."

"Not just coffee, right? Because that's dehydrating. I don't want you getting sick."

"We're only walking like three blocks. We'll stay in the shade. And it's cool at Moushoom's."

"Okay. I'm going to grab a water bottle for myself. You want one?"

Christina patted her leg to call Stella to her and gave Margie an annoyed look. "Yeah," she agreed finally. "Grab me one too." She sighed dramatically.

Margie went to the kitchen and grabbed a couple of water bottles from the bottom of the fridge. She knew she should be using a filter and refillable bottles instead of the cases of bottles that she had picked up at the grocery store, but it had been more convenient to just grab the flat. It was bad for the environment, and she should be doing more to take care of Mother Earth.

Christina snapped the leash onto Stella's collar and slid her feet into her sandals, and they were off.

CHAPTER EIGHT

Moushoom's room was cool compared with the temperatures outside and at Margie's house. Warmer than she would have kept it if she had central air conditioning, but older people were often cold, so she imagined that was why it was as warm as it was. She was relieved, at any rate, that everything was working as it should. She always worried about the elderly in extreme temperatures. Without fail, whenever they had extreme hot or cold snaps, elderly people died.

But those were mostly people living by themselves or on the street. Not people in care centers like Moushoom. If they had problems with the air conditioning, they would have someone in right away to fix it. They would let Margie know if there were any concerns about her grandfather's health or their ability to provide for his needs.

At least, she hoped so.

There were other family members in town, but Margie was the closest to him, both by blood and distance-wise, and the others had been happy to put her name down as his emergency contact once she had moved in.

She'd heard horror stories about the conditions in care centers, especially at the beginning of the COVID crisis. People living in filth and without the necessities, alone and isolated, bodies piling up too fast to be dealt with. She'd been relieved when she moved to Calgary and found Moushoom in a clean, neat, well-ventilated room with diligent caregivers close at hand, an emergency alarm on his wrist, and allowed visitors if they were masked and sanitized.

"There are my girls," Moushoom said with pleasure, a big smile on his face.

Margie's heart felt as if it would burst. She loved him so much and had only been able to see him once or twice a year when she had lived in Winnipeg. Now that they were close at hand, they were making up for lost time.

"Hello, Moushoom!" Margie bent down to give him a hug around his thin shoulders. She remembered Hungry Bear's grandmother, how old and wizened she was. But still so strong. It had taken a strong will for the past generations to survive and go on to raise their families, despite the best efforts of the government to stamp out the traditional ways. She could see that strength in the survivors. "How are you feeling today?"

"I am ready to go for a walk."

"I'm sorry… it's still too hot out. It's supposed to cool down on the weekend, and then we'll go out."

"A little warm weather never hurt anyone."

"These temperatures do. We have had several deaths. I'm not risking losing you."

Moushoom scowled, but then turned it off and spoke to Christina. "And where is my hug?"

Christina was happy to give him one. Margie could see that Moushoom was not really angry or upset. He had expected her answer. As soon as the weather broke, they would take him out again.

Margie brought over chairs and she and Christina sat down close to Moushoom to talk.

❧

THERE WERE FIREWORKS AT ELEVEN. Margie stepped outside for a moment to watch them, then she went back into the house. The house was holding on to the heat of the day. The temperature outside had finally dropped to the high twenties instead of high thirties. Margie's bedroom was the only room that was reasonably comfortable, so that was where they were hanging out.

"Do you want another movie?" Christina suggested, tapping her iPad.

"No. I need to get to sleep. I have work tomorrow, and it will be busy with this new case."

"Can I watch it still if I put on headphones?"

"Sure."

Margie dropped off to sleep more quickly than she had expected to. Her brain was whirling with thoughts of Hungry Bear and his family and where the case would lead. But she'd been up early for her run, and it had been a hot, busy day, so her body took charge, and she was soon off to sleep.

A crash woke her a few hours later and, disoriented, Margie thought at first that it was more fireworks, then maybe a truck crashing into the house, and, finally, logic reasserting itself, she realized that it was thunder. The loudest, most aggressive thunder she had ever heard. And she had seen some storms in Winnipeg.

"What was that?" Christina grasped at Margie. "Are you okay?"

"It's okay. Just thunder."

"Thunder?" Christina's hand worked its way up Margie's arm and shoulder and touched her face. Christina leaned in close in order to see her. "I thought you got shot!"

"Oh, baby." Margie pulled away from Christina to turn on the bedside lamp, then returned to her previous position and cuddled Christina to her again. "I'm just fine. It was only thunder. Maybe you had a dream to go with it."

"Yeah." Christina's eyes searched Margie's face and then did a quick scan of the rest of her body. Apparently convinced that Margie was telling the truth and she had not been shot, Christina relaxed and put her head against Margie's. "Yeah, just a dream. That was really loud."

Stella whined, squeezed up against Christina's other side. She wasn't supposed to be on the bed, but neither of them tried to tell her that. They lay there watching the startlingly-bright flashes of lightening and listening to repeated peals of thunder. After a few minutes, it stopped. Margie waited for the rain, but not a drop fell.

"I guess that's it for tonight," she told Christina. "Just nature's way of showing up the fireworks."

Christina giggled. "Yeah. *I'll* show you a light show."

"Are you okay? I'll turn off the light and we can go back to sleep."

"I'm fine." The girl yawned, and Margie found herself doing the same. Back to sleep, then; she would need to be up for work in a few more hours.

CHAPTER NINE

$\mathcal{M}$argie was in the bullpen early, reading through the reports in her email and jotting down notes for the squad's stand-up meeting, where she would be expected to report on the progress in the Hungry Bear case.

There was always a certain level of stress, anxiety, and energy in the room when they had a new case. Although it could take months or even years to clear a homicide file, they all knew that the progress they made in the first couple of days was vital.

But there seemed to be something different about this case. The Hungry Bear death seemed to have affected people differently. Maybe it was just the holiday. People had taken the Thursday off to be with their families, and then had to come back in on a Friday to deal with a death that, in all likelihood, would be cleared as an accident within a few days. Maybe they just didn't feel like getting into it.

Margie nodded to Katelyn Jones as she came in, to Cruz, and to the others on the team who walked by her desk and gave her a smile, nod, or thumbs-up. Margie's initial worries over being accepted by the team when she had first moved to Calgary had mostly faded. They were all willing to work with her and treated her pretty much like any other member of the team, but Margie worried that there were still some reservations. People were still watching to see how she would act at annual review time, when salary increases or promotions came down, the first time she used her gender or her cultural heritage to get special treatment. It was ingrained. Most of them were probably not even aware of the biases they held.

"Let's go," Mac called out as he left his office and headed to the conference room for the morning meeting. Margie glanced at the system clock on her computer. He was five minutes early.

Could she safely take the last five minutes of time to prepare? Or did she need to stop what she was doing and give her report, feeling rushed and not quite fully prepped?

She decided that being seen as arriving late would be a bigger blot on how she was perceived, even though she wasn't actually late. She could go ahead with the points that she had, and answer anything additional with an "I don't yet have that information."

Five minutes more preparation wasn't going to make that much of a difference.

"Ready to go?" Mac asked, the moment Margie stepped up to the table and set down her papers.

She had never known him to be so impatient. "Yes, sir."

"Let's start with your new case."

Margie nodded. She glanced around at the attendees. There would be a few stragglers. The team wasn't used to Mac jumping the gun like that.

"I think everybody already knows the basics. The body of Bruce Hungry Bear was discovered in Valleyview Park by a runner—myself—yesterday morning. He had clearly been dead and in the water for a few hours. No attempts at resuscitation were made. Dr. Galt attended on behalf of the Medical Examiner's office. He made a cursory investigation at the scene and brought the body back for further examination. I attended at the morgue early this morning, and the preliminary report showed…" Margie took a deep breath, bracing herself for their reactions. "Hungry Bear died from a blow to the head, not drowning."

"Really?" Jones blurted. She blushed slightly, a charming shade of pink that set off her blond, wavy hair. She grimaced and shook her head, not happy being the first one to ask for more details. "So…how does that play out? He was in the water when you found him."

"Yes," Margie confirmed. "But during the autopsy they found that he did not have water in his lungs. He didn't drown."

"Was he in the water when he died? Like he was walking over slippery rocks, and he fell and hit his head and died in the water without breathing it in?"

"There are drag marks on his knees and shins."

The room was silent, as if everyone were holding his breath. Margie was holding hers for sure. She waited, looking around at all their faces. She knew what they had all thought to begin with. That Hungry Bear had just been a drunk who had happened to fall into the water and drown. But that was not what had happened. No matter what anyone had thought, that had been an incorrect assumption, and they had begun the investigation with that bias.

MacDonald's face was stern, almost angry. "This was supposed to be an accidental death."

"But it wasn't."

"The Stampede starts in one week. We have delegates coming in from out of town. We need this to go away."

Margie shook her head. "Why would anyone coming from out of town be concerned with it?"

"We missed the Stampede last year due to COVID. For the first time ever. That lost the city a lot of revenue. This year, the border is still closed, so it is only Canadian tourists. They need to at least recover costs. And if people are hearing about a homicide instead of the grandstand show…"

The rodeo, fair, exhibits, and musical performances of the Stampede were a big deal to Calgarians and, as Mac said, brought in a lot of revenue.

"I don't see what this has to do with people going to the Stampede. It isn't as though we have a serial killer attacking tourists, or someone threatening to bomb the events. One suspicious death has nothing to do with the Stampede or tourists."

"There has been a lot of… negative news lately. I've already been called by several different offices requesting that we keep this out of the news except to say that it has been cleared and there is no danger to anyone visiting or living in the city."

A lot of negative news lately. That would be the graves at the residential schools, along with calls to cancel Canada Day. Celebrations had been canceled in several municipalities, but Calgary had chosen to go ahead with theirs, paying some lip service to the tribal elders and saying that the fireworks would be in memory of the children who had died.

Margie had never attended a memorial service or vigil with fireworks.

"Did you see the news last night and this morning?" Detective Gagnon asked. "Ten Catholic churches vandalized in Calgary, statues of Queen Elizabeth and Queen Victoria and early explorers vandalized, knocked down all over Canada, even thrown into the harbor in Vancouver. And Calgary's masking bylaw still in place even though we are over 70% vaccinated." His voice was loud with frustration. He wasn't the only one who was frustrated. A lot of people who were promised that everything would be back to normal in July were not impressed that the requirement for masking had not been lifted.

Society had changed in the last year and a half. Maybe some things would never go back to the way they had been.

MacDonald nodded. "The fact that Hungry Bear was Aboriginal will play big in the news. It's going to be connected to all this other genocide stuff, even though there is no connection. And with a name like Hungry Bear, everyone will know that he was an Ind—Native person. We really need to clear it quietly. Before the Stampede parade."

Which, Margie knew, was a week away. Homicides weren't cleared that fast. It would barely be enough time for the ME to declare the manner and cause of death. If it was murder, a week's investigation was not going to put it to bed.

"With all due respect, sir... I don't think that's possible."

"I need you to be behind me on this. Whether you think it is possible or not, I need you to put all of your effort into it. Make sure that it is *old news* by parade day."

Margie swallowed. She looked down at her notes, trying to

arrange her thoughts into bullet points. "Tox screen was negative for alcohol or street drugs."

"Maybe it was a wild animal," Jones suggested, playing devil's advocate. "There are animals over there, aren't there? Maybe it was a coyote attack. An animal could have dragged him."

Margie gritted her teeth and pretended to consider it. "Definitely something to look into," she agreed. "But as there were no teeth marks on Hungry Bear, and it took two of us to pull him out of the water... I can't see a coyote being able to drag him anywhere. And why would it drag him into the water?"

Jones couldn't come up with an explanation. Crocodiles pulled people into the water, but there were no crocs in Calgary. They didn't have any large predators living in the pond. Margie briefly entertained the idea of informing the press that maybe they had a lake monster like Nessie or Ogopogo in Valleyview pond. But that probably would not go over well.

"Detective Cruz and I talked to Hungry Bear's roommates and his family yesterday. None of them were aware of any of the circumstances surrounding his death. The parents believe he was going to spend the evening with friends. I will be following up on that today. If we can get his phone logs, I can start identifying who he has been in contact with in the last week. Detective Cruz got some information off of his computer." She looked at Cruz for him to fill them in.

"I got a few names from his social apps," Cruz acknowledged. "It will start us off."

"Anything suspicious in his email?" Mac asked. "Any red flags?"

"No. Everything I saw was innocuous. Spam and shopping. I'm told," he glanced over at Margie, "that young folks these days don't use email."

MacDonald cleared his throat. "Right. Anything in his social apps, then?"

"It all looked pretty vanilla. No criminal activities that I could spot. No threats or cyberbullying. From what I can tell, he lived a pretty quiet life."

"Give me an update at the end of the day," Mac instructed. "I expect to see some progress. Detective Patenaude, would you stay after this meeting, please?"

Margie nodded. "Yes, sir."

They moved on to the other cases that were being actively investigated. Margie looked through her notes, but tried to keep focused on what the others were saying so that she would know the status of each case and if there were parts of the investigation that she could assist with.

CHAPTER TEN

In half an hour, they had touched on each of the active files, and Mac dismissed the group. They all headed back to their desks, leaving Mac and Margie to talk. Mac shut the door.

"I'm sorry things didn't go the way you expected," Margie said tentatively, wondering if this was a private dressing-down for not agreeing that the Hungry Bear death was an accident.

Mac nodded and waved the comment aside. "Not much we can do if the evidence points in another direction… but I'm sure this is a pretty simple case. Don't make it more complicated than it is."

And keep it out of the papers.

"No, sir. Of course not."

"I wanted to talk to you about the complaint you submitted on Oliver Symons."

"Oh." Margie nodded. She swallowed, trying to dispel the lump in her throat and butterflies in her stomach. "Yes, I was pretty shocked."

Mac looked at her and didn't say anything for a minute. "Well… I didn't find anything particularly shocking about it. I would have taken it as an off-the-cuff remark. A poor attempt at humor."

"You can't deny that it was racist."

He was silent.

"If you're concerned about people hearing that an Indigenous man was killed after hearing so much in the news focusing on Indigenous harms, then how do you think a comment like *this* from a municipal employee would play in the media?"

"I don't deny that it was inappropriate. But I think you're making too much about it. I want you to consider whether you really want to submit that report or not. Because I think… you don't want to."

"Why not? Because I should *take it?*"

"Because no harm was done. It wasn't aimed at you. It wasn't aimed at anyone who could be hurt by it. Yes, it was inappropriate. But it was gallows humor. It's just a stress relief valve."

Margie breathed in and out in long, slow breaths. "Number one, drawing attention to someone's ethnic or Indigenous name is a microaggression. An ethnic name is just as normal and valid as any white European name. Second, saying something negative about someone's ethnic name or mocking it is overt aggression and racism. Symons made fun of the name Hungry Bear. Third, by calling him Thirsty Bear, Symons implied that he was a drunk and that was why he had died. Knowing nothing about the man except for the fact that he had an Indigenous name, he made the assumption that he was a drunk. Hungry Bear didn't reek of alcohol. He wasn't carrying a flask. There was nothing to indicate that he was drunk or had died because of it."

"That's just because we had a death there previously due to someone intoxicated wandering into the pond. I understand what you're saying, but I think that filing an official complaint against the guy is taking it too far. Symons is a good forensics tech. He just needs to learn to watch his mouth."

"And maybe a reprimand will remind him to do that next time."

"I feel for the guy. You haven't been policing here very long and were never on a beat here, so you don't know what it's like. But most of a beat cop's contacts with the Native population are for drunk and disorderlies and domestics involving alcohol. That's fact, not bias. Alcoholism is rampant in that population. That's just the way it is here."

"Symons isn't a beat cop. He's just a racist. I'm fully aware of the alcoholism endemic in the Indigenous community. More so than you are. It doesn't excuse making assumptions and racist comments about victims of homicide or anyone else."

Mac held up his hands in surrender. "Fine. You're entitled to your opinion, and you're absolutely entitled to file a report on what you saw and heard. I just wanted to give you a heads-up and see if you wanted to rethink your decision. If you're determined to file it, then go ahead. I'll sign off on it."

Margie stared at him for a moment, then nodded. "Thank you, sir."

"Of course. And… if anyone on my team were to make similar remarks, I assume you will come directly to me."

Because he wanted to know about it and handle it immediately, or because he wanted the chance to bury it or talk her out of filing a report on a member of the homicide squad?

She chose to believe the best of MacDonald. If something happened, she would take it to him first. And if it wasn't dealt with, she would take it to Professional Standards.

∾

MARGIE'S CELL PHONE RANG. Sliding it out, she saw Christina's name and picture on the screen. She swiped to answer the call.

"Hi, honey."

"People suck!"

Margie laughed. "Well, yes, sometimes they do. What's wrong? What happened?"

"You know I've been bagging up all of the empty bottles for the fundraiser for residential school survivors?"

"Uh-huh?" Taking empty drink containers to the bottle depot earned them ten cents for small containers and twenty-five cents for anything over a liter. Christina had been diligently collecting all their cans and bottles and even discarded beer cans she found on the street, to donate for a fundraiser that would benefit IRSSS, the Indian Residential School Survivors Society.

"I was going to put them in the shed, so I had them out in the back yard…"

"Yeah?"

"And somebody stole them! Somebody walked right into our yard and stole my bags of bottles!"

"Oh, honey. No! I'm sorry about that!"

"I can't believe they would do that! It isn't like I put them in the lane with the garbage bins. They were right in our yard. I was just going to take them all the way to the shed later, after I dressed."

"How many did you have?"

"Five bags. And I was going to go around the neighborhood and see if I could get some other people to donate their bottles too. Why would somebody do that?"

"Well… hopefully it was somebody who really needed the money. But I'm sorry. You've been so good about making sure nothing gets thrown out or recycled if we can get a deposit on it."

"People just suck," Christina repeated. "That's all there is to it."

CHAPTER ELEVEN

Margie started with the names that Cruz had pulled off of Hungry Bear's social networks and ran some initial background checks against them. They were not criminals. Any priors were for teenage hijinks, moving violations, that kind of thing. No drug dealing or violence or human trafficking. All pretty clean. A look at their social networks—not Facebook, because again, young people had moved away from Facebook when their parents had started getting accounts—showed that they were all pretty wrapped up in themselves. No hint of anything unsavory. Gaming, parties, pictures of products they were selling or closets they had dejunked, some family shots with extended family members. None of them appeared to have children of their own yet. Some mentioned their jobs, but most had no means of support that could be gleaned from the social network feeds.

Margie started making phone calls, and immediately discovered that the friends knew something was up. Maybe Hungry Bear's mother had known who her son had been going to see after all, or maybe she had just called a couple of friends that she remembered from his high school days and they had spread the word. Or maybe they had missed him, but had heard of the body discovered in the park and put it together.

"Could we all get together to meet with you?" the girl named Kennedy asked. "I mean… he was with all of us on Wednesday night, and… I'm not really comfortable talking to you alone. It would be more efficient for you to talk to us all together, wouldn't it?"

Margie grimaced. "Well, it is really better if we can talk to you separately. It is easier for us to find out what each individual knows that way."

Easier to spot discrepancies in their stories. To ask one what they thought of the other. To make sure that they weren't covering for each other.

"Well… could you anyway? I mean, none of us really know anything. And I wouldn't want to come in myself. That's just so…" Margie could practically hear her shudder. "It's like TV or something. I can't believe… I don't want to believe that anything happened to Bruce. I want to help, but I just can't. I can't do it on my own. You should come and talk to all of us at once. I'll even set it up for my house. That's how much I want to help."

"I appreciate that." Jones looked up from her work and Margie rolled her eyes at her. "I can come to you, of course, and if you'd be more comfortable with someone else there… but maybe we could limit the numbers…"

She hoped that the young woman's mother would not be there, helicoptering around her, trying to ensure that the police did not do anything to upset her child.

Jones responded with an eye roll of her own, acknowledging Margie's opinion. Margie did her best to get the meeting set up with Kennedy, who promised to call back once she had a time nailed down with her friends. Then they could all get together.

It could be a ploy, designed to put Margie off. Say that they were going to arrange it, and then never settle on a time. They would keep telling Margie, "Don't call us, we'll call you," or whatever the modern equivalent was. "I'll message you. Promise."

After hanging up with Kennedy, Margie turned her attention to the files in the workspace that had been set up for the case. She had already at least skimmed all the written reports, her own among them. Just to make sure that it was complete and that she hadn't already forgotten any of the details of the scene. It was a bit different being a witness as well as the primary investigator. Homicide detectives did not normally go around finding bodies themselves.

The photography was another story. Margie was familiar with the park and had seen everything that was there to see, so she hadn't bothered to spend much time on the pictures. But it was time to remedy that. She might have missed a clue with adrenaline pumping from her discovery, a little tired from the first half of her run, trying to preserve the evidence and keep people back from the scene before she had any way to rope off a perimeter.

There were a few establishing shots of the park, showing a pulled-back view of the pathway, pond, and the area around it. Similar to what Margie was used to seeing when she went to the park, either with Stella or on her own as part of her new morning run routine. Similar to the pictures that she took when the sky was still pink or the water was particularly glassy and clear.

The next pictures, though, were far different from any that she had taken. Hungry Bear's body where she and the bystander had pulled him up out of the water. Still stomach down because that was the way they had pulled him out. Close-ups of any mark or foreign object on his clothing. Pictures of the bruise on his head. Hungry Bear's bloated face.

Then more shots after he had been taken away. The pond, anything they found on the ground that might have had something to do with his death. Shots of the bystanders and of Margie herself, standing there talking to Cruz.

Margie wrote down a couple of pictures that she wanted to print or review over again later. The next set of photos was for the garbage excavations. The techs had emptied each of the garbage bins in the area Margie had indicated. She was sure they were just delighted with her suggestion that each needed to be checked. Especially considering the fact that they had found nothing of interest. No bloody bludgeon. No bottles of alcohol. No nasty notes about how Hungry Bear needed to be killed.

There were 7-Eleven bags and Tim's coffee cups. Chip bags and half-eaten muffins. And lots of dog poop bags. The park was well used.

"Sorry guys," Margie muttered to herself. She was not sorry that she had not been personally involved in excavating the bins one layer at a time, pulling out all those doggie doo bags. Some of the 7-Eleven bags had been used to pick up poop too, only it wasn't obvious until the techs uncrumpled the bags and spread them out. What a job.

She skimmed through the garbage pictures quickly. She wasn't expecting to find anything in the garbages related to the investigation, but one never knew. Canadians were well-known for their manners, and leaving a murder weapon or other evidence on the grass or in the water would have been very rude.

The techs had also itemized the contents of each of the bins, and each bin was marked on a map so that Margie could see where each had come from. She looked through the itemized lists for anything sinister.

Baby wipes and diapers. There were a few needles in addition to the other crap. Needles that should have been properly disposed of in a sharps box. They didn't need the techs getting stabbed while they were working.

Broken toys. Shoes. Teddy bears. Margie frowned, wondering if a neighbor's memorial to the dead residential school children had been stolen and thrown in the garbage.

&

THE PHONE RANG. Margie was so deep into her notes that it made her jump. She took a breath, finished the sentence she was writing so she wouldn't lose her thought, and looked at the caller display. Kennedy Johnston, the young woman who she had been talking to earlier.

Margie hadn't expected to hear from her again so quickly. She figured they would be exchanging phone messages back and forth for a few days, with both of them trying to find a time that would work for everyone.

"Detective Patenaude."

"Oh, hi… this is Kennedy? We were talking earlier about Bruce?"

"Yes, I remember, Kennedy. Have you already been able to set something up?"

"Uh, yeah, actually. Would you be able to come to my place this afternoon?"

"I'll make the time. What is your address and what time should I be there?"

Kennedy gave her the pertinent details, stammered a little about seeing Margie later, and hung up.

Detective Cruz had been good with Hungry Bear's roommates and family, but he was busy on his own cases, and Margie asked Jones whether she would be able to attend the interview with her. They had worked well together on other cases and Margie wanted Jones fully onside with the fact that it was not a case of accidental drowning. The evidence said that it could not be.

"Sure, I could do that," Jones agreed pleasantly, looking at her computer screen for her schedule. "I don't have anything I absolutely have to be here for."

"I'd really appreciate it. I know it's out of your way and it's not your case…"

"They are all everyone's cases. We're not going to get them cleared without everyone helping out."

Margie nodded. The homicide team was very good that way, but she still wanted to be careful not to impose on the others or to imply that her case was any more important than anyone else's. The Hungry Bear case was starting to get hot politically. They had all heard Mac say that he wanted it cleared within a week. It probably wasn't possible, but Margie needed to be able to show that she had used every resource within her reach to do so. Including human capital.

She gave Jones the details of where and when, and the blond nodded agreeably. "That gives me half an hour to clear my desk. I'll just tie up a couple of loose ends here and make sure that I'm ready to go."

CHAPTER TWELVE

o you know exactly where this is?" Jones asked, peering out the window and studying the street signs.

"Well… not exactly. I looked at it on the map before we left, but I don't remember the exact turns. I think it's… over there?" she gestured to the right. A guess. Her phone was clearly being affected by the clouds gathering overhead and was rethinking the route.

"I think it's one of these backward lots," Jones said.

"Backward lots?"

"These ones," Jones gestured toward one of the alleys. "The fronts face onto green space and a shared multiuse trail. The backs are the only way to get to them by car; you have to go through the alleys to make deliveries or to interview someone."

Margie turned into the alley, reading the street sign as she went by it. The alley was, in fact, the street. But it was still full of garbage bins and broken-down cars and falling-down fences. It hadn't been made more presentable because it was the only way visitors could access the houses.

There were numbers on some of the fences, but not all of them. Margie shook her head in irritation. There was a bylaw that people had to have their house numbers in the back for law enforcement, first responders, and garbage collection. But a lot of people didn't know or didn't care about the requirement.

"If we're on the right street, it could be this one," Jones gestured to a house squashed away in the corner.

The GPS program on Margie's phone suddenly sprang to life, blitzing through several screens too fast to follow, showing a few different routes with the turns mapped out, and then finally settling on a picture of her car on the map and a blue dot representing her destination right on top of the corner house Jones had indicated.

Margie eased the car forward until she was as close as she wanted to get to the garbage and the decrepit fence that might blow over onto her car at any moment. She turned on her police flashers to deter thieves and busybodies, and they got out of the car and put on their masks.

"What a junkyard," Margie said, looking around.

"I know. But that's what it's like in the poorer neighborhoods. They don't have the money to have stuff hauled or to pay the disposal fees at the dump. They've got three cars in hopes of being able to get one running. And it's probably like Hungry Bear's house, with several people sharing the rent or mortgage."

Margie nodded. She'd seen it all before. It wasn't anything new. But she always felt bad when she saw neighborhoods like that. Bad that the people were so down on their luck and bad that everyone else had to look at it. The little house in Dover was only a kilometer or two from Margie's own house in Southview. Margie's area had definitely been kept up better, but that didn't mean the people in Dover were lazy. Just that they didn't make as much money.

There was a cord tied around the gate post that they had to untangle in order to open the gate and get into the yard. Margie looked for a "Beware of Dog" sign, but there wasn't anything to indicate that they might be attacked the instant they opened the gate. She could hear dogs barking nearby. Hopefully, they were caged or chained, wherever they were.

Margie had been bitten a couple of times in Winnipeg. Luckily, in both cases she had been able to find the owner and to confirm that the dog's vaccinations, including rabies shots, were up to date, which meant that she'd been able to avoid having to get shots of her own. But she wasn't eager for a repeat of the experience.

Eventually, Jones worked the cord loose and opened the gate. They walked through it and pulled it shut behind them, wrapping the string loosely around the post so it would be easier to get back out.

It felt like an invasion to walk in through someone's back yard and approach the back door. Different from when it was a friend and she just knocked on the kitchen door and went in.

Kennedy was apparently watching for them and opened the door as they approached.

"Hey. Hi. I'm Kennedy."

She held her hand out tentatively. Margie glanced over at Jones, then back at Kennedy. "I'm sorry, we're not supposed to shake. Department policy. So many police officers got sick at the beginning of COVID..."

Kennedy shrugged and withdrew her hand. "We're supposed to be back to normal now. Fully open. I know Calgary still has to cancel their mask bylaw, but this isn't a public place; it's my home. You don't have to wear them."

"It is still recommended by CPS. It's for your protection as well as ours."

"I'm vaccinated. I don't care."

Margie nodded agreeably. "So, are the others here?" she asked, prompting a subject change. She had learned not to argue hygiene measures with civilians. It never got anywhere, and people just got hot under the collar. It was hot enough without throwing irritated, opinionated people into the mix. Thinking about the temperature, Margie ran a finger around her collar. It was cooler than Canada Day had been, and it looked as though it might start storming any minute, but it was still 27 degrees.

"Yeah, come in," Kennedy agreed. She turned around and led the way into the house. Margie followed close behind her, with Jones bringing up the rear. Margie looked around alertly for anything that was out of place. There was a danger that came with walking into someone's house, into their territory, where they might feel the need to protect themselves, where they could lay a trap or just happen to have a firearm hidden somewhere close when things got emotional.

The house was somewhat untidy, but not a hovel. Cleaner than Hungry Bear's house had been. Tidier than the junk outside had suggested. Kennedy apparently did take some pride in her house.

"We're meeting in the game room downstairs," Kennedy led them to a stairway that led down from the kitchen. "It's a lot cooler down there."

It was. Margie could feel the chill as she walked down the stairs. They had left their shoes on, but she was sure if she hadn't, the floor would have been icy through her socks. Tile over concrete.

The basement was mostly the game room, which included a wet bar. There was a sliding pocket door to one side that Margie assumed was a washroom. Most of the room was empty, with some folding tables against the wall that were normally used for whatever games they played together. Role playing games, Margie guessed by the posters on the wall. She had never gotten into them, and neither had Christina, but they both knew people who were heavily into D&D and other games.

There were several other members of the group of friends waiting, sitting in chairs around the room. Margie and Jones were apparently the last to the party.

"Okay, so this is Alex, Evander, Roger, and Susan. And I'm Kennedy," she added, in case they didn't remember from the phone calls and the introduction upstairs.

"It's good to meet you," Margie said to the group.

"You want to sit down?" Kennedy pushed a couple of folding chairs in their direction.

After considering for a moment, Margie took one of them and sat down. It would be easier to talk to them on their own level. She wanted them to feel comfortable, as if it were a friendly conversation, rather than feeling threatened by a police interrogation. Jones followed her lead and sat down. Margie saw the slight movement as she readjusted her concealed holster to make herself more comfortable.

"So… I guess I'll start with whether you have any questions for me," Margie said. "I gather from talking to you on the phone that you know the sad news about your friend Bruce."

Kennedy shook her head. "I can't quite believe it. I mean… are you sure? I couldn't get him on the phone, but I never thought that something *serious* had happened. He was just here Wednesday night. How could something have happened to him in that short period of time?"

"I know. It's quite a shock, and it takes time to adjust to the idea. I'll just confirm what his family probably already told you…" Margie waited for some sort of indication that it had been Bruce's family who had told Kennedy and the other friends Bruce was dead. They looked at each other, but no one offered anything by way of explanation. "Yeah. So Bruce's body was found early yesterday morning. You know where Valleyview park is?"

They all nodded. "Of course we do," Kennedy said, rolling her eyes. "It's just over there." She made a movement to indicate one direction. Margie was too turned around to know whether she was right or not. She had to assume that Kennedy knew what she was talking about. They lived in the neighborhood; of course they knew where the park was.

"It was… in the water. Bruce was dead." Again, taking care not to use euphemisms that might confuse things and leave the friends thinking that Bruce was just hurt or traumatized rather than deceased.

"What happened to him?" the other woman asked. Susan. Kennedy was blond, Susan had dark brown hair. Poker straight.

"We are still investigating the cause of death," Margie said, giving nothing away. Hold back. Always best to hold back and see if people gave themselves away by knowing details that they had not been given.

"It just doesn't make sense," said the slight, dark-haired man who Margie thought was Evander. She hadn't had time to anchor the names to the people yet.

"It's Evander?" she checked.

They all shook their heads. "I'm Alex," the man corrected. "So what happened to him? I mean, he was playing here, it was getting late; he left to walk home. It isn't that far, just a few blocks. He should have been home in ten minutes."

"Alex. I am sorry for your loss. I understand it must all be very confusing right now. Maybe if I could ask you some questions, I would have a better idea of how things happened. It will help to set the stage."

Alex frowned, irritated by her non-answer. She had asked them if they had any questions, and then she hadn't answered his.

"Just like I said," he snapped. "We were playing games until late. Here." He raised both hands to indicate the expanse of the room. "Like we always do. No different from usual."

"Were you drinking?"

"There were drinks," Alex said a little belligerently. The others looked at each other.

"Some of us were drinking and some not. No one was drunk. We just like to do a little social drinking when we're doing our thing." This explanation came from Susan. She had a straightforward, matter-of-fact manner. Telling it like it was. Margie decided to dig a little deeper.

"Was Bruce drinking?"

Susan shook her head, eyes widening slightly. She looked around at the rest of the group. "Bruce didn't drink anymore. He was out of the closet."

Margie frowned and tried to reconcile this declaration with the rest of the conversation.

"On the wagon," one of the boys corrected. "He was never *in* the closet."

Margie smiled, understanding the mistake. Bruce hadn't come out as gay; he had stopped drinking.

"Is there a reason for that? Has he had troubles in the past?"

"No."

"He had," Alex said. "A few years back."

Susan shook her head adamantly. "No, not Bruce…"

"It was before you were around."

Susan looked at the others, who nodded. She still didn't look as though she believed this fact, but she shrugged. "Whatever. He wasn't drinking Wednesday. I've never seen him drink."

"I see. Could he have been on anything else?"

They all looked at Margie blankly.

"Drugs?" Margie said. "Maybe some weed?"

"No. Why are you asking these questions?"

"I just want to be sure that we have all the facts," Margie assured them. "A death like this… sometimes alcohol or another drug is involved."

"He hadn't been drinking or using drugs that night," Kennedy said firmly. "Not ever. Alex is right. After the trouble he had a few years back, he got into a program. Cleaned up his act. Even though we usually had booze around these meetings, he never had any. Just kept to soft drinks. We used to joke that he was the designated driver."

"Why is that a joke?" Jones asked. "He didn't drive?"

"No. He was close by; he just walked home. Everyone either stayed here overnight or walked. None of us ever drove drunk."

"Ah. That's wise. The rest of you stayed here?"

"Yeah, the rest of us did."

"Who was drinking and who wasn't?"

Walls went up. No one wanted to be judged for being a drinker. The non-drinkers didn't seem particularly interested in declaring themselves either. Margie shrugged and took over again.

"That's fine. We don't care either way. We're just trying to build a picture. Everything that happened Wednesday night. Do you usually party on a Wednesday?"

"No, we don't usually *game* on a Wednesday night," Evander corrected. "It wasn't a party. Just a game night. And usually, people have work Thursday. But because of Canada Day, we didn't. We didn't have to get up Thursday morning. We were going to play some more in the afternoon."

"You were going to? But you didn't end up doing it?"

"No." Kennedy spoke up. "Bruce was supposed to come back over, but he didn't. And we didn't feel like starting on our own and then being interrupted an hour later when he decided to show up. We called him… kept getting his voicemail."

"And I wasn't feeling well," Susan contributed. "I had a killer headache from *the heat* and couldn't play a game. So we just kind of hung out. Watched some Netflix, had a few drinks. Tried to stay cool."

Margie assumed Susan was one of those who had been drinking. She didn't want to admit that she'd woken up hung over, so it was the heat rather than the drink. The two combined could be a pretty potent combination. People got dehydrated faster, woke up sicker.

"Can you believe the heat?" Margie asked rhetorically.

Most of them nodded and made comments about just how hot it had been. Record breaking.

"It's a good thing you have this basement," Margie said. "It's really nice and cool down here."

Various nods of agreement, declarations that it was too hot to do anything but play games in the basement.

"So… how did Bruce seem Wednesday night?"

CHAPTER THIRTEEN

The friends all looked at each other. Margie wished that she had been able to convince them to do their interviews separately. So that they weren't all just giving the party line, making sure that each account fit with the others.

"He seemed fine to me," said Roger, who had been quiet until then. "He'd had dinner over at his mom's. He was chill, didn't act like he'd had a fight with them or anything."

"Did he usually have fights with them?"

"No." Roger shrugged. "But some people do. People aren't always cool meeting with their parents. Bruce liked his okay. Had disagreements sometimes, but he didn't get really worked up about them."

The others nodded.

"He wasn't upset about anything?" Margie tried.

There was a hiccup of silence. Everybody quiet for just a moment too long, looking at each other, weighing their answers.

"So, he *was* upset?" Margie suggested.

"What's to be upset about?" Kennedy asked. "It was a holiday. He had a nice dinner with his parents. Was having a nice time playing with friends. No worries about work the next day or anything. Just vibing with friends."

"That doesn't mean that he had nothing to be upset about. Sometimes something that you wouldn't think was a big deal can tip someone over the edge."

They shook their heads, sticking to Roger's and Kennedy's stories. No, he wasn't upset about anything. Just hanging out.

Margie looked at Jones for a moment, letting her mind worry over the possibilities. Had Bruce had an argument or altercation with someone in the group? Or had it happened earlier when he'd been at his parents' house? What had been on his mind?

"Who won the game?" Jones asked.

"What?" Evander said blankly, then apparently remembered that they were supposed to have been playing a game that night. Maybe they hadn't had the time to get down to these details in the story? Why would a cop care about who won the game? "Oh… we didn't finish. We were going to finish on Canada Day. Pick up where we left off. Only… Bruce wouldn't answer his phone. He didn't come back. So we couldn't finish it."

"Was he mugged?" Susan asked. "Is that what happened? Somebody wanted his money?"

"He wasn't mugged," Alex told her. "They didn't say he was mugged. Just… that he died. It must have been an accident. Maybe… he tripped and fell into the pond?"

"Maybe," Margie said neutrally.

That started them off speculating, and Margie and Jones listened carefully to the various scenarios. He was mugged. He tripped. Someone pushed him in for no reason. A gang initiation thing. A dog or a wild animal scared him. They were creative; Margie had to give them that. From what she understood, role playing games involved a lot of storytelling. They were good at spitballing, coming up with some ideas that Margie hadn't considered. But they didn't match the forensics. And no one suggested it could have been intentional or that Bruce had been confronted by someone who knew him, who was angry at him for some reason. All of their suggestions involved strangers or accidents.

❦

"We would like to get your contact details," Margie told the group of friends as they prepared to leave. "In case I have any further questions or things that need to be cleared up." It was too late to get an untainted story. But maybe they would still be able to separate the truth from the lies and would be able to gradually pick apart the story the friends had woven, to get down to what had really happened when Bruce had left Kennedy's house that night.

As they climbed the stairs to the kitchen, there was a crack like a gunshot. Both Margie and Jones ducked and flattened themselves against the wall, looking around quickly for the shooter, evaluating escape routes and how to protect each other.

"Thunder," Kennedy said, laughing. "Sounds like the storm has hit."

They didn't immediately accept this explanation, looking up and down the stairs and listening for anyone moving toward them. Kennedy stood on the stairs looking down at them, amused. Back in the game room, they could hear the laughter of the friends, relieved that the police were leaving and also startled by the thunder. A bit giddy. They would be breaking out the drinks soon, Margie was sure.

There was a low rumble of thunder and another crack. Enough to reassure Margie that Kennedy was telling the truth. It was just the storm. They continued up the stairs. Before they reached the door, Margie could feel the fresh, wet air blowing in through the screen door. It was starting to rain, but not yet in earnest. As they stepped out the door, Jones looked worriedly up at the darkening sky. The temperature had dropped considerably and the wind was brisk.

"It's not going to be pretty," Jones predicted.

They got back into the car just before the hail started. Margie flinched every time a big piece of ice hit her windshield or side window. "Do you think… I should drive?" she asked Jones. "See if we can get out from under it?"

"No. We're kind of sheltered by the house and tree here. Try to drive through this and you might get your windows broken."

They sat in silence for a few minutes, watching the hail pour down around them and bounce off of the car and the roof covering the porch behind Kennedy's house. Some of the hailstones were as big as a nickel.

"Do you mind if I call Christina?" Margie asked, pulling out her phone.

"Of course, go ahead."

Margie tapped on Christina's name and listened to it ring.

"Mom?"

"Hi, honey. Just wanted to make sure you're okay."

"Wow, are you in this? What a storm! Stella is scared, but other than that, we're okay."

"No broken windows? I guess this will be the test as to whether the basement leaks."

"Yeah, everything is fine. I haven't checked the basement, but everything is fine up here."

"Good. We're close by; I just don't want to drive until the hail stops."

"Okay," Christina agreed cheerfully. "I wouldn't want to be driving in this either."

Christina had her learner's license, but tended to be a nervous driver. Margie made a mental note to herself that they needed to spend some more time practicing to boost Christina's confidence. And she needed to get the girl into a driver's ed class.

"She's good?" Jones asked.

Margie nodded. "She's good. I didn't know you got storms like this in Calgary."

"A few years ago, we had a series of big storms, and that combined with the meltwater from the mountains and poor reservoir management cause flooding all over the city. Pretty much the entire downtown was under water. We couldn't get into the office. A bunch of the riverbanks in Inglewood crumbled into the Bow. Do you know the train bridge you can see from the pathway between here and the zoo? From Pearce Estate or crossing the Deerfoot pedestrian bridge from Max Bell?"

Margie nodded slowly. She had seen the latticed bridge during her Google maps exploration of the pathways to downtown.

"The deck of that bridge was actually under water. Over by the zoo, it was up over the handrails along the pathways. They had to move some of the animals because the river was up over the banks and into the zoo."

"I think I remember seeing pictures of all of that." Margie could vaguely remember the story in the news. It had been some time before she considered moving to Calgary, so it hadn't really registered. She had been concerned about her family members in the area, of course, but everyone had been okay, and she hadn't thought more about it. There had been deaths, but no one she knew.

Eventually, the hail stopped and there was just rain.

"Think it's safe to go?" Margie asked.

Jones nodded. "Yeah. Let's give it a try. But be ready to pull over under a tree if it starts up again."

Margie pulled out and made a tight three-point turn to get out of the alley. Jones was tapping on her phone.

"Are you getting directions to get out of here and back to the office?" Margie asked.

Jones shook her head. "I know the way. I'm just looking at Twitter…"

Margie rolled her eyes. "Can you tell me which way to go, then…?"

Jones didn't look up from her phone. "Hmm… might not be the best idea to go back downtown. A lot of streets have flooded. They'll drain once the rain slows down, but if you drive into a flooded street, it will stall your car and wreck your engine."

"Is there another way we can go?"

"I wouldn't count on it. You're good up here on the hill, but if you go down any of the lower-lying streets you might end up in trouble…"

Margie was just creeping along the street, uncertain which way to go. Luckily, there were not many other cars on the move, and no one honked at her to speed up.

"Why don't we go back to your house until the water goes down?" Jones suggested. "If you don't mind me hanging out for a while. Once the rain stops and the streets drain, I can just catch the Max downtown."

The Max Purple bus route ran from Seventeenth Avenue to the downtown core pretty frequently, but Margie wouldn't want Jones to get stranded if the downtown were flooded and the bus had nowhere to go.

"We can go to my place," she agreed. "I'll drive you back once we know it's safe."

"We'll talk about it. Sorry about imposing myself on you."

"No, that's fine."

Jones raised her eyes to the road, then looked at Margie. "To your house, then."

"I don't know the way. I got turned around."

The other woman laughed. "You'll get it eventually," she promised. "Some neighborhoods are easier than others. It's nice when they are on the grid system, but all the new developments are full of cul-de-sacs. This area really isn't bad once you get used to it. Just confusing because of the backward houses."

She gave Margie directions until she hit Twenty-Sixth Street and recognized where she was. "There's the park," she pointed Valleyview out to Jones. "That's where Hungry Bear's body was."

Jones craned her neck, but couldn't see the pond because of the trees and hill that were in the way. She nodded. "Don't think I want to explore it in the rain."

"Yeah, I'd rather stay dry."

In a couple of minutes, they were back home. Margie went in first, tapping on the door and calling out to Christina. "I've got company," she announced. "Hide the drugs!"

She could hear Christina's laugh at the back of the house. Stella padded out to greet them, but was not her usual exuberant self. She whined at Margie and pushed her muzzle into Margie's hand for comfort. Margie scratched her ears and jowls and crooned to her that the storm would end soon and Stella would be all right.

Christina joined them. "Isn't it so nice? It finally cooled down!"

The breeze was blowing through all of the house's open windows, cooling the house down for the first time in a week.

"It is. You remember Detective Jones?"

"Kaitlyn," Jones corrected. She had stayed with them overnight when Margie and Christina had been in danger from a killer who had targeted them. So Christina and Jones were on a first name basis.

"It's good to see you again!" Christina greeted. "Are you going to stay for dinner?" She flashed a look at Margie that said, "And what are we going to make for her?"

"Oh, it will probably just be a few minutes. There's flooding, so I wanted to wait until the rain stops and the water goes down." Jones looked out the window. "Hopefully, the weather will break before long."

Margie looked at the ominous, swirling clouds. It didn't look to her like it would break in a few minutes.

"Yeah, we'd better get something on," she told Christina. "At least it's cooled down enough that we can use the oven!"

"Yeah." Christina brightened. "We can put a pizza in!"

"Good idea. And I'll make a salad to go along with it. Just so we can feel virtuous." She laughed.

"I really don't want to be any trouble," Jones protested.

"You're not. We have to eat anyway. We've been terrible this week, just eating junk food and sandwiches, because we don't want to heat up the house by actually cooking anything. A pizza will be a nice change."

"If you're doing it anyway. Just don't go out of your way for me. I'll just stay out of your way."

"It's nice to have company," Christina assured her. "It's just me and Mom all the time."

"You can actually have friends over now," Margie realized. "Now that the restrictions have been dropped."

Moving to Calgary during the COVID lock-down had not exactly been easy on Christina. She was naturally social, but she could only see her friends at school; they weren't allowed to go to each other's houses. Margie knew that a lot of the teens went shopping or did things outside together, but she'd tried to keep Christina close to home to minimize the chances of infection.

"Yeah!" Christina looked surprised. "I guess I can."

It occurred to Margie that Hungry Bear and his friends had been breaking the gathering rules, since it had only been June 30 when they had gotten together for their gaming night, and the restrictions hadn't been dropped until July 1. And from their conversation, she thought they had been meeting together regularly even before that.

It was no wonder infection rates had gotten so high.

CHAPTER FOURTEEN

They had eaten the pizza while looking at the pictures on Twitter and Facebook showing cars up to their windows in water and people canoeing or kayaking down their streets. Margie's throat got tight looking at all that water.

But by eight o'clock the storm had petered out. Jones called the police dispatcher to find a clear route back to her house, since it was too late to bother going back to the office. She directed Margie, and then helped her to set up the Maps app on her phone to take her back home by a safe route.

"If you run into any flooded streets, then stop. Don't drive into the water. Call me, and we'll figure out a different route."

"Okay." The way there had been clear, so Margie thought she would be fine, but had to admit to herself that she was still a little nervous. She didn't like water, and the thought of driving into a flooded street and being trapped in her car with the floodwaters rising around her sent her heart into wild contortions.

"It will be fine," Jones assured her.

"Yeah. I'm sure it will."

The other woman gave her a reassuring smile and pat on the shoulder. "Thanks for supper. That was a lot of fun."

"We'll have you over again. I really enjoyed it."

"We don't have to wait until the next storm. And I'll supply the dinner next time. It will be my treat."

Margie watched her walk into her apartment building and waited a few extra minutes just to make sure that she hadn't run into any trouble. Then she steeled herself and headed back for home.

SATURDAY MORNING, Margie got up early for her run. It was only supposed to get up to 27 degrees, but she wasn't counting on it. She didn't want to wait too late and be running in the heat of the day. It had stayed cool all night, so the house was comfortable and the temperature outside was cool, just right for a nice run.

She hesitated about going back to Valleyview, even though it was her usual route. Would everyone there look at her differently, now that they knew she was a police detective? Oscar certainly hadn't been impressed when he had discovered what it was that she did. And there were also Margie's worries that she would find something else unexpected in the park or have flashbacks. Of course she wouldn't actually find another body, but that was now her strongest association with the park. And what if it were flooded from the storm the previous night? It was part of the stormwater management system. What if the entire park was now covered with water? Then she wouldn't go in, of course. She'd just stick to the Twenty-Sixth Street pathway, which was at the top of the hill and would not be flooded.

It was best to confront any thoughts of anxiety or flashbacks head on. Face her fear right away, and it would not be able to settle in and take over her life. If she avoided the area, the fear would just grow and become more entrenched. She would have a big hole in the middle of the neighborhood, an area that she could not go to. It was a great place for walks, runs, and throwing the Frisbee for Stella, and she would not let it become a place she had to avoid.

So she forced herself to cross Twenty-Sixth Street and enter the park. It was a little strange to see it empty again after having been filled with police cars and vans and all of the investigating team and spectators two days before. It was as if nothing had changed, yet everything had changed in her own mind.

Margie made one loop around the pond, watching the ducks and red-winged blackbirds and looking for the muskrat. The muskrat did not put in an appearance. Across the field, a group of gulls was congregating, mostly black-headed Franklin's gulls, which she hadn't seen much of in Calgary. She hadn't noticed any in Valleyview park before.

There was an older couple walking around the pathway together at a leisurely pace. The man had a long grabber tool that he used to reach over the short chain-link fence to the splash park—which was still padlocked early in the morning—to snag pieces of litter and put them into a shopping bag that hung on his other wrist. They strolled along, picking up trash along the way. It was no wonder the park was normally so pristine. Margie smiled and nodded as she went by them. She didn't stop and give them a chance to realize that she had been there on Canada Day and had been the one to find the body.

She looked around for the other couple, the two who had been out walking their dogs. The man who had helped her to pull Hungry Bear's body out of the water. But she didn't see them. Maybe they didn't walk there every day or were on a different schedule on the weekend. She was sure she would see them again at some point.

Margie stopped for a quick swig of water, then pushed herself to run faster around the long pathway, then back across Twenty-Sixth Street to head home.

&

SHE WASN'T SCHEDULED to work on Saturday, but she headed downtown anyway. She wanted to transcribe all of her notes from the interview with Hungry Bear's gaming friends while it was still fresh in her mind. She was also determined to go through all the reports and photos one more time. And maybe she could start making individual calls to the friends to see if she could shake anything loose.

As much as she tried to make Hungry Bear's death fit the scenario for a mugging or gang activity, it just didn't fit the pattern. He'd had a wallet on him but no cash, it was true, but fewer and fewer people carried cash anymore, especially since the pandemic had hit and people had been encouraged to tap rather than handling cash or using the touch pad, reducing the number of times a point-of-sale machine had to be wiped down. If he'd been mugged, the thief would have just snatched Hungry Bear's wallet and phone, he wouldn't have asked for his cash and let him keep the rest.

And gang violence? A single blow to the head didn't look like gang violence. There was nothing on Hungry Bear's record to indicate that he'd had anything to do with gangs in the past. Dire Facebook warnings notwithstanding, attacking or killing strangers was not a typical way to initiate new gang members. Not in Calgary, anyway. Even with blood-in gangs, initiates tended to target people that they knew or who were members of a rival gang, not complete strangers.

Margie called Jones, hoping she wasn't too busy, and asked her for her impressions of the interview with the friends. They had briefly discussed it in the car and while Christina was out of the room making pizza, but not in any depth. Just agreeing that the friends had intentionally gotten together to make sure they all told the same story. Whether that was because they were trying to hide something or protect one of their number, or just because they were nervous about being questioned by the police and wanted the moral support, was not yet clear. Margie would dig down and try to get to the truth when she followed up with them individually.

"Made it home safe?" Jones asked cheerfully.

"Yes. And downtown without any problem this morning. There are a lot of disabled vehicles still on the road, though. You can tell that something happened."

"I don't envy Traffic Division."

"No... I guess they'll be out there ticketing and towing. I hope they give people time to retrieve their own vehicles, though..."

"I imagine they will. They won't be looking for more work. Easier if people pick up their own vehicles."

"So... just wondering if you have a few minutes to talk through the interview last night. I'll get your notes on Monday, but if you had any feelings, any red flags..."

"Well, just the fact that they circled the wagons and wouldn't talk to us separately says something to me."

"You don't think it was just because Kennedy was anxious and wanted someone else there?"

"No… she didn't strike me as the nervous kind. If it had been Susan, okay, I could see that. If it had been a group of all girls, I could see how they would want to band together. But Kennedy seemed pretty strong and put together, and the boys were confident enough. Susan is the weak link."

"You think I should talk to her first?"

"Definitely. If anyone is going to talk, it will be her."

Margie nodded thoughtfully. She clicked through photographs of the scene while she talked to Jones, looking for anything out of place or unusual. Sometimes there just weren't enough clues at a crime scene to come to any conclusion. It wasn't like on TV when there was always enough evidence to catch and convict a killer.

"Do you think one of them knows what happened? Or all of them?"

"It just seems 'off' to me. They all stayed overnight except for Hungry Bear? They just sent him off on his own late at night? Why didn't he stay?"

"His house was close by."

"They are all close by. Relatively, anyway. I looked at their home addresses. They're not all in Dover, but most of them could walk home if they wanted to. So why didn't they? And why *did* Hungry Bear?"

Margie thought about the dynamics of the group. What had they learned?

"Maybe there was an argument or a fight? The others were drinking, tempers might have been high. Or they might have been pressuring him to drink and he knew he needed to get out of the environment."

"Could be," Jones agreed. "If he was trying to stay clean, and they weren't supportive of his sobriety, that would be good reason to leave, even if it was late. Maybe especially if it was late, since inhibitions are reduced as you get more tired and he would have known that he was more likely to take a drink the later he stayed."

"They said they didn't have much to drink."

"So they said."

"Yeah. That's not necessarily true," Margie admitted. "It was a party. Get together and play games, get a head start on celebrating the holiday."

"Uh-huh. I suspect they had more to drink than they told us. They wanted to show themselves in a good light. Portray themselves as some friends who got together to play a game and have a glass of wine or bottle of beer."

Margie pictured the wet bar. It had appeared to be well-stocked but, of course, she had not gotten behind the counter to have a good look at it. Any empties had been cleared away, there were no bags of bottles to be returned for deposit. Margie frowned, clicking through the photos on the screen.

"If they hadn't already cleaned up, we could check fingerprints on the glasses or bottles, see how much they had each been drinking in reality."

"I suppose. But what would the point be in that? Hungry Bear wasn't drinking, or it would have shown up in his bloodwork. No alcohol, no drugs."

"Just to show if they were lying, I guess," Margie admitted.

"You're not going to get a warrant from a judge based on 'we think they're lying about something, but don't know what.'"

"Uh, no."

"I don't think there is anything we can go after them for until we get confirmation from one of them that someone is lying. Preferably someone with a motive to kill Hungry Bear."

"*Did* someone have motive to kill him? We haven't really talked much about motive." Motive is always the crux on TV. In real life… not so much.

"Maybe he was too friendly with one of the girls?" Jones suggested.

"Or one of the guys?" Margie countered wryly, grinning. "Jealousy? Or protecting someone's virtue? It's always possible. There's nothing that gets people upset as fast as a love triangle."

Margie looked down at her notes for a moment, considering each of the members of the group of friends. She hadn't noticed any romantic attachments between any of them. There had been no long looks or flirting. When they talked about staying over for the night, there hadn't been giggles or significant looks. No discussion of bedroom assignments or other sleeping arrangements. They had just acted like friends.

But that wasn't conclusive. Some people wore their emotions and attractions on their sleeves and others did not.

Christina, for example. Margie had been watching for signs that she was attracted to anyone at school or pairing off when school let out. But so far… nothing. She told herself that Christina was just still trying to fit in and make friends. She had put in a full year at a new school, but with all the back and forth between online schooling and in-person schooling, and time off for quarantines half a dozen times during the year, it seemed as if she had never been at school for more than a couple of weeks at a time. And when they weren't allowed to have other people in their house, it was pretty hard to tell who Christina was friends with, other than through overheard conversations.

Margie reached the itemized lists of what was in the garbages, skimming over them quickly for anything that shouldn't be there. It was a long shot, but sometimes people did throw things into public garbages just out of habit. Or someone else picked up something that had been dropped to put it into the garbage himself.

CHAPTER FIFTEEN

O h!"

Jones had been speaking, but stopped at what she heard in Margie's tone. "Oh, what?"

"It isn't something that is there. It's something that is missing."

There was silence on the other end of the phone. Margie pulled up each of the garbage inventories, looking through them carefully.

"I missed it," Margie murmured. "We all missed it."

"Missed what? Do I dare ask? Have you broken the case?"

"I don't know. It's probably nothing. But we also might be missing evidence from our crime scene."

MARGIE LOOKED through the pictures taken of the people hanging around after the body was discovered, rubberneckers trying to catch a glimpse of the body or something equally horrifying.

She recognized a lot of the faces she had seen there on her morning runs or evening dog walks. It was a well-trafficked park, a place to go and watch the children play in the water or the playground, watch a volleyball tournament, run, bike, walk your dog, sit on a bench and visit while watching the ducks… Despite how small it was, many people made use of it.

Frustratingly, she couldn't find the couple she was looking for. It would have been so much easier if someone had taken their statements. She would have names, addresses, and phone numbers to go with the faces. But apparently, they had not stayed around to find out what was going on. Or maybe they hadn't even been there that day and she was on a wild goose chase.

Margie and Christina took Stella to the park to play ball and Frisbee Saturday afternoon, and Margie returned on her own on Sunday morning to watch the walkers and look for familiar faces. The old man with the cane went walking every morning on his slow circuit around the pond. Lots of dog walkers, including the one who had helped Margie to pull Hungry Bear out of the water. She got out of her car, admired the dogs, and thanked him for his help.

"I'm just glad *you* were here," he said. "I wouldn't have known what to do by myself."

"You would have called 9-1-1 and they would have sent help, just like they did. I didn't really need to be there for that."

"Maybe… but it was nice to have a cop there who knew what she was talking about."

The man's girlfriend gave Margie a friendly nod but didn't have much to say. Margie let them continue on their walk and sat on one of the benches by the pond, overtly looking at the ducks, but also watching the people in her peripheral vision. They didn't have any reason to avoid her, but people didn't like knowing they were under surveillance.

And then she saw them. The tall, slim man with a garbage grabber and his wife or friend, taking a leisurely stroll around the park, eyes open for any litter to be picked up. Making the world around them a better place. Margie waited until they were closer to her before standing up. She let them approach her, trying to look non-threatening. Just another person enjoying the beauty of the park.

"Hi. Nice day."

"Cooler," the woman agreed. "Nice to have a break in the weather. Between the heat and the storm…"

Margie nodded. It was an overcast day, and would probably rain later on, but there at least weren't any thunderstorm warnings. Yet.

"I'm actually with the police department. I wonder if you could help me out."

They exchanged looks.

"We're not doing anything wrong," the man protested.

"No, no, this is not about anything you have done wrong. It's about the body that was found here on Canada Day. You heard about that?"

They nodded in unison. "Horrible thing," the woman observed. "I guess he was drunk and fell in?"

"It doesn't look like it, no. But I can't discuss the specifics with you. But you may be aware of evidence that could help us."

"We don't know anything."

"I've seen you here before, picking up garbage."

The man nodded. "I want it to look nice here. People litter, or stuff blows in from somewhere else… I don't want kids picking it up, or dogs eating it, or just having it cluttering up the park. So I pick up a little each day." He looked around, admiring his handiwork. "And it helps to keep things looking nice."

"That's so admirable. I'm really impressed that you do that."

That seemed to relax him a little. Margie smiled, trying again to reassure them that she wasn't there to accuse them of anything.

"You may not know, but we took all the garbages from this area and looked through everything for any evidence."

"Evidence of what?" the wife asked, her brows wrinkling.

"Anything. Anything at all related to the victim's death."

The man spoke up. "And what does that have to do with us?"

"I realized yesterday when I was looking through all of the garbage that had been inventoried… there were no bottles."

"Well, no. You don't throw out bottles. They're worth money if you take them back to the depot."

"Yes. My daughter is doing a fundraiser by collecting cans and bottles for refunds."

"It adds up. Might just be ten cents here and twenty-five there, but it adds up once you've collected a few bags."

"I wondered… whether you collected any bottles from the park."

They looked at her, not answering. Still thinking they were going to be accused of something.

"I clean up the park. There's nothing wrong about that."

"No, there's not. You're doing the community a service. There's nothing wrong with you picking up cans or bottles if you find them here."

He nodded slowly.

"I imagine that sometimes people throw them in the garbage can. And if you open it up to put the litter you have picked up in there and you see bottles or cans, you would probably retrieve them. They shouldn't just be going to the dump."

"No, that's right."

"So if there were any bottles on the ground or in the garbage, you would pick them up."

"Sure."

"Again, there's nothing wrong with that and I'm glad that you're taking care of the park and keeping it so nice for everyone. But I would like to see any beverage containers that you have picked up here since Wednesday."

He stared at her. "Why?"

"Because it might be evidence. There's no guarantee that it is, or that it will have any significance at all… but if I can get those bottles, they could be very important."

"I don't see how," he grumbled.

His wife gave him a little tap on the arm. "Myron. There's no reason to act that way. This officer has been very polite. She's trying to solve a homicide!"

"If you're going to take my bottles, I'm going to expect to be paid for them."

Margie blew out her breath in relief. "I would be happy to."

She wasn't in the habit of paying for tips, but giving Myron a twenty for what might be important evidence? She could do that.

"Well, then…" Myron brightened. "What are we waiting for?"

CHAPTER SIXTEEN

Margie had each of the friends back in over the weekend to review their testimonies and get their fingerprints, which she told them would be used to eliminate any of their fingerprints found on Hungry Bear's possessions. Margie did her best to find out more details of what had happened that night while the techs analyzed the evidence, hoping that she could make some progress on the case independent of the physical evidence. But the friends all stuck to the same story, with little variation. A sure sign that they had discussed the details among themselves to make sure that they all told the same story.

It wasn't until Monday that she was ready to move forward.

She welcomed Alex into the interview room and offered him a seat. They were both wearing masks, so it wasn't easy to see his expression, but in the past year she had grown more skilled at watching the eyes and the other muscles of the face to discern a person's expression behind the mask. People seemed to be freer to let their faces shift while they were wearing a mask, assuming she couldn't see a smile or scowl behind it.

Alex looked around the room, uncomfortable. He had trouble choosing a chair to sit in for their interview. He dithered between two or three chairs before finally choosing one. It wasn't like any of them were farther away from the bottle that sat in the middle of the table.

"Thanks for coming in," Margie repeated, smiling at him and being sure to make her voice pleasant and soothing. "I know that you must have a lot to do, probably back at work today, so I appreciate you taking the time."

"I don't understand why you needed me to come in today." He looked around, as if waiting for her to bring the other friends in. Had he already talked to them? Did he realize that he was the only one who had been called in?

"Well, I just had a few more things that I was hoping to cover with you, like I said on the phone."

"We've already told you everything that happened that night. None of us know what happened to Bruce." He gave an exaggerated shrug. "We weren't there."

"Hmm." Margie looked at the bottle in the middle of the table. "I think that one of you was."

He kept his eyes away from the bottle, as if it were invisible and he didn't know what she was talking about. Margie continued to gaze at it, until he felt compelled to follow her eyes and acknowledge the presence of the bottle.

"What's this?"

"It's your bottle."

"My bottle?" He rolled his eyes. "I don't even drink that brand."

"Interesting… then why would your fingerprints be on the bottle?"

"I don't know where you got it. I don't know that it *does* have my prints on it."

"This is the bottle you were drinking at the party Wednesday night. The bottle that you took with you went you left the party with Bruce."

"We were just gaming together. That's all. You make it sound… like it was more than it was. Just some friends getting together for some wholesome games. We weren't out on the streets making trou-ble. We don't run with a gang or deface property or anything like that. And we don't go around…" He twirled a finger, at a loss for words.

"Killing each other?" Margie suggested.

"No. We don't. Look, I've never been in any kind of trouble, and I've answered all your questions. Can we just wrap this up? If you're going to make ridiculous suggestions, then we're done here."

"Did you and Bruce leave together? Why? Were you walking him home?"

"No. I didn't go anywhere with him. I told you that."

"How did this bottle with your fingerprints on it come to be in the park, then?"

"If it has my prints on it, I probably just moved it to the side that night. You know, pick it up and move it over so I could grab a beer."

"The positioning of the fingerprints suggests that you drank from the bottle, among other things."

He shifted in his chair. "But you can't tell whether I did drink from it or not, can you?" He looked triumphant. "I can hold a bottle like I'm going to take a drink of it, and then not. Right? You can't tell the difference."

"Maybe by DNA swabs of the mouth of the bottle," Margie suggested. She shrugged. "It doesn't really matter whether you drank from the bottle or not, though, I just wanted to establish that you had it with you went you went to the park. With Bruce."

He shook his head. "No. I don't know what you're talking about. I don't know how it got to the park. Maybe one of the others went over there looking for him after I fell asleep."

Margie stared at him steadily. "That doesn't sound very likely, does it?"

"But you can't prove that's not what happened."

Margie leaned back in her chair and raised her eyes toward the ceiling. "I would just like to know what really happened. I can't figure out why you would want to hurt Bruce. Did the two of you have a fight? Did you think he had done something to you? Maybe both of you were interested in the same girl and you thought he was weaseling his way in on you?" She didn't see any response to this scenario in his eyes. "Or maybe you were interested in Bruce, or he was interested in you?"

"No!" She could see his grimace of disgust behind the mask. That wasn't it then, but that still left many other avenues open.

"No? What was it then? What was it that made you so angry?"

"I wasn't there."

"The bottle was there. Your fingerprints are on the bottle. And not just in the position they would be for you to take a drink. There were also prints in the right position for you to swing the bottle and bring it down on someone's head. To bludgeon them."

Alex's eyes were icy. He was doing everything he could to look casual and not at all concerned about the accusation. He had friends, after all. Friends who would back his alibi and say that he had never gone out of the house. He had been there all night, sleeping over like everyone else.

"You hit him from behind," Margie said. "Why? What reason did you have to sneak up behind him and—"

"Sneak?" Alex objected "What are you talking about, sneaking?"

"Why else would he have his back to you? You don't turn your back on your enemy. In the middle of the night, in the dark. Why would he do that?"

"We weren't enemies, we were friends. We all told you that."

Margie waited, letting the silence draw out, compelling him to fill it. The silences in an interview were just as important as the words.

Alex looked at the bottle again. His expression under the mask shifted, but it was too subtle for Margie to tell exactly what had changed. He sniffled.

"He was my friend," Alex insisted. "We were friends long before anyone else in the group. I knew him from the time we were in junior high. When it was just him and me, learning how to play D&D, the geeks that no one else was interested in. He was *my friend.*"

"Tell me what happened that night."

"I've already told you."

"No, you haven't. And if he was your friend, then don't you think it's time to clear this up? His family needs to know what happened. Why this happened. Don't you owe it to Bruce?"

"You think his parents would want to know—" Alex cut himself off, shaking his head.

Would they want to know that he had been killed by his best friend? Was that really what would make them feel better about their son's death and help them to find peace? Margie doubted it. But she was a seeker of the truth. She had to follow this line of questioning to its conclusion. Just like when breaking the news of a death to a family member, she had to hear the true story, unvarnished. No hiding behind euphemisms, just the cold, stark truth of it.

"Yes. The truth needs to come out. It will be better for you. It will be important to his parents. All of us need to be able to close this chapter. We can't begin to heal until the truth is known."

Alex's eyes flared. He shook his head angrily. "You sound *just like* him!" he blurted. "Talking about truth and healing. I was so sick and tired of it!"

Margie's own anger flared, but she kept it hidden. He wasn't attacking her. He was reliving what had happened between him and Bruce. And if something she did or said prompted him to do that and to tell her about it, then that was what needed to happen.

"What was Bruce talking about?"

"It never stopped. I grew up with the guy. I knew the kind of home he came from and the way he grew up. He didn't live on the reservation and he went to the same schools as I did. Not some residential school where he was abused."

Margie nodded encouragingly, a picture starting to form in her mind.

"All night while we were gaming, he was on about this 'hashtag Cancel Canada Day' and 'No Pride in Genocide' stuff. He just wouldn't shut up about it. We would change the subject, and he would be right back to it two minutes later. No one wanted to hear it. We were there to have a good time together, not to rally against the government. Everyone was sick and tired of it."

"He didn't go to a residential school, so it had nothing to do with him?" Margie asked.

"He had to go all the way back to his grandma to find someone who had gone to residential school. So how does that affect him? She wasn't one of those little kids who died. He didn't go to residential school, and neither did his parents. Why did we have to keep hearing about all of the abuses? That stuff is all in the past and there's nothing we can do about it." He met Margie's eyes. "Can you explain that to me? What exactly are we supposed to do? *We* aren't the ones who abused anyone. We had nothing to do with it."

Margie could have given him a list. Pressure his elected officials to follow through on their promises and the recommendations of the Truth and Reconciliation Commission. Support Indigenous outreach and counseling programs. Help with memorials for those whose deaths had been ignored or hidden. Or just be a supportive ear to a friend who was dealing with inter-generational trauma.

"And you were fed up with it," she suggested instead. "You didn't want to hear any more."

"Exactly. Just shut up already. It was getting late, so... I said I'd walk home with him. I'm a good friend. I didn't just tell him to get lost. I could tell it was getting on everyone else's nerves too, so I said I'd walk home with him. He probably just needed a good sleep, and then he'd feel better about it. He wouldn't be so wound up. It was just because he'd been with his parents, you know. He wasn't usually like that with us."

"He just acted like a normal white guy with you."

"Normally," Alex agreed. "We're not racist. We don't look at him and say that he's brown so he can't play with us. I don't see color. He's just my friend."

"So..." Margie gazed at the empty bottle on the table. "What happened then?"

"We went through the park. He was getting on my case. Saying why didn't I stand up for him, if we were friends? Why did I just sit there like I didn't care? I told him he was the one being rude, tiring everyone out with his complaining about something that didn't even affect him." Alex rolled his eyes up toward the ceiling. "I told him if he wanted to play with us on Canada Day, to leave his agenda at home."

Margie nodded.

Alex shook his head, eyes glistening. "I just don't know why he had to be so up in our faces about it. He said it wasn't an agenda, it was who he was, and that I could go... *you know.* And he turned around and started to walk away from me."

"And..." Margie said gently, trying to encourage him to complete his statement. "It was just too much for you...?"

He put his hand to his face, rubbing the bridge of his nose with the back of his thumb. "I'd had a bit to drink. It all happened so fast. I was mad, he was mad, we were yelling back and forth. He told me to... just walked away from me, like nothing that happened in the last ten years meant anything to him, that we weren't anything."

"And you hit him."

Alex shook his head, staring at the bottle. But it wasn't a denial. Maybe disbelief. "I'd never hurt Bruce. He was my best friend. He used to be."

Margie nodded.

"I hit him," Alex admitted, staring down and talking to the table. "I never meant to do anything to hurt him. And when he went down, I laughed, and I expected him to get back up. He'd be boiling mad, but I wouldn't care. As long as he got up again."

But he hadn't gotten up again, and Alex had been left with the body of his best friend on his hands, the murder weapon in his hand. Drunk, he had made the wrong decisions.

"Why did you drag him into the water?"

"I just thought... that would be more natural. Someone could see that he'd just fallen in. An accident. There was a body discovered there a couple of years ago, you know, and the police said right away, not foul play. And I figured they would again. Just a... tragic accident."

Margie breathed out slowly. And there it was. The explanation of what had happened to Bruce Hungry Bear and how he had ended up dead, floating in the pond Canada Day morning where Margie had found him.

Alex raised his eyes to Margie. "What's going to happen to me now?"

"You are under arrest. Charges will be brought. You'll make a court appearance. You'll want to get a lawyer, talk with him about what you will plead to."

"I'm not going to have to go to prison, am I?" He stared at her beseechingly, clearly not understanding the full impact of everything he had said. "It was just an accident."

"Tripping and falling is an accident," Margie told him softly. "Whacking someone over the head with a bottle when his back is turned… that's something else."

Mac had been pleased that Margie had put the case to bed so quickly. He was happy to write it off as a drunken argument between friends, something that he could explain away to any higher-ups in the city's organizational structure, to any Stampede officials, sponsors, or celebrities. It could all be explained away and there was no need for anyone to be concerned that Calgary was a dangerous city.

Margie reported back to Hungry Bear's heartbroken family that it had been a fight between friends, not a premeditated murder or a hate crime. She pictured the face of the white-haired grandmother, someone who had already been through so much in her life, seen so many of her friends and loved ones die. And now Bruce.

She didn't tell them what the fight had been about.

Wednesday morning, she reached the crosswalk across Twenty-Sixth Street to Valleyview park, and didn't hesitate to cross for a loop or two around the pond. From the top of the hill, she could see West Dover school. Low fog clung to the grassy fields. She could see the orange ribbons still tied along the fence.

Margie watched the ducks and the blackbirds as she circled the pond. She no longer felt anxious and afraid that the park would always represent something ominous. It was still the same place it had been before she had discovered Bruce Hungry Bear's body immersed in the pond.

As she ran by the fence of the splash park, which Myron had diligently cleared of all litter, she saw that there was something tied to that fence too, between the signs warning pathway users to stay two meters apart from each other. Orange paper hearts with pictures glued to them tied together in a chain. Printed on each heart: *An act of reconciliation.*

She read the explanatory card at one end of the chain and thought about the two school pals whose friendship had ended on almost that very spot. The school children who had made the paper hearts had no way of knowing that. Hopefully, their offering would help to heal other wounds, so that other friends could be reconciled.

VALLEYVIEW PARK

While Valleyview Park is the tinniest of the parks so far, it packs a punch, with a pond, a playground, a children's splash park, beach volleyball courts, baseball diamond, and soccer field, along with a few park benches and picnic tables. There was also a fire pit there for a few months earlier in the year, though it has disappeared again.

Just across 26th Street from the multi-use pathway, leash-free area, and a lookout platform, Valleyview Park is well-used by neighbourhood walkers, runners, and dog-walkers. The red-winged blackbirds, ducks, and a muskrat enjoy the use of the pond, and you can occasionally spot coyotes, foxes, and rabbits in the fields.

The multi-use pathway runs under 17th Avenue to the Max Bell Arena pathways, then over Deerfoot Trail to the east side of the river, past the zoo, and downtown. There is also a connection over Deerfoot Trail beside the Max Purple bus route, then under 17th Avenue/Blackfoot Trail to the Bow River Pathway (west side of the river), through Pearce Estate Park and Inglewood downtown.

SKIMMING OVER THE LAKE

A PARKS PAT MYSTERY #5

For those who feel differently

CHAPTER ONE

Margie was settled in front of the TV with her teenage daughter Christina as the Calgary Stampede parade began. The Stampede had been canceled the previous year due to COVID so everyone was eager to see its return. The much-shorter parade could only be watched on TV and not attended in person. At least it was still going ahead.

It had been a long time since Margie had seen the rodeo/fair, dubbed "The Greatest Outdoor Show on Earth," while visiting cousins in Calgary over the summer.

"Do you think we can go to the Stampede?" Christina asked. "There will be lots of stuff to see. Including the Bow River Camp."

"The Bow River Camp?"

"What used to be the Indian Village. Tipis and dances and other Indigenous culture. You want me to go to stuff like that, don't you? To be educated about my background?"

Margie pushed her own long, black hair back over her ears, smiling at Christina. "You really don't need to pull the 'culture' card to go to the Stampede."

Christina had a sip of her coffee. "I didn't think it could hurt."

Margie chuckled at this. "Well, we'll see. I don't really have anything against it, other than crowds and noise and possible contaminants. And people drinking and getting out of control. The heat and the dust, or the rainstorms..."

Christina shook her head. "Maybe we could take Moushoom down if they have a seniors' day. He remembers what it used to be like; he can tell us how it compares."

"I don't know that I want to be taking an old man down there." Margie thought about the hazards that she had already mentioned. Her grandfather's immune system wasn't as strong as a young man's. He could be a target for drunks—someone small and frail who couldn't fight back. He would look strange to them in his brightly colored clothes and buckskins. And the heat was more likely to affect a senior. "Maybe we could take him to one of the pancake breakfasts around here. Or find something that is closer to home. Taking him in his wheelchair on the bus and train..."

"Why can't we drive?"

"Because there isn't much parking, and it is expensive. The Stampede gate tickets are expensive enough without having to spend a hundred dollars on parking. Or on hiring a taxi or Uber."

"Can't you park for free with your police tag?"

She had a point. But Margie would only use her police tag if she were actually on the job. She wouldn't use it just to get more affordable or convenient parking. She was scrupulously careful in not taking advantage of anything because she was a police detective. Or playing the race or gender cards, for that matter. She was determined to only get what she had worked hard to earn.

"No, I can't," she told Christina flatly. "That's not the way it works."

Christina huffed and rolled her eyes. Stella, lying at her feet, opened one eye to examine her to see why she was making such a noise, then decided it was not anything to be concerned about and closed it again. She made a little groan and rolled over so she was right on top of Christina's foot. Christina wiggled her toes. "Hey! It's too hot to have a fur rug on my feet. Get off."

Stella didn't, and Christina didn't immediately pull her feet out, but instead reached down to scratch Stella's ears and then her belly. Stella's tail thumped loudly on the floor.

"There are the Calgary Police!" Christina exclaimed, as a series of police cars and motorcycles led the parade. "Do they have a float too, or is that it?"

"I think the mounted unit is in it later."

"It's a good thing that you're a homicide detective, so you don't have to be downtown blocking off streets and keeping drunks away from the parade."

"You're right." Margie was very happy to be right where she was, watching the parade from the comfort of her own home. The convenience more than made up for any pang of regret that they could not see it in person.

They were watching the Native Princess who had been appointed parade marshal when Margie's phone rang. She looked down at it, hoping that it would not be work. She'd even take a telemarketer. Which was easy, because she didn't have to answer the phone for a telemarketer. She'd even take a call from Christina's school saying that she hadn't handed in some final assignment or they had lost her final exams.

It was work. The name and picture on the display were Detective Siever's.

She didn't know Siever well. He was pretty quiet. Good with technical stuff. If she had a computer problem or was trying to figure out how to process a large amount of data, he was the one she would go to. They hadn't worked very closely on previous files. He seemed to prefer staying in the office over getting out and doing field work. More comfortable with a computer than real people.

Maybe it was just a call to let her know that she had a new login or hadn't responded to an email he had sent previously.

Margie looked at Christina, who was watching her closely.

"That had better not be work," Christina warned.

Margie raised her brows in an expression of surrender and swiped the screen to answer the call.

"Detective Patenaude."

"It's Siever. I'm heading in your direction. Looks like we might have another case for 'Parks Pat.'"

Margie thought immediately of Valleyview Park, her last case, just barely put to bed. It couldn't be another death in Valleyview.

"What's going on? Where?"

The other possibility that presented itself was Ralph Klein Provincial Park. It had almost been a year since that one, but Siever would still consider it to be "in her direction." It was only a fifteen-minute drive away. Margie hoped it wasn't Ralph Klein. She did not like the murky black water in the reservoir beside the education center. The canals and other waterways caused her anxiety enough; that black pool was so ominous and foreboding.

"Elliston Park. You know it?" Siever asked.

"Uh… no, I don't. I've heard of it. I think it is east down Seventeenth Avenue?"

"That's right. Surprised you haven't taken your dog there. It's a nice area."

Margie had plenty of multi-use pathways close to the house and hadn't ventured much farther than Valleyview Park. Or north to the winding pathways around Max Bell Center.

"It's on my list."

"Well, today you get to see it in person."

Margie looked over at Christina, sighing. "Do you really need me there?"

"I'd appreciate it. I know everyone is supposed to be off today, but homicides don't wait for anyone. You're the closest one, it would disrupt your schedule the least."

"I'm watching the parade with my daughter."

"She's a teenager, isn't she? She can look after herself until you get back. It will be an hour. Maybe two. You can DVR it and watch it with her later. Fast forward through the boring bits and watch the good stuff over again. Much more entertaining."

"How long until you'll be there?"

"I'm about ten minutes out. Probably going by your house about now. I'll meet you in the east parking lot. You know how to get there?"

"No." Margie's stomach tightened. "There is more than one parking lot?"

"Sure."

And probably only the main one would show up on GPS. By the way Siever said she should meet him in the east parking lot, she assumed that it was not the main entrance.

"Maybe I should use the main parking lot. You can secure things on the east, and I can see if there is anything of note going on in the..."

"The west access." Siever was silent for a minute. "I don't think there is going to be anything on that side. The vic's car will be in the east lot. That's where we will be collecting evidence."

"We won't know if there is anything of note in the west end unless we check. I may as well do that."

"Do you think you can find your way from the west end to where the body is?"

Margie had an uncomfortable feeling that he knew or guessed more about her lack of sense of direction than she had ever told anyone. Why else would he have asked that?

"How big is this park? Are there are lot of pathways?"

"Not really. They're just in a loop around the lake. Sort of an outer loop and an inner loop."

"Okay. And which should I be on?"

He considered for a few seconds. "Fine. Shortest to go around the north side of the lake. If you're facing the lake from the west parking lot, that's the left. Doesn't matter which path you take. The outer loop will be longer, obviously."

"I can do that." Margie grabbed a pen and a flyer from the coffee table and scribbled down his instructions. "I'll be on my way in five minutes."

He grunted and hung up the phone.

Christina looked at Margie, one eyebrow raised. "First, no Canada Day, and now no parade day?"

"I'm sorry, honey. Like Detective Siever says, you can DVR it and we can watch it together later."

"I don't want to watch it later; I want to watch it now. With you. Not a taped version later. We can just watch the news or YouTube for that."

"I'll be back as soon as I can be." Margie knew there was no point in arguing. It wouldn't get them any closer to overcoming the disappointment that once again, Margie was being taken away from Christina on a day that was supposed to be set apart for the two of them. Christina wasn't the only one who was upset about her being called in.

"I can't control when the bodies are found." Margie divided her hair into sections behind her head and began to braid it. She would have to change out of her casual shorts and t-shirt and into something more appropriate for a homicide detective. And then jump in the car and get to the park as quickly as she could. She didn't want to keep Siever waiting for too long and it was going to take time to walk to his location.

She hadn't even asked him how far a walk it would be.

CHAPTER TWO

*S*he was right about the GPS on her phone only giving her one option for a route to Elliston Park. She didn't even see the second parking lot marked.

Happily, there wasn't much traffic on Seventeenth Avenue and she was able to get to the park in good time. There were more cars than she expected in the parking lot. Apparently, a lot of people did not care about watching the Stampede parade. It might be sort of a holiday to Calgarians, especially those who normally worked downtown, but there were obviously plenty of people who didn't watch the coverage.

It was a sunny day, the sky a clear, pale blue. Margie could see people walking dogs, carrying little children on their shoulders, and strolling around the park at a leisurely pace. No one seemed to be aware that there was a dead body somewhere at the other end of the park. It was just a normal day for them.

Getting out of the car, Margie put on a mask and consulted the corner of the flyer that she had torn off and put in her pocket. *Facing the lake, take the left-hand pathway.*

There were several pathways to the left, and not all of them appeared to loop around the lake. But they might meander other directions first and then turn around. Margie walked slowly, trying to fix the other end of the lake in her mind. She would keep going left, or clockwise, and she would eventually meet up with Siever on the other side.

Margie walked past flower beds vibrant with colors. Keeping left, she discovered some kind of monument and walked closer to take a look. Various cylindrical concrete blocks stood in a half circle, numbers on top of them. There was a grid of months and horseshoes embedded in the pavement in front of them and a starburst shape like a sun or a compass at the top. Margie looked at it, bemused. Public art? A puzzle?

"It's a sundial," said a voice behind her.

Margie turned and looked at the woman behind her. Shoulder length brown hair under a baseball cap, somewhat overweight, in a t-shirt and shorts, pushing a stroller with fat wheels seating two toddlers. The children were lolling over, eyes glazed, obviously tired out from walking or playing.

"A sundial?" It didn't look like any sundial that Margie had ever seen. There was no pointer to cast a shadow on the numbers. The pillars themselves cast shadows, but Margie couldn't figure out how that would tell her the time.

"You stand on the month," the mother instructed, pointing to July.

Margie positioned herself on the rectangle.

"Then put your arms over your head like this." She demonstrated, pressing her palms together, arms extended over her head.

Margie did so.

"Now look at your shadow."

Margie followed her shadow out to the numbers and found it falling between the eight and the nine. She looked at her phone, thumbing on the screen. Eight-thirty. "It worked!"

The woman laughed. "It does," she agreed. "Every time."

"Except if it's too cloudy or dark to see your shadow," Margie pointed out.

"Right. Of course." She gave Margie a broad smile. "Reliable enough for me to know that it was only six o'clock when they were racing those stupid boats."

Margie looked toward the lake. She couldn't see any boats from where she stood and didn't remember seeing any from the parking lot. There were no cars with boats in trailers. Maybe in the other parking lot, where Siever had gone.

"They were racing boats in here?"

Margie would not have thought it large enough for a boat race. It wasn't just a pond like the one in Valleyview, but it was nothing like Chestermere Lake or the reservoir.

"RC boats."

"RC?"

"Remote control." The woman mimed working a controller in her palm. "Little remote control boats. They play with them out on the lake."

"Oh, I see." Margie nodded. "Six o'clock does seem a little early to be playing with remote control boats. I suppose whoever it was had the morning off for parade day. But maybe he has to go into the office in the afternoon."

"Maybe. I still don't like having the serenity of the morning broken by those whining, whizzing boats. They go so fast. Did you know they can go, like, two-hundred-fifty kilometers per hour?"

Margie tried to picture it. She shook her head. She had been thinking of the remote control cars some of her cousins had had when she was a kid. They didn't go any faster than a brisk walk. Slower if their batteries were getting low. She had pictured something similar putting along the surface of the lake. But that wouldn't have irritated the woman so much. It would have been quiet. Little boats going over two-fifty, though… that was a different story. Margie could just imagine them screaming over the water.

"That's incredible. I had no idea."

"It's cool to see people playing with them here. The kids like it. But you would think people could be more considerate and not do it while people are trying to enjoy the peace and quiet of a morning walk."

"Mommy…" one of the toddlers whined, not sitting up, but still lying back, looking exhausted. "I'm firsty…"

The woman shook her head at Margie. "When we get into the car, I'll give you a juice box," she promised.

"I'm firsty too!" the other insisted more loudly.

"I'm sure you are. We'll be in the car in a minute."

The woman waved at Margie. "Well, I guess I'd better get on my way." She looked Margie over, taking in her slacks and blazer. "You… know where you're going?"

"Just around the lake," Margie said lightly.

"There's something going on down the other end. I don't know what. Saw a bunch of flashing lights and uniforms. Maybe some vandalism or a homeless person causing trouble. They camp out here in the trees sometimes."

"I'll watch out," Margie promised.

"Okay. Have a nice day."

"You too."

The woman pushed her stroller back toward the parking lot. Margie reoriented herself to the lake and followed the path that ran along the edge of it.

Ducks and other waterfowl floated serenely on the glassy surface of the lake. The skies were blue with big fluffy white clouds. She could see a few Canada geese floating at the end of the lake as well, one of them clambering up onto the shore to poke through the grass for something tasty. Margie didn't know as much about wildlife as she should, but she knew enough about Canada geese to give them a wide berth. Being attacked by one of those big birds and their hard beaks was something she would prefer to avoid. They might look like stately, graceful creatures, but cross one, and you'd better be ready to run. It was probably too late in the year for there to be goslings to protect, but Margie was not going to find out.

The single pathway split into two, and Margie hesitated over which to follow. Siever had said that there was an inner loop and an outer loop. She could stay on the inner loop, where she could keep the lake in sight. It would be a shorter distance for her to walk. But if the woman was right and there were sometimes homeless people camped in the trees, then maybe she should take the path that led into the grove of trees. There might be witnesses to interview.

Evidence that someone had discarded in the trees in the hopes that the police would never see it.

It would take longer, which would probably irritate Siever. But it would be more efficient and save time in the overall investigation.

Margie unlocked the screen on her phone and tapped Siever's recent call record. She walked into the trees as she waited for him to answer.

"Did you get lost?" Siever asked dryly.

"No, your directions were good. I'm on my way around to you. I just thought I'd let you know that I'm taking the longer route, through the trees. I could see a good deal of the shore, and I don't see anything suspicious by the lake. But something could easily be hidden in the trees, and a woman I just passed said that sometimes the homeless camp out here. So I'm going to take a quick walk through to see if there is anything that we need to take a closer look at."

Siever was silent for a moment, considering this. She waited for him to tease her that he thought she had gotten lost and was just looking for an excuse for her lateness. Cruz or Jones would have. But Siever was quieter, a bit shy or awkward. He didn't press it.

"I suppose if you think that's the best course," he allowed. "You're the one with experience in parks."

She didn't have *that* much experience. She certainly wasn't a tracker of any kind. She hadn't inherited that gene through her Cree or European explorer ancestors. But Siever had agreed to her chosen course.

"Thanks. I'll see you in a few minutes, then."

CHAPTER THREE

Walking into the trees, it was almost as if the rest of the world ceased to exist. There were still occasional traffic sounds, but all the busy-ness of the walkers and other park users disappeared and she was alone, her view limited by the trees that pushed close in on the trail. Birds chirped and twittered. She had expected to hear a lot of red-winged blackbirds, like she did at Valleyview park, but she couldn't pick out their songs. She heard many sparrows and smaller birds like she often heard from her yard. Always fighting and bickering with each other, declaring their territory, calling back and forth.

It wasn't a paved trail like at the other parks she had been to. A worn footpath rather than a multi-use pathway. It was kind of nice that way, making her believe that she really could be in a forest, removed from the constant hum of civilization, rather than walking beside busy Seventeenth Avenue.

"Coming through!" a voice called out.

Margie looked up, startled, to see a bicycle hurtling toward her. She stepped to the side, off the worn path.

"Thank you!" the cyclist called out as he whipped past her. And in a few seconds, he was gone again.

So much for being isolated. Margie laughed to herself.

She was there for a reason, and it wasn't just to take in the trees and nature around her. She was supposed to be looking for anything that was out of place. Any homeless encampments or possible evidence. She scanned back and forth, looking for anything that might have been dropped or thrown to the side.

Like the other Calgary parks she had been to, it was pretty clean and tidy. Not much for her to find.

A few minutes later she could see a large rock that was obviously out of place. The forest ground cover was mostly grass and pine needles. It was a river rock, round and smooth. And it had been painted. Margie left the trail to look at it.

It was robin's egg blue and painted on it in a cursive script were the words "Pray Always."

Margie studied it for a moment. Was it evidence? There was nothing to indicate it had been placed there recently. There was no blood spatter or other obvious contaminant. Did it indicate that someone frequented the park who was evangelical? Maybe even a religious zealot who would rail at and try to convert park goers? Religious mania could sometimes lead to violence.

The two painted smiley faces on the rock dissuaded her from this line of thought. A violent zealot might have painted fire and brimstone, but not smiley faces. Still, the rock was out of place and she should make note of it. Margie took a couple of pictures with her phone. Using the toe of her shoe, she lifted the edge of the rock, and could see by the dampness of the ground underneath that it had been there for some time. Not just dropped there the night before.

She returned to the trail and continued through the trees. The next people who came through from the opposite direction were a man walking a big, black dog, and two more cyclists. Margie would not have expected so many bikes through there on a trail that wasn't made for them. She wouldn't have wanted to be bumping over all of the rocks and roots on a bike.

As she emerged from the grove of trees, an older woman, thin and deeply wrinkled, was walking toward her. She nodded a brisk greeting at Margie.

"You might not want to go this way," she told Margie. "They're blocking the pathway. You can't get around."

"Oh, okay. Thanks." Margie smiled and nodded. "Any idea what's going on?"

Sometimes there was more to be learned from gossip than through official channels. Margie was curious as to what people were saying about the police activity.

"Police roping off the area. I guess they think it's unsafe. The lake is a stormwater catchment, maybe they're worried about it getting too deep with the last couple of storms."

"Oh, okay." Margie nodded. "There has been some spectacular lightning lately, hasn't there?"

"Yes, and there was a lot of flooding last week with that sudden storm. Lots of people got stranded in their cars. Dangerous to be near a basin like this if there is a sudden downpour."

"That makes sense. Thanks."

Margie continued to walk in the direction she had been.

"You can't get by them," the woman warned again. "You can't get all the way around."

"That's okay. I don't need to get around."

The woman frowned. Then she shrugged. She had done her neighborly duty by informing Margie of the problem. If Margie still wanted to follow the ill-advised route, then that was her own business. She would just find herself blocked at the other end of the lake anyway.

They went their own ways. A leg of the lake jutted out to the left and, as Margie started to follow the perimeter, she realized that the lake was bigger than she had thought. She hadn't been able to see all of it from the parking lot.

Which meant it would take that much longer to get to Siever and the body.

Margie picked up her pace.

CHAPTER FOUR

It felt like it took a lot longer than it should to get around the lake. Margie had thought that it would take her only a few minutes, but it took nearly half an hour, and she was drenched in sweat once she got there. She should not have worn her blazer when she knew she was going to the park. Homicide detectives were supposed to look professional, but she probably would have looked more professional in khakis and a white t-shirt than dressed for the office and drenched in sweat.

She approached Siever, trying to look as calm and cool as possible. He glanced over her. He was heavyset, his face slightly rounded with extra weight. Hair buzzed short. His expression, what she could see of it around his mask, was neutral. "Glad you could make it. Ready to go?"

Margie nodded. "Yes, what have we got?"

Siever pointed at something in the lake. Margie could see a brightly colored inflatable raft and some other indiscernible shapes. She squinted, trying to force her eyes to adjust to the bright reflection of the sun on the surface of the water.

"And we think that's a body?"

He handed her a pair of binoculars. Margie put them up to her eyes and adjusted the focus. She could make out an arm and hand protruding from under the raft. There was also a smaller boat; Margie assumed it was the RC boat that the woman at the sundial had been complaining about.

"So… is someone coming to tow it all to shore?" *She* certainly wasn't going to be swimming out there to get them.

"Fire department has some boats. They're going to send someone over."

So Margie had not held anyone up in taking so long to get to the scene. They still couldn't even access the body. She took a few pictures of the raft with her phone, though she knew that the chances she would actually be able to see anything significant in the pictures were extremely low.

"I would think that they would be faster getting someone here. We can't even confirm that the guy is dead. What if he's just injured?"

"Hasn't moved for an hour and he's under the water. I don't think there's any chance of a successful rescue."

"Who found him?"

Siever motioned to one of the spectators standing close by. "Dog walker. His dog kept going into the water and banging into the boat. Eventually he figured out that something was wrong. A birdwatcher had binoculars," he made a gesture toward a tall, gangly woman who was also waiting and watching the water through binoculars. "She was able to see the arm once the dog had moved the raft enough."

"Do we know who he is?"

"Hopefully, he'll have some ID on him. Otherwise, we might have to wait until the parking lot clears out and see which car is left."

"He could have walked in."

"Not with a raft and other equipment," he pointed out.

"Oh." Margie nodded. "No, not very likely. How big is the parking lot at this end?"

"Smaller than the one you saw and less well-known."

"So now we're just waiting."

Siever shrugged. "Forensics is on their way. Mostly, it's rock by the edge of the water, but I could see some footprints, so we want to keep everyone back until they have documented everything."

Margie looked around. He had taped off a nice wide perimeter, and no one seemed inclined to cross the barrier. People stood back watching the activity or looking into the lake and pointing at the raft, but so far no one of the type who thought they had the right to march into an area, caution tape notwithstanding.

"Looks good."

She was regretting that she had hurried to get there. Margie took off her jacket and folded it over her arm. She was probably showing huge sweat rings under her arms, but there was no point in getting overheated or dehydrated because she was dressed too warmly.

"So… what do you think happened? He had a problem with his remote control boat and went out to get it?"

Siever nodded. "Probably. And then he overturned or fell out reaching for it. Wasn't as strong a swimmer as he thought or hit his head on an underwater rock. Freak accidents happen."

They listened to the whoop of a siren making its way down Seventeenth Avenue and looked toward it, though their view of the traffic was blocked by the trees. It pulled into the parking lot behind them and turned off the siren, still out of Margie's view. It sounded big and heavy, so she assumed it was the fire department, not another police car.

In a few minutes, a group of firefighters came out of the trees carrying a boat. It wasn't an inflatable like the raft on the lake and required several firemen to carry it.

"Just over here," Siever directed, pointing to the raft. "There's a body under it."

"What a pity," one of the men said, heavily accented. Bahamian, maybe? West Indies? He certainly wasn't a Calgary native.

Siever directed them around the tape perimeter, so that they wouldn't go walking across the area he believed the evidence was in. They set the boat into the water, talked back and forth for a bit, getting everything ready, and then started the motor and buzzed slowly over to the bright yellow raft. Margie tried to see what they were doing, but their boat blocked most of the view as they turned the raft right side up and examined what they found underneath for a few minutes, talking to one another, before they worked together to heave the body out of the water into the rescue boat. Margie found herself tensing, her own body remembering pulling a man out of the Valleyview pond. She hadn't been able to do it herself, but had needed help to lift his weight and break the surface tension to get him out of the water.

She tried to relax her muscles and breathe evenly. She wasn't the one doing the physical work this time. The firefighters would bring him to shore, the death investigator would examine him and take him away in his van, and Siever or one of the others would attend at the autopsy. Eventually, Margie would get the medical examiner's report in her inbox, neat and tidy.

It was a few more minutes before the rescuers tied the raft to their boat and putted back to the shore, again staying well away from Siever's evidence. Margie walked along the tape perimeter down to the water's edge. She could get close to the water without getting anxious, as long as she didn't have to step into it or take a bridge over it. Then things got complicated. But she was fine standing on the shore to get a good look at the victim and any of the evidence that came with him.

He was a large man. A good thing that they'd had several firefighters to pull him out of the water. One or two wouldn't have been able to manage. His t-shirt had pulled up, exposing a wide expanse of white belly and rolls of fat. He was sandy blond, with short, thinning hair. His face had not yet begun to swell, which indicated to Margie that he hadn't been in the water for very long. But she already knew that. The mom with the stroller had said that she'd heard him running the RC boat, alive and well, at six o-clock.

The firefighters left the body in the boat as they pulled the boat up onto the rocky shore, not stretching him out on the grass to be on display to all the spectators. Pulling the tow rope attached to the inflatable raft hand over hand, the Caribbean firefighter smiled at Margie, flashing bright white teeth at her before pausing to pull up his mask as she approached.

"You are a detective?" he asked. "I don't think I have met you before."

"Yes, I've been in Calgary less than a year, so… that's not surprising. Detective Margie Patenaude." Margie didn't bother offering her hand. Besides the fact that many people no longer felt comfortable shaking hands, he was obviously occupied with his job. He pulled the raft up onto the shore and started to look it over carefully.

"Anton Carter," he introduced himself. "Parks Pat!" he said after a minute. "I have heard of you, ma'am."

"Well, yes, that's what they've been calling me." Margie was a little embarrassed by the name. But it was so much better than the other names that she imagined her fellow law enforcement officers giving her, she didn't fight it. Parks Pat was a little ostentatious, but that was all.

"You are the lead?"

"No." Margie pointed to Siever. "Detective Siever is in charge. I'm happy to help, of course, in any way I can, but I'm only assisting on the case."

"I do not see anything wrong with the raft." Carter poked and prodded at the seams. "And it should be sturdy enough to hold his weight, even though he is a big man."

"What do you think happened, then? He fell out?"

A nod. "That's usually what happens in these cases. Like falls off of ladders while people are painting. They think they can reach farther than they can, and overbalance."

"I guess you probably see a few of those too."

"Ladders? Yes ma'am. If we're the closest first responders, we will take the call until paramedics can get there."

Another of the firefighters showed Margie the remote control boat. She leaned in closer and studied it with interest.

It wasn't like she would have imagined a remote control boat. She had pictured a child's toy, like a normal boat, only reduced in scale and made of plastic. Like she had played with in the tub as a child. But it was wider and flatter, not looking much like a pleasure craft or any speedboat she had seen in real life. She wasn't sure what it was constructed of, but it didn't appear to be plastic or metal.

"Where is the engine?"

He turned it around and opened up an access panel to show it to her. "This one takes nitro. There are others that are solely battery powered."

"Which is better?"

"You could research that all week long and not be able to decide. Everybody has a different opinion. It really just comes down to your personal preferences."

"Do you have one of these?" She assumed by his familiar handling and lingo that he knew something about it.

"My brother does. I gave it up years ago because he always beat me or wrecked my boats. It can be an expensive hobby. We've had a better relationship since we aren't competing against each other. I can just go to a race day and cheer him on."

"That's too bad. It sounds like it could be fun."

"Yes, if you don't get too obsessed about it and are just in it for the fun. But many people… take it too seriously. Takes the fun out of it, in my mind."

He had the experience, so she assumed he knew what he was talking about.

"Do you know the victim? If you've gone to your brother's races, maybe you've run into him at some point."

The firefighter shook his head. "No, I wouldn't recognize anyone. Don't go often enough to remember anyone else from one meet to another."

He looked the boat over one more time and then handed it to her. "I guess you're going to want that."

Margie pulled on a pair of gloves before taking it. "Yes, I guess we'll need it as evidence until the ME confirms that it was an accidental death."

CHAPTER FIVE

he van from the medical examiner's office and techs arrived at around the same time, and neither of them paid any attention to the fact that there was no road from the parking lot and simply drove out onto the grass. Margie could understand their not wanting to carry a heavy stretcher all the way across the grassy expanse or to have to carry their various bits of equipment from the van to the scene to collect the forensic evidence.

Margie stood back and let Siever give directions to the team. Not that he needed to tell them where to go or what to do; everyone knew his job without being told. Margie nodded at them as they went by. They went to the body first so that the techs could gather any necessary evidence before the investigator touched the body. They took pictures, tweezed a few bits that Margie couldn't see from where she was standing, and eventually nodded to the death investigator that he could go ahead. Margie watched him check for a pulse and put on a stethoscope to check for respiration or a heartbeat before starting. Despite the fact that they all knew the body had been face down in the water for over an hour already. Margie didn't see how he could have survived that, but supposed that it was part of the prescribed routine.

The death investigator took some pictures of his own, examined the body in situ, and looked out to the point that the firefighters pointed to on the lake. Carter showed him the raft that they had brought back in and described the positioning of the raft and the body.

During his examination, the man retrieved a wallet and held it out to Margie. She opened it up to reveal that the victim was one Simon Hustler. She did a quick flip through the wallet but didn't find anything of note. No pictures of family, but who kept those in their wallets anymore? It was all on phones.

"Did he have a phone?" Margie asked, looking back at the body. The pathologist patted all the likely places. "Not that I see yet. Maybe it went in the drink." He looked over his shoulder to the lake. "Or maybe it's with his things by the water."

Margie looked at the backpack and luggage that Hustler had obviously used to carry his boat and equipment in, which he had left on the shore when he went into the raft to go after his RC boat. She hadn't touched anything yet. Let the tech guys go through the cases and contents and collect any evidence they needed. If there were a phone in there, it would turn up. But if it were in the water…

"Maybe he dropped it in the water and that's how he ended up tipping out of the raft. Trying to dive after it."

A shrug from the investigator. "Possible."

People kept their lives on their phones and, even if their information were stored in the cloud, it would be natural for Hustler to reach or jump after it in a split-second of panic, only realizing afterward that he had made the wrong choice.

Eventually, the remains were bundled up in a double layer of body bags and prepared for transport.

"Do you have a preliminary cause of death?" Margie asked, unable to hold her tongue.

The pathologist raised his brows at her. "Nothing to indicate that it was not drowning. Pretty good guess, to begin with. We'll know better after the autopsy."

Margie nodded.

Her last drowning case had turned out not to be drowning.

But this one seemed to be pretty clear. Guy had been out there alone on a raft, retrieving a boat that had stopped working. Somehow, he tipped himself into the water and wasn't able to recover.

It would be an open and shut case, easy to clear.

EVENTUALLY, all the evidence had been collected and taken back to the lab. Siever talked to the dogwalking man and the birdwatching woman, getting the same statement that he had gotten from them the first time. Margie couldn't detect any discrepancies or any sign that either one of them was not telling the full truth.

Neither of them professed to know Hustler from other visits to the park. They had just happened to be the lucky ones to stumble across the body.

Margie knew what that was like!

Her stomach was growling loudly and she felt like it was going to eat itself from the inside out. She should have grabbed a couple of granola bars on her way out the door. Just drinking a cup of coffee was not nearly enough to last her all morning. Had she even finished her first mug of coffee? Margie suspected that she had not. Siever looked around the scene for anything that they might have missed.

"You didn't find anything significant in the trees on the way over here?"

"No," Margie admitted. "Oh—but I did run into a woman who was complaining about the noise of the RC boat this morning. She said that six o'clock was too early to be racing it out here, that it disturbed everyone's peace and quiet."

"She was sure of the time?"

"She used the sundial in the corner. It's pretty accurate; I tried it out myself."

"Well," Siever nodded. "Assuming she did it right, that gives us a window for time of death."

"She showed me how to use it. So she definitely knows how."

"Did you take her name and contact details?"

"Uh… no. It was just a casual conversation while I was coming to see you. I should have. I'll come back here a few times to see whether she comes back. Sorry about that. She seemed to know the place pretty well, so maybe she walks here every day… or at least a few times a week."

"Yeah… if you could find her, that would be good. We can find out if there are cameras recording people as they walk into the park. Or taking pictures of their license plates. I assume there's some kind of security other than just saying it is closed at night."

"If we're done here… I should be getting home to my daughter."

"Do you want a ride back to your car?"

Margie looked across the lake to the parking lot on the far side. It was a beautiful day, the clear blue sky reflected in the water. But she had been on her feet for hours and didn't really feel like walking all the way back, either the way she had come or via the other side of the lake, which she had not yet walked.

"Actually, that would be really nice."

He started to take down the yellow tape to allow people to walk through the area. "You should have just come down this end to start with."

Margie shrugged. "Then I wouldn't have run into the woman at the sundial. So it's probably a good thing that I did."

Siever tilted his head, then nodded. "Maybe you're right."

Margie started at the other end of the tape and they worked together to take it down, meeting in the middle.

❧

SIEVER DROPPED Margie at her car. She got settled and touched Christina's name on her phone before pulling out.

"Hi, Mom."

"Hi! How was the rest of the parade?"

"There were different floats, marching bands, and stuff. There were a couple of Indigenous groups. The Stoney Nakoda and Niitsitapiiks. The parade was kind of cool. Seemed more… small town-y than I expected."

"It had become pretty big and commercial the past few years,"

Margie said. "Probably good for them to scale back a bit. Are you hungry? I thought I would stop for something on the way home."

"Yeah, lunch would be good."

"Burger King?"

"Get me an Impossible burger?"

"Sure. You want a shake? They have those mini ones right now."

"Yeah. Strawberry."

"Okay, I'll be home soon!"

෴

THE AFTERNOON WAS MORE RELAXING. Margie watched a few highlights of the parade and discussions of the special rules the Stampede was working under and gave Stella a thorough brushing, which hadn't been done for a while. Margie figured she had enough extra fur for a whole new dog.

"I'm going out with Tracy for a while," Christina told her, marching into the living room and tucking her phone into her pocket.

"Whoa, wait! I thought we were going to go see Moushoom."

"Tonight, you said. I can go out for a few hours."

"With Tracy?" Margie remembered that Tracy was a boy, not a girl, from Christina's school. Were they dating now? Was this a thing? "Why didn't you mention anything before?"

"We just decided. We were both kind of bored and didn't want to stay inside all day. You said you wanted me to have friends and that I'd be able to do things once the restrictions were lifted." Christina stood there, looking expectant, one eyebrow raised.

"Sure. I didn't say you couldn't," Margie reassured her. Though she wished that she had a good reason to ask Christina to stay home. "I'm just surprised. You kind of ambushed me."

"I'm just hanging out with a friend for a while. It doesn't have anything to do with you."

"I was planning on us having the afternoon together, that's all. Since it was my day off."

Christina rolled her eyes. "Yeah, and I thought we were going to have the morning together, *since it was your day off.*"

Touché.

"Okay, well… say hi to Tracy for me. What are you guys planning to do?"

Christina's stance relaxed slightly, reassured that Margie wasn't going to go all hardcore and insist that she had to stay home. "Like I said, we're just going to hang out. Go to the mall maybe, since we don't have to wear masks and social distance and all the capacities are back to normal. We can just… be normal again."

They had been under health restrictions ever since moving to Calgary, so Christina hadn't yet had the chance of a normal life and normal relationships there. It had been nice to cocoon at home and not to worry about her getting into trouble as much, but Christina had to spread her wings and have some independence. Hopefully, she would make good choices. Margie couldn't help worrying about what else they might decide to do now that they were allowed social gatherings.

"Have a good time. And you'll be back in time to see Moushoom?"

"Yeah. Of course. We're just going out for a few hours."

Christina was out the door, jogging down the sidewalk to get into the car that pulled in at the curb. Margie hadn't even had a chance to ask whether Tracy had his full driver's license yet.

CHAPTER SIX

After a long weekend, Margie felt refreshed going back to the office. She had not spent as much time as she had hoped with Christina, but it had been nice to have a little downtime, and she had been able to catch up on some of the cleaning and home maintenance stuff that had fallen behind lately. She'd actually unpacked the last of the moving boxes. Only seven months after their move; that wasn't so bad.

Except for the boxes that she had decided didn't need to be unpacked, that would just stay in storage in the basement. She wasn't sure how they had accumulated so much stuff or why she had decided to move everything she had. They could have had a garage sale or given some items to relatives. But they had just packed everything up.

Margie took a few minutes to look through her in basket before going to her email. Despite the promise of the paperless office and having had to work from home as much as possible during the pandemic, there was still a significant amount of paper floating around the department. And too much of it was just printouts of what she had already received in mail or seen posted on the case file virtual workspaces. They just went straight into the garbage, because Margie didn't want to keep track of physical paper as well as everything else. Filing everything twice was not efficient.

She moved on to email and reviewed everything that had happened over the weekend. Most of it she had already skimmed over anyway, unable to just disconnect from work, even when she was supposed to be off. She saw that the medical examiner had posted his report to the workspace for the Hustler file and clicked through to have a look at it.

Hustler's death had been determined to have been caused by drowning, Margie was happy to see. She hadn't expected to have two cases in a row where an apparent drowning had turned out not to be a drowning. That would have been too coincidental. But as she read on, she frowned.

"What are you looking so glum about?" Kaitlyn Jones asked as she walked past Margie's desk to get to her own. "Didn't you have a good weekend? Or maybe you had too good of a weekend and didn't want it to end." Jones gave her a wide grin. Though she had her hair pulled back in a bun, a few tendrils of wavy blond hair had escaped and framed her face, making her look younger and less like the seasoned homicide cop she was.

"It was good," Margie said. "This isn't anything about my weekend."

"What's up, then?"

"You heard about the new case on Friday? A body found in Elliston Lake?"

Jones nodded. "Sure, I saw that. And of course Siever pulled you into it. You are Parks Pat, after all."

"I think it was more the fact that I'm just ten minutes from there. So… yeah. Body floating in the water, face down, under a raft that had tipped over. It looked pretty obvious that he just fell in while trying to reach for his RC boat."

"Uh-huh."

"But the ME hasn't made a finding of accidental death."

Kaitlyn's brows went up. "Really?"

Siever apparently heard the conversation and wandered over to join them. "You talking about the Hustler case? He said it needs further investigation. I really don't understand why. It's open and shut."

Margie read over the words on her screen, trying to take them in. She felt like the screen was too far away from her, the words difficult to concentrate on while the other two looked at her, waiting for her response.

"He says that there was a lot of perimortem bruising. Which I guess would be unusual if this guy just happened to fall into the lake…?"

She looked at Jones and Siever for their thoughts.

"I guess," Jones said, shrugging. "But he could have gotten bruised from a lot of different things. Not necessarily anything to do with the accident."

"And I guess that's what he wants to establish. Where the bruises came from."

"Click the pictures," Siever instructed, looking over Margie's shoulder.

She was sure that he would already have looked at all the pictures on his own computer. But she did as he suggested and brought a couple of them up on the screen. Blue-purple bruises on white skin. At seemingly random places on Hustler's shoulders, arms, chest, and face. In a couple of places, it wasn't just bruising, but tearing of the skin as well.

"What the heck caused that?" Jones wondered, leaning in closer for a better look.

"I have no idea. And I guess the ME didn't either, or he would have made a finding based on that. What do you think?" She turned her head to face Siever. "Can you think of anything at the scene that would have caused that?"

Siever shook his head slowly. "I initially thought maybe he hit his head on the bottom of the lake, diving after his phone or something. And he could have been bumped by the boat. Even though it was an inflatable, those things still have some hardware and can do damage."

"I can't imagine this being done by a collision with the bottom of the lake or the raft. It would have to be multiple collisions."

"Ready to go?" Sergeant MacDonald asked as he walked by the bullpen. Siever looked uncomfortable. He waited until MacDonald was in his office, then looked at Jones and Margie.

"What am I going to say? Mac is going to be expecting us to put this one to bed, but I can't do that with the ME saying that it needs to be investigated further."

"Just tell him that, then. You can't control what the ME finds," Jones told him. "You're not responsible for that. You just summarize it and figure out what we're going to do next."

Siever looked a little green. "You're so much better at this than I am."

"What's Mac going to do? He's not going to fire you. He can't even criticize you for continuing the investigation, considering that is what the medical examiner says to do. Now if you tried to close it, that would definitely be a problem." Jones laughed. She went over to her own desk, putting down her purse and straightening things on her desk. "We'd better get ready, then; looks like he's raring to go."

According to the system clock on Margie's computer, they still had another twenty minutes before the scheduled stand-up meeting in the conference room. She looked at Siever. "We still have time to prep. No one can tell you that you're late just because Mac is eager to start the meeting. Why don't we take one of the small meeting rooms, and we'll go over your notes and what you want to say? You can write down bullet points or rehearse or whatever helps you."

Siever's eyebrows went up. "You would do that?"

"Sure. Grab your stuff and we'll do a quick run-through. Mac doesn't need to hear everything; it's only supposed to be a brief."

Siever returned to his desk to grab a folder of loose papers and his tablet. They closeted themselves in one of the small interrogation rooms and bent their heads over the papers.

It wasn't a particularly comfortable setting. The plastic chairs and wobbly table were not meant to make suspects feel good. While on the surface, a suspect was kept comfortable and given everything he needed, there was subtler effort to keep him off his game. To make him want to get out of there as soon as he could.

But Margie knew she and Siever were only going to be there for fifteen minutes. How comfortable the furniture was didn't come into it. Siever briskly paged through the reports and statements in his folder. He opened a note on his tablet and began to type bullet points. Margie didn't really do anything other than to act as a sounding board and encourage him to get down what he needed to in order to be comfortable.

"It's okay if everyone's questions are *not* answered," Margie reminded him. "People will ask questions and the answer will be 'we don't know' or 'I will look into that.' That's perfectly reasonable. Today may officially be day four, but it is really only day one. We didn't know this could be classed as anything other than an accident until today. Now we will start making inquiries of a more personal nature."

"What about the scene? Should we have done anything else at the scene to preserve evidence? Was there anyone else that I should have talked to, or any other follow-up?"

"You followed all the correct protocols. Even though it looked like an accident, you taped off the perimeter, identified forensic evidence beside the lake, and stayed out of the way to let the techies' and ME's office handle the evidence collection. There wasn't anything else to find."

"And you helped to establish time of death," Siever pointed out.

"Yes." Margie flipped through the ME's report and saw that his time of death window had been much larger. Because Margie knew that he had still been alive and playing with his boat at six o'clock, the TOD had to be between then and when the first witness had spotted the body under the raft, sometime around eight. It was good to have a narrow window. It made it much easier to identify or eliminate suspects.

Were they looking for a suspect? Of what? Murder? It seemed bizarre that they would be thinking about suspects instead of just an accident. How could it have been anything but an accident?

"The death occurred between six and eight," Margie said. "That is something that we know. Concrete."

"Yeah. That's good. When we look at the video coverage, we can eliminate anyone who left before or came after that." He caught Margie's eye. "As a witness, I mean. It will help us to identify witnesses."

"Yes. Someone might have seen something without even knowing that it was important."

Siever made a couple of additional bullet points and was looking far more relaxed. He nodded slowly. "This is better. Thank you. I just needed to get my mind around it all. You really helped."

Margie checked the time on her phone, though she had been watching it pretty closely throughout their meeting. Having a prep meeting was great. Showing up late for Mac's stand-up meeting would not be.

CHAPTER SEVEN

As usual, the stand-up meeting moved briskly. It was a chance for everyone on the team to hear of the latest developments on each active case. They gave reports, asked questions, and spitballed solutions at a rapid pace.

She listened to Siever's efficient outline of the Hustler case and what they knew so far. He gave no sign of his earlier anxiety, sounding confident and self-assured.

"Any idea what it was that caused these bruises?" Mac drilled.

"We don't know yet. We will need to investigate further."

"There wasn't anything on the scene that you could identify as a weapon?"

"There were plenty of rocks, some sticks or branches. But whatever it was didn't break the skin most of the time. Only once or twice. There were no signs of blood on the shore, but it's rocky; they could have been missed. But he died of drowning, not the blows or any blood loss. My guess would be that whatever hit him was in the water." Siever shook his head. "We just don't know what that was yet."

"What about this dog that found him, that kept swimming out to the boat. Could he have shifted the boat and caused the bruising?"

"Not with the number of bruises that he had. It wasn't just the boat landing on top of him. It was multiple blows or collisions."

Margie tried to envision what might have happened and still couldn't fathom it.

"Is it something that happened before he went out on the water, then?" Cruz asked. "Maybe he had a fight with someone. Then he went off to get the boat, overturned, and presto, we're back to accident again."

"Could be," Siever agreed. "We'll need to find out if there were any bad feelings with anyone. If he was the kind of guy who normally got into physical fights. Questions for family and friends."

"Was anyone there with him?"

"Not that we're aware of. We have some video footage of traffic going into or close to the park. I'll be watching to see whether anyone arrived at the same time as Hustler, or sometime during the time of death window."

The discussion went on to other cases. Siever's shoulders relaxed slightly. He stayed engaged, commenting and asking questions on the other cases that were presented. The meeting dismissed and they all headed toward the door. Margie hung back a little so that she could exit behind Siever. She slapped him on the shoulder. "Good job."

"Thanks again for the prep."

Margie nodded. "So, what do we tackle first? You have the names of his family?"

"His mother. Father is either dead or not in the picture. Hustler wasn't married, no children."

"Well, that's something, at least. Those little guys… they just tear your heart out."

Siever nodded his agreement. "I did the death notification Friday and explained that I would be doing the investigation into her son's death and would be in contact if I had any further questions. So now… I guess we go ask her further questions."

"Was he an only child? Is she on her own now?"

"Yes. All alone."

Margie sighed. "Poor woman."

"Hopefully she has friends, maybe extended family. She couldn't have just relied on her son for all of her social interaction."

❦

MRS. HUSTLER, the decedent's mother, lived in a small home by herself in Inglewood. It was an older part of town, and Margie suspected that she had probably lived there all of her life. Or at least since she had gotten married and/or had her son. Everything about the house spoke to it having been there for a long time, with Mrs. Hustler making only the very necessary technological advancements as time marched by her or upgrades when something fell to pieces. It was like walking into a church, only less cheery.

Mrs. Hustler herself was not that old. Certainly not as old as the house. If Hustler had been forty, she was probably sixty. She looked older than that, but she wasn't a wizened, tottering old woman. She had wrinkles, extra weight, and what Margie suspected was a wig. She moved decisively, showing Siever and Margie into her living room and showing them to their seats. She offered them tea, which both turned down, and she sat down in a chair a few feet away from them. Margie looked over to Siever to see whether he would start the questioning. He looked back at her, widening his eyes slightly in an expression that Margie thought was intended as *go ahead.*

"Mrs. Hustler. We are terribly sorry for your loss. And sorry about having to come back here to bother you with more questions."

"Yes, I know," she agreed. "Nothing one can do but go on."

"You remember Detective Siever. And I'm Detective Patenaude. Some people prefer to just call me Detective Pat."

"Okay."

"Had you seen Simon recently? How long was it since you had seen him?"

"We Skype every week. I have not seen him face-to-face in months. With the pandemic, you know."

Indoor gatherings had been prohibited for some time prior to July 1. Although a woman living on her own, as Mrs. Hustler was, was allowed two regular visitors. It was odd that her son hadn't been one of hers.

"So what day did you usually talk to him?"

"Sunday."

"And did you talk to him last Sunday?"

Mrs. Hustler hesitated. "Sunday a week ago, yes."

"Had you talked to him any time since? Emailed or messaged?"

"We might have emailed during the week. I would have to check."

"But nothing that jumps to mind."

"No. If we did… it was just to share a joke or a news article, that kind of thing. Nothing important."

"How was he when you talked to him on Sunday?"

She thought back, leaning her head back on the headrest and closing her eyes. "I don't remember very much about it, I'm sorry. They all run together after a while."

"Was there anything that he might have been upset about? A complaint about someone else?"

"Oh… he *always* had grievances, that boy." She shook her head. "I don't know why he chose to be so miserable. He had a good life. You know, before you have children, you have all these wonderful ideas of what kind of a parent you will be. How your children will be so well-behaved because you know how to do it all. Other people's children act up because they weren't raised right."

"Uh-huh…?" Margie could see where this was going and smiled slightly.

"And then you have your own child. Welcome to reality. You find out that they come with their own personalities and sensitivities, their own ideas about how the world should work. We do our best to lead and guide them, but they aren't just miniature versions of ourselves. We can't just train them to be the way we think they should be."

Margie nodded. "I have a teenager."

"Well then, you know. During the teen years… you can do nothing right. You don't know anything about anything. And they do."

Margie chuckled. "When you're right, you're right."

"Simon was miserable as a teenager… and he never really grew out of it. It's like he got stuck on that one track, complaining about everything and being unhappy about the rest of the world and how they treated him. And he could never appreciate the good things about his life."

Margie jotted a couple of notes in her notepad. Not because there was really anything to write about Simon Hustler having a bad attitude about life in general, but because she wanted Mrs. Hustler to get used to seeing the pen and notepad in Margie's hands, so that when she did have something important to write, it wouldn't distract the woman from what she had to say.

"What was his life like? I understand that he wasn't married, didn't have any children?"

"No. And he had a lot of sour grapes about that. No woman ever saw what a great catch he was. He was so smart and would be a good provider. She could stay at home with the kids and be the kind of mother that he always wanted. But the women that he was interested in were never interested in him. Sometimes he would go on a date or two, but it never lasted."

"That must have been disappointing for him. And for you."

"You want to die knowing that your children are cared for and are in good hands. I always wanted him to find the woman that could be… a soul mate for him. Someone who understood his quirks and could put up with his nonsense when he got worked up. He was never violent. He just… had a lot to say."

Margie nodded. "And no relationships that produced children?"

"Certainly none that I was ever aware of. And I think that he would have told me if he'd had any. He would have been so proud. But as it was… No. I won't ever have any grandchildren. He even tried doing the big brother thing for a while. I don't know which organization it was, but one of these programs where they mentor children. Uncles or brothers or whatever."

"But that didn't work out the way he hoped?"

"No. He went through two or three different children, but it was the same as the dating game. He would see them a few times, and then he would be assigned someone else. They never told him what he was doing wrong or if the children were complaining about him. He just bounced from one to another for a while… and then they stopped assigning him. They told him they would call when they had a match for him. And then they never called."

If he had been as negative as his mother perceived, then Margie could understand that. That wasn't a good influence around children. They would either be irritated by his attitude, or they would copy it and drive their parents and everybody else crazy. Mentoring programs had very high standards and, if he had failed a few times, they might have decided to just let him down easy. Ghost him until he got the message and gave up.

"That's too bad. It would have been rewarding for him if it had worked out."

"Maybe it would have," Mrs. Hustler agreed. "Or maybe it wouldn't. He didn't seem to… feel the happy stuff. The negative stuff, yes; he would talk about it for hours. But the good stuff never seemed to lift his spirits. I suppose they have a name for that now."

"Depression?" Margie suggested.

"Alexithymia," Siever said.

Margie looked at him, surprised. Mrs. Hustler frowned and leaned forward.

"I've never heard of that. What is it?"

"Well… it's sort of a broad term for not being able to feel emotions or to identify the emotions you are feeling. Sometimes it can be like you said, never being happy about things." Siever shrugged. "I don't know if he had that… but it's a possibility."

Mrs. Hustler nodded slowly. "Could you write that down for me so I could look it up later?"

Siever's brows drew down, studying her. Then he took out his notebook, wrote the word down carefully, and tore the page out of the notebook for her. Mrs. Hustler put it on the side table under the lamp and put a pen on top of it to keep it from fluttering away in the breeze from the fan oscillating back and forth.

"Did Simon get cross-threaded with people?" Siever asked. "Was there anyone in particular who had a problem with his personality or negativity? Maybe someone at work?"

"I don't remember him talking about any one person more than another. Simon… complained about everyone at some point or another. I hate to think about what he might have told people about me. I'm sure he wasn't any happier with our relationship than he was with any other. He didn't shy away from saying hurtful things to my face. I can only imagine what he might have said behind my back."

"So at work… there isn't anything that jumped out at you lately that he was unhappy with?"

"No. No more than usual."

"And what about his social life? I know you said he didn't get along well with women… but did he have any friends that he spent time with? Somebody who might have gone with him to the park for a stroll…"

"The only people I know of that he ever met at the park were those boat people."

"Those boat people?" Margie echoed.

"His club. The group that he ran. Racing the toy boats. They were always getting together. Not a lot during COVID, maybe, but whenever they could. They met a couple of times a week, normally."

Margie captured this point in her notepad, leaving Siever free to continue with his questions.

"He didn't just use the RC boats by himself."

"Oh, no. There was a big group of them. He was very well-regarded by them. They made him the president of their club. If that's what you would call it. He could talk for *hours* about his boats and racing on the lake."

"So there was something that he enjoyed in life," Margie suggested.

"I suppose so… though he wasn't ever telling me about how wonderful things were going. If he didn't win a race, there was always a reason, the other boaters cheated or didn't follow all the rules like he did. If he did win, then he would complain about how the others hadn't congratulated him or had complained about something he had done that was totally within the rules. They were very competitive, from what he said."

Margie remembered the first responder at the park saying the same thing about his brother. How it had become too competitive for him and he had had to bow out to keep their relationship intact.

"I never even knew about RC boat racing before this case," Margie said. "But you must know a lot about it."

"More than I ever wanted to, my dear. I wish I had never bought him that first boat!"

"He got into it when he was a boy?"

"I'm not sure how old he was… a teenager, probably. Yes, I remember the principal at his school saying that he needed to find a hobby. Something to keep him busy. I think he was rather disruptive in his classes. He was very bright and not shy about letting everyone know it. They didn't want to put him ahead, so he was bored. We went to the hobby craft store… the same one as is still there on Thirty-Second Avenue. I let him browse around to see what caught his fancy, and it was those boats. I thought they were just model boats to start with, and I thought that gluing together all those little parts would be a nice, quiet hobby for him to occupy himself with." She shook her head, laughing at herself. "Well, I have gotten my education since then!"

The boat that Margie had seen hadn't looked like a model boat. No tiny pieces to glue together and then show the completed piece on your mantle or float it in the bathtub. The boats had been much sturdier and utilitarian rather than showy. She nodded her understanding.

"Well, it must have brought him a lot of joy over the years. So even if it was an irritation to you… at least you know that it was something he loved."

Mrs. Hustler considered this. "I don't know if it brought him joy… but he did love his boats."

CHAPTER EIGHT

Margie looked out the window again, wondering where Christina was. It had been easier during the lockdown, when her daughter had either been home or at school. There hadn't been much opportunity for her to go anywhere else. But now that the health restrictions had been repealed and school had let out for the summer, it was a double whammy. Christina was free to go wherever she liked and when Margie was at work, there was nothing she could do about it. She wasn't sure there was anything she could do about it if she had been home either. Christina was at the age where she should be more independent, but Margie had hoped that she would still let her know where she was going to be and when she would be home. And maybe that they could talk about the appropriateness or inappropriateness of her activities.

But Christina was being like any other teenager. Close-mouthed about what she was up to, irritated and oppositional if Margie asked too many questions about it or hinted that she would like Christina to be home or thought that she might be getting herself into a situation that was not ideal.

And what could Margie say? She really didn't know anything. Tracy seemed like a nice enough boy, though all Margie had been able to do so far was to wave at him from the front step as Christina climbed into the car. But Christina never came home with bruises or mentioned any trouble from the police or anyone else. Margie had talked discreetly with the school resource officer, and he said that Tracy was a nice boy, not the kind to cause any trouble, not into drugs or drink or gangs, as far as he knew. Christina said that they just hung out, which was not very enlightening. She didn't like the thought of Christina hanging around malls where kids could get into trouble. There had been trouble at the malls with assaults and robberies by or aimed at teenagers in the past. She had checked.

Maybe she shouldn't have checked. Maybe she should have just been another oblivious parent, thinking that kids were perfectly safe if they were meeting somewhere in public.

She sighed. She had made supper and Christina had said that she would be home for it, but there was no sign of her. Margie eventually sat down to the vegetable stir fry with rice by herself. Christina was mostly vegetarian, so Margie had fried up just a bit of chicken for herself and kept it in a separate dish. A little bottled sauce from the cupboard, and it made a nice meal. But not one she had intended to eat alone.

She texted Christina as she sat down to eat. She tried not to constantly phone and text Christina, figuring that if she did, the girl would just tune her out like so much background noise. If she only made occasional contacts when she really needed something, Christina would be more likely to pay attention.

I'm going ahead and eating. Will you be home in time to visit Moushoom?

She switched her phone over to one of her social networks immediately after sending the text, so that she wouldn't be staring at the texting screen wondering whether Christina was going to text her back and how long it would take if she were. The time would pass much more quickly if she weren't waiting for those little dots to appear on her screen, indicating that Christina might be typing a reply.

The vibration and banner across the top of her phone came just a minute or two later, and Margie tapped the banner to switch back to the text messages.

Sorry got held up will be home soon see moushoom

Margie read the message a couple of times and let out her breath in a slow, controlled stream. Christina was fine. Nothing untoward had happened. And she would be home soon. That was all that Margie could hope for.

She tried not to gobble the meal down, but to go slowly and savor it. Eating alone didn't mean that she couldn't enjoy herself and what she had prepared. Maybe Christina would be home quickly enough to have a bite or two to eat before they went over to Moushoom's. Or maybe she would eat some after they got back, when she was looking for an evening snack. She might have already eaten somewhere with Tracy.

Margie was just putting the leftovers away when she saw Tracy's car drive up to the curb. Christina did not get out immediately, apparently taking a minute or two to wind up their conversation and say goodbye. Then Christina popped out the door and jogged up the sidewalk. The front door banged open.

"Hi, Mom! Sorry to be so late. I didn't mean to be."

Christina bounced into the kitchen and gave Margie a quick kiss on the cheek.

"Really, I'm sorry."

"No problem. Maybe you could just pop me a text next time. Let me know you're running late and what your plans are."

Christina nodded. "Yeah, I should have. That smells good, how was it?"

"It was good. Plenty left if you want some later."

"I might."

"So how is Tracy? What did you guys do?" Margie was careful not to put too much emphasis on the words. Just a casual conversation. Two people who lived together asking each other about their days.

"He's good. We had a nice time. Went over to his sister's house to help her pack for a move. I didn't know that it would take so long."

"Oh," Margie was a little surprised at this news. She added the tidbits of information to what she knew about Tracy. He had a sister who also lived in Calgary. She would be older than he was if she had a place of her own. Margie knew that Tracy's family had immigrated from China, so she assumed that there was probably only one sibling. "Well, that sounds like a lot of work. Maybe you'd better have something to eat before we go out." She paused in putting the leftovers into the fridge.

"No, it's okay. We had pizza earlier and I'm still full."

"Okay." Margie put the last plastic container into the fridge and closed the door. "All taken care of, then. Are you ready to turn around and go right back out, or did you need to freshen up first?"

"We can go. I'll relax while we're visiting."

Margie nodded. "Do you want to walk over or drive? Are you tired?"

"Umm… maybe drive over in case Moushoom wants to go for a walk when we get there. I don't think I can walk over *and* go for a walk with him *and* walk back."

If Christina had spent a good part of the day packing for a move. Margie was inclined to agree. She grabbed her purse. "Let's go, then. Stella! Go for drive?"

Stella jumped down from the couch where she had been sleeping and ran over to the door. Margie had to laugh at how eager she always was to go out.

Christina got to the door first and gave Stella ear scratches, cuddled her face, and kissed her on the snout. "How is my Stella? How is my doggie? Did you miss me today?"

"I'm sure she did," Margie obliged. "She isn't used to you being gone so long."

"Oh, poor Stella." Christina loved her some more. "She's used to me going to school, though, and that's all day."

"You're usually back before supper. That's different for her."

"I guess." Christina grabbed Stella's leash from the peg beside the door and clipped it onto the D-ring on her collar. "Come on, then, girl. Go for drive!" She opened the door and took Stella out to the car. Margie locked up and followed them.

"Can I drive on the way back?" Christina asked. "I need to get more practice time in."

It was only a two-minute drive. Margie shrugged. "Sure, of course."

They took Stella into Moushoom's building with them. Margie had been hesitant to do that at first, thinking that people would be averse to having a strange dog in the building. There were bound to be rules about dogs, especially larger dogs. But she had found that the opposite was true. Whenever they took Stella in with them, it took three times as long to get to Moushoom's room, because everyone wanted to say hello to Stella and to give her a pet and a kind word. Margie didn't hurry people, thinking of it as sort of a service to them. Not a formal visiting-dog program, but something that brought them joy and should not be rushed. So she just provided them with a wipe or squirt of sanitizer so that Stella did not become a vector to transfer diseases from one resident to another.

Eventually, they reached Moushoom's door. They knocked and went in. Moushoom was asleep in his wheelchair in front of the TV, and it took a few minutes of gentle prodding before they were able to wake him up.

Moushoom looked at them for a moment, eyes blank, not taking them in. Then all of a sudden, a smile bloomed across his face and he reached for them. "There are my girls!" He gave them both hugs, and Margie brushed his wrinkled cheek with a kiss.

"*Boon swayr,* Moushoom. How are you?"

"I am good. *Maarsii.*"

"Are you tired? We can help you to get into bed?"

"Oh, no." He shook his head briskly at this. "I'm not ready for bed. And I am not so old that I cannot get myself into bed anymore."

"Okay. I just wanted to make sure. We wouldn't want to wear you out."

"I was just napping so that I would be ready when you came. Now I'm bright-eyed and bushy-tailed."

Christina laughed. Moushoom scratched Stella's ears, smiling at her. "She reminds me of a dog I used to have," he reminisced.

Margie and Christina had heard this story many times from him, but neither gave him any sign that it was one they already knew.

"Tell me about your dog," Margie encouraged.

"She was just a stray when I got her. I guess we didn't have the humane society back then, or maybe people just didn't use it. There were a lot more stray animals around. She kept hanging around my back door, and I started feeding her some scraps. She was very skittish, did not like people approaching her. But she got more used to me, always coming back for more scraps, until she would come right up to me and eat out of my hand. And then I started being able to pet her. And eventually... to give her a wash with the garden hose and brush her..."

"What was her name?"

"Queenie." Moushoom's eye were far away. "She was a good dog. She would never come into the house, but we were used to keeping dogs outdoors. It wasn't a big deal back then. Now, I suppose if you had a dog that you kept outside all the time, the bylaw people would come and take her away. But whatever had happened to her before she started showing up at my back door... she would never let herself be tricked or tempted into going inside."

"She was probably abused," Christina said.

Moushoom nodded. "Probably. I don't know who had her before she showed up at my door. But we got on very well, once we were friends."

"Did you want to go for a walk today?"

"Yes. It looks like a beautiful day out there." Moushoom looked toward his window and the bright blue sky.

"There are some clouds coming in. We'll have to come back if it starts to rain."

Moushoom leaned back in his wheelchair, looking serene. "I will not melt in the rain."

Margie chuckled. "No, but you might catch pneumonia. I'm not willing to risk it."

"You don't want to go to hospital during COVID," Christina said wisely. "Especially not with pneumonia."

Margie nodded her agreement. "We want to keep you as far away from infections as possible."

Moushoom threw up his hands in surrender. "You are like two mother hens. How is a man supposed to fight both of you?"

"You're not supposed to fight us," Margie told him, bending down to give him another kiss on the cheek. "You're supposed to do what we say when it is for your own good."

He looked again at the window. "We'd better get outside before it starts raining."

CHAPTER NINE

Margie was at her desk looking through some of the surveillance video footage of Elliston Park when Siever texted her. She looked at the message and then looked across the room to where he was sitting at his own desk.

You want to go back to the park?

Margie could have texted back to him for more details, but it seemed a little silly to be texting across the room when she could just go over and talk to him. It wouldn't disrupt anyone else's work. She got up and went over to his desk.

"What's up?"

"Apparently, the RC boat club that Hustler led sometimes meets at Elliston Park on Tuesday mornings. Around ten o'clock."

Margie looked at the time on her phone. It felt like she had just gotten into the office, but she had been there an hour already.

"Sure. I'm up for checking that out. Do you want to drive together?"

"If you want to come back here afterward to pick up your car. If you're going to go somewhere else or go home after, it would make more sense for us to take separate cars."

Margie considered. While it would be nice to just spend a couple of hours at the park and then go home and work from there, she wasn't sure how productive she would be. It was easy to get distracted at home and to start on something else not work-related, when she really needed to focus.

"I think I'd better come back here after and keep looking through those videos."

Siever nodded. "Sure. I'll drive, then. Unless… you want to drive." He looked at her, cheeks getting a bit pink. "I don't mean to dictate that I should drive. If you wanted to."

Maybe it had occurred to him that when a male and female law enforcement officer went out together, it was almost always the man who drove. But there was no reason it should be that way. But she imagined Siever fidgeting in the passenger seat beside her with nothing to do and decided she would prefer his driving.

"No, that's fine. I don't mind."

"Okay." He looked relieved. "If you really don't mind."

"I don't. I won't tell you one thing when I really mean another."

Siever didn't move, very still as he considered her statement. In the end, he shrugged it away. Margie suspected he didn't believe it. He had dealt with too many other people who said one thing when they really felt a different way. He'd learned to accept it as a human behavior and wasn't willing to believe that Margie would be any different.

Siever put the papers on his desk neatly into one file and put the file into the file drawer in his desk.

"Just give me a sec," Margie told him. She went back to her desk to lock her screen and get out her purse and water bottle. She checked that her notepad was in her purse where it was supposed to be, then nodded to Siever. "Okay. Let's go."

It didn't take as long as Margie expected to get from downtown to the park. Really, no longer than it would have taken Margie to get home, and it was much faster late in the morning than it was during rush hour. It made a difference when they didn't have to deal with bumper-to-bumper traffic.

Siever went directly to the parking lot he had used the week before. Margie looked around, assessing everything. Had Hustler been there alone or with someone else? Had someone else gone separately? Or had he gone with someone? Had they met there intentionally or by accident? Or were they wrong in assuming that someone else had been there? Maybe the bruises were from something that happened before he got to Elliston Park. Maybe not even that day. Sure, the medical examiner could guesstimate when the bruising had occurred, but doctors could be wrong. It was still a guess.

Siever stood waiting for her. Margie shrugged. "Just getting a feel for the place. Seeing if I can picture what might have happened."

He nodded.

"Lead the way," Margie invited. It was true that she had gone out that way the previous week, but she wasn't sure how many ways there were in from the parking lot and how easy it would be for her to get lost.

Siever didn't have any trouble finding his way through the trees to the end of the lake where they had watched the firefighters retrieve the body and the boats. Before they even got there, Margie could hear the high, whining buzz of the little boats.

"Looks like you were correctly informed."

Siever nodded. "You must be able to hear them all over the park. So your witness was probably telling the truth. Both about being able to hear Hustler's boat and about it being annoying to those who come out here to walk in peace and quiet early in the morning."

"Yeah, it would be."

They walked in silence the rest of the way to the east end of the lake, where there were now a number of portable tables set up where various club members had their boats displayed or awaiting launch. The club members were not concerned by their approach. They were probably used to all kinds of people asking them questions about what they were doing. It was something new and interesting to many people and would attract attention.

"This looks like fun," Margie offered, raising her voice so that they would all hear her over the noise of the boats that were skimming over the surface of the lake. Despite the fact that they didn't look a lot like regular manned boats, they were very fast and maneuverable, making hairpin turns and avoiding each other when there were more than one out on the water.

A couple of the men who were waiting for their turn to put their boats in the water turned toward them. Margie suspected that they must only allow a certain number of boats on the water at the same time to avoid collisions.

"It is fun," a man in a red ball cap answered, giving Margie a tolerant smile. "Nothing like getting your boat out on the water."

"Are you here often? Is this some kind of club?"

He nodded. "Once or twice a week if I can. We are a loosely formed group. Not a club, exactly. But it's more fun to enjoy the boats together than separately, so we get together when we can."

"Do you have a lot of members?"

"There's a core that is generally the same." The man gestured to himself and the others who were there, some of them listening to the conversation and others ignoring it as they worked their boats out on the water. "And then there are others who come and go. People who are just starting out, experimenting, or new in the city."

"And does Simon Hustler play with your group?"

The members looked around at each other. "Well… yes, he's here sometimes."

"Pretty often," offered a woman with long gray hair. A couple of dogs stood near her, watching everything she did. They were obviously well-trained not to go into the water after the boats. Margie wasn't sure how hard it would have been to train Stella not to go after little boats. It would be doggie heaven for her to have something to chase in the water. "He was an enthusiast."

"I heard that he was the president of this club."

There was a snort from a dark-haired, heavyset man. He looked at Margie and rolled his eyes. "He told you he was the president of the club? I'll just bet he did. No, we don't have a president. We meet together as friends and enthusiasts when it is convenient. There isn't anyone in charge. Not Simon. Not anyone."

"You don't have anyone who… makes the decisions? Recommendations?"

"No. Everyone does their own thing. And if you can meet when everyone else can meet, then you get together and do it. If you can't… then you try to rearrange your schedule for the next time. There's no… special privileges for anyone."

"Aren't there rules?" Siever spoke up.

"Well…" the gray-haired woman conceded this point. "There have to be rules. For races or meets. But they were just established over time. There wasn't any one person who created them and who enforced them for everyone else."

There was a pause as several of them looked at each other. Of course, they were going to have some thoughts that they didn't think were appropriate to share. Were they thinking about Simon and how he'd tried to enforce rules? Or was he a rule breaker? Margie couldn't be sure from all that had been said so far.

"And Simon doesn't try to enforce the rules?" Siever asked. "Or to make any changes to them? To report people when they aren't following them?"

"He might," the heavyset man conceded. "But what I'm saying is… he doesn't have any special privileges or duties over anyone else. We all just take care of ourselves and our own equipment. If you're going to fight and argue with people, no one is going to want to run their boats with you."

"What was Simon like?" Margie asked.

At their sudden looks of surprise and alarm, Margie realized that she'd done it. Siever glared at her. She'd blown any effort that he was making of being quiet and round-about in his questioning. One wrong question, and everyone knew something was up.

Margie opened her mouth to correct herself, then decided there was no point. They weren't going to believe it and, sooner or later, they would find out the truth, so there was no point in trying to lie now.

"I'm sorry. I mean…"

"What *was* he like?" asked a man with a controller, watching the boat that he was guiding out on the lake. "Did something happen to him?"

"I'm afraid so," Margie said. "I'm sorry, I hadn't planned to put my foot in my mouth like that. I don't mean to be insensitive."

"What is it, then? What happened?" the gray-haired woman asked.

"He was killed last Friday."

"Killed? What does that mean? In an accident?"

"We are investigating his death," Siever said. "We don't know yet."

The members of the group were all turning around to look at the two of them. Those who had boats on the water cut their engines and left them floating out on the lake while they turned their attention to the detectives.

"What are you talking about?" the woman asked.

"I'm sorry, we can't give you any details at this time. It is under active investigation."

Margie studied the faces of each of the members of the group. Were they upset or just shocked? Was there anyone who was closer to Hustler than the others? Who had spent the most time with him? Known him for the longest? Were there any reactions that seemed wrong or out of proportion with the rest?

"You're cops?"

"Maybe we could get everyone's names," Siever said. "It will be easier if we know who we are talking to, and then we can contact you when we do know something."

People were not eager to hand out their names and contact details, but they came forward gradually. The more people who introduced themselves, the more the remaining members of the group were under pressure to comply as well. No one walked away or refused to give their names.

The gray-haired woman was Monica Ellis, the dark-haired stocky man was Michael Richards, and the one in the red ball cap was Larry Brown. One of the men with his boat on the water was Terry Hall, and the other was Vernon Nash. Siever diligently wrote down everyone's names, phone numbers, and email addresses. He didn't get addresses, but he would be able to pull up their driver's licenses to figure those out, and they could do background checks on each of them.

"So you can't tell us what happened?" Monica demanded. "It

seems like you should be able to tell us something. Obviously, if you are investigating it, Simon didn't just die in his sleep."

"Unless someone poisoned him," Larry pointed out.

"I'm sure no one poisoned him," Monica snapped.

"The police are investigating it; he could have been."

Monica turned to Margie, maybe picking her as the softer target. "Simon *wasn't* poisoned, was he?"

"The medical examiner's findings have not been released yet," Margie fudged. If she told them that he'd died of drowning, then they would know why she and Siever were there at the lake. It wouldn't be too hard to figure that out. "He said that more investigation was necessary."

Margie and Siever both watched everyone's faces for any tells. Terry Hall and Michael Richards were both wearing masks, though Michael pulled his down occasionally to have a drink of water and grab a few breaths of fresh air. The others, maskless, were easier to read. But none of them were giving anything away.

CHAPTER TEN

"When was the last time each of you saw Simon?" Siever asked.

They looked at each other.

"He wasn't here Sunday," Larry answered. The others were giving him dirty looks for being the first to speak up, but he ignored them. "Was he here last Tuesday? He's usually here every time I am… he likes to get his boats out whenever he gets the opportunity."

"He was here Tuesday, a week ago," Vernon agreed. "Same as he is every week."

"Were you surprised not to see him on Sunday, then?" Siever pressed.

"Well, yes. A couple of us said something about it. Wonder what happened to Simon. Maybe he's sick. Just the usual stuff in passing."

"Anyone call him to find out if everything was okay?"

Heads shook. They weren't close enough to be comfortable calling him up, even if they thought that he might be sick. But of course they hadn't had any reason to believe that anything bad had happened to him. Just because a guy didn't make it to one regular boating day, that didn't mean that there was anything wrong. He could have been working, visiting his mother, getting a vaccination. A hundred other things.

"So the last time any of you saw him was last Tuesday?" Margie asked.

They all nodded, some more emphatically than others.

"How did he seem then?"

Looks were exchanged. People thought back, tried to remember clearly.

"No different than usual," Larry said. "Simon was Simon."

"Yeah. Just the same," Monica agreed.

"He wasn't upset about anything?"

"Well… Simon was usually upset about something. He liked to complain and make a big drama over little things," Larry contributed, picking his words carefully.

"Larry!" Monica reprimanded.

"Well, it's true. Are you going to deny that it's the truth?"

"No… I just don't think… you need to make it sound like he's a bad person. He complained, but a lot of people do. Something bothers you, you go rant to your friends about it for a while, and then you feel better. That's the way society is these days. Did he argue any more than the average person…?" Monica opened her mouth to answer her own question "No," then stopped, looking stricken.

"Yes," several of the others answered together.

They all looked at each other. Monica was still trying to bring herself to say no, he was just like anyone else, but she couldn't seem to manage it, knowing that it was a lie.

"Well… maybe," she admitted. "A little."

"A lot," Larry corrected. "He always had something stuck in his craw. You know it's true."

"But that doesn't mean that he was dramatizing. Some people just have… a more negative outlook at life. Maybe he had a difficult childhood."

"I'm sure his mother thought he had a difficult childhood," Terry said dryly.

"You guys! I don't know how you can joke about this, or not think about the fact that Simon is dead! He's dead, and you're joking about him or saying things about him that are… exaggerations."

"Was there something in particular that he was upset about on Tuesday?" Margie interposed.

"That's a long time ago now," Larry said, shaking his head. "I'm lucky if I can remember what I did before breakfast. Last Tuesday...?" He looked at the others, hoping one of them would remember.

"This and that," Monica said, shaking her head. "I can't think of anything in particular. He was looking for a part that the hobby craft store didn't have and wouldn't order in. He said something about his mother. I forget what, that he had to go see her to help her with the garden, or something. I think. Anything else?"

"Work?"

"Maybe."

Simon had been an accountant, according to the background they had gathered on him. Margie was sure that an accountant would always have something to complain about at work. Clients who didn't know what they were talking about. The other accountants in the firm. A messed up financial statement. A missed delivery. A CRA audit. There was plenty that could go wrong in accounting.

"Was he here most of the days that your club meets?" Margie asked.

"Sure. He was almost always here. If he missed, it usually meant that he was sick. He didn't skip out because he had something else going on."

Margie nodded. "And what about days that you guys aren't here? Did he come on his own too?"

Monica and the others looked at each other. "I guess so," Larry said. "Most of us only get here on either Tuesday or Sunday, not both, but I know Simon sometimes mentioned being here other days too, in case anyone wanted to join him."

"And did anyone ever take him up on it?"

There was a definite hesitation, the group not wanting to answer the question.

"Not anyone who knew him well," Michael said finally. "A newbie might, someone who wants to get some more time in or thinks it would be a good time to pick a pro's brain about some of the ins and outs of the craft..."

"But those of you who knew him well, you wouldn't come here to boat with him?"

They shrugged or shook their heads. "Simon was quirky," Monica tried.

"Simon was a pain," Michael countered. "I know he probably couldn't help it, but the guy drove me up the wall. His voice, his negativity, his… social skills, I guess? Always wanted to talk about himself, made inappropriate comments, would change the subject and try to take over the conversation if he wasn't interested in what someone else was talking about. He was just awkward, I guess. Not someone I enjoyed being around. I put up with him in order to meet with the others and have a chance to try out my boats or have a race, but come here with him on another day? No, not me."

Margie looked around and the others in the group. "Was that the general consensus?"

They looked up or down or out at the lake at the boats bobbing on the surface.

"He was awkward," Larry agreed.

Margie made some notes in her notebook, but she didn't see how any of it could relate back to Hustler's death.

CHAPTER ELEVEN

Margie was frustrated by the lack of progress on the case. Some cases took months or years to close, of course, but the Hustler case had seemed so open and shut that she was irritated that they hadn't yet been able to establish the manner of death and to move it forward.

She and the others spread out a representative sample of the photos of the body on the conference room table and printed off the medical examiner's preliminary report and emails regarding what they knew about the bruises so far. They ordered sandwiches for lunch and all walked around the table looking at the pictures and rereading the description of the object or objects that had caused the bruises.

Margie worried that it was a wild goose chase. What if Hustler had sustained the bruises earlier in the day from something that was totally unrelated to his death? None of them could identify anything that had been out in the water that might have cause the bruises. Would they have to drain the lake or send in divers to see if there was something under the surface that was dangerous? People sometimes disposed of old cars or other junk in lakes like that. Margie couldn't understand why they would since there were plenty of auto junkyards and the dump right beside the park.

But there could be something under the surface that he had run into while trying to save his dropped phone. It was really the only logical assumption.

"They're all on his upper body," Cruz observed, "nothing below the shoulder blades or chest."

"Do you think that he could have dived down and gotten caught in something?" Margie suggested. "He had to fight his way out...?"

No one seemed to think this was a possibility.

"Blunt object, sharp edges," Jones mused. She examined a couple of pictures, holding them close to her eyes and turning them around to see them from all angles. Margie wasn't sure how that was going to help. The bruises were not giving much away.

On TV, there were always distinctive chain patterns, an emblem, or some other shape that could be matched directly with one unique item. But in real life, bruises were usually indistinct, and a person had to be able to connect the dots and be creative in trying to think of what object or activity had caused the injuries.

"And a lot of force," Siever pointed out. "This wasn't something that he just bumped into. He was hit with a fair amount of force."

"But we don't know exactly how long it was before his death," Margie said. "I don't think there's an exact science to how well the bruises would be developed by the time he died."

"They were new bruises. Not purple or yellow. Still fresh," Cruz said. He looked at the array of pictures. Shades of red. Blood collecting under the skin. Nothing, as he said, that could be days old.

"But minutes or hours?" Margie asked. "What if he'd had a fight with someone earlier in the day?"

"Earlier than six o'clock?" Jones asked. "Who would he have fought with before six o'clock in the morning? He didn't live with anyone, right?"

"No. No family or roommates."

"Then it wasn't likely a fight with anyone. And those aren't from a car accident. Whatever happened to him must have happened in the park." Jones asserted.

"Well, the only things in the water were the raft and his RC boat."

"You got pictures of the RC boat?"

Margie went to the laptop on the boardroom table and browsed through the pictures in the workspace for the Hustler file, eventually bringing a couple of pictures of Hustler's RC boat up on the screen.

"Here it is."

Everyone grouped around the laptop to look at the pictures.

"Well," Cruz ventured, "It could be from the boat, don't you think? That would explain why everything is shoulders and above. He's in the water, the boat is floating on top of the water; it would hit his head and shoulders."

Margie looked at the picture and shook her head. "It makes sense, but it doesn't. Why did he go out on the lake? Because something was wrong with his boat, and he had to retrieve it. So it was disabled, it wasn't going anywhere."

"How fast did you say those things could go?" Siever asked.

"The woman I talked to said two hundred and fifty kilometers per hour. We could talk to one of the other guys in the boat club to verify that or look it up online."

"It's good enough for an estimate. Something that can move like that over the water, it could cause some pretty good bruising."

"Bruising?" Jones asked. "It could take your face off. It obviously wasn't going that fast."

"But his boat wasn't operational. He wouldn't go after it in the raft if it was working."

"Maybe something else was wrong with it," Cruz suggested. "Maybe the controller wasn't working properly. Or the brakes. Maybe he couldn't get it to stop, and he didn't want to run it aground."

The shoreline had been very rocky. Trying to run the boat aground at a high speed would have destroyed it.

"But even then, he wouldn't have been in the water with it. He would be in the boat."

"He reached out to grab it and overbalanced, just like we thought in the first place," Siever suggested.

It could fit. Almost. But Margie still couldn't play it out in her head. Hustler ended up in the water, and the boat kept hitting him? Multiple times from different sides? How could that have happened? He was using the controller to drive it toward himself, but couldn't catch it and just kept smashing it into himself? He wanted to drown? The RC boat developed sentience and decided to kill its creator?

"What?" Cruz asked, studying Margie's face.

"There's only one solution that fits," she said finally.

"Which is?"

"Someone else was there with another boat."

CHAPTER TWELVE

hey all looked at her and thought it through.

Margie played it through in her head. It was the only scenario that made sense. He wasn't there by himself. He wasn't controlling the RC boat and it wasn't trying to kill him by itself. Someone else was there with another boat, and *that* was the boat that had hit him multiple times.

Hit him over and over again until he could no longer fight back or escape it, out there on the water, far from the shore.

"And… it was intentional," Margie said. "It wasn't an accident."

"It would fit," Siever admitted.

"Yeah."

"The people in his club seemed pretty nice. I didn't get the sense that any of them had anything against him. Not anything serious. Just that he was annoying."

"Then I guess we'd better dig deeper and see if we can figure out who *wasn't* so nice."

SIEVER TALKED to the medical examiner on the phone and described the RC boats and their theory in as much detail as possible. The pathologist agreed that it was a possibility. The bruises could very well have been sustained from an RC boat while Hustler was in the water. It wouldn't have needed to get up to top speeds to have caused the bruising they had seen. And it would have been very painful. It would easily be enough to make someone panic and drown, even if they were an experienced swimmer.

While Siever was talking to the medical examiner's office, Margie started running the names of the members of Hustler's RC boat group through the computer to see what she could find on them. She saved each report to a folder with the person's name. Driver's licenses to start with, which established their addresses. Any criminal charges against them. Credit checks. Complaints made by them against someone else. General background, including their social media accounts.

Everybody seemed pretty clean. Larry had a couple of drunk and disorderlies, but Margie figured that probably spoke *against* his being in the park at six o'clock in the morning.

There were others who were part of the group too, though. People who might have attended other meetups and just hadn't happened to be there when Siever and Margie showed up to talk to them. They could get the names of some of the other members of the club. Maybe there was someone with a grudge against Hustler who had judged it better not to show up at the club's next few gatherings. Or someone who happened to have work on a Tuesday morning and couldn't adjust his schedule to give him the time to attend.

Some of the participants had been carrying quite a bit of equipment. It had to take time to get everything together and set up, play for a while, and then take everything back down and pack it away. And maybe then to take it home and put it in the garage until the next time. It would take a half day. Hustler could apparently take off a morning each week, but not everyone could. There would probably be more people there for the Sunday meets.

And it was customary to give employees in Calgary parade day morning off.

"ANYTHING PROMISING?" Siever asked, hovering over Margie's shoulder.

"Well… nothing that really points one direction or the other. I've started to get a clearer picture of the group, but I wouldn't put my money on anyone at this point. There might be other members of the group that we don't know about yet. We can start by re-interviewing some of the people we talked to this morning and ask each of them for the names of other people who are regular members of the group."

"It's too bad there's no members roster. At least an email list that they give out for people who want to be notified of the next meet-up."

"That would be helpful," Margie agreed. She sighed, leaning back from the computer screen into her chair. "Do you have anyone in mind who you would like to interview first?"

Siever shook his head slowly. "I'm not great with people. I would just pick someone at random."

"Then I'm going to say Monica first. I think she might have said more if she had been alone."

CHAPTER THIRTEEN

"Thanks for having us here to talk to you," Margie told Monica. She looked around at the inside of the house. It was neat and tidy. Not quite a "little old lady" house. Way too many RC and model boats around for that. Margie could see that the dining room table was not set with dishes for company, but held a case, with tiny individual drawers containing different parts for building or repairing the boats, and a roll-up tool case.

The nautical theme extended to paintings on the walls and the white-on-white wainscoting around the living room. Monica appeared to be just a *little* obsessed with boats. Margie hoped that she had grandchildren to share her passion with. What little boy wouldn't love a grandma who built and played with boats?

"I don't think there's anything that I can tell you that we didn't already cover this morning," Monica said. "So I'm hoping that this won't take too long."

"Our investigation has been proceeding, and new facts have come to light. With each new fact, there are new directions for us to investigate, new questions for us to ask," Margie explained.

"You can take those masks off. I find it really hard to understand what people are saying with them on. They aren't required anymore, and I, for one, never saw the need for them."

They were far enough away from Monica that there really wasn't much of a chance of infection unless she started singing or screaming, and she didn't look likely to do either. The CPS rules were flexible enough that they could use their own judgment and take off their masks despite strong recommendations to continue using them.

Margie looked over at Siever, saw that he agreed that it would be appropriate since she had trouble understanding them otherwise. They both removed their black masks. Margie smiled at Monica. "How's that?"

"So much better. I never realized how bad my hearing is until people started wearing the darn things. Between people's words being muffled and me not being able to see their lips, it makes it really difficult to communicate sometimes."

Margie gave a nod. "Anyway, as I was saying, new facts have come to light..."

"What new facts?"

"I can't give you that information. But if you could answer my questions, we would really appreciate it."

Monica leaned back in her seat, giving a shrug that indicated *ask away*.

"I gathered from our discussion this morning that there wasn't anyone who was particularly close to Simon?"

"No... not that close. I mean, we all talked to each other and boated together, but... we weren't particular friends with each other. Sometimes someone brought a little Christmas cheer or we marked an important holiday, but it was just... a meetup. A couple of times a week, we got together and played with our boats."

"Was there anyone who was antagonistic toward him?"

"No."

"The men that we talked with this morning didn't seem to have much of a connection with him. Were there any... ongoing feuds or arguments? Even just a feeling of not being able to click together?"

With her finger, Monica traced the piping in the arm of the couch she was sitting in, frowning slightly.

"I don't think so. Not really. You know how men are, they enjoy being competitive. Badmouthing your friend isn't really badmouthing them. It's just something you do to show that you like them."

"So you think they were just teasing each other? Being macho?"

Monica nodded. Her eyes slid to Siever, analyzing what he thought of this suggestion. Siever didn't look like the macho type, but you couldn't always tell by looking at a person. Someone might have to wear a suit to work but still be a redneck with his buddies.

"What kind of things did they say about him? What things did they compete in?" Margie asked.

"I don't know. Just being sarcastic, saying silly insults to 'burn' each other. And as far as competing... we were all competing with each other all the time. Not just Simon. We try to build our boats to be lighter, faster, and more maneuverable. We tweak them with different ignition systems, replacing this valve with that, trying a new fiberglass shell. Getting a new boat with all of the latest advancements... electrics, computer controls, AI. You wouldn't believe the number of options. It's what keeps us going back year after year, tweaking, and buying new stuff and testing it out. Just like a kid with a new toy. There's always something shiny to grab our attention and then we aren't happy until we have that too. I have a garage full of old boats. And some of them were barely even used before I jumped onto the next thing. I've got old wooden boats with gasoline engines. Fiberglass with nitro. Electrics of all sorts." She shrugged. "It's more than just a hobby for me. Some of the guys have families, work, school, wives, and all kinds of other commitments and the only time they can take for themselves is Sunday morning. I don't have a lot of other things to occupy my time."

"You sound like you've got a really good collection," Siever said. "I don't suppose we could see them...?"

Margie hadn't heard him say anything about enjoying boats during the investigation, so she glanced over at him, trying to analyze his angle. She decided that he just wanted to have a chance to see if any of her boats could have inflicted the damage that they had seen on Simon Hustler's body. Chances were, most of the boats would have been capable of such damage. And if she'd gotten Simon's blood on the boat, chances were that she would have washed it well after-ward. Probably with bleach.

"Yes, maybe," Monica agreed. She looked a jeweled watch on her wrist. "We'll see how the time goes."

"You're sure that there wasn't anyone who had a particular grudge against Simon?" Siever asked. "No one who you thought… was going overboard on the insults. Or who seemed to mean them more. Or just that you thought… things were off between them, more than normal."

"Simon wasn't an easy guy to get along with."

Margie nodded understandingly. "Maybe there were a few people who would rather not be around him or to have to hold a conversa-tion with him."

"I really couldn't say. I always thought that… he tried to get along. He had goals that would require him to get along with people. But he just… didn't have the right personality to make friends"

"But there was no animosity?"

Monica stared off into space. She wasn't denying it, and Margie thought it best to wait and see what came out if Monica were left in silence for a while.

"I thought…" She was still hesitant. Margie and Siever gave her time, both sitting still and waiting for her to get it out. As much as Margie wanted to jump in and offer suggestions, she knew that it wasn't the right time. Monica had to come up with it on her own. They didn't want to be accused of implanting memories or suggesting what testimony they wanted her to give. "I thought that Terry Hall was kind of… He really didn't want Simon around. Avoided him rather obviously… said things sometimes that were… more than teas-ing. Kind of cruel."

"Oh? Like what?"

"I don't know if I can think of anything specific right now… I tried to ignore that kind of thing and just go on with my own stuff. There's no point in worrying about anyone else's issues. We have enough to do dealing with our own."

"There wasn't anything particular that you thought Terry had against him?" Siever asked.

"No. I don't know. I thought maybe that they'd had an argument, something outside of the meetup. But no one ever said what it was."

"Did the others notice this tension as well?"

"I don't know what anyone else noticed. We didn't talk about it. 'Oh, what's going on between Terry and Simon?' No, nothing like that."

Margie thought that Monica was done, but as she prepared herself to ask another question, Monica said as sort of an afterthought, "Terry *did* damage one of Simon's boats once."

"He did?" Siever asked. "I don't imagine that was looked on too kindly by the others."

"No. Like I said, we were competitive, but damaging someone else's boats, that's going beyond. We don't do that. We're always very careful, we have rules about how many boats can be in the water at a time, and about taking turns and such. And of course no one ever touches anyone else's boat without permission. You wouldn't just walk up to someone's table and pick up their boat or take it out of the water. Nothing like that."

"What did Terry do to damage Simon's boat?"

"They were both in the water at the same time. I'm not sure what Simon did to get Terry's goat, but it seemed like Terry was really upset about something. He had his kids there that day, and maybe Simon had said something that he shouldn't have in front of them. I don't know. He was the kind of guy that would do that, and then look at you and ask what your problem was, because he really was clueless."

Margie and Siever nodded, encouraging Monica to go on and explain what had happened. "They both had crafts out on the water, and Terry was in a bad mood. He knocked Simon's boat off course and made it run into one of the rocks on the shore. Damaged one ski pretty badly. Simon freaked out, said that it had been on purpose... we all told him that it was just an accident, but I think we all knew that it wasn't."

"Did Terry apologize? Give an explanation?"

"No. Didn't say sorry or that it was an accident. Just said that Simon had better keep his boats to himself and watch where they were going?" Monica's voice rose at the end of the statement, turning it into a question. "That's paraphrasing, I can't remember his exact words. It was sort of strange, anyway."

"And you weren't aware of any incident leading up to this? Simon having bumped one of Terry's boats or cut it off? Nothing that you think would have explained Terry's words?"

"No. Nothing that I knew about. But something could have happened the week before that I didn't remember. Or something might have even happened there that morning, and I just hadn't noticed it. I do tend to get pretty wrapped up in my own boats."

"Sure," Siever nodded. "We all do that sometimes."

He waited for a few seconds, letting the silence grow. Monica looked uncomfortable but didn't seem to have anything else to offer. She looked at her watch. "I really should be getting back to things now. I've done my best to answer your questions, but I'm still not sure where they're supposed to be going. Whatever happened to Simon, I'm sure it couldn't have had anything to do with our boat club. It wasn't even one of our days."

"Maybe we could see your boats before we leave?" Siever asked, voice slightly wheedling. Margie was surprised. She'd never heard that tone from him before. Was he really interested in the boats? As someone who was into technology, he too might be attracted by shiny objects and want to try his own hand at the RC boats game.

"I don't think so," Monica said stiffly. "This has really taken enough of my time. I didn't expect to be taken away from my work for so long."

She had told them that she didn't have much else to do, so Margie couldn't feel too bad about the amount of time they had taken. Monica was just trying to express her displeasure at having to talk to them again when she didn't know what it was all about.

Siever and Margie stood to go. Siever gave Monica a grave nod. "Thank you for your time, ma'am. We do appreciate it."

Her cheeks turned slightly pink, and she escorted them to the door.

CHAPTER FOURTEEN

They were not able to schedule an interview with Terry until Wednesday. Margie felt like they were right on the edge of figuring out what had happened to Hustler but tried not to let it affect her. If they could discover the truth from Terry Hall, that was great. But he might not know anything. He might have some petty reason for holding a grudge against Hustler and yet never have mentioned it to anyone else.

There was no guarantee that their discussion with Terry Hall would lead them any closer to Hustler's killer.

While they usually like to invite people in to the homicide department meeting rooms for interviews, that wasn't always possible. Sometimes people didn't want to come in. It was inconvenient. Parking was terrible. They didn't want to deal with traffic. Or maybe they didn't even have a running vehicle and it was a pain to get there on the bus or on foot. Terry said that he could not spare enough time to make it all the way downtown, and if they wanted to talk to him, they could come to his house. So they did.

Terry lived in Applewood, a neighborhood adjacent to Elliston Park. Nice and handy if he ever wanted to pop over there and play with his boats for a while. Margie and Siever were greeted at the door by Mrs. Hall, a short Filipino woman who smiled and nodded a lot and probably missed half of what they were saying. Margie was sorry they hadn't known ahead of time that she was Filipino. They could have brought Cruz with them. Or Cruz could have gone in Margie's place, as the three of them ganging up on the family would probably be too much.

Instead, they smiled and nodded and tried to speak slowly so that she would be able to understand them.

Margie wondered how she liked her husband's boat hobby. Did she think it was silly? A good thing to relax and de-stress? Something that took too much of his time and attention? Margie saw a couple of giggling children run across a hallway behind her. They were perhaps four or five and cute as buttons. A boy and a girl.

Mrs. Hall had them sit down and bustled into the kitchen to fix a beverage or snack; Margie wasn't sure which. In a few minutes, Terry Hall joined them in the living room.

"I hope this doesn't take too long," he said. "It's my daughter's birthday today, we have a special evening planned."

"Oh, is it? Well, happy birthday to her. How old is she?"

"Four. We're going to go out for supper, and then go to the park for a while, let them burn off some steam. Have some cake. A few of our friends are going to join us there."

Margie had a feeling that "a few of" their friends probably had the same meaning in the Filipino community as it did in Margie's family. Somewhere under three hundred people. She smiled.

"How nice. I'm sure she'll love that. We'll try to wrap things up here pretty quickly."

"I don't know what happened to Simon. I thought I made that clear. I don't know anything that happened and I can't think that anything I could tell you would be helpful." He shrugged. "You're wasting your time."

"If we could just go over things again. Sometimes being in a quiet setting, where you are not distracted by the boats and everything else that's going on, makes a difference. I'm sure it won't take long."

Terry shrugged and folded his arms, a closed-off gesture that told her he wasn't going to be trying too hard to help her out.

Mrs. Hall returned carrying a tea tray. She said something aside to her husband, then encouraged everyone to take some tea and the other treats that she had prepared for them. Or had pulled out of the freezer so that it would look like she was prepared for company when she was not. She spoke to them mostly in Filipino, pointing to the tea and cookies and asking her husband in English if there was anything else that he wanted her to do.

"It's fine, honey," Terry assured her. "They're just here to talk to me. Not to have dinner."

She nodded a few times and eventually retreated, leaving them alone to discuss the case once more.

"When was the last time that you saw Simon?" Siever asked.

"Tuesday before last. I think. The days run together sometimes. It's hard to remember what happened at one meeting and what happened at another."

"No problem." Margie smiled. "Just do your best to answer the questions, and we'll try not to take up any more of your time."

He nodded.

"Had you ever gone to the park with Simon? Just with the two of you, I mean?"

"No. Why would I? The guy bothered me when we were together with a group. I wouldn't want to spend *extra* time with him."

"What was it that bothered you about him?"

"Just a personality conflict. He rubbed me the wrong way." Terry's face was a mask; expressionless. "That kind of thing happens. Just because we were both interested in RC boats… that doesn't mean we were best buds."

"I heard that there was some kind of problem with the boats. You hit Simon's boat with yours?"

"I think they just got too close together and he panicked. I don't think that they actually collided."

"How did that happen?"

"He didn't stay to his side of the course. If he had, I wouldn't have spooked him."

"So it was his own fault. And his boat was damaged?"

"The boats are made of lightweight materials. They don't fare well when they collide with rocks."

"I don't imagine so," Siever agreed dryly.

Terry smiled at the irony in his voice. He appreciated having someone there to share his wry sense of humor.

"But Simon blamed you for the damage done to his boat?"

"Yes. He did."

"Did you apologize? Agree to help him out with the cost?"

"No. Like I say, it was his own fault."

The two children came thundering down the stairs, then stopped where they were and hid behind the banister post, peering around at the two police detectives.

"They can still see you over there," Terry told the children. "You guys need to leave me alone for a few minutes, and then I'll get ready to go."

"Cute kids," Margie said, smiling at the children. This made them giggle and duck down to hide again.

Terry gave her a wary look. "Thank you."

"Do they like racing boats?"

"Yeah, what kid wouldn't? They don't usually come with me, but sometimes as a treat or to give my wife a break, I bring them along."

Margie smiled at the children again. But Terry didn't invite them to come closer and she didn't want to disrupt the interview or irritate him, so she turned her attention back to him, resolved to ignore the children's giggles. They would get bored and go play until Terry was finished and ready to take them out to eat.

As she turned back to Terry, she noticed his eyes on Siever, watching him with a frown. Siever had been looking at the children but, like Margie, apparently decided that the best course of action was not to engage with them, and his attention turned back to Terry.

Sometimes it was helpful to admire or talk to the interviewee's children. With mothers especially. They became more engaged and liked to show off their offspring. But Terry was clearly not one of those people. He had already told the children to go and did not talk to Margie and Siever about them without encouragement. When Siever turned his attention away from the children and back to Terry, Terry's shoulders dipped down and the tightness in his face softened.

"How long ago was this accident with Simon's boat?" Siever

asked. "It sounds like it was recent, but I might be making a wrong assumption."

"It was a few weeks ago. Not long."

"And was Simon still upset about it?"

"We weren't speaking to each other. Which was fine with me. I assume that means that he was still upset about it."

"How did Simon feel about the children?" Margie asked. "Did he enjoy having them around? Was he irritated or distracted by having them around when they came?"

Terry's face immediately contorted into a scowl. It was something that he felt so strongly about that he was not able to control his expression for a second or two. The change in expression was not subtle. Terry ground his teeth and didn't answer at first.

"Simon seemed quite comfortable around children," he said through gritted teeth.

Margie tried to reconcile the words to Terry's reaction. Most people would be happy that other people didn't mind kids around. It would be a problem if the opposite were true and Simon Hustler hadn't liked having kids there when they were playing with the boats. Margie could understand a bachelor being irritated by kids getting underfoot, asking a lot of questions, and squealing at the boats racing around the lake.

"Why does that upset you?" she asked finally, unable to find a more tactful way to approach it.

"I didn't like him around my kids."

"Oh. Why is that? Was he mean toward them? Too loud?"

Terry shook his head. "No. He was… too close to them."

argie studied Terry's expression and then looked at Siever. *Too close.*

"Did he behave inappropriately toward them?"

"Depends what you call inappropriate, I guess. I kept a close eye on him, made sure he couldn't do something behind my back. But he… he'd get down on their level, close to them, hug them close to show them something. Patting their heads or shoulders. Sometimes he would bring them treats or toys. Something from the hobby craft store."

That all sounded pretty innocent to Margie. Things that anyone engaging with a child might do. But what sounded innocent and what looked innocent to Terry could be two totally different things.

"And that made you uncomfortable."

"You know what they say about grooming children. About the molester making friends with the parents and the kids, giving the kids presents, building a special relationship with them. Seeing how close they can get to desensitize the parents."

Margie nodded slowly. "Yes… you're right about that."

"That's what he was like. Showing them more attention than anyone else. Doing things to get them to like him. Touching them too much. Buying them things. I didn't like it, and I told him to stay away from them."

Margie met Siever's eyes. This was a new direction. One that they hadn't foreseen.

"You need to go with your gut," she acknowledged. "A parent can't afford to take chances."

"Did he listen to you when you warned him off?" Siever asked.

"No. He didn't."

"The man with the boats?" the little boy piped up, still watching them from behind the banister. "We like the man with the boats like Daddy's."

However much Margie wanted to start asking the boy questions directly, she had to school herself not to. Terry had already demonstrated that he was protective of them and, if she showed them what he thought was too much attention or he thought that she was scaring them or putting words into their mouths, he would not like it. Their interview with him would be over.

She could already see him shutting down at the little boy's words. Closing everything off.

Siever followed Margie's lead and did not ask the boy anything directly.

"How did that make you feel?" Margie asked. At Terry's look, she clarified. "When you told him to stay away from your kids and he didn't?"

"How do you think it made me feel? The guy should know better than to mess with someone else's kids. If I tell someone to stay away from them, I expect them to do it. I could call the police, tell them that he was causing trouble. I could get a restraining order."

Margie wasn't so sure that he could get anything on the basis of not feeling comfortable with Simon being friendly with his kids. There wasn't much the police would be able to do other than to advise Simon that he needed to listen to the children's parent and stay away from the kids. And to advise Terry to stop bringing the kids to the park for the meetups.

Take the kids to the lake on days when the rest of the group wasn't there.

Margie made a few notes in her notebook, more to avoid looking at Siever or Terry than because she was afraid she might forget anything. She documented the meeting with Terry and wrote down her thoughts about Simon and the children.

"Was there anything else?" Margie asked eventually. "Any other disagreements with Simon? Problems with his behavior?"

Terry shook his head, his mouth an angry straight line.

"How about the others? Are you aware of any disagreements between any of the others in the group and Simon?"

"You would have to ask them. I don't know anything about any of them."

"You don't think that anyone had a grudge against him?"

It gave Terry the opportunity to point the finger away from himself and focus the police department's attention on someone other than him. But he didn't take her up on the opportunity. He just shook his head.

"Nothing I know about. You would have to ask them."

MARGIE WAS sure when they got back to the car that she and Siever were both thinking the same thing. She pulled her seatbelt across her body to buckle herself in and looked at him.

"He thought Hustler was a pedophile," Siever said.

"Yeah. That certainly puts Terry at the top of my suspect list. If I thought that a predator was hanging around my daughter..." Margie's heart started to race and she felt a warm flush over her skin just at the thought of it. "I wouldn't wait until he hurt her."

"He told Hustler to stay away from his kids, and he didn't. He kept behaving inappropriately..." Siever hesitated. "If what Hustler did was inappropriate...?"

"Even if he didn't mean any harm, he should have backed way off when Terry told him that there was a problem."

"Yes," Siever agreed. "Once he knew there was a problem, he should have backed off. Stopped talking with the kids or bringing them presents. Just ignored them when they were at one of the meetups."

Margie flipped through her notepad, thinking. "His mother told us about him trying to become a mentor. An uncle or big brother through one of those programs."

Siever nodded, remembering. "But they kept switching kids on him. And then they ghosted him."

"I think we should find out what they knew."

IN ORDER TO join the mentorship program, Hustler had been required to go through a police check. That police check was clean; he didn't have any accusations or charges against him. The results had been sent directly to the organization, so they knew which one Hustler had applied to.

Siever managed to get an appointment with Amanda Sorken, the director of the program, within a few hours.

Sorken was a tall, dark-haired woman. She offered to shake hands with each of them, and Siever and Margie both shook, though they preferred not to have physical contact with more people than they had to. They were all seated in Sorken's small office. There were stacks of paper everywhere, on the desk, the shelves, and even a few piles on the floor.

"We are required to keep things confidential," Sorken started delicately. "For the sakes of both our children and our mentors. We need to be very careful of anything we say."

"Simon Hustler, the man that we are inquiring about, is dead. So you don't have any requirement to keep anything regarding him confidential. You can keep the names of the children involved confidential for now. I can't promise that records won't be subpoenaed later but, for now, we don't need any names."

She didn't look quite comfortable with this declaration. She sat stiffly, waiting for their questions.

"From what we understand," Siever said, "Hustler was assigned several different children to mentor, but each one lasted only a few meetings. They would meet together once or twice, and then he would get changed to another child."

Sorken nodded. "Yes, that's a fair summary."

"Were there accusations against him of inappropriate behavior?"

She shook her head. "There were not."

Margie let out a breath. That, at least, was a relief.

"Were there any red flags in his behavior that led you to believe that he might not be an appropriate person to mentor these children?"

Sorken had to think about that one. She waffled, shaking her head and making several false starts before she was able to get going. "Not in the way you are thinking, no."

"What am I thinking?"

"There wasn't anything that made me or anyone else think that he might be abusive in any way. But as far as being the appropriate person to be a mentor… that's a different question. A mentor should be someone that the children look up to. A good example of what they can achieve. Something that they can reach for."

Margie nodded. She thought about what she knew about Hustler. A bachelor with a very negative world view and an obsession with RC boats. He had things going for him—he was an accountant, so he had succeeded in his schooling and post-secondary training and was at least competent at what he did. His mother had said that he was very bright, that she had fought to have him moved ahead in school because he was bored. He was diligent, getting to all of the RC boat get-togethers. And he had shown interest both in mentoring children and in the children of his fellow enthusiasts. All positive traits.

"He just wasn't a very good fit for this kind of work," Sorken said. "He had… a certain social awkwardness. Saying the wrong thing or saying it in the wrong way. Blunt. Critical."

"The children didn't like him," Siever suggested.

"No. They didn't. He was 'creepy.' He leaned too close. He breathed on them. He 'told it like it is' when they needed tact and understanding. We tried to find a child that he could get along with. Someone with similar interests or a compatible personality. But we did not have good success. We were still trying to find someone…

told him to wait and we would see what we could find… but eventually, we knew there wasn't going to be anyone. He just didn't have a way with children."

"Did you give him any advice about it?" Margie asked. "Give him some tips on improving his relationship with the children? How to get along without creeping them out?"

"We really don't have time for any kind of intensive training. We expect people to have a basic understanding of how to get along with others."

"So you didn't give him any information at all about what the problem was or how to deal with it?"

Sorken looked at her for a moment, then shook her head. "No. We did the best we could with what we had, but we were not prepared to train him or impose him on any more children."

Siever was making a few notes in his notepad. "Did anyone else ever inquire about him? Make a complaint about him?"

"No." Sorken shook her head. Then she stopped and thought for a moment. She shook her head. "There… might have been one. Someone who wanted to know if he was still registered with us… I'm afraid I don't remember the details. We don't give out any information on individuals, so the answer was no, we don't give out that information."

"And that inquiry didn't come from another organization that was vetting him. It was from an individual?"

"Yes, I think so. I'm sorry to be so vague. We get a lot of calls through here, and if I don't write them down, I don't remember."

"And you wouldn't have written that one down?"

"No. I would write down a call that someone needed to follow up on. No one needed to follow up on this one, because we couldn't give him the information he wanted."

"Male?"

"Um… maybe. That's what sticks in my mind, but I don't know. I might have everything backward."

"How long ago was this?" At Sorken's bewildered look, Siever clarified. "Days, weeks, months…?"

"Days. I don't think it was much more than a week. Maybe. Maybe two weeks at the outside. But not long."

Siever looked at Margie. Two weeks. Just a short time before Hustler had been killed.

They finished up with the interview, then sat in the car in silence for a few minutes.

"So is this what we're thinking?" Margie asked. "Terry Hall thinks that Simon Hustler is a pedophile, trying to groom his kids and mentoring teens in his spare time. He knew that Simon was going to be at the park with his boats. He either said that he would join him, or just 'accidentally' met him there. Then what? How do we get from A to B? Or D, or however many steps it takes. They're both at the park…"

Siever closed his eyes, thinking about it. "Terry Hall rams Hustler's boat. Disables it."

"The only way for Hustler to get his boat back, even just to see what damage there is, is to take the raft out on the lake to go retrieve it."

Siever nodded. "Right. So he does. Maybe he thinks that Terry has left, or maybe he just isn't worried about Terry still being there. What's he going to do? He doesn't know that Terry has it in for him."

Margie nodded. "So he goes out on the raft. Which Terry knew he was going to do, so others must have seen him use the raft before."

A fact that they could verify. Others in the group would know that Simon had a raft he would use if his boat couldn't make it back to shore on its own.

"And then… what? He reaches for it and falls in?" Siever suggested.

"No, Terry uses his boat again at that point. Bumps the raft or knocks the boat farther away. Something that makes Simon overbalance and end up in the water."

"Could he bump the raft hard enough?"

"If those things can go two hundred and fifty kilometers an hour? I should think so. Maybe he could even puncture the raft. Maybe he thought that it would. Deflate the raft, Simon goes down with it, end of story."

Siever grunted his agreement with this.

"So then Simon Hustler is in the water." Margie said.

"If it was just a prank or a warning, then he could have left it there," Siever pointed out. "He could give Simon a scare, tell him to straighten up and fly right—or whatever the appropriate nautical metaphor would be—or something worse would happen to him."

"But he didn't leave it at that." Margie rubbed the palms of her hands on her jeans, frowning. "Is it as hard for you to believe that he would intentionally kill someone over something like this as it is for me?"

Siever's brows drew down. "I guess not. It seems pretty straight-forward to me. This wasn't just one RC boater getting angry at another for crossing him off or damaging his boat in a collision. He was afraid that Hustler was going to molest his kids. That maybe he already *was* molesting others with his mentoring gig. You said your-self that you would do whatever you had to if someone was a danger to your daughter."

Margie swallowed. "Yeah. When your children are threatened, or even being hurt already... So... Hustler is in the water," Margie returned to describing the scenario, making sure that all of the other pieces fit. "Terry is still around and has his boat in the water. Maybe he pretended to leave or maybe Simon just didn't think there was anything to fear from him. And Terry rams him with his boat."

"Multiple times."

Margie tried to remember if the medical examiner's preliminary report had said how many bruises Hustler had sustained. She couldn't remember. But she did remember looking at photo after photo of bruises.

"And kept hitting him until he let go of the raft. Until he went under the water and didn't come back up."

Siever nodded his agreement.

"However much this guy thought he was in the right, we need to prove that he did it," Margie said quietly.

Siever nodded again.

CHAPTER SIXTEEN

Margie looked in on Christina before she went to bed.

Now that it was summer holidays, there would probably be a lot of days that Christina stayed up to watch TV or chat with her friends after Margie had gone to bed. She still had work and Christina hadn't landed a job for the summer. She hadn't even tried, really. Margie couldn't blame her. Things had been so strange in the past year; Christina probably just wanted some downtime to assimilate and try to get back to normal again. With the restrictions having been lifted, it was the first time that Christina could actually go out places with her face uncovered and be places with her friends without being accused of breaking the rules for gatherings.

But she had been out with friends all day and had come home exhausted. She had spent a lot of time outside in the heat and Margie made her drink plenty of water, even though Christina protested that she didn't want to be up twenty times during the night to pee. She had almost been nodding off during dinner like a toddler, and soon after everything was cleared away, she had collapsed into her bed and not moved.

Now that she had her own air conditioning unit in the window, she could be comfortable in her own room and not have to go to bed with Margie in the only cool room in the house.

She was still sleeping soundly. Margie could hear the rhythm of her slow, steady inhales and exhales. Not quite snoring, but a little loud.

It was good to know that her daughter was home safe and well.

Margie didn't have to lay awake wondering what she was up to or what time she might make it home. Or if she even would make it home. Margie had seen too many parents of teenagers in Winnipeg come in to file missing person reports on their daughters. And there had been nothing that Margie could do. She would take the report and see that all of the appropriate actions were taken, but she knew that in many of those cases, they would never know what had happened to the girl.

In some of them, they would know what had happened, but it would be too late to save them.

Too many missing and murdered.

But Margie knew where her daughter was and that she was safe.

❦

AT THEIR REQUEST, Terry Hall came downtown for a second interview. Or a third, if you counted the first meeting with the whole group. Margie could picture Terry that day—just two days ago—a stranger to her, concentrating as he ran his boat out on the water, looking as though he knew nothing about what had happened to Simon Hustler.

They had said that it might be better for him to come downtown this time. Rather than worrying his wife and kids with another visit to the house. But of course, it was far less convenient for Terry. He was impatient when he got in, having had to make the trip downtown and to find and pay for parking. And then he would get to do the reverse after the interview, dealing with downtown traffic and the drive back to his house. All for the convenience of the police department, a couple of bumbling detectives who couldn't seem to get their story straight and get all of the information they needed the first time.

"Thank you for coming in, Mr. Hall," Margie told him pleasantly, setting him up in the interview room with coffee that was fairly fresh, but not hot enough to do anyone damage. "Hopefully today we'll be able to get this all wrapped up."

"I don't see why I'm here. We already went over everything."

"We didn't, actually." Margie shook her head. "And I wouldn't have wanted to do all of this in front of your wife and kids."

She left him to think about this, while Siever came in, set the folder of evidence on the table in front of his chair, and sat down. Even sitting and with his jacket off, he looked very stiff and official. More than he usually was when Margie watched him unobserved. He really didn't like dealing with people face to face. And this interview in particular was going to be an uncomfortable one for everyone involved. But it needed to be done.

Terry looked at Siever, waiting for him to begin. The silence drew out, making everyone uncomfortable. Even knowing that Siever was using it as a tactic to make Terry want to talk to fill the silence, Margie still had a hard time with it. She looked down at her nails and picked at the tip of one nail to clean it.

"You haven't told us everything," Siever said in a flat, serious tone. "Don't you think it's time that you told the whole story?"

"I've answered all of your questions," Terry snapped. "I don't know what else you're looking for."

"No?"

Terry shook his head. "No. I've answered everything you've asked me, and I've come down here, and if you have anything else you want to know, then you should ask me now. Because after that, I'm done. I don't want to keep running around. I don't want this to be a part of my life and to be disrupting my time with my family."

"Family is very important to you, isn't it?"

"Yes, of course it is."

"You are lucky, having a wife and children. A happy family. A lot of people would like to have that who don't."

"It isn't something that you just fall into by accident. I've worked hard for what I've got."

"Yes, you have, haven't you?"

Terry looked at Siever, not liking the tone. But he didn't argue it or challenge him to explain why he was sounding so sarcastic. Maybe Siever had gotten up on the wrong side of the bed that morning. Maybe he hadn't had enough coffee. Maybe he was just naturally a grumpy, sarcastic kind of person.

"Some people would like very much to have what you do," Siever repeated. "Simon Hustler would have liked that kind of life."

"What was stopping him? He could have made the same kind of decisions that I had, and then he would have a happy family."

"What is stopping him is that he's dead," Margie said. "He can't really correct any of those decisions anymore, can he?"

"That's not my fault."

"It's the fault of whoever killed him."

"Exactly," Terry agreed.

"You were up pretty early last Friday morning, weren't you?"

"I don't really remember… no earlier than usual, I don't think."

"Maybe your wife would remember what time you got up." Siever suggested.

Terry looked wary, like they might already have captured his woman and be talking her into testifying against him. "I doubt if she would either. She's usually still asleep when I get up. She gets up when the kids get up, a couple of hours later."

"Didn't the kids want to go to the park that day?"

"They were still sleeping. I like to get up early and get some work done."

"Or to go for a walk?"

"I guess. Sometimes."

He didn't sound like it was something he would ever do. A workaholic, one who tackled things early to leave time for his family later.

"Maybe a walk in Elliston Park," Margie suggested.

Terry shrugged and didn't answer.

"Did you ever go to the park early in the morning to play with your boats?"

"No. I only went on the days that the group meets."

"One thing that kept us from figuring things out as quickly as we might have was that there was no other car in the parking lot during the right time frame that led anywhere. No one who had any connections with Hustler. Mostly they were regulars who were there every day. None of them showed up on the lists of people who have been at any of the meetups lately."

Terry nodded. "I don't see how anyone from our group could be connected. It just doesn't make any sense."

"But then there is you. You live close enough to the park that you could have walked there."

"Yes," Terry shrugged. "If I wanted to lug all of my equipment there. I don't know how I would do that on foot. And I didn't. I don't understand why you would think that I had anything to do with it. Or anyone in the group."

Margie leaned in closer to him. "You knew he was grooming your kids. And even when you told him to stop, he wouldn't. You knew that he had contact with other kids. He told you guys that he was mentoring teenagers. You knew that he was up to no good, and that no matter what you said to anyone, he would just be allowed to continue. All of those kids, Terry. All of those innocent kids. Yours included. He bribed them, made them like him. You could tell them to stay away from him, and maybe they will at this age. Maybe you can scare them into listening to you. But when they're teenagers and are rebelling against you and think that they know more than their old man... what then?"

Terry's face was as white as a sheet. He licked his lips. He took a sip of the lukewarm coffee, then a few more swallows, as if trying to fill a hole inside of him.

"Predators like that... I've read the stories. I've seen how they can destroy lives. I'm not going to let that happen to my own family."

"You're the protector," Siever said.

"Yes. If I can't protect them from pedophiles and drug dealers and all of the other scumbags out there, then who will? They say it's people that you know. Your own family and friends. Parents can't be complacent and think that everybody around them has good intentions. I could see what Simon was doing. I wasn't going to let him hurt them."

"So you decided that you would meet Simon out there at the lake. A friendly little get-together. Simon wanted friends. He would have jumped at the chance to do something with one of his fellow enthusiasts. You walked over with your boat, and then you saw to it that he would never return."

Terry shook his head, in full retreat. "No. That never happened. You can't prove any of this. You have *no* evidence. I was never at the park that day."

"Because you couldn't have carried your boat all that way," Margie offered.

"They're lightweight, but they're large and awkward. You don't want to have to carry one more than a block, and it's a couple of kilometers to the park. And that's just the boat, not any of the other equipment that we take along."

Siever took a large, printed photo out of his file folder and laid it on the table in front of Terry. "That's you, isn't it?"

Terry looked down at the picture of himself early Friday morning, pulling a wheeled case on the sidewalk behind him, the skis of the boat sticking out the top. Terry's mouth opened. "Where did you get this?"

"You thought that by using the pedestrian entrance on Seventeenth Avenue you would avoid any parking lot or traffic cams."

"Where did this come from?" Terry studied it, trying to orient himself as to where it was and where the camera had been located.

Siever took out several more photos, all similar, and laid them out in front of Terry. "In case you're thinking that it's just one picture…"

Terry just sat there with his mouth open. He clearly hadn't expected there to be any evidence to show that he had gone to Elliston Park that morning with his boat to meet with Simon Hustler.

"A lot of your neighbors have security cameras now," Margie explained to him. "Mounted on their garages, up under the eaves, doorbell cameras, there are so many choices these days. It's hard to go three or four houses now without finding at least one security camera. We can follow the trail all the way from your house to the park."

"But those… those are private, you don't have access to them."

"The first thing we do is ask. If people say no—and they rarely do when they know there is a criminal stalking their neighborhood—then we can get a subpoena. But there are enough of them that we rarely go that route. We just use the ones that people agree to give us."

"I didn't… *mean* to hurt him," Terry tried, changing tack. Knowing that he was caught, that they could put him in the park, he had to move to a different explanation. "I was only there to talk to him. To explain how he needed to stay away from my kids. And anyone else's kids. Or I would turn him in. He could go to prison for what he was doing. He just laughed and said that he'd never hurt anyone. He didn't know what I was talking about."

"Maybe he didn't."

"I saw him with my kids. I know what he was doing."

"You saw him talk to them. To get down to their level and show interest in them. To buy them gifts because he liked them. You never saw him touch them inappropriately, or show them pornography, or any of those other things. You just didn't like him talking to your kids."

"Those are grooming behaviors."

"They are also steps to building a friendship."

"Not when it is a grown man and a four-year-old."

"Maybe you hadn't noticed Hustler's social awkwardness. He sent the wrong signals. His timing and judgment were off. Yes. It seemed inappropriate. But he'd never been accused of pedophilia."

"That doesn't mean that he wasn't one."

"Until there is some kind of evidence… we need to withhold judgment."

"And that's exactly what you would have told me if I had come to the police for help," Terry said, sitting back again with his arms folded. "You would have said that there was nothing you could do until I had proof that he'd hurt one of my kids. Until then, he's innocent. You wouldn't do anything about it."

Margie looked at Siever. They didn't work those cases, but Margie knew that what Terry said was true. They couldn't just arrest someone on suspicions. They couldn't arrest someone for pedophilia before they had actually broken a law. They had to wait until someone got hurt.

Only this time, the innocent victim had been Hustler.

CHAPTER SEVENTEEN

It was a clear night. The sidewalks still held the warmth of the sun, but the air had cooled when the sun disappeared below the horizon. Margie bent down to make sure that the blankets around Moushoom were tucked in and that he wasn't getting cold.

"How are you doing?" she asked him. "Are you cold? Tired?"

"I am just fine, little girl," Moushoom laughed. "You worry like your mother."

Margie nodded her agreement. As a teen, she had sworn that she would never be anxious or as careful as her mother. She would do whatever she wanted to and not worry about the rest. She would be confident in herself and not worry about other people. But all of that had changed when they put Christina into her arms. Then the weight of the world landed on her shoulders, and she worried not only about Christina, but the community that she was going to grow up in. Events on a global scale. Illnesses that Christina would face, meningitis and pneumonia and appendicitis. She had known nothing about pandemics back then. But she had known that there were ills that no one could vaccinate her little baby against.

And as a mother she seemed to have become responsible for the other children in her community as well. And the elders. Her extended family. The women and children living on the streets in Winnipeg. The addicts and drunks.

And the others who were vulnerable.

Margie patted Moushoom's hand. "We'll have some hot chocolate when we get there. We filled a thermos with Tim's."

The stars twinkled overhead. In a few minutes, Christina, Stella, Margie, and Moushoom were at the "ditch," close to the edge of the embankment, looking across the city at the downtown buildings and watching the sky to the right for any changes.

At eleven o'clock, they saw the first Stampede fireworks of the night go off. Soon the sky was ablaze with color and motion. Margie poured out cups of hot chocolate for the humans and gave Stella a doggie biscuit that she'd hidden in her pocket before leaving. Stella had known it was there and kept watching her with hopeful, soulful eyes. Setting her cup where it would hopefully not get kicked over, Margie squeezed Christina to her on one side, and Moushoom on the other.

"Do you know how much you guys mean to me?"

"We know, Mom." Christina leaned over to give Margie a peck on the cheek. "We know."

ELLISTON PARK

Elliston Park is home to Elliston Lake, the second largest body of water in Calgary. There are a couple of walking loops around the lake, an off-leash dog area, playgrounds, including an accessible or inclusive playground, picnic tables, a rose garden, and a sundial. Calgary's Globalfest Fireworks competition is held in Elliston Park each year.

Home to many waterfowl, from ducks, loons, and gulls to the occasional Canada geese, the park was named after the Ellis family in 1995.

An RC boats group meets here a couple times a week, though meetups were less frequent during covid restrictions.

INDIGENOUS PEOPLES IN AND AROUND CALGARY

Calgary is built on Treaty 7 land. Treaty 7 was signed in September 1877 between the Canadian government and five First Nations: the Siksiká, Kainai, Piikani, Stoney-Nakoda, and Tsuut'ina. This Treaty granted the Government of Canada a 130,000 km2 tract of land and did not allow them to continue their traditional lifestyles. The Treaty resulted in significant hardships and suffering for those Nations, although they continue to show their strength and resilience today.

Three First Nations (Siksiká, Stoney Nakoda, and Tsuut'ina) have their territory just outside of Calgary city limits. In addition, many Indigenous people live within Calgary, representing a multitude of Nations from this continent.

Some of the Indigenous Nations mentioned in this series include:

Métis - The Métis are a constitutionally recognized Indigenous Peoples (Métis Nation) in Canada. Their culture emerged from the association of European explorers and traders with the nations already living in what would come to be called Canada. The only remaining Métis self-governing land base in Canada is located in northern Alberta, with communities known as the Métis Settlements. For some

Métis, their language is a mixed language of Cree and French, called Michif. There are several variations of Michif, and it is currently spoken by fewer than 1000 people.

Siksiká Nation or Niitsitapiiks - part of the Blackfoot Confederacy. Their community lies to the east of Calgary. They speak Siksiká, an Algonquian language.

Stoney Nakoda - historically referred to as Rocky Mountain Sioux or Plains Assiniboine. Their communities lie to the west of Calgary. Composed of three Nations: The Bearspaw First Nation, Chiniki First Nation, and Wesley First Nation. The Stoney language is a variety of Dakota Siouan and is closely related to Assiniboine.

Tsuut'ina - historically referred to as Sarcee, which is considered offensive. Their community lies between and slightly to the south of the Stoney Nakoda and Calgary. Calgary is currently building a ring road through what was, until recently, Tsuut'ina land. This project has displaced a number of Tsuut'ina families.

HAZARD OF THE HILLS

A PARKS PAT MYSTERY #6

For those standing close to the edge

CHAPTER ONE

argie studied Christina as she prepared to go out with her friends.

"Hat? Sunscreen? Bug spray?"

"Mom!" Christina gave her most exasperated-teenager groan to the word. "I don't need any of those things. It isn't like I'm going to get sunburned."

"Even with your dark skin, you can still get sunburned," Margie told her, smiling at the rich brown tone of Christina's skin, very close to Margie's own. Christina's Cree features were a little less pronounced than Margie's. Anyone looking at Margie immediately knew she was descended from one of the First Nations. Christina was most likely to be considered Indigenous, but her smaller nose and more rounded cheeks left enough doubt that people would ask rather than just assuming. "I remember going to an air show in Winnipeg once where I—"

"Was standing outside in the full sun looking at the sky for ten hours," Christina finished. Apparently, Margie had mentioned the story once or twice before. "And your skin peeled."

Margie nodded. "Exactly. You get a burn like that once, and your chances at getting skin cancer skyrocket. It isn't worth the risk. If you would at least wear a hat to keep the sun off your face…"

"No. I don't want a hat on, and I'm not going to be looking at the sky for ten hours. We'll be outside for a few minutes, and then be in one of the buildings to eat or look at exhibits. I don't need a hat and I don't need sunscreen."

Margie didn't bring up bug spray again. Christina was rarely bothered by the mosquitoes. And it was going to be a warm day. The mosquitoes wouldn't be out until the evening.

"Okay? I'm going now," Christina informed her. She leaned down slightly to give Margie a hug and kiss her forehead as if she were the child instead of Christina. "Stop worrying. I'll have my phone with me, there's security, and you raised me well, so there's nothing to fuss about. I'll be fine."

Margie knew that she probably would be, but that didn't stop her from worrying. Things could still happen. Girls could be lured and trafficked. There was, unfortunately, an increase in trafficking around the Stampede, with extra girls brought in to serve the tourists and locals looking for some Stampede side action. What if some of those traffickers were looking to increase their stables? Christina was an attractive girl of the right age. And as sophisticated as she was, there was no guarantee she would recognize the danger if she were approached by a teen boy who showed her interest.

"Who is going with you? You guys will stay together, right?"

"We're going as a group," Christina said, which didn't actually answer the question of whether they would stay together all the time. "It's just some friends from school. You don't know all of them."

"Is Tracy going?"

"Yes." Eye roll. "Tracy is going."

Tracy, a boy, not a girl, would help to deter approaches by young men, but also brought more worries.

"You won't go off on your own? It's not safe for you to just wander by yourself."

"It will be perfectly fine," Christina insisted. "I will be okay, Mom, I promise."

"Maybe I should come along. Seeing as it is Community Spirit Day, and I really should go see the Elbow River Camp. I went a couple of times when I was a little girl, but that was a long time ago."

"You are *not* coming with me."

Margie smiled and gave her daughter a squeeze. "Don't give me reason to, then. Be safe. Take all the precautions, even if you think that I'm being silly and you don't need to. Remember I'm a cop, I've seen a lot more than you."

"Yes, Mom." Christina's tone was pained. "Now I have to go. They're texting me." She flashed her phone at Margie to show her how impatient her friends were. "I'll talk to you later."

"When will you be home?"

"I don't know. It might be late. We might go to Peters' and then find a place to watch the fireworks."

Margie salivated as she remembered her own trips to the drive-in with her friends those summers she had visited her Moushoom. Peters' burgers, milkshakes in unending varieties so thick you could hardly suck them through a straw, and big baskets of fries. Back in those days, she could eat things like that without putting on weight.

"Call or text me a couple of times during the day just to touch base," she told Christina. "Then I won't call you."

"Okay, Mom. Bye."

Christina touched Margie fleetingly on the arm to soften her abrupt reply and dashed out the door. As she left, Margie saw that she was wearing sandals. If she walked in those all day, the backs of her heels were going to be raw.

Christina had promised that she would be okay. She was sure that she could control the outcomes, when all she could really control were her own choices.

&

ONCE CHRISTINA WAS on her way, Margie did a quick sweep through the kitchen and the rest of the house to make sure that all the dishes were in the dishwasher and clothes from the previous night were in the hamper. The house looked reasonably tidy. Christina didn't always remember to pick up after herself, but she was pretty good about it. Better, Margie was sure, than she herself had been as a teenager. She hadn't made the best choices herself, becoming pregnant with Christina when she had been barely older than her daughter was now.

The thought made her shudder.

She had thought that she was so grown up. Such an adult. She hadn't known how much growing up she would be forced to do in a short time to keep her daughter and get herself back on track.

Margie's phone vibrated in her pocket. She pulled it out, expecting to see a text from Christina, but it kept vibrating in her hand, a picture of Kaitlyn Jones, one of Margie's fellow homicide detectives, on the screen. Blond, friendly, smiling in the picture. She had made Margie feel immediately welcome in Calgary when Margie had arrived less than a year before.

Margie swiped to answer the call. "Detective Patenaude."

"Is this Detective Parks Pat?" Jones asked smartly.

Which meant that Margie's assumed specialty in solving homicides that took place in Calgary's parks was being called upon. She let out her breath. "What have we got?"

"I don't have many details yet. Body found in Edworthy Park. A woman. That's about all I know so far. Meet me there?"

"Will do," Margie agreed. "Will it be on my GPS?"

"I'm sure it will be. And the scene is actually fairly close to the south parking lot, so it shouldn't be hard for you to find once you get there. Just look for the yellow tape and people trying to see what's going on."

"Okay." Margie headed over to the door to put on her shoes. "Tell me there isn't any water at Edworthy Park."

Jones laughed. "It's on the river. But you're in luck this time. The body is not in the water."

"Thank goodness for that. I'm beginning to think that I'm going to have to invest in a life jacket as part of my on-scene uniform."

Jones chuckled at that. "See you there," she said, and hung up.

CHAPTER TWO

The route that the GPS app showed on the map of Calgary was convoluted, and Margie hoped that she wouldn't miss any exits, or she would be driving all over Calgary before she managed to find Edworthy Park. The computer voice would yell at her to perform illegal U-turns and cross medians while Margie tried to keep an eye on the screen and on the traffic and exit signs all at the same time. One thing that she wished was different about Calgary was how much area the city covered. It was not neat and compact, that was for sure. And very little of it followed the grid system that the city's forefathers had envisioned.

Margie finished braiding her hair and pinned it up into a bun.

"Okay, be nice to me," she told the GPS voice, and pulled away from the curb.

She did manage to miss a couple of turns but, thankfully, the GPS was able to compensate without making her perform any illegal turns. She did not get pulled over by a traffic cop. Explaining that she was a police detective and couldn't follow navigation directions was not how she wanted to start the case.

It was nearly half an hour before she made it to the signs designating the park. There was a steep hill down into the park with switchbacks back and forth. She was immediately surrounded by an impressive growth of trees and bushes, giving the illusion that she was out in the wilds rather than in the middle of a busy city. When she got to the bottom, she could see the series of parking lots for public parking. There was a squad car with flashing lights blocking off one access and a cop redirecting traffic away from it on foot. Margie followed the road that curved through the parking lots, aiming for that entrance.

The traffic cop bent down to talk to her when she stopped, half of his face obscured by a black mask. "Sorry, ma'am, this area is restricted."

Margie held up her police identification. "Homicide."

"Ah. Give me a sec." He moved away from the car and grabbed one of the orange A-frame barricades that also blocked the road. He pulled it to the side so that Margie could get her car past the police car, then pulled it back into place as she drove farther down the road.

Margie continued to follow the road and the waves of various law enforcement officers or park conservation officers along the way until she reached what was obviously the staging area. She stepped out of her car and was met by Detective Jones.

"Didn't take you too long," Jones observed, her eyes smiling. "I take it Edworthy Park was on your GPS?"

"Yes. Didn't lead me astray this time. Which means I'll have to be all the more careful next time…"

Jones nodded. "We're this way."

She led Margie at a quick clip to a patch of browning grass and dirt with narrow tire impressions, and there it was. Margie stayed well back from the body, looking around to see whether the forensic techs were there yet. There were a couple already geared up and waiting in the shade of the nearby trees. She made a slow circle of the body but couldn't see much other than what Jones had already mentioned. That it was a woman, and she was dead. The crumpled form was face down, limbs askew, and it was not immediately apparent what had happened to her. She wore a light jacket and long pants, so it had probably been cool when she had gone for a walk in the park and… Margie had to stop there, because she really didn't have any idea what happened next. The clothes were scuffed and had holes in them. A homeless person?

"Any idea what happened to her?" Margie asked. "Who found the body?"

"Dog walker." Jones motioned in what appeared to be a random direction, since Margie didn't see a man with a dog waiting to be interviewed. There were privacy screens up, though, and there might be a witness in one of the blind spots. "As usual. And as far as the cause of death, I would think that was pretty obvious."

Margie looked again for any sign of violence. There was no spreading pool of blood, no visible bullet or knife wound. No vomit puddles nearby indicating poison or overdose.

"I guess I haven't had enough coffee yet this morning. What's obvious?"

Jones pointed up. Margie raised her head and followed the direction of Jones's index finger. "What...?"

The hill beside them was steep, nearly a cliff. But as Margie looked at it, she realized that the stripes down the side were trails worn by bicycle tires. Margie would not have attempted to walk up or down the steep incline but, apparently, bikers used it regularly. Margie looked at the tire marks through the clearing. What amazed her was how many tire tracks and worn trails there were. It clearly wasn't just something that one daredevil had attempted, surviving the plunge to the bottom, but something that was done with regularity.

"You've got to be kidding me."

"I wish I was."

"She fell?"

"Looks that way. Went out for her evening constitutional, and..." Jones made a whistling sound.

"Ai-yi-yi! Why isn't there a fence or a barrier at the top? This is dangerous!"

"They've had fences. They gave up because they kept being pulled down by the downhill bikers."

"They should be put in jail. Or in some kind of institution. How could anyone sane even consider that?" Margie stared up the hill. "I mean seriously, is biking down there even possible?"

"I don't think I would be able to watch."

Margie took another look around, analyzing the positioning of the body once more. Not someone who had just collapsed there, but someone who had taken a tumble down the hill and landed in a heap there. The dirt and tears in her clothing not from living rough or sleeping outside, but from falling down the hill head over heels.

"How high is the hill?"

"I asked one of the CO's. Apparently, it's about 70 meters."

Margie automatically converted it in her head. Over 210 feet.

"Crap. She must have been terrified."

Jones nodded soberly.

"Well, I don't think we're going to figure out much more standing here, so let's have the experts take a look."

"Yup." Jones raised her hand high over her head, motioning for the forensic guys to come over. They looked at her for any detailed instructions she might have. "I'll leave you to it. I don't have any particular insight into people who fall over cliffs. I guess we should look for anything that she might have been holding and dropped. But I don't see anything obvious. Record everything you can, and then we'll have the death investigator take a look at the body and arrange transport."

They didn't tell her that they already knew the protocol, just nodded politely and went to work. Margie and Jones scanned the ground for anything that might have been dropped or fallen out of the pockets of the deceased. There was some litter, more likely left behind by the crazy downhill bikers, but it would all have to be gathered together for analysis anyway.

"You can't be over the police line!" A strong male voice was raised over the chatter of police radios, bystanders, and various people involved in the scene. Margie looked around one of the privacy screens to see what the commotion was about. Detective Gagnon, whom she'd not had much opportunity to work with previously, was telling off one of the bystanders, who was, in fact, properly behind the yellow police tape. Margie turned her head to frown at Jones, who was also looking at the scene with some consternation.

"You want me to confiscate that?" Gagnon demanded.

The man he was talking to had something in both hands like an electronic game. His head was down and he was working the controller in his hands. He glanced up at Gagnon, scowling, and said something back to him.

Margie wanted to go see what was going on, but if she and Jones both went over, it would look like they were questioning Gagnon's judgment or all ganging up on the bystander, neither of which was a desirable scenario.

"Go ahead," Jones said. "See if he needs a hand with anything and I'll supervise here."

Margie nodded and moved off to join Gagnon at the perimeter. "Anything I can assist with, Detective Gagnon?"

He cast an irritated glance at her, which Margie fully understood. She wouldn't want anyone trying to poke their nose in when she was handling a situation either. Only sometimes, it did help to have someone else on hand.

"This joker thinks that he doesn't have to respect the police line," Gagnon pointed out.

Margie looked at the man a few feet back of the police tape. But as she stood there, something caught her attention out the corner of her eye. She turned her head and looked up. A bird or squirrel? But the movement hadn't been an animal in the trees. It was a small box floating in the air. There was a very faint whirring coming from it that she could barely hear over the other ambient noise of the murder site.

A remote-control drone of some kind. And it was, in fact, significantly inside the police line. In a position where its camera would be able to view over the privacy screens to where the body lay. Margie looked back at the man with the controller in his hands.

"Do you want me to arrest him for obstructing an investigation?"

Gagnon's jaw clenched and he gave a curt nod. "Might as well, he won't listen to anything else."

Margie took a step toward him. "Sir, I'm putting you under—"

"I'm not doing anything!" the man protested, looking at her for a moment before looking back down at the controller in his hands, twiddling the joystick that controlled the craft's direction. "I'm not interfering. I'm back here behind the police line, just like he said. I haven't touched anything or gotten in anybody's way."

"You've been told that thing can't be over the police line. You've failed to comply. So I'm putting you under arrest. We'll impound the drone and the judge can decide whether—"

"It's here. It's here, it's not over the line anymore." The little box hovered over the man, then ducked slightly behind him, as if it were a child hiding behind his father.

"What's your name, sir?"

"Howard Ross."

"Have you got some ID?"

He looked as though he would argue. Then he bit his lip and used his controller to bring the drone down to the ground, so that he could put the controller down to go through his pockets. He pulled a wallet out of his breast pocket and dug out his driver's license for Margie to look at. He had given his correct name, and she quickly jotted down his name, address, and birth date, as well as the operator's license number in her notepad.

"Have you ever been arrested before?" she asked him.

"You can't arrest me! I'm doing what you told me to."

Margie looked at Gagnon, raising her brows. "I'm pretty sure I can," she argued. "Wouldn't you say?"

"Of course."

Margie nodded. "So, is this the first time you've been arrested?"

"I've never been arrested before. Look, all I was doing was using my drone. I didn't think there was any harm in it."

"When a peace officer gives you a command and you don't comply, you're in the wrong. Period. It doesn't really matter what you *think*."

He opened his mouth to argue, then apparently thought better of it. "Yes, ma'am."

"This is a police perimeter. You can't cross a police perimeter with a drone."

He nodded his understanding.

"I think you owe Detective Gagnon here an apology."

"I'm sorry," Ross said immediately. He turned slightly to face

Gagnon directly. "I'm sorry, sir. I should have listened to what you said. I really don't want to be arrested. I wasn't trying to do anything wrong. Do you think…"

Gagnon gave him a fierce look, unblinking. Ross lowered his eyes and looked at the ground near his feet.

"I am. I'm sorry. I'm not just saying that. Please don't arrest me or confiscate my drone."

"Why don't you pick up your drone and get out of here?"

"Okay. Yes, sir. I will." Ross turned around and bent down to pick up the small drone and beat a hasty retreat.

Gagnon turned and looked at Margie.

"I hope you don't think I was interfering," Margie said. "I was just offering to help out."

"You have a teenager at home?"

"Yes," Margie was surprised that he knew. She hadn't had much to do with Gagnon at the office, and she didn't talk a lot about Christina or have pictures on her desk. She tried to keep her personal life and job from intermixing too much.

"I thought so. There's no one as intimidating as a mom with a teenager."

Margie laughed. "Thanks!"

"He didn't back down for me," Gagnon pointed out. "But he wasn't going to cross Mama Bear."

CHAPTER THREE

The medical examiner's van had pulled into the scene. Margie nodded to Gagnon and returned to the area behind the screens. She waved at Jones, who had noticed her return. While the techs stood to the side once more, the death investigator from the medical examiner's office leaned over the body. Margie had met him before.

"Dr. Kahn."

He looked up for a moment. "Parks Pat," he greeted, tone slightly mocking.

"That's Detective Pat to you."

He was wearing a mask and face shield, but she saw the fan of wrinkles that sprang from the corners of his eyes when he smiled at her comment.

"I suppose you're expecting me to declare cause and manner of death on the spot."

"Oh, Detective Jones has already done that," Margie said, waving a hand airily. "Accidental death caused by a fall."

"It wasn't the fall that killed her," Kahn said.

"Oh?"

Everyone nearby froze and looked at him, startled by this announcement.

"No. It was the landing that killed her."

Margie groaned. Everyone resumed their conversations, their eyeballs nearly rolling out of their heads. "That's really bad, Dr. Kahn."

"I thought you would appreciate it."

"I'm not sure *appreciate* is the right word."

He chuckled and resumed his examination of the body. Margie was hesitant to look too closely, but now that the woman had been turned over, she leaned in for a better look at the face. The fall had done a number, but she was still recognizable. Since the impact had killed her, there hadn't been any swelling. If she had survived, Margie was sure her face would have been too swollen for her own mother to recognize her.

"Do we have an identity?"

"Patience."

"Patience who?"

He ignored her. After a few minutes, he patted her pockets. He shook his head. "No wallet on her. You've looked around the area to see whether it fell somewhere close by?"

"We didn't find anything," Jones confirmed.

Kahn looked up at the hill. "Then I guess you should look at the top and follow her path down. See if she lost a wallet or purse along the way. It could be caught on a clump of leaves or a depression in the ground."

They all looked at the 70-meter climb. No one volunteered.

"Do you think it's best to go down from the top, or up from the bottom?" Jones asked Margie.

"Top down, for sure. But with a harness and rope. I'm not taking the chance of landing beside our mystery woman."

"Try the Fire Department Vertical Rescue Team," Kahn suggested. "They love stuff like this."

Margie didn't mind the idea of adding a little adventure to someone else's day. If the Fire Department would enjoy belaying down the hill, who was she to step in the way of their good time? "I'm on it."

She called the non-emergency line and explained to the phone operator what she needed. In a few minutes, she was talking to Captain Burrows, head of the Vertical Rescue Team. She smiled at the excitement in his voice when he heard that they had an actual crime scene to help out with. Not just an exercise, but not a life and death rescue either.

"We'll be there as soon as possible, detective."

"Do you need coordinates or a more accurate description of where it is?"

"Oh, trust me, I know where it is."

Margie laughed and hung up. "They'll be on their way soon," she told Jones.

"Excellent. You don't know how glad I am that no one is going to be lowering me down that hill on a rope. Do you know how long it would be before I got tripped up on a slope like that?"

Jones was a little overweight and not in the best physical shape. Unfortunately, detectives spent a little too much time at their desks and didn't get the kind of exercise that a beat cop did. She wasn't particularly clumsy that Margie had noticed, but Margie wouldn't want to be going down that hill without a safety harness either. She couldn't imagine looking down from the top of the hill, balancing on a bike, trying to work up the courage to rocket down it. It was amazing they didn't have regular calls out to the location. Maybe that said something about the common sense of most bikers. But not all of them.

She looked back at Dr. Kahn and the victim. "Was she killed instantly?" She wasn't sure she wanted to know the answer to that one. But it was something they would need to know.

"Very little blood or perimortem bruising. I would say that she probably died on impact." He was working his way around the victim's head, fingers quick and light. Margie was reminded of checking a melon for soft spots. The thought stirred a little nausea and she turned away to look around the scene.

"At least this one is clearly an accident," she offered to Jones.

"Don't jinx it."

"By saying that it's an accident?"

Jones nodded. "Yeah. You don't want it to turn out to *not* be an accident, do you?"

"No. But I don't think I can say anything now that will change it."

"Just don't bring the wrath of the universe down on you by saying we know something before the medical examiner confirms it. You know how complicated things can get when you think it's an accident but then it isn't."

Margie rolled her eyes. Yes, she had seen that on a few cases. "Okay. I'm not saying anything. Unhear it and forget all about it. We don't know anything yet. I sure hope that the medical examiner decides that it was an accident."

Jones groaned.

Margie looked at her. "Not that either?"

"No."

Margie lapsed into silence. Apparently, she was not supposed to say anything.

&

THEY COULD HEAR sirens off in the distance, apparently getting closer and, after a few minutes, the sirens cut off somewhere close by. Margie looked up at the top of the hill. It wasn't long before she could see tall dark figures silhouetted at the top of the hill. It made her dizzy just looking up at them.

Didn't they get dizzy looking down?

Jones waved up at them and a few of the men waved back. They stood at the top discussing things for some time, then retreated.

By the time Dr. Kahn and his assistant had removed the woman's body from the scene and were transporting her back to the van, firefighters were starting down the hill, strolling along as if they were just out for a Sunday walk. But Margie could see that they had safety harnesses attached to ropes being belayed by men up above. They worked their way down the hill slowly.

Margie gasped when she saw one of them slip and ski down the hill for a few feet on loose dirt or gravel. She could hear the sound of the skid and found herself reaching toward him as if she could hold him back. She laughed at herself, covering her mouth with her hand to prevent herself from gasping or shouting out again. But she'd heard several other gasps around her too. She wasn't the only one captivated by the sight of the strapping young men working their way down the dangerous slope.

One of the men called out and held a hand up to stop the others. Margie couldn't hear what he was saying and took a couple of steps closer, hoping that if she concentrated, she would be able to hear what he was saying.

Her phone started buzzing in her pocket. Margie answered it and heard Captain Burrows's voice.

"What do you want us to do about any evidence that we find?"

"Well… it will need to be documented." Margie stared up at the hill, where they were gathered around something. "Can they take pictures? Something close up, with an object to show scale, and some shots showing context—the area it is in. We'll have to mark it all on a map of the hill afterward. Do they have gloves and evidence bags?"

"Yes, I did think that much out ahead of time. We can manage that."

"Okay. Have one person do all the collecting, he'll need to initial the evidence bags and sign an affidavit so that we maintain the chain of evidence. What did they find?"

"Couple of credit cards. No purse or wallet yet. Maybe she just had them loose in her pocket."

"Oh, well I guess you don't need to show scale for credit cards. They're all the same size."

"Got it. Thanks."

❧

MARGIE'S PHONE vibrated again as the forensic techs were gathering up the last of their evidence and equipment. She instinctively looked up the hill to see whether it was Burrows again but, of course, he wasn't standing on the edge looking down at her.

She slid out her phone and looked at the face, but it wasn't Burrows this time. It was Christina.

"Hi, sweetie." Margie glanced around her. She'd hardly even been aware of the passing of time and didn't know at first whether Christina would even be at the Stampede yet. But judging by the short shadows on the ground it was noon or close to it. "How has the morning gone?"

"Really good," Christina enthused. "There were some really good bands, and we even got to talk to some of the musicians. There aren't a lot of people down here like you would expect there to be. Except with COVID, you don't know how many people to expect. But it isn't crazy crowds like I had imagined."

"That's great. What else have you done?"

"A bit of this and that. Some games and rides, a couple of exhibits. I'm going to go have lunch in the Elbow River Camp. See what's going on over there."

"That sounds great. Say *Taanishi* for me."

Christina sounded like she was smiling as she answered. "Okay. I just wanted to let you know that I was still alive and haven't been kidnapped by head hunters. We're having a good time, and everyone is fine."

"Thanks for letting me know. Call me again later."

CHAPTER FOUR

argie followed Jones's car up to the top of the hill where the vertical rescue team was staged. They were met by Captain Burrows, a tall, broad-chested man in his thirties who would certainly not be out of place on one of the fundraising calendars that the fire department put out. Margie gave him a warm smile behind her mask and strove to remain professional.

"I'm so glad that we had your team available. I would not have wanted to search that slope by myself."

He nodded his agreement. "It really isn't safe. Can't believe that people would actually use it for downhill biking. Some people are crazy."

"Or suicidal," Margie agreed. "I can't imagine doing that unless you were."

"The people who do things like that don't usually think about consequences. Teenagers and young people whose brains haven't fully developed. Thrill seekers. No real concept about the kind of suffering it could bring to them or their families. Plenty of my guys are thrill seekers. It's the nature of the job. But going on a bike down that slope… that's beyond the pale."

Jones and Margie both vigorously nodded their agreement.

One of the other team members joined them, smiling in greeting. "And you must be the detectives."

"We are," Jones agreed. She nodded to the bags in his hand. "My evidence?"

"Yes. Can you walk me through what I'm supposed to do to preserve the chain?"

Jones had him seal and initial the bags and took down his name and contact information in her notepad. "I'll send you an affidavit to fill out. At some point, you could be called upon to testify, but considering that this is ninety-nine percent likely to be classified as an accident, probably not."

He nodded and handed the sealed paper bags to her.

"Did you see the name on the credit cards?" Jones asked.

"Evie Wyler." The firefighter spelled it for Jones.

"Great. Much easier to identify the body when you have a name to begin with."

They chatted for a moment, some small talk. Margie cocked her head. "Is there music?"

Burrows pointed. "It's the Wildwood Stampede Breakfast. Just over there. We've been invited to join them if you'd like to come along."

"No, we should be getting back to the office." But Margie was already salivating at the idea of a pancake breakfast. She'd had her usual coffee and toast and normally tried to stay away from big breakfasts full of greasy sausages and fake maple syrup. But she could smell the grease and syrup in the breeze and it brought back memories of Stampede breakfasts she'd had as a child when she had been visiting her Moushoom or other relatives in Calgary.

"I don't know how many opportunities we're going to have for pancake breakfasts," Jones said, looking longingly in that direction.

"Maybe… we should conduct some community interviews," Margie suggested. "People in this area must know about the hill. Evie Wyler might have come from this neighborhood. Must have if she was out walking at night. You don't drive to another part of town to go for a midnight stroll."

"Unless you're casing out houses to burgle," Jones put in.

Margie grinned. "Well, obviously."

"I think we should check it out. Keep our fingers on the pulse of the neighborhood. Identify suspects. Find out if she had friends and family in the area. Or if anyone was aware of any problems she might have been having."

"Problems?"

"Threats. Depression." Jones shrugged. "We won't know until we ask."

Margie nodded. "Really, we'd be negligent if we didn't."

"I agree."

"You call it in," Margie told her. "I'll go scout ahead."

"You can leave your cars here," Burrows advised. "There isn't much parking over there because they're using the community center parking lot for the breakfast. It's just a few blocks. That way you work off the calories walking there and back," he told her with a knowing grin.

Looking at his physique, Margie had a hard time believing that he ever had to worry about counting calories. Though, maybe that was how he had gotten into such fine shape. She should take his advice. "Okay, that sounds good," she agreed.

Jones made a quick phone call to check in as she walked to her car and locked the evidence into the trunk. She slid her phone back into her pocket. "I saw him first."

"Who?" Margie laughed. "Captain Burrows?"

"Yes."

"I talked to him before you saw him."

"Doesn't count."

Margie chuckled again as they started walking toward the vertical rescue team, who were heading down the street toward the faint music and smell of sausages. "I don't need that kind of complication in my life right now. You go right ahead."

"He's just the kind of complication that I do need in my life."

"He's all yours. With a teenager in the house, I'm really not into dating right now."

"Why does having a teenager in the house matter?"

"If she isn't totally mortified at the idea of her mother having a boyfriend or... extracurricular pursuits, then she repeats back all of the motherly advice that I ever gave her. It's one thing when she's telling me to eat a proper breakfast or to make sure I eat enough vegetables. I don't think I'm up for *that* talk from my daughter."

❦

THE COMMUNITY CENTER was a little farther away than Margie would have guessed. The music was very loud and the breeze blowing in just the right direction to carry the food smells to them. Margie looked around at the long tables set up in the parking lot to eat at and the grills lined up nearby. The smells all mixed to produce that distinct *Stampede Breakfast* perfume. People were milling around, talking excitedly with one another and enjoying the band. Some wore masks, and others didn't and were quick to greet each other with friendly hugs.

"Come on over here for your breakfast," a stout woman in a plaid blue and white shirt instructed. "Free for emergency responders, of course. You can get whatever you want. Tables are set up if you want to eat there. If you want to social distance, then pick a spot on the grass."

"Thank you," Margie nodded at the woman. "This looks really great."

"It's so nice to be able to do something as a community again. I feel like we've been in prison for a year and a half and have finally been let out. It's so nice to be back to *normal.*" She shrugged, looking at Margie's and Jones's masks. "Well, as normal as possible."

"Do you know an Evie Wyler?" Jones asked the woman. "I thought that she might be here." Jones faked looking around for her.

"Wyler... I'm not sure. I've seen her name on the Facebook page, but I'm not sure that I would recognize her. Charles...?"

A tall man with a bushy mustache and a straw cowboy hat turned from his grill to face her. "Yep?"

"Evie Wyler? Do you know her? These ladies were hoping..."

"Wyler. Evie. No, can't say I do. You can look around. We're only here until eleven, so she'll have to come before then if she's going to have any pancakes."

"Thanks," Jones said with a nod.

❧

MARGIE HAD BEEN to Stampede breakfasts where the pancakes were burned on the outside and raw on the inside, but the ones at the Wildwood breakfast were remarkably good. Margie and Jones and the vertical rescue team sat on the grass, but keeping social distance proved to be impossible, as all the kids wanted to talk to the cool firefighters. Plenty of the dads too. They weren't quite as interested in the lady detectives. Dressed in suits rather than uniforms, it wasn't immediately obvious what they were, or maybe there would have been more interest.

No, Margie decided. To be fair, the brave, handsome firefighters would always attract more attention than a couple of cops, even if they were homicide detectives.

A couple of men appeared to be making their rounds through the crowds. Stopping to talk to people and shaking hands or bumping elbows. They were not wearing masks and had bright-white smiles. They were wearing matching black cowboy hats, western style shirts probably from Lammles, and shiny new cowboy boots that had never met a cow patty. Tourists?

It wasn't long before they made their way over to the firefighters and police detectives on the grass.

"Vincent Skinner," the taller of the two greeted, reaching out his hand.

Margie nodded and decided to remain occupied with her plate and fork, leaving no hands free to shake. "Detective Patenaude," she introduced herself. "And Detective Jones."

"Detectives! With our city's finest?"

"Yes." Of course. What did he think she meant? She didn't add that they were on the homicide team.

"We're certainly glad that you could join us today. We're always happy to have the city's first responders at our community events."

"Just in case someone chokes," Jones suggested.

He laughed heartily. "Just in case… yes, exactly. And this is Harland Roberts, my campaign manager."

"Campaign?" Jones repeated.

"Yes! I am a mayoral candidate."

"Oh." Margie was surprised. She had been surprised by the number of election signs already up around the city. "Isn't it a bit early to be campaigning?"

"It's never too early to start getting your name out there. If I waited until September, I wouldn't have nearly enough time to meet all the constituents that I would like to."

"July just seems like an awfully long time until municipal elections in October. Aren't you afraid that people will forget your name during that time?"

He shook his head. "People need to see you out there. And that's what the big signs are for. Get my name and face firmly implanted in people's memories. Lots of exposures between now and then."

Margie supposed that a longer lead-up did give people more opportunities to get his name implanted in their minds. They said it took seven or more exposures to a brand before people were ready to purchase. The same must apply to politics.

"Well, it's good to meet you."

"I have a lot of ideas of things that will be very beneficial to Calgarians. With me as your mayor, we could move things forward in this city. Jobs, transit, improved economy." He nodded. "It's time to move out of the stagnation of the COVID lockdown into a new and brighter future!"

Jones nodded. There were murmurs from a few of the firefighters, but Margie couldn't tell whether they were moved by his speech or thought he was full of hot air. Skinner was impressive, at any rate.

Skinner looked around at them all, as if expecting them to say that they would support him, or that they must have questions to ask him about his campaign. Maybe closer to the election, people would, but they were at a Stampede breakfast, not exactly a place to talk politics and municipal development. People were there to relax and enjoy the food and the music. Across the field, children were jumping and squealing in a blow-up bouncy house.

"Have you been to the Stampede yet?" Skinner tried.

"No. I don't know if I'll get down to the grounds this year. But my daughter went today with a group of friends. It's Community Spirit Day, so cheap gate admission."

"I hope she enjoys it. Will she see the Grandstand Show?"

Margie looked down at her food to avoid rolling her eyes. If the girl couldn't or wouldn't pay full price for the gate admission, what were the chances that she could afford the limited seating at the Grandstand Show?

"No, she and her friends will probably find somewhere good to watch the fireworks. After Peters', of course."

"Ah, Peters'…" Skinner got that faraway look of a true Calgarian, remembering trips to Peters' in days gone by. Margie had to smile, despite not really liking Skinner. Could a man be all bad if he loved Peters'?

"So, do your people still have a presence this year?" Skinner asked. "Or has that all been kiboshed with all of this… *cancel Canada* stuff." Then realizing that his words might possibly be offensive he quickly added, "Not that there isn't good reason for it."

Margie stared at him, trying to form an answer that was polite and courteous as befitted a member of the Calgary Police Service, but would clearly inform him that he was treading on thin ice if he wanted votes from "her people."

"I mean," Skinner clarified, "do they still have the Indian tipi village, or whatever they call it now?"

"The Elbow River Camp. Yes, we are still trying to educate the public about our cultures."

He gave her a bland smile and started to move away, his pale campaign manager tugging at his arm, quite possibly sensing the chill coming from Margie's direction.

CHAPTER FIVE

There was a lot of work to do the day that a file was opened. Margie and Jones headed back to the office after having had their fill of Stampede pancakes and, as their stomachs tried to process the unusually large morning meal, flipped through photographs of the scene, collated data, transcribed the notes in their notebooks to electronic notes in the newly opened virtual workspace, and made sure that all departments involved had the proper coding to ensure that the forensic and pathology results would be properly routed to the workspace and their individual inboxes.

Margie had started to run background on Evie Wyler, gathering as much information as was readily available. It didn't take long to find her operator's license. Margie compared the photo with one of the accident scene photos of the victim's face to make sure it was the right person. Someone else could have lost something out of her pockets on that hill. Anyone who had gone down that hill might have left their own contributions behind.

The faces did match. Wyler's address was in Wildwood, close to the hill. Her car was probably still parked in her garage at home, as it wouldn't have made much sense to drive that distance and look for legal parking. Margie tried to imagine what Wyler had been doing. They didn't have a time of death from the medical examiner yet, so she didn't have any idea whether it had been an evening, middle-of-the-night, or early-morning stroll that had led Wyler to the top—and then bottom—of that hill. Margie had been assuming that it was dark, since that would explain a fall and her body being found early the next morning. But there was a whole range of possibilities.

Wyler had no criminal record. Not even a speeding ticket. She had made 9-1-1 and 3-1-1 calls in the past to report activities or concerns around her neighborhood. Nothing that had been flagged as a nuisance call.

She found a couple of social media accounts in the name Evie Wyler and opened the first one.

It hit her like a gut punch. She should have known that a young urban professional was unlikely to be living alone in a family neighborhood like Wildwood. Nice houses, close to the park, popular for retirees and families, but not single young men and women.

The cover image on the account showed Wyler holding a little girl of about three, both of them laughing. There were plenty of pictures of both the daughter and her husband in the feed that followed.

Margie groaned. "Wyler has a family."

Jones looked up from her work, her face pinched into a frown. "What? I checked and there was no marriage record."

"Maybe they're not married. But she has a little girl and a man in her life."

Jones swore, echoing Margie's sentiments.

"I was hoping she was single. Informing parents is bad enough. How old is the little girl?"

Margie turned her monitor for Jones to see the tiny, laughing blond.

"Oh, isn't she precious." Jones's eyes teared up, and she turned away to reach for a tissue. She dabbed at her eyes. "We'd better get over there to do the notification. Will you come?"

Margie nodded. "If you want me."

Jones glanced toward where Gagnon was sitting at his desk. "I'm sure any of the detectives would do just fine, but you have… a light touch."

"Okay. I'll come. Did the husband not file a missing person

report? He got up in the morning and his wife wasn't there, and…?" She thought back to the Roscoe case, a file she had been involved in shortly after her arrival in Calgary. A high percentage of murdered women died at the hands of their husbands or intimate partners.

But Wyler's death had been an accident, not murder. If her husband had not reported her missing, there was a reason for that. Or he had reported her missing and the file simply hadn't been posted to the system yet or matched to their file for some reason. Technology didn't always work the way it was supposed to.

"I guess we'll get around to asking him that," Jones said. "Once we've done the notification."

THEY BOTH HOPPED into Jones's car and headed back out to Wildwood. It was a family-friendly area, lots of bungalows, mostly family housing. Some of them looked as if they had been built in the 60s and some were brand-new with huge, black-tinted windows.

At the community center, the band and the bouncy house were gone. All the tables and grills had been put away. Everything was tidy and clean, as if the pancake breakfast had never happened.

"It should be up here, I think," Jones said, looking at the GPS unit to identify their target. Margie scanned for the house numbers, which at least were reasonably visible during the day. Identifying house numbers after dark could be a nightmare. They found the right house and looked at it for a minute before getting out of the car. A nice house, brick or faux-brick siding, tidy gardens and lawn. Every-thing appeared to be freshly painted. There were no children's toys in the yard.

Jones led the way up to the front door. Everything was quiet; there was no indication that someone was anxiously looking out the window, waiting for his wife to get home or for the police to show up and help. They stood to the side of the door and rang the doorbell. In a few minutes, the man she recognized from Evie Wyler's news feed opened the door. He looked at them and shook his head slightly.

"Yes? Can I help you?"

"Calgary Police Service, sir. Are you Mr. Wyler?" Jones asked.

He laughed. "No, there is no Mr. Wyler. I'm Trevor Vance. Are you looking for Ms. Wyler? Evie?"

"Could we come in to talk?"

He looked as though he would deny them, but eventually he shrugged and stepped back from the door, allowing them in. The inside was mostly beige and darker browns. Neat and tidy. Vance bent down and picked up a stuffed rabbit, which he held in his hand, unsure of what to do with it.

"Let's have a seat," Jones suggested.

Vance gave a slight laugh as they sat down. "You're making me nervous now. What is all this about?"

"According to her driver's license, this is Ms. Wyler's residence?"

"Yes, that's right."

"And are you her partner? Nanny? What?"

"Partner, yes. I've got Ada today, but it really depends on our schedules as to which one is home to take care of her."

"It's your wife's workday today?"

He nodded.

"Where does she work?"

"From a coffee shop, most of the time."

At their quizzical looks, he explained further. "Remote work, you know, but working with the little one underfoot is distracting. She likes to work from the coffee shop, or somewhere else she can just sit and work and not be disturbed. Now that we're allowed to be in restaurants, of course. She couldn't while there were more restrictions."

"What does she do?"

"She's a teacher. Not on Zoom or somewhere they meet face-to-face, obviously, since she's in the middle of a coffee shop. But people complete online units, and she grades them, gives feedback, suggests additional resources, that sort of thing. For online accreditation."

"They don't just have the computer mark the tests?" Jones asked.

"If there is a multiple-choice section, then yes, the computer will mark that portion and just give Evie the results. But there are short answers, essays, oral reports on video, all kinds of different responses. And computers don't do very well at that kind of thing."

"Ah." Jones and Margie nodded. "So she would be at the coffee shop right now?"

"She had to go in to the physical campus today. It's in Red Deer. A bit of a drive, but she doesn't have to be there in person very often."

"So what time did she leave this morning?"

"I don't know. I slept until eight. She was gone when I got up." He looked from Margie's face to Jones's. "That's not unusual. She sometimes gets up at five, five-thirty. Goes for a walk or run. Gets started on her work early so that she will be done by early afternoon. Then she has time in the afternoon and evening for family or other things."

"Sounds like a reasonable plan," Jones agreed. "If you can get up that early."

"Me, I can't. But her body is set differently than mine. For her, sleeping in until eight would be impossible. But so is staying up until midnight."

"So you keep different schedules and don't try to match each other's rhythms."

"Yeah. When we're together, we're together. If we have different things to do, that's okay too. We're both open to the other person being independent and having a life of their own. That's what works for us."

Margie wondered if this was the new euphemism for an "open relationship." Polyamory of some flavor.

Vance looked at Jones, raising his brows. "So… I've answered your questions. Now you want to tell me what this is about? Is Evie in trouble for something? Outstanding parking tickets?" He smiled, waiting for an explanation that he was sure would be bland and unworrying.

"Mr. Vance, I'm sorry to give you this bad news, but Evie's body was found this morning. She is dead."

His mouth fell open. He looked back and forth at them, gave a little smile as if it must be a joke he was supposed to find funny. Maybe they were recording him and wanted to see if he would cry and wail, then they would tell him he had just been punked. Margie and Jones both continued to look at him steadily, waiting for it to sink in. For him to see their grave expressions and realize that no, it was not a joke. It was the end of the relationship and the start of a new life that he had not anticipated.

"My... Evie? That can't be. Are you sure it's her? Maybe someone... stole her wallet or her computer. If something had happened to her, wouldn't I know it...?"

"Some people do get premonitions," Jones offered. "But most people don't. For most people, it is quite a shock. Like for you."

"She was just here. I looked in on her before I went to bed. She was fast asleep. Everything was just fine. Normal."

"You sleep in separate rooms?" Jones asked.

"Yes. It's easier that way, with us going to bed and getting up at different times. Trust me, there's always time for intimacy whether you're sleeping in the same room or not. We just have two beds to choose from." He gave a little laugh. He'd explained this before. Their friends probably all thought they were a little weird. He had the patter memorized. It came out automatically, without the appropriate emotion.

"Well, if one of you snores, that makes a lot of sense," Margie offered.

"No, not usually. But Evie talks in her sleep. Or gets up to write or work on the computer when she can't sleep. And we're up and down at different times. Of course, there's Ada too. She still gets up the night sometimes, wet or with nightmares. So one of us can take care of her without waking the other one up."

"How do you decide which one of you takes care of her?"

"She's big enough to get out of bed herself, so she chooses which room she goes to." He hesitated. "Usually me."

"Dads are more fun at night?" Jones asked. "Big surprise."

They were both watching him carefully, waiting for it to sink in and start becoming real to him. It was easy to chatter on about Ada and their domestic life and not really think about what they had said. He could almost forget it.

Almost.

Tears gathered at the corners of Vance's eyes. "She can't be dead," he said pleadingly. "There's been some kind of mistake."

"We will need to verify her identity. At this time, a visual match has been made, comparing her face to the picture on her driver's license. But we'll need something more definitive than that. Don't worry about that part right now. What we are going to need you to talk about right now is the last time that you saw Evie, and what has happened since then."

"I just told you. I looked in on her before I went to bed. She was asleep. I went to sleep. I got up around eight when Ada got up. Had some coffee, puttered around on the computer. That's it. Played with Ada, gave her breakfast. It's summer, so she doesn't have any preschool to get to. It's just her and me today, until Mommy gets home… at two o'clock or so." He swiped at a tear on his cheek with the back of his hand. "Only…"

Only this time, Mommy wasn't ever coming home. She never would again.

CHAPTER SIX

"You said that Evie would get up early to walk or run or work. And that sometimes she got up in the middle of the night when she couldn't sleep."

"Yes."

"And you don't know what time she got up this morning or last night and left the house."

"No."

"Does she take her car or transit?"

"Her car, usually." Vance got up from his seat and walked to the back of the house, where he apparently looked through a connecting door into the garage. He returned, looking stunned. "Her car is in the garage. So she didn't go out to one of her favorite coffee shops. She just went... out for a walk?"

"Apparently." Jones waited to see what his response would be. That this was normal? Unusual behavior? That she had been anxious lately and the separate bedrooms were still quite a new arrangement?

Vance shrugged and scratched his forehead. His arms were shaking. He sat back down. "I... don't know. I have no idea what to think of this. I just thought when I got up this morning that she'd already left for work. I didn't even know there was anything wrong. I wouldn't have known until this afternoon."

"You don't talk or text during the day?"

"Well, often, yes. We send each other messages or relax for a few minutes and call to see how the other one is. But there isn't anything *set,* you know. If one of us is super busy or stressed, then we might get through the day without ever connecting with each other. And then we just try to have a nice evening together and get caught up. Even if we had gone all day without talking to each other or without getting a text from her, I wouldn't have been worried that something was wrong."

Margie made a couple of discreet notes in her notepad.

"What... happened to her?" Vance asked tentatively. "Was it a car accident or a heart attack?"

He seemed to have forgotten that the car was still in the garage. He was just looking for something that would make sense. People didn't just die without warning in his world.

"The autopsy hasn't been completed yet," Jones said. "But it looks like it was a fall. An accident."

"She fell and... hit her head, or something?" Vance asked. "Is that what you mean?"

"We won't know for sure until we get the ME's report. But please try not to obsess over that. From the preliminary information we have, it was very quick. She did not suffer."

"But... a fall. What kind of freak thing is that? People don't just die from a fall. Maybe they get a broken bone. *Maybe.*" He shook his head. "They don't die."

"I'm sorry. We'll provide you with as much information as you need later, when we have it. For now, you're just going to have to be satisfied with what we can give you. It is an active investigation and we're limited in what we can tell you."

"An active investigation. You mean you're from..."

"We are homicide detectives," Margie confirmed.

"You mean this was murder? You're investigating this as a murder?"

"No, Mr. Vance. We believe it was an accident. But each case needs to be investigated until we are satisfied that there was nothing suspicious about it. No foul play."

"There couldn't have been. No one would ever do anything to hurt Evie. She was so kind and sensitive. I don't know of anyone who didn't like her."

Jones smiled reassuringly at him. "She was well-liked? And nothing had happened lately to stress her out? Getting up late at night or early in the morning wasn't because something was on her mind? Worrying her?"

"She worried about everything." He shrugged and puffed out his cheeks, then let the air go. "She's the kind of person who always got all twisted up about injustices. People or animals or protected areas that were being threatened. She wanted to live in harmony with nature and with everyone around her. Hated hearing anything about child abuse or cruelty to animals. Always taking up a new cause."

"And what was bothering her the most recently?"

"I don't know. There was the residential school thing. That bothered her a lot. And our, uh, discussions over Ada and her diet, and whether it was okay for me to feed her meat when she was with me and we were eating out somewhere. Evie kept a vegetarian household," he explained. "And everything had to be cruelty free, but she didn't try to force other people to do the same things as she did. I'm not vegetarian, but I eat vegetarian when I'm here. But not when I go out. I figured Ada should be allowed to choose when we went out too. At least to be exposed to other foods. I told Evie that when people are deprived of a thing for their whole lives—sugar, or meat, or alcohol, or whatever—then they just go crazy when they are old enough to make their own decisions or have their own money. The kids without any self-control or adults who are immediately addicted, that's because their parents kept them from experiencing those things. If they had allowed some choice and moderation instead..."

"So you wanted to be able to raise your daughter to be an omnivore." Jones asked.

"Yes. Or to choose for herself."

As if a two- or three-year-old was old enough to make a choice like that. A child of that age would happily choose a grilled cheese diet. Or a pizza pocket diet. Preschoolers were not well-known for making wise, well-balanced decisions.

Margie didn't look up from the notes she was making in her notepad as she asked her question. Jones would be watching him carefully for his reaction. "How intense did these discussions get?"

"How intense?" Vance sounded for a moment like he didn't understand, then all at once, he did. "No, it wasn't like that. We didn't fight. There was never any violence in our relationship. Evie would never have stood for that. Neither of us were inclined that way."

"Raised voices?"

"No. Well… maybe raised voices. But no threats, no violence. Just… active debate."

Margie nodded and looked up to assess his face. No obvious tells. But she had been fooled before. People could lie well, were psychopaths, or had another reason for not feeling guilty about what they had done or the stories they were telling her. She could rely on her eyes and ears only so much.

"Was there anyone else around last night? Company over for wine?"

"No. Just Evie and me and Ada. And Ada was off to bed, of course. So it was just the two of us. Watching some TV, talking about our days, relaxing at the end of a long day."

So no witnesses.

"What was Evie's day like? What did she tell you about it?"

He thought back, licking his lips. "Umm… well…" He rubbed at the corners of his eyes again, though they didn't seem to be producing any more tears. "Pretty much the same as usual. She has her work. Sometimes she tells me about funny answers students have put on tests. Computer problems she might have been frustrated by. The meeting in Red Deer was kind of out of the blue, I hadn't known that she was going out there."

"Did she seem concerned or agitated about that?"

"No. No, I don't think so."

"Did she seem relaxed? Say or do anything out of the ordinary?"

"I really can't think of anything. You don't think that something happened and someone killed her, do you? That doesn't make any sense. She was a mom. An online teacher. Not the kind of person who attracts a lot of attention. No enemies or jealous coworkers."

"The two of you saw other people?" Margie asked. She kept her voice casual, as if this would be a normal arrangement. They were sleeping in separate rooms, after all. They might very well have other relationships, approved by the other.

But Vance's face portrayed shock. "Saw other people? Certainly not! Why would you think that?" He looked suddenly more anxious. "Was there something that made you think there was someone else? She wasn't… with another man, was she? Or in a hotel, or…" He shuddered, scaring himself with the direction of his thoughts.

"No, nothing like that," Margie assured him.

"We're just covering all the bases," Jones said blandly. As it was natural to ask how many other lovers a spouse or intimate partner might have. With the direction society was headed, it seemed like there were more and more of those "open" relationships going on than ever. Or maybe people just talked about it more, with the explosion of personal information being revealed on social media. What was a shocking secret a hundred years ago was now a social media post.

"We were committed to each other. We were exclusive. Neither of us saw anyone else."

"You didn't have any female friends that you saw occasionally?"

"Friends, yes. But not lovers. That's different."

"Did you see them with Evie, or on your own?"

"On my own. We didn't share a lot of friends. We had very different interests, weren't into the same things."

"And Evie saw people on her own. Female and male."

"I suppose so."

"And it never concerned you? You were never jealous or suspicious? She didn't seem to be keeping anything from you?"

"No. There was nothing like that. We both chose to be here, to be in this relationship. No one forced us into that. And we didn't force each other to stay. If one of us didn't want to stay together… then we would have dealt with that."

"Whose name is the house in?"

"Evie's. But that was just for convenience. So that if we needed to sell the house, she could sign everything."

Margie made a note about that. And who would get the child? Evie, presumably. The courts still favored mothers over fathers. So if Vance had wanted to terminate their relationship, but to keep the house and his daughter…

She finished her note. It wasn't murder. There was not anything to indicate that it was anything other than what it looked like. Evie had gone out for a walk. She had fallen down the hill. End of story.

Vance rubbed a hand over his face. "When can I get her cell phone back?"

CHAPTER SEVEN

Margie and Jones exchanged glances. While they had been able to find a few credit cards, they had not turned up a wallet or purse. No cell phone. Evie's personal effects consisted of some pocket litter and what she had been wearing when she died.

"We have not found a cell phone," Jones said. "Is it possible that she left it here by mistake? I know it is rare to go out without a cell phone these days, but she might have left it on the counter and meant to grab it or been distracted by something."

"No, I would have noticed if she had left it lying around."

Vance looked vaguely around the room. He again retreated to the back of the house to check the table or the counter beside the coffee pot, places where Evie might normally have lain her phone down and then not picked it up again. He wandered for a moment, then returned, shaking his head. He pulled out his own phone and dialed.

Everyone waited in silence, ears pricked for the ringing of Evie's cell phone, or the low rumble of a phone vibrating on a hard surface. There was no sound. Margie watched Vance's face for any changes as he held his phone to his ear, listening to the ringing on his end, as if it might all be a mistake and Evie would answer her phone and explain it all away.

Then his face fell. He paused for a moment, then pressed the end button on the call and slid his phone away.

"She must have it."

"It wasn't on her body. Maybe she dropped it," Jones suggested.

"*How* could this happen? How could something like this happen?" He stared at them, his eyes rimmed with red.

There was a small noise, and Margie turned her head to see a little angel emerging from the hall that led to the bedrooms. Mussy-haired Ada went to her father. He picked her up and held his face against her head, eyes full of tears once more. How was he going to tell this little darling that her mother was dead and would never return home again?

But he wimped out and didn't tell her right away. Maybe he needed some more time to prepare himself. A good sign. If he had been involved in Evie's death, then he would have been thinking of how to break it to Ada. He'd have a script prepared, something gentle and honest. He might have looked up on the internet how to break bad news to children.

Ada took Vance's face in her hands, one on either cheek, and rubbed her face against his.

"Daddy owie," she said. She rubbed her cheek with her hand, then put her hand back on his cheek and rubbed it. Margie could hear the scrape of his whiskers and understood. She smiled. Ada didn't like the scratchiness of Vance's whiskers.

"My sister's son said that his dad had 'dangerous sharp things' on his face," Margie told Ada. "Does your daddy too?"

"Yes." Ada gave a definite nod. "Yes, dang'rous sharp tings."

There was a lump in Margie's throat. She swallowed and tried to continue as if unaffected. They needed to be professional. Ferret out everything they could in case the significant other had any reason to want the victim dead. Do the official notification. Ask if he needed anyone to stay with him.

"Is there anything we can do for you, Mr. Vance? Is there anyone you would like us to call for you? Maybe someone who can come and sit with you and help with Ada?"

"No. I'm used to looking after my own daughter. Anyone else would just be in the way."

"You will want your loved ones around you. Are your parents in town? Siblings? Friends?"

"No. Not yet. I don't want to do this yet."

By "this," Margie assumed he meant that he couldn't accept that Evie really was dead and wasn't going to do anything that might concede that she was gone. By avoiding the truth, he could keep her with him just that little bit longer.

"I'll give you my card," Jones said. She reached into her pocket and thumbed one out. She looked at Margie, who handed her one of hers. Jones nodded and passed both of them to Vance. "There you go. That's both of us. If you need to talk, please give us a call. And we can refer you to some community resources. Grief counseling. Other supports."

"Not yet," Vance murmured. "Not yet."

At home in the evening Margie was still thinking of Evie and Ada. She played some upbeat music on her iPhone and danced around the kitchen while she searched the fridge for ingredients and prepared her meal, trying to lift her spirits. She talked and sang to Stella, who sat watching her with a doggie grin, happy to have the attention, whatever the reason.

It was important not to bring all those work worries home with her. She could not fix everyone's lives or protect all the family members from feeling the effects of what had already happened. She could do her best to bring the families answers and closure, and that was all. Worrying about it at home wouldn't improve her work. The best thing would be for her to go into work the next day rested, refreshed, and ready to tackle the case again, and that meant she needed to let it all go.

She felt very virtuous making herself a vegetable stir-fry. Since Christina wasn't home, she threw the leftover chicken in as well. She considered leaving out the noodles and rice to keep her calorie intake down, but she really couldn't have stir fry without rice or noodles, so she went ahead and warmed those up as well. A run in the morning would help combat the extra calories. No reason she couldn't enjoy a little extra here and there if she were increasing her activity level.

"We'll go for a walk after supper too," she told Stella. "I can do a nice long walk today, as long as it isn't too hot."

The last couple of days, the weather had moderated a little due to the amount of smoke in the air from the BC forest fires. The temperatures had still been getting up to 29 or 30, but without the direct sun, it was much more tolerable, except for those first couple of minutes in a hot car. She had also figured out the best places to put fans in the house and it really hadn't been too bad.

But if she took a long walk, her legs might not be ready for a run in the morning. So maybe just a medium walk.

Her music stalled, a call coming through on the phone. Margie clicked her earphones to answer it without checking the caller ID first.

"Detective Patenaude."

"Your daughter," Christina snapped back, and laughed.

"Oh, hi sweetie. Sorry, I'm working hands-free and didn't know it was you. How are you doing?"

"Good. Lots of fun at the Stampede, but I'm exhausted. That's a lot of walking around. And my feet!"

"I wondered whether sandals were a good idea for all that walking around. If they're broken in, then they might be okay, but those ones were pretty new."

"Well, I guess they're broken in now. Or my feet are broken in. Ouch."

"Did you get some band-aids on them?"

"Yeah, but the straps keep rubbing against them and pulling the band-aids off. I just went to the first aid place the first time, but now I've got a box of band-aids in my backpack and I'm replacing them like every hour." Christina sighed. "The things we do to look good," she said dramatically.

Margie laughed. "Glad you're looking after them. So have you had something to eat yet? I mean other than deep-fried Twinkies and mini donuts."

"None of us are very hungry right now. Just tired. So we're going to take a break in the park, just stretch out in the shade. When we've finished digesting all of those Twinkies and donuts, we'll go to Peters'."

Margie could hardly even think of Peters' after all the other Stampede junk food without feeling a little queasy. But the teenagers had iron stomachs.

"Then we'll go find a place to watch the fireworks. I hope we can still see okay with all this smoke."

"I saw some pictures on Facebook. I think you'll be able to see just fine. It's the 'Fireworks Spectacular' tonight. Should be the best night to watch them."

"They're at eleven." Christina yawned. "Then I'll be home after that."

"Are you sure you don't need to come home and go to bed right now?" Margie teased.

"Mom! I just need a little nap, then I'll be just fine."

"Okay. You guys be careful going to sleep. Make sure your electronics are safe and out of sight and have someone stay awake to keep watch. Don't make yourselves a target."

"I promise we'll be fine," Christina reassured her.

Which didn't reassure Margie.

She sighed after the call was disconnected, then grabbed her dinner and sat down at the table to eat alone. But with the TV on and Stella at her side, she didn't feel quite as lonely.

❦

AFTER DINNER, Margie clipped the leash onto Stella's collar. "How about that walk now? We'll get some fresh air and exercise, see if there are any squirrels or gophers, and check out all your scent posts. How does that sound?"

Stella's mouth was wide open as she panted her approval and her tail wagged back and forth so fast they didn't need a fan.

"Yes? Yes, you're ready for walkies?"

Stella gave one excited yip, then pointed her nose at the door, waiting for Margie to follow.

"All right. Let's go." Margie opened the door for both of them to step out, then locked it behind her. She let Stella pull her to the city sidewalk and start walking toward the multi-use trail along Twenty-Sixth Street.

When they reached Twenty-Sixth Street, Margie's eyes widened in wonder. She wasn't sure what to say or think. There was a teddy bear or other stuffed animal fastened to each fence post between the pathway and the road. She knew instantly what it was for. People had been setting out their own memorials of children's shoes and stuffed toys on their porches to memorialize the children who had died at the residential schools. The toys on the fence posts were clearly a continuation of this idea. They extended down the road as far as Margie could see. There were, she suspected, 215 bears, each symbolizing a grave discovered with ground-penetrating radar at the old residential school site in Kamloops.

Margie pressed her finger to the bottom of her nose for a moment, trying to quell the emotions rising up within her. It had already been an emotional day, discovering that their victim was the mother of a little girl. A sweet little angel who would grow up without her mother, and probably remember nothing about her as an adult.

"Okay. It's okay," she prompted herself. Though the raw wound she had felt each time new gravesites were acknowledged had been starting to heal, it was good to stop and acknowledge those children once more. Someone in the neighborhood—more than one someone, considering the number of toys that had been collected for the project —was mourning with Margie. She was not alone.

Despite the deniers and the people who thought that Margie should "be over it already," since she hadn't gone to a residential school herself, there were still others out there who were looking for ways to express their grief and to memorialize the deaths of the children far away from their families.

Margie tried to swallow the lump in her throat. She looked down at Stella, who was sitting beside her patiently, staring up at her and wondering what was holding her up.

"Let's walk," Margie told her lightly. They crossed the street at the crosswalk, and Margie looked for a sign explaining the memorial and who had placed it there. There was a yellow sign to the right where the line of animals started, so Margie turned right so that she could go read it.

There was no signature. No name of a school or other organization that had arranged the collection and installation of the animals. Just the words

In memory for the children found

CHAPTER EIGHT

argie stayed up reading until Christina was dropped off by her friends. She entered the house quietly, then raised her brows at her mother sitting up on the couch.

"You didn't have to stay up for me, Mom," Christina whispered, as if she might wake someone else in the house up.

"I wanted to make sure that you got home safe. I know you think that I worry too much. But you don't know how much I've really dialed back. If you knew the level of worry that I *started* at, you would be really impressed."

Christina laughed. "Well, I've seen you worry, so I think I know. But I'm home safe. Nothing happened to any of us. It was a good day." She yawned widely, not bothering to cover it until she had closed her mouth again, politely patting her lips. "We had a really good time. Just—a long time."

"You'll have to tell me everything that happened."

"I will. Tomorrow. Did you know *Marianas Trench* was there? They were so good. And…" Christina yawned again. "And there was a bannock booth at the Elbow Park Camp. Mmm." She patted her stomach. "So good."

"Did you bring me some?"

"Nope." Christina's look was mischievous. "We'll have to make some."

"Oh, I see. Well, we will soon. Brush your teeth before bed."

"Yes, Mom."

Margie closed her eyes as Christina headed to the bathroom. It felt good to have everybody home.

❧

"WE HAVE A SURPRISE," Jones announced when Margie answered her phone, not even bothering to say hello and exchange social niceties. "So you should come out to Edworthy again today. Is that okay? Are you already on your way in?"

"I was just heading out the door. And I still have it in the GPS from yesterday, so that isn't a problem. What's up? I thought we finished with the scene yesterday."

"Didn't I just tell you it was a surprise? See you when you get here." Without waiting for an answer, Jones hung up.

Margie looked at her phone for a moment, then put it down on the counter and poured her coffee into a travel mug. So much for having a leisurely coffee before work. She would drink it on the way instead. At least she had driven the route once before, so she wouldn't be as worried about not being able to find it.

Half an hour later she was blasting the wrong way down Bow Trail and looking for a way to get turned around. After forty-five minutes, she was finally pulling into the park, sweat dripping down her forehead and back, not from the heat but from the stress and embarrassment of getting lost despite the GPS and the flak she anticipated she would get from the other law enforcement officers for being so late.

There were no barricades this time. Margie got as close as she could to the staging area from the day before, and saw several vehicles pulled up on the grass. She followed their lead and drove her car out of the gravel of the parking lot. She drained the last of her coffee, very cold and bitter, and climbed out of the car.

"Here's Patenaude," someone called out.

Margie looked around and saw Cruz, a Filipino native, motioning to her, the others standing around in a loose grouping. She walked toward them.

"Sorry to be so long," she apologized. "Traffic. So what's going on? What are we doing back here today?"

"I was talking to Siever last night about the case," Cruz said, nodding in Detective Siever's direction. "We were bouncing ideas around. Got to talking about the fact that the victim didn't have a phone or wallet on her. Or keys. Jones said that you guys talked to the husband yesterday, and same thing, where is her phone? It's not at home, so where did it go?"

Margie turned and looked at the hill. It was a long way to the top. And she wasn't climbing it for another search. Not after seeing the vertical rescue team navigate it with safety harnesses the day before. She didn't need that kind of excitement.

She looked back at Cruz, who was nodding. "None of us are going back up there for a grid search," he confirmed. "Besides, what if it is somewhere you can't see or reach from the ground?" He motioned to the trees. "A purse strap could easily get caught in the branches of a tree. She's not going to hold on to it all the way down. It's going to get airborne at some point, and then… where? We don't know."

"Right. So are you hiring a pack of squirrels to search the trees, or what?"

Cruz raised one eyebrow. "That would be pretty nutty," he deadpanned.

Margie smiled, glad that she and the others on the team could talk to each other and keep things light without worrying about offending each other. Some teams were so serious that just surviving through the day was like going to battle. At least with her homicide team, she knew she could count on them to try to keep each other from getting dragged down by the gloom that came with working in dark places.

Jones walked up and handed Margie a device with a joystick.

"Are we playing video games today?" Margie asked. "That's a nice break from the job."

"This one is yours," Jones said, pointing to a drone on the ground nearby. "Flip the switch to activate it."

Margie flipped the on/off switch. The drone buzzed to life, the rotors starting to spin immediately. A screen on the controller lit up so Margie could see that it had a camera installed and ready to go. "Okay. How do I do this?"

"You'll get the hang of it really quickly. These are the sticks," Jones pointed to the two joysticks, "and those control your direction and height. You can see your progress on the screen, and an aerial of the ground below." She pointed to each control and explained what she needed to know. It was all a little overwhelming, but Margie had seen a four-year-old flying his father's drone at a family picnic back before COVID, and she figured if a four-year-old could figure it out, she could eventually be taught how to operate one too.

In a couple of minutes, Margie had the drone in the air, and Jones ran her through a few exercises to make sure she got the hang out of how to move it around. She pointed to the hill.

"This area is yours. Everything left of that tree. You see the tall one there, with the weird branch to the right?"

"Yeah."

"So just fly this baby around, over the trees, down close to the ground, behind bushes, everywhere you can think of that the fire-fighters might not have been able to see when they helped out with the search yesterday. Siever, he's got one with a grabber, so that we can retrieve whatever evidence we might find, but it needs to be documented first, just like normal. All the footage is being recorded, so just fly around, get as many angles as you can if you find something interesting."

"And call Siever to pick it up."

Jones nodded. "Exactly."

CHAPTER NINE

$\mathcal{M}$argie found that she could only operate the little craft for a certain amount of time before things started to blur and she was no longer seeing what was on the screen clearly, but just going through the motions and not absorbing what she saw.

Everyone had the same problem to one degree or another, so Margie wasn't the only one taking breaks to put down the controller and walk around looking at the ground and trees from their usual perspective for a while. Other than Siever, who seemed to have become one with his drone controller and was able not only to fly the drone much more skillfully than Margie, but to carry on conversations, walk around, and do other things while he was flying.

Margie called Christina when she was taking a break from flying.

"Hi, Mom." Christina yawned into the phone. "How's it going?"

"I hope you're not still in bed."

"No. I've been up for a long time. I was actually thinking of having a nap soon."

"I figured with how tired you were yesterday you would be asleep until noon today."

"No. I was up at eight-thirty. Something like that. I already took Stella out for a walk," she informed Margie, anticipating what she would say. "Hey, did you see the memorial over on Twenty-Sixth Street?"

"Yes, I just saw it yesterday. I was going to tell you about it, but you were so tired last night."

"Yeah, I was dead to the world in about thirty seconds. I don't think I would have remembered anything you said between the door and my bed."

"Good thing I made you brush your teeth."

"Did you? See, I don't even remember that."

Margie laughed. Christina had had that zombie look when she had walked from the bathroom to her bedroom. Already asleep on her feet. "Guess what I'm doing today?"

"Well, you don't usually sound that perky, so I'm going to say… running away from home?"

"No. I'm flying a drone."

"Really? Like Uncle Dave had at that last reunion?"

"Yep. I am now as cool as Uncle Dave."

"I wouldn't push it. You don't actually *own* a drone. I hope they didn't give you the kind that drops bombs."

"No! I don't think anyone would dare do that! These ones just record camera footage."

"That sounds like a lot of fun."

"It is."

"So who gets to *review* all of the camera footage?"

Margie groaned. "You had to say that, didn't you?"

"Sorry. Just being practical. Learned it from my mother. If you're out there recording the drone's feed all day, then it will take at least as long to watch all the footage."

And with several of them flying drones, there would be even more.

"I don't think we're going to review all of the raw footage," she told Christina, crossing her fingers and hoping it was true. "Just if we find something, they'll chop it up into stills. If we need them as evidence."

"What are you trying to find? I hope it's not a skeleton."

"No, not a skeleton. We already have the body. We're just looking for any other personal effects that might be close by."

"With a drone? Where exactly was this body?"

"I can't give you details."

"Have you found anything yet?"

"No… nothing significant. But there is still a lot of area to search."

"Well… good luck. I hope you find something. Stella says hi. When we go see Moushoom next, we should take him to see the memorial, if the weather is good. I think he'd really like to see that. To know that his friends who died aren't forgotten."

Margie nodded her agreement. "For sure. I think he would like that too."

"And bannock. Can we take him some bread? And maybe some stew? He always loves it when we take him traditional food."

It was too bad that the dining room didn't explore options from other cultures. Everything they served was so uniformly "American." None of the foods from Indigenous cultures. Margie had seen other cultures represented in the people on Moushoom's floor as well. Hispanic, Italian, Russian—they had some very different backgrounds. Maybe the kitchen staff could try a traditional recipe from one of those cultures every week, instead of always just serving bland hamburger, chicken, and meatloaf day in and day out. Margie felt bad for Moushoom when she saw the dinners they served him.

"I'll schedule some time so we can make some bannock together, okay?"

"Okay," Christina agreed. "I could probably make it myself. It's not that hard."

"Yes, if you want to. But I enjoy cooking with you."

"Me too." Her daughter's voice was warm and happy, satisfied that Margie hadn't said that bannock was too hard for her to make by herself or that she wasn't allowed to have the stove on while Margie was at work. The girl was a teenager. She could probably have made bannock herself when she was five. As she'd said, it wasn't exactly a difficult recipe.

"I'd better get back to flying. Have a good day and don't try to do too much today. After everything you did yesterday, you don't want to wear yourself out. You know you get sick when you are exhausted."

"I'm not exhausted. I slept good. And I'm not going anywhere today. Everybody is just gaming or chatting today."

"Good." Margie was glad that Christina was happy to stay home for a quiet day and she wouldn't have to worry about what Christina was up to and when she would be home. "I love you, honey. Talk to you later."

"Have a good flight."

❧

IT WASN'T a surprise to anyone that it was Siever who made the only significant discovery. He had probably checked his own area and everyone else's three times over and had incredible control and attention.

"There's a purse," he announced, raising his voice above the other chatter going on around him.

Everyone crowded in close around him to look at the screen as he lowered the grapple toward the red purse, lodged in the branches of one of the trees. Margie looked at the sky, straining to see where the drone was. They were surprisingly hard to see against the trees. The drone was close to where they were gathered, just a few meters from where Evie Wyler's body had landed.

She looked back at Siever's screen again. The clawed grapple was close to the purse. He inched it closer, coaxing the hooks around the strap of the shoulder bag. The claws fell into place, and he pulled the drone up. The claws closed more tightly around the strap and, in a moment, the purse started to lift.

Margie cheered with everyone else and clapped her hands. "Detective Siever wins the prize. Nice work!"

"It was his idea too," Jones reminded everyone. "Well done, Siever."

His cheeks were a little pink and he split his focus between the screen on the controller and the drone in the sky, flying slowly home. He flew the little craft up to Detective Jones and hovered there. Jones put her hand around the strap of the purse, and he released the grapple.

"Show off," Margie laughed.

Siever brought his drone down close to the others on the ground. "Is that it, do you think? Or should we keep looking?"

"I think we've been over this area as much as we can justify," Jones said. "They won't want me using too many man-hours for something that might not even be there. This was a brilliant find. Really good work. I didn't think we were going to find anything after the number of times we have gone over this area"

"How can something bright red have been that hard to find?" Margie marveled.

"It was well-disguised by the leaves," Siever said. "I just caught a flash of something behind them. It could have been a kite or a bit of a plastic bag."

"Good eye."

Jones took a cursory look through the purse to see what it contained. She just touched the edges of the items with her purple gloves, being careful not to smear any fingerprints or obscure any other evidence.

"Zipper was open; contents of the wallet have spilled inside the main compartment of the bag. That would be how the credit cards were lost in the fall. But… I do not see a phone."

"She had to have a phone. Where else would it have gone?" Cruz asked.

"It might have fallen out, like the credit cards. And if so, it could be anywhere."

They all looked up into the trees and the hill that they had already searched.

"Wherever it is, I don't think we're going to find it," Margie said, rubbing the back of her neck. There was only so much that they could do. Especially when they were just investigating an accident, not a murder. They couldn't put all kinds of hours and other resources into an accidental death. It didn't benefit anyone.

CHAPTER TEN

There was a briefing in the conference room once they had all returned to the office. Mac was pleased with the discovery of the purse, and gave compliments all around to the team, but especially to Siever, who blushed again at the praise.

"That was a significant find. Unfortunately, we are still left with the loss of the cell phone, which is unfortunate. Have we made a request with the service provider to give us the last known GPS location or cell tower ping?"

Jones nodded. "I've got a request in. But you know how long they can take sometimes."

"I do," Mac agreed. "And even if we get that information, it might not help us at all. Do we have progress in any other directions? How did the autopsy go?"

"Death by fall from height, blunt cardiac trauma," Jones replied.

"Which is what we expected."

Everyone nodded.

"Anything else we need to follow up on?"

Margie raised a tentative hand.

Mac nodded to her. "Patenaude?"

"I'm just… a little confused about the purse and the credit cards."

He blinked at her. "Jones said that there were cards in the main section of the purse and that the zipper was open."

"Yes, exactly."

"That explains how the credit cards fell out onto the hill."

"Yes, but what explains the purse being open and the cards spilled into the main section?"

Everyone looked around at each other. Jones started to nod, thinking about it. "The cards clearly belonged inside the wallet."

"Then who took them out? Why would Wyler take a bunch of cards out of her wallet and just leave them loose in her purse? And why would she leave the zipper unzipped? I know it's mostly men in this room, but a lot of you are married. Do your wives leave their handbags unzipped when they are out in public? With their cards, and phone in clear view? That would just be marking them as a target. You don't need to be a skilled pickpocket to grab a wallet from an open purse. Wyler was out walking at night or in the early morning with her purse gaping open? Why?"

"There's a simple enough explanation to that," Siever pointed out. "The zipper caught on a branch. Or the impact of getting caught on the tree burst it open. It probably landed with a lot of force. A car hitting a pedestrian can blast them out of their shoes. I'm sure that there would be enough force to unzip or split open a zipper."

Margie had to admit he had a point there. But it didn't answer the other question. Why were the cards outside of her wallet but inside the purse?

"How did the cards on the hill get out of the purse if it didn't open until impact?" she asked, cocking her head at Siever. "It had to be open while it was airborne."

"Hmm." Siever nodded. "You're right."

"Why would she take the cards out of her wallet?" Jones asked Margie, turning to her. "Do you ever just randomly start pulling cards out of your wallet while you're out for a walk?"

Margie laughed. "No. I take a card out to pay for something. Maybe to swipe for loyalty rewards. Umm, my health care card at the doctor's office or driver's license at a traffic stop."

"Right. The only time you take your cards out is to use them. And you don't use multiple cards in one location, except maybe loyalty card plus credit card or somewhere you have to give two forms of ID. But this was something else."

"Reorganizing them?" Cruz suggested. "Someone had put the cards away in the wrong slots."

"She wouldn't have been reorganizing them in the middle of the night," Jones countered.

"Nothing to say that she was." Cruz stared up at the ceiling, thinking it through. "She might have been doing it during the day and gotten interrupted. Kid wanted to show her a picture or fell off the couch. Or it was time to make dinner. So she just left them loose in her purse until she could get back to them and complete the project."

Margie nodded. "I suppose I could see that. Then she picks it up when she's on her way out in the dark and doesn't realize that she's left it undone."

"Either that, or someone else rifled her purse," Siever said.

Margie looked at him thoughtfully. But who would have gone through Wyler's purse? Vance, looking for evidence that she was seeing someone else? Her daughter, playing "store"? Or something more nefarious? Someone who had looked through her wallet to verify her identity. Maybe when she was already disabled or dead.

"There haven't been any indicators of foul play," Jones countered.

"This could just as easily be homicide as accident. Someone pushed her. She knew the area; it wasn't like she would just walk off a cliff because she didn't know it was there. Or that she would decide to explore a steep trail down the side of a steep hill in the middle of the night. Has the tox screen come back? Was she drunk? Under the influence of some drug? A sleeping pill? Did she really just walk off a cliff?" Siever asked.

Margie shifted uncomfortably. They had all just been going on the assumption that there was no one else involved. Wyler could have misjudged the edge, slipped, or dropped something and fallen trying to retrieve it. But was that more likely than being pushed?

"There wasn't any evidence that anyone else was there," she said.

"There were other footprints. Other people had been up there. We just can't determine who was there when. She wasn't necessarily walking alone."

"She could have been meeting someone," Margie mused.

Siever nodded. He sat back, looking satisfied that someone else had heard him.

"The husband didn't say that she walked in her sleep," Jones said, her thinking obviously off in another direction. "But people do. They can do all kinds of things while sleepwalking. Including driving a car or cooking on the stove. Or walking off a cliff."

"The husband would have noticed if she was sleepwalking when she got up, wouldn't he?" Cruz asked.

"No. I'm not sure you could tell." Gagnon had been mostly quiet until then. "And if it was at a time when she normally would have been up…"

"They didn't sleep together," Jones told him. "They had separate bedrooms."

Gagnon blinked, thinking about that. "I suppose she could have been sleepwalking, then."

"So, it's possible," Siever said a little aggressively. "But is it likely? What's more likely? That she was sleepwalking or that she met someone?"

Margie thought of the sweet little girl. Evie Wyler seemed like she had the ideal life with Vance and their little girl. She had a comfortable house to live in, good job, a partner who seemed fully committed to her and participated in the childcare. He was even the one that Ada chose to go to when she woke up from a nightmare, which suggested that he was a loving and attentive parent, not one who just did what Wyler told him to.

Would Wyler leave all of that for an illicit affair? She thought she needed more excitement in her life? She wasn't happy with her situation? Would a woman who had so much allow her head to be turned by a passing attraction to some other man?

Margie had been a cop long enough to know that it was a possibility. People didn't behave logically, they behaved emotionally. Maybe Evie Wyler wasn't the greatest mom in the world. Maybe she regretted having had a child. Maybe she wanted out of the situation she was in or wanted something else that she wasn't getting in her relationship with Vance.

Her social media posts seemed to indicate that she was happy with her family and that things were going well for her, but people didn't post the deep dark secret thoughts of their lives in public areas. Usually. They posted the superficial happy stuff, making their lives look normal and perfect, and kept the dark things hidden.

"Her phone logs may show if she was having long or frequent conversations with someone else," Margie said. "That might help sort it out. It would also show whether she had a phone call that morning that precipitated her leaving the house."

"Good thought," Mac agreed. "That will give us some more context. Maybe we should talk to a few friends and family members other than the husband, get their perspective on just what the relationship was like."

"I can reach out to some of the people on her social media," Margie said. "Since the next of kin has been notified, we can talk to other people about her death."

"When were her last posts on social media?" Siever asked. "That might help to narrow our window. And if they have a location code as well…"

"I don't think there was anything since before bed," Margie said. "I'll have to check." She made a note in her notepad.

"Location tracking," Cruz mused. "Does she share her location with any apps? Some people track their walking or running routes."

"Yes… and some people share their locations with family members or friends," Siever said, straightening up. "Does she have location sharing with her husband?"

"It might be worth taking a look at!"

"Wouldn't he have said so when he asked us about her phone?" Jones asked. "He'd be able to look at it and see where her phone was."

Siever shook his head. "He might not pay any attention to it. Some people like to watch their loved one's location, and others don't care. He might not even know he has the ability to check her location, if they happen to have a shared family account and he's never actually tried it."

"Let's find out," Margie encouraged. "Do you want me to give him a call and find out if knows if they have location sharing and to get their account information?"

"No."

Margie looked at Mac at his flat refusal.

"You get a warrant for his phone and any other electronics," Mac said, "and you go over there with it in hand. You don't give him a heads-up that you want his phone or his account information. We don't want him wiping it and deleting their accounts."

"Oh, right." It made logical sense, but Margie hadn't thought about Vance being a suspect in his wife's death. They had been thinking of it as an accident rather than a homicide, which made him a victim as well as her. But if someone had killed Evie Wyler, then the intimate partner was always the first suspect on the list.

She couldn't see him leaving little Ada asleep in bed and taking Evie Wyler to the top of the hill to have a talk with her, then pushing her over. He had come across as an honest, trustworthy, caring person. A nurturer.

He could have motive. The house was in her name and she could sue for sole custody of the child. If Wyler were having an affair, he had a lot to lose. There was a lot to be gained by disposing of his lover rather than trying to work things out and convince her to give him what he wanted. And he would be sad, devastated, the target of much sympathy from all those who knew him.

"I'll start working on a warrant," Margie offered. "Can I run it by you before we submit it? Make sure we're not missing anything?"

Mac nodded. "Of course. But if you're working on the social media follow-up, maybe someone else on the team should draft the warrant. Jones? Did you want to make the assignments?"

"Yes, sir." Jones looked at Margie. "Yes, if you could stay on the social media, I'd appreciate that. Gagnon, if you can draft the warrant. Patenaude and I can serve it once it's issued. We are both familiar to him already, so he should be more relaxed with us, more likely to hand it over without any trouble."

Margie was glad that she would still be able to be a part of serving the warrant.

Knowing where Wyler's phone had been and what had happened to it would be very helpful.

CHAPTER ELEVEN

As Margie had suspected, Evie Wyler had not posted anything on social media after retiring to bed the night of her death. No early-morning shots of the sun coming up or something of interest in the neighborhood.

So they ended up at the house in Wildwood again on Sunday morning. They might even wake Vance up. He said that he usually got up around eight, so he might be up already or still be in bed. It probably depended more upon what little Ada wanted than on Vance's preferred schedule.

He came to the door in boxer shorts and a house coat, wrapping the housecoat around him and tying it up when he saw who it was. "Officers. Is there something I can do to help?"

Jones held the warrant up. "We have a warrant for your phone, sir. With the unlock code. And any electronics that belonged to your wife."

He stared at her. "What?"

"We would like to see your phone, please."

"Well…" he patted at the robe pockets and came out with his phone, but didn't immediately hand it over. "I need this, though. I can't just give it to you."

"It's evidence. You are ordered to hand it over."

He shook his head in disbelief. "You really don't know… you can't understand. I need it for my business. For everything. My life is on that phone."

"And if you dropped it in the toilet, you would find a way to replace it," Jones said unsympathetically. "We are investigating the death of your partner. One would think that you would want to help out with that."

"Of course I do. But I don't see what this could have to do with anything."

Jones put out her hand, and Vance handed it over, looking sick.

"Thank you, sir. Can you tell me whether you have any location sharing apps on the phone?"

"What? Location sharing? I don't think so."

"The ability to see where Evie was. Where her phone was. Is."

He stared at her, blinking, trying to process her words. "No, I don't think so."

Jones looked down at the phone. "Are you both on the same account? Your phone service providers?"

"Yeah. She got onto a good plan, so I switched over to it a year or two ago."

"You're on a household plan?"

"Maybe. I guess so."

"I need both of your phone numbers and your logins for your phone provider and the cloud services you use. And Evie's email address account info."

"I have her address, but I don't know her login. Her password."

"Why don't you write all of the information you know down for us," Jones suggested. "The sooner we have everything we need, the sooner you'll be able to get your phone back."

But Margie suspected he would never get the phone back. If Wyler's death was found not to be accidental, they would need it as evidence. She was starting to be swayed to Siever's thinking. Why would Wyler go out for a walk in the early morning and just walk off the edge of the hill? Drugs or alcohol? Sleepwalking? Suicide? Just tripping or stepping over the edge seemed less and less likely the more she thought about it.

It was another hour before they had all of the information they thought they needed from Vance. It was probably more than they would use, but they didn't want to have to keep going back to him multiple times and wanted the ability to be able to get into whatever of his or Wyler's accounts they could. Something in there might tell the story about what had happened to Evie Wyler.

As soon as they returned to the office, Siever was there, waiting to take the phone and see what secrets he could find.

"We should be passing it directly on to the tech unit," Jones said. "What if there is sensitive information on there that could be destroyed by us accessing it?"

"You got his unlock codes, right?"

Margie and Jones nodded.

"Then I'm not going to destroy anything. Just have a little look around. If I come across something I can't open or something that we need recovered, I'll send it over to IT recovery."

Despite her suggestion, Jones seemed to be perfectly comfortable in having Siever look at the phone. She handed it over to him without further argument. Siever cradled it in his hands like it was a small, injured animal. "Give me a few minutes and I'll figure it out."

MARGIE FIGURED that a few minutes would turn into a few hours. Computer jobs always took significantly longer than she figured they would to get done what she wanted. And everybody she had dealt with on technical issues had been the same way. "Just one minute…" quickly turned into a few hours or a few days.

But Siever had some preliminary results in less than an hour.

The bullpen was quiet; it was just the three of them there on a Sunday morning. Siever hustled them into the boardroom and pointed the remote at the big screen at one end of the room. Turning it on, he quickly worked to get a few reference slides up on the screen.

"I have a few coordinates for you," he announced, looking at the screen rather than his coworkers' faces. "From the night before."

The dot on the map on the big screen showed the location of Evie

Wyler's Wildwood home. She nodded. Just where they expected her to be.

"The phone is on the move just before six in the morning. Wyler is out of her house and walking down the street."

A couple of slides to show the dot getting farther away from her home.

"Between six-thirty and seven, she is hanging around a single location."

Margie wasn't good at visualizing maps when looking at the real world and, conversely, had trouble translating a flat map into the actual buildings and roads around her. Satellite imagery helped, but was still not enough to be able to fully translate between the 3D world and the 2D world.

But the big green blob on the map had to be Edworthy park, and that particular shape, the hill that they had stood at the bottom of, looking up.

"So she went there on her own, but then waited." Margie took a swig of her cold coffee. "So now we know for sure. She was meeting someone."

"I haven't gone through all of her previous activity," Siever warned. "It could be that she goes and sits there with a coffee and a journal each morning. Or something good to read. Or just her phone."

"Okay... it *appears* that she was there waiting for someone."

Siever nodded, happier with this statement. "Shortly after seven..." He changed the slide. The dot was farther inside the park. After the fall.

"So it is still out there," Margie observed. "Is this map accurate enough that we can use it to find the phone now?"

"It would be," Siever said, flipping to another slide. "If it were still there."

Margie stared at the map without any dots on it. "Wait, what?"

"Someone removed it from the scene"

"Maybe it just ran out of juice," Jones suggested.

Siever shrugged. "It's possible... but I don't think so." He flipped through a number of screenshots. "It disappeared within a few hours.

Most people don't want their phones dying halfway through the day. They charge them during the night so that they are fully charged and ready to go before work in the morning. But Wyler's phone dies far too early for that." He left up the last screenshot before the phone disappeared off of the map.

Margie checked the time stamp. "That's right after we released the scene."

Siever nodded. "That's what I figured too."

And if it wasn't coincidence that it had disappeared right after they released the scene, then what?

Then someone had picked it up and shut it off or destroyed it.

CHAPTER TWELVE

"Who saw it and removed it from the scene?" Jones asked.

They all looked at each other, thinking back to the scene that day and trying to figure it out.

"The first scenario is that it was just picked up by someone random. People find dropped and lost cellphones all the time," Siever contributed.

"Right. They might have turned it in or advertised it somewhere but, since no one has identified it as Wyler's phone, no one has claimed it," Jones agreed.

"But right after we released the scene?" Margie asked. "And it was turned off, not transported somewhere else."

"Yeah. That's weird."

"It could have been damaged in the fall," Siever said. "And it just didn't die immediately. If it was wet or the battery damaged, it might have taken a few hours to short out."

"That makes sense." Jones nodded. "And if so… we should still be able to find it at the location on the map."

He nodded. "Possibly. And the other possibility is… someone was looking for it, or knew where it was, and was just waiting until we released the scene so that they could get their hands on it."

Margie had a knot in her stomach. Was that possible? Had they been working under the eye of a murderer, just waiting for the chance to wipe out any clues of his presence?

Margie rubbed the bridge of her nose. She was starting to get a headache. She really did not like where the investigation was going. It had seemed so obvious that it was an accident. To have everything turned around now…

She could accept that one of the other possibilities was more likely. She liked the idea that it might have been damaged in the fall and had survived Wyler by a few hours. Then it could still be an accident. They could go back to the park and referring to the phone's last known location, find the broken phone.

Or maybe not, if the parks service or someone else had already picked up the broken phone and tossed it in the garbage.

"Do we have pictures of the bystanders?" she asked Jones

"They might appear in a couple, but no… we were taking pictures behind the screens. We did some wider scene shots for perspective, but we didn't intentionally take pictures of all the bystanders. Most of them arrived there quite some time after the body was discovered. They were just attracted by all the activity and wanted to know what was going on."

"Most of them, probably. But people do return to the scene of the crime. They want to make sure that everything is unfolding the way they expected, that nobody suspects them, or that they're getting the kind of attention they wanted to. *If* Wyler was pushed, it's possible that the killer attended at the scene later to see how things were playing out. And it's possible that he could have seen her cell phone and removed it later." Margie shook her head. "It really seems like a long shot. How would he see the phone when we didn't? We didn't see it when we were looking for evidence at the scene, and we didn't find it when we went back with the drones."

"The drones," Jones repeated.

"The phone wasn't there anymore when we took the drones," Siever reminded them. "It was removed on Friday."

"But there *was* a drone. There was the drone that one guy was using at the scene. Gagnon was trying to get rid of him." Jones looked at Margie. "And you got him to go. Did you get his name?"

"Yeah. I wrote down all his information." Margie opened her notebook and flipped back, looking for the details. "I wanted to put a scare into him. Make him fly straight." She chuckled at her inadvertent pun. "Make him fly straight and respect the law in the future. Here it is. Howard Ross. And I've got his address, driver's license, and birth date."

Jones grinned. "Color me impressed. I'll reach out to him. See whether we can get him to send us a copy of the pictures."

"I'll see whether I can plot the last location of the phone against the scene photos that we have," Siever offered. "In good conditions, we should be able to plot it within five to ten feet."

"Sounds great." Margie had an impulse to offer to do something that would help them to clear the case as well, but there wasn't much else she could do at the moment. It was Sunday and she should be home with her daughter, not hanging around the office any longer than she was required to be. "I think I'll head home, if no one has any objections."

She gave them all the chance, but no one spoke up. Margie nodded. "See you tomorrow, then. I'm looking forward to the morning briefing."

"See you," Jones agreed. "Maybe we'll have it solved by then."

IT HAD BEEN a cooler day and Stella had more energy than she had had in the recent heat. She jumped up when she heard Margie at the door and pranced around her as she walked in. Margie was happy to see her having fun. Too many days recently, Stella had just wanted to lie on the floor, panting, too hot to show any excitement.

"Hi, Mom!" Christina called out from her bedroom in the back of the house. Margie went to the doorway and looked in on her. Christina was stretched out on her bed, phone in one hand, tapping her tablet on the pillow with her other hand. Margie smiled.

"What are you up to?"

"Looking at the pictures of the fire last night. Some of my friends posted or forwarded videos of the flames and the firetrucks."

"What fire?" Margie's mind went immediately to the BC forest fires. But there was no way they had reached Calgary. Especially not the far side of Calgary. They couldn't exactly jump over the entire city to land on the other side.

"There was a fire on the train tracks night before last. Sparked by one of the train wheels, probably."

"Where, exactly?"

Christina motioned to the south. "Erin Woods. Just over there."

Margie knew where Erin Woods was. A little community a fleeing murder suspect had ended up in one day the previous year. Margie's skin prickled with goosebumps and she had a chill, remembering.

Not her best day. But they had caught him. And they would catch Wyler's killer too, if someone had caused her death.

CHAPTER THIRTEEN

Howard Ross had, perhaps unsurprisingly, provided copies of his drone footage to the police when requested, so they hadn't had to chase down a warrant. Margie suspected that Jones might have had something to say about confiscating his drone so that they could get the pictures off of it themselves and to make sure that he hadn't tried to delete any evidence. He wasn't likely to want to give up his bird. Who knew when they would give it back, if ever?

Siever had already gone to work sorting out geotags so that the pictures could be arranged by the area they were taken in, giving them the ability to pinpoint the area that Wyler's phone had been in at the time of her death.

Margie and Jones sat at their desks, looking at the photos on their own computers. Margie started with the pictures that were closest to the phone. Not as helpful as it might have seemed, since all that gave her was a big tree with lots of leaves and branches. The leaves were too thick to see through, so that if the phone were in the tree branches or on the ground beneath it, she couldn't see it. She started moving outward from the tree, looking for anything else that might be helpful.

Maybe the phone had been stolen by some bird that liked shiny things. Though Margie thought that a phone would be too big and awkward for a bird to carry. Some of the ravens up north might snatch it, but most of the birds she had seen around Calgary were small and would not be able to lift something like that.

She widened the perimeter so that she should see the privacy screens, and then over them into the accident scene, including Wyler's body. She shook her head in irritation at Ross for using his toy to trespass on the scene and to scope out the dead body. There was really no excuse for that.

She remembered Siever using the grappling hook on his drone to retrieve the purse that had become lodged in the branches of the tree. What if Ross had used the same trick to retrieve a phone from the big tree? Once they had cleared the scene, he was free to go back there, and people wouldn't think there was anything strange about his flying a drone around the park once more. He was probably there often and would be invisible to the regular park users.

But why? Was he somehow connected with Wyler? Or had he just been interested in retrieving what was lodged in the branches of the tree for sport? Or out of macabre interest? Did he now own the phone of a dead woman? And if there were any evidence on it, how were they going to prove that he had it, unless he turned it over voluntarily?

There wasn't anything enlightening in the photographs of Wyler's body. She looked it over carefully, remembering everything in as much detail as possible. Was there anything out of place? Anything they had missed? Evidence on the body or nearby? Some small detail that would make a difference to the investigation?

Margie moved on to the photos taken on the other side of the tree. Not toward Wyler's body, but the interested onlookers, craning their necks for a view of a dead body. Who wouldn't be excited to go home at the end of the day and tell their loved ones around the dinner table that they had seen a dead body in the park that morning? Or to post it on their social media and get all kinds of views and responses?

Some of the faces were easier to see than others. Ball caps and cowboy hats used to shade the spectators from the sun also shielded their faces from the drone. Most of the time it was too high to get a good, identifiable view. She studied each of the people who were watching the scene. Was one of them a killer? Someone who had shown up not just by accident but because he wanted to view the aftermath, and to make sure that no one had seen or suspected him?

"Detective Jones?"

Jones turned away from her monitor to look at Margie. "Find something?"

"No. Maybe."

Jones got up and looked over Margie's shoulder for a better view. "Okay, what are you looking at?"

"You see how everyone is looking in the same direction?"

"Mostly, yes," Jones agreed, nodding.

"But what about this guy?" Margie pointed to a head that was turned at a different angle from everyone else. Black cowboy hat. Western shirt. Like many of the people who attended Stampede functions around the city, both on the Stampede grounds and off. Or even just people who enjoyed dressing up a little for Stampede when they weren't going anywhere. Margie herself had been tempted to pull out some of her traditional Métis clothing a couple of times during the week, but she wasn't sure how it would go over at work and when dealing with the public, so she had not. Cruz, a Filipino immigrant, had been wearing a different western shirt and belt buckle every day of the week. People were fine with the cowboy-themed stuff, but Margie wasn't sure they would be quite as accepting of her traditional dress. Fine for the Elbow River Camp, not so much everywhere else. There was a lot of prejudice toward the visibly Indigenous, even in times when they were supposed to be sensitive about racial bias.

"What's he looking at?" Jones mused.

Margie switched pictures to one that was pulled a little farther back, giving a bit more context.

"At the tree. Where the phone was at the time."

They both studied it. Margie zoomed in on the tree, hoping to be able to spot the phone in the branches. But she suspected she would have to be on the ground like the cowboy hat dude. Or like Ross, to have a drone that she could send closer to have a look around. It had been fun operating the drones as part of their search for Wyler's phone and the purse.

"Some of the later pictures are lower and have a better angle," Jones said, pointing to the file explorer on Margie's screen. "When you made him land his drone."

Margie started to page through the photos, looking at the spectators, keeping her eye on the man in the black hat. As the drone got lower and closer, he started to look more familiar. Who was he? Where had she seen him before?

"Oh!" She and Jones both got it at the same time.

They had seen him at the Wildwood Stampede breakfast. When they had been approached by the schmoozing Vincent Skinner, mayoral candidate, and his campaign manager.

CHAPTER FOURTEEN

"What is he doing there?" Margie demanded. She pulled out her notebook to find the notes she had made while at the breakfast to refresh herself on the names. "Harland Roberts."

"Maybe… he was just hanging around, getting ready for their appearance at the Stampede breakfast, and he was attracted by the lights and sirens, decided to go see what was going on."

"All right," Margie said slowly. "Then why wouldn't he be rubbernecking like everyone else? Trying to catch a glimpse of the body or overhear our discussions? Why is he looking over there?"

Jones nodded. "Because he saw the phone."

"And wouldn't normal Joe Public point that out to the police? Be helpful and get brownie points for helping with an investigation? Especially someone like this, so used to spinning stories for the media and getting all the attention for the campaign that he could."

"Yeah. Of course he would." Jones's lips pressed together. "It's not proof, but it's compelling. We need to know what he did with the phone. And what his connection is to Wyler. Were they lovers? Is that who she was waiting for when she was standing at the top of the hill?"

"Or is he there for Skinner, Mr. Elect-Me-Mayor? Maybe Skinner sent him to clean things up. Make sure that there wasn't anything left behind to implicate him."

Jones *hmmed* and nodded. "Can't rule that out," she agreed. "We need to find out which one of them was connected to Wyler, if one of them was. This can't be a coincidence. He didn't just happen to be there to see what was going on, and see a phone, and then not point it out to the police. And then go back and take it once the scene was released."

"We got her computer on that warrant too, didn't we?"

"Yeah. Siever's got it. Siever, you still have Wyler's computer?" Jones called across the bullpen, but walked closer to Siever's desk as she spoke to be polite.

"Better," Siever said, holding up a small, oblong box, "I've got a copy of it."

"How is that better?" Margie asked.

"Because we can play around with it all we like and not mess up the original, which forensics has. We don't have to wait for anyone else, if you know what you're looking for."

"Well," Margie looked at Jones.

"It turns out we do. We're going on the working theory that Harland Roberts or Vincent Skinner are involved in this and have some kind of connection with Wyler. Can you search that for any reference to either of them?"

"Sure, I can do that."

"I'll call the husband and ask him whether he knows either of them or if there is some way that Wyler could have run into them," Margie offered.

"And I guess I'll run background and see if there are any court cases or charges that the two of them were both involved in. See if there are any intersecting interests or favorite haunts," Jones decided, though she didn't look too excited about the prospect. Computer background was not her favorite thing, but Siever was already tied up with seeing whether there was anything on Wyler's computer to do with the case.

Margie could swap jobs with her. Jones was the primary, so she was entitled to make assignments. But Margie didn't really want to be stuck doing background all day, and Jones decided to let her do what she had volunteered for.

Margie turned back to her computer and closed the various pictures, except for the one that showed Roberts's face. She brought Vance's number up on her screen and dialed the phone.

❧

Margie, Jones, Siever and the others all gathered around the conference room table later for a quick bull session, making sure that everyone was up to speed on all the progress on the file.

Jones shook her head in disgust. She stretched, showing that she had been hunched over a computer keyboard for too long already. "I wasn't able to find any connections between either Skinner or Roberts and Wyler. Other than that Skinner was scheduled to campaign in the area the day that Wyler died. That's not a connection that we could use to convince a judge of anything."

"So Roberts just happened to be at our accident scene for no reason that day? I don't believe that," Margie offered. "I talked to the significant other, but he couldn't connect them either. He'd never heard of Skinner or Roberts. Wyler had never mentioned them."

"Wyler doesn't have any credit card charges to a hotel nearby or anything like that," Jones said. "I don't see any suspicious spending patterns."

They looked at Siever. The other detectives in the room quieted, waiting for his response.

"No mention of Skinner or Roberts on the computer," Siever said. "I've done a full search of all files, and neither name is ever mentioned."

Jones groaned. "So it's a dead end."

"I did get access to their phone bills through Vance's phone, though. Logged into their service provider."

Margie remembered asking Vance for the information that he had on passwords and providers in hopes that it would help them to track the location of Evie Wyler's phone. That had paid off in more ways than one.

"What did you find?" Jones asked, her voice squeaking slightly. It was clear that Siever must have found something. He wouldn't tell them that he had logged in to the phone service provider just to tell them that it was a dead end.

"There were calls and texts to a burner phone in the days before her death. Phone was registered to a fake name and address."

"Which may or may not have anything to do with Skinner," Jones said, let down.

"Before she started using that number, there was a call to Skinner's campaign office."

"What?" Jones slapped her notepad down onto the boardroom table with a crack. "We know she called Skinner?"

"We know she called Skinner's campaign office," Siever corrected precisely.

"Well it comes out to the same thing."

He shook his head. "We don't know who she talked to at the campaign office. Was it Mr. Mayor himself? I don't think so. He probably just goes by there once a week to wave to people and tell them what a great job they're doing."

"But Roberts would be there almost full time," Margie said. "So maybe when she called, it was Roberts she talked to."

There were nods around the room.

"No guarantee," Siever said, "but that would be my guess."

Margie didn't sugar coat it. "We have her calling his office, and we have him showing up at the scene of her death. But we don't have anything to show what they talked about or if he had anything to do with her death. Maybe Roberts was who she was waiting for when she died. Maybe they missed each other and he was still waiting when he heard the sirens."

"And maybe they found each other, and he took care of her," Jones said, her voice clipped. "He pushes her off the cliff, opens her purse, rifles through the content and checks her identification to see who she is. Or if she is who she says she is. Then he tosses it over as well."

It fit the evidence. It could have happened that way.

"But what started it? Why did she call the campaign office to begin with? Obviously, it wasn't because she was there to make a campaign donation. She would have just sent it electronically or put a check in the mail. They wouldn't have had to have an ongoing conversation and more than one meeting for that."

"Unless she was working with a foundation that would give grants under certain circumstances, and they needed Skinner to get all his ducks in a row before she would send it. Sometimes those kinds of thing take several meetings," Gagnon suggested.

"It's possible," Jones said, but shook her head. "But I don't think she was working with anything like that. What was it her husband said she was doing?" She looked at Margie.

"Online teacher. Grading papers and such."

"Right. I don't see how that would have anything to do with Skinner's mayoral campaign."

"I don't either," Margie admitted.

It was frustrating to be able to see that there was some kind of connection there, but unable to figure out what it was.

"With her calling the campaign office, it doesn't sound like an affair," she said.

"No. I think you're right," Jones agreed. "Unless they started an affair after the first time she called, and that's why he switched to a burner."

Margie thought of little Ada. How could Wyler have done anything to hurt her? It happened, of course. Parents had affairs all the time; it didn't matter how close they were to their children. Even those who appeared to be so close to their spouses could wander.

"What about asking around at the coffee shops?" Gagnon suggested. "If that's where she often worked from, it may also be where she met up with him."

"Yes. Good idea," Jones agreed. "Oh, and while I'm thinking of it… let's do a garbage search on Roberts. If he retrieved Wyler's phone and threw it out at home, or if he threw out other evidence that connects him to this case, that would be a starting point."

Margie glanced around the room, not expecting anyone to jump in and offer to do that job. Everyone was looking away, checking their watches or phones, attempting to look as though they had somewhere else to be. Margie smiled at Jones.

"You'll help out?" Jones asked, letting out a sigh of relief.

"Sure, why not? I want to get this guy."

CHAPTER FIFTEEN

Despite the fact that it was a cooler day with the sun blocked by the smoke of the BC fires, sweat trickled down Margie's forehead. She used the back of her wrist to wipe it away. They had turned up the van's air conditioning as much as possible, but it didn't seem to be doing much. Probably because they also had the windows open in an effort to circulate air so that Margie and Jones wouldn't die from the stench of the garbage bags.

Margie had hoped that a guy like Harland Roberts would be a bachelor subsisting mostly on restaurant food, so that his household garbage would be mostly paper products, plastic wrap, and whatever other non-recyclables Roberts went through.

But bless his heart, he was not a bachelor, but married with two young children. Two very young children. Children still in diapers. And the diaper changers did not seem to put all the used diapers into one diaper pail bag, but into whatever garbage happened to be closest at the time, so every bag they had pulled had little—and not so little—stink bombs lurking amid the rest of the refuse.

Margie gagged. Was she ever glad that she no longer had a baby or toddler. Little children like Ada were wonderful to be around for a few minutes, until they stopped acting like angels and had explosive diarrhea. Which happened all too often for Margie's tastes. She was so glad to have a teenager who could take care of all of her bodily functions herself.

And the food… it appeared that Roberts, and maybe Skinner too, were dressing above their class. They had looked like the rich and powerful businessmen that she associated with mayors and their offices, but Roberts didn't appear to be making enough money to take people out to fancy restaurants. There was a lot of KD, frozen burritos, and Ichiban noodles. The family threw a lot of leftovers out in the trash instead of the green bin, with only the occasional fast-food wrapper thrown in. And after sitting outside for a week or more in thirty-degree temperatures, everything was rotting and liquefying.

Jones's phone rang. She crouched there for a moment looking at the garbage, then straightened. She slowly stripped off her gloves, wiped sweat from her face, and answered the phone.

"Hey, Cruz. Tell me you have some good news."

She listened, nodding and making sounds of acknowledgment. "Okay. All right. Thanks for letting me know."

She hung up the call. Margie looked at her, eyebrows raised.

"Did he find anything? Tell me we don't have to go through any more garbage."

"Well, no one said that they had seen Roberts at the coffee shops."

Margie groaned. "So that's a dead end. And I seriously don't think that we're going to find anything in here." She looked at the heap of trash they had already been through.

"Yeah. I think this is going to be a bust too. But… one of the coffee shop employees did remember seeing Wyler."

"We already know that she frequented coffee shops to do her work. That doesn't mean anything."

"He said that he saw her there with another woman."

"Okay." Margie considered. "Is there something about this other woman that helps us?"

"I don't know. I'm thinking about it. Her job is online, on the computer. Vance said she didn't do any face-to-face tutoring, even virtually. So who was she there with?"

"A girl friend. If you know your best friend is at a coffee shop all day long, why not stop by at some point for a cup of coffee and a visit?"

"Maybe," Jones admitted. "But if that's where I went to get away from the distractions and get some work done, I'm not sure I would tell any friends where I was, for just that reason. Everyone would think it was okay to interrupt."

"So what are you thinking?"

"The witness said that the other woman seemed to be upset about something. He thought maybe Wyler was trying to pressure her into something."

"Wyler was trying to pressure someone else into something?"

Jones nodded. "I'm wondering… maybe this was blackmail. Wyler was trying to get someone to pay up. Maybe this girl was having an affair with Roberts, and that's the tie between them." Jones looked at the trash around them. "I mean… I could understand if he didn't want to come home to this. A politician with a girl on the side, that's not exactly a shocker, is it?"

"No. So would she be able to blackmail him for something like that?"

"Sure. Just because it's common, that doesn't mean that he wants everyone to know about it. If it's Skinner, he doesn't want his public to know that he's not the perfect family man. If it's Roberts, he doesn't want his boss to know that he's got a girl on the side. It's bad optics, if he gets found out. So if Skinner finds out Roberts is playing around on the side, he's gone."

"Maybe. It does seem like they're both trying really hard to appear to be something that they are not."

"Fake it 'til you make it. That's the world of politics."

"So how do we find out who has a girlfriend?"

"See if we can get the phone logs for the burner phone, to start with. See if there is another number that it calls regularly. If he had a different phone to talk to Wyler, that's probably the same one as he used to talk to his girlfriend."

"Nice. We can do that."

"We may as well go back to Vance too. See if he knows anything about this woman Wyler saw at the coffee shop. Maybe we're wrong and it's his sister, or someone else from work, or a best friend. Maybe he can tell us something. Whether we're on a wild goose chase."

Margie wiped her face. "I think we'd better get cleaned up first."

CHAPTER SIXTEEN

*V*ance did not look too impressed when he saw the women on his doorstep. Margie felt like checking the mirror again to make sure she hadn't missed a smudge or something else offensive. He should be happy that they were clean and presentable. He wouldn't have liked it if they had shown up on his doorstep half an hour earlier.

"You again." His forehead was creased. "Do you have news? Are you closing the case?"

"We're getting closer," Jones said with a bland smile. "We'll be sure to let you know our findings when we have something to report."

"Then what are you here for? You already got my phone and Evie's computer. I don't know what else to tell you. She fell down and died… it was an accident. I wasn't there. She just… I guess she just tripped and fell. Sometimes that happens. People do trip and fall."

"Can we come in to talk?" Jones asked.

He looked like he would say no, but good manners prevailed and he motioned for them to enter. "I only have a few minutes… I don't mean to brush you off, but I do still have my work to do and Ada is down for a nap. She doesn't sleep for long, so I need to use the quiet time to my best advantage."

"We shouldn't be too long," Margie assured him.

They all sat down. Jones looked around the pleasant little living room. "You have a very nice house."

"Thank you. It's very comfortable. Evie was always good at… making people comfortable. Knowing just the right touches to make a room seem friendly. Me… I have no sense of style. My idea of decorating is Ikea shelves."

Margie laughed. "There are some very nice Ikea shelves. And you know what I always loved about Ikea, besides the cool decorating ideas? That they have a kids' play place and you can just walk around and look without little ones underfoot. And then there's a restaurant at the end where you can have meatballs and a hot dog…"

Vance gave her a more genuine smile. "Date night."

Margie nodded. "And you don't have to feel guilty, because the little one has a blast too. Shopping, together time, dinner, and a happy, tired kid. It's the best."

Jones didn't have any children. She just looked at Margie and shook her head slightly, bemused. "Why not just hire a babysitter?"

"Because the play place at Ikea is *free*."

"Not if you spend hundreds of dollars on furniture you don't need."

Margie couldn't help chuckling. "Oh, believe me, you *need* the furniture."

They were all smiling. Vance was getting more relaxed. But they did want to move quickly, to get as much out of him as they could before Ada got up from her nap. She would be distracting. They wouldn't get far once she was underfoot again.

Jones began delicately. "Mr. Vance. Trevor. We've been making some inquiries at the coffee shops where Evie might have gone to do some work."

"Inquiries… about what? What could that possibly have to do with her death?"

"We're just exploring all avenues. Going where the evidence takes us." Soothing words that meant nothing.

"But she fell down a hill. What does that have to do with working in a coffee shop?"

Jones didn't try to explain it to him. He was the one who wanted them to move along. "At one of the coffee shops, they mentioned seeing Evie, and also said that she had been there with another woman."

"Another woman. Who?"

"We're hoping that you can help us out with that one."

"I don't know who she would have been there with. Someone else who hung out there to work and they got talking? It could be anyone."

"I'm thinking it was someone she knew outside of the coffee shop. Did she have a best friend that might have dropped in to see her? A sister? A client?"

"She went there to work, not to visit. But I don't know. She could have asked someone to meet her there. We didn't keep tabs on each other. She didn't tell me everyone she talked to during the day, and neither did I. We did our own things and spent time together when we were able to."

"It seems like you were more roommates than partners. Was Evie seeing someone else?"

"I told you before, no. I don't know why that is so hard to believe. We didn't have other people. Friends, yes, but not partners. Casual friendships."

"This woman was blond, a little shorter than your wife, hair in a pixie cut…" Jones offered.

Vance scowled, shaking his head. "No, I can't think of who that would be. Maybe it's just somebody who was having coffee and they got to talking. Evie was a friendly person. She liked interacting with other people. She worked on her own, but she wanted to be around other people still. Grown-up people, not two-year-olds."

"Sure, of course. So you think it was just someone she happened to meet. The witness said it seemed like Evie was trying to talk her into something."

"I don't know," Vance said blankly. He looked off into the distance. "Maybe she thought that the woman would like to take one of the classes that Evie offered. Trying to talk her into giving it a try. People are leery about trying something new."

"What kind of classes did Evie teach?" Margie asked.

She imagined some work by Shakespeare or Dickens. Maybe a whole English lit course. Or maybe she was into history. Or home decorating.

"She taught different classes at different times. But the backbone of her work was ethics."

"Ethics," Jones repeated, looking as surprised as Margie felt. She had assumed that it would be something in the arts. Something creative. What a sexist assumption. There was no reason it couldn't be math, or hard science, or ethics. "What was her background?"

"Journalism and law. Pre-law. She was taking some night classes, or online classes, through the same company as she worked for. But she wasn't sure if she was ever going to get a law degree. She really liked what she was doing. And she was very good at it. She got really high ratings from her students. I'm sure a lot of people get into this kind of teaching online thinking it's going to be simple. A walk in the park. But it was a lot of work. Like I said, it wasn't all multiple-choice tests that the computer could mark. She had to grade essays and all kinds of other projects. Her students really liked her."

"And she never saw any of them face to face?"

"No. They were all over the world. Not just local."

"And she didn't ever meet any of the local students? Maybe have a pub night at the end of the class with anyone who was in Calgary or Red Deer?"

"No."

Jones and Margie posed a few more unimportant questions, and then excused themselves, telling Vance that they were done and he could get back to his work. Which he seemed quite happy to do. He saw them out at the door, promised to let them know if he thought of anything, and they promised to let him know when there had been a resolution on the case, and they went their separate ways.

CHAPTER SEVENTEEN

*M*argie and Jones got into the car without saying anything to each other. Then before starting the engine, Jones turned to her and said what they were both thinking.

"She was teaching ethics. You don't suppose that the woman she met in the coffee shop was a student, do you?"

"One who had written an essay about someone local who had poor ethics?" Margie suggested.

Jones nodded. "Exactly what I was thinking." She pulled out her phone and dialed in, on speaker so that Margie could hear.

"Siever."

"Do you still have that copy of Wyler's computer handy?" Jones asked, knowing that he would. It was an active case; of course he still had it on his desk.

"What are we looking for?" he asked, bypassing any unnecessary discussion.

"Wyler taught ethics. We think that the meeting in the coffee shop might have been with one of her students. Someone who had written something about Skinner or Roberts."

"What meeting at the coffee shop?"

"Cruz and Gagnon were checking out the coffee shops that Wyler might have gone to in case she had been seen there with Roberts. No one saw her with *him*, but they did see her with another woman, whom she seemed to be pressuring. If this woman was a student and had written something about Skinner or Roberts, then she might have been trying to get her to report them to some authority or the media."

"There are a lot of documents on this computer," Siever warned. "And we've already searched it for mentions of Skinner or Roberts. There are no files that mention either of them by name."

"She might not have named them. Look for something about a politician or candidate. It should have been received shortly before Wyler called the campaign office. She couldn't get the student to report the guy, so she thought she would have a go at it herself."

"And written by a female student. Well, those parameters will help to narrow it down. Are you coming back here?"

Jones looked at Margie, who nodded. "Yes," she told Siever. "If we can figure out who the woman is, we might be able to pull this all together."

SIEVER HADN'T FOUND the essay by the time they got downtown, but he'd made some good inroads and was reading through the files that he had filtered out.

"I could never be a teacher. All these typos and incomplete sentences…"

Margie laughed. "Luckily, you don't have to grade them. Just to find the one that made Evie Wyler reach out to her student."

"You're sure that's what happened?"

"Well… no, we can't be sure, but it's a good theory. One that we have to run down."

Siever nodded.

"Do you want to split the files between us and we can each read a few?" Jones asked.

He glanced at the file list on his screen. "No. I've just got a few left. It wouldn't be worth my time to divvy them up."

"Anything interesting so far?"

"It's an interesting topic. But I wouldn't want to spend hours reading them."

"Well… we'll just be over here, pretending that we're not waiting to see what you find," Jones said, motioning to their desks. Like he wouldn't know where to find them once he had finished his review.

Siever gave her a brief smile, then dove back into his document review.

❧

EVENTUALLY, Siever joined Margie and Jones with a couple of printouts. He handed them each one. "I think this is the most likely candidate. If it's not the right one, there are some other possibilities. But a local woman, in that time frame, writing about a politician… this is your best bet."

Margie took her copy and focused on it, tuning everything else out. It was the story of a hit and run driver. A woman had been killed crossing the street. But the driver would not turn himself in. The passenger had a number of reasons for not reporting him herself, including the fact that she had been drunk and high at the time. She had done her best to forget about it, to push it far away into the back of her mind.

And then the driver decided to run for office. The hit and run had never been attributed to him. As far as anyone was concerned, he had a clean record. Everyone except the passenger. But she had built a life for herself. She supported herself and did good work and service for others. If she reported it and ended up being arrested as well as the perpetrator, she would lose her child and the community would lose the other good work that she had been doing. Wasn't it better for her to remain in the community where she could continue to do good?

"Bingo," Jones said. "This has got to be it. Skinner was the hit and run driver."

"And Wyler knew that the student was local, so she tried to convince her to report it like she should."

CHAPTER EIGHTEEN

*J*ones and Margie took the chance that Kimberly Martin would be home in the evening. If she was an online student, she was probably working during the day and upgrading at night. Of course, she could be working at night and doing school during the day, but it was worth seeing whether she was home. If not, they could try to reach her in the morning.

The woman who answered the door fit the description of the woman at the coffee shop. A cute blond bob, about Margie's height and similar to her in age, though the fine smoker's wrinkles around her mouth made her look older. It was a vice that Margie was glad she had avoided.

Kimberly raised her brows, looking them over warily.

"Yeah? Can I help you?"

"Miss Martin? We're with the Calgary Police Service. Could we come in to talk, please?"

She stood there for a moment considering, then stepped back and let them into her apartment. It was small but neat. She had obviously been eating sitting in front of the computer; whether to do school-work or watch Netflix, Margie couldn't tell from her angle. They all sat down in the worn furniture arranged in a conversational grouping.

"What's this about?" Kimberly asked nervously.

"Have you ever met this woman?" Jones showed her a picture of Wyler, taken from her Facebook page.

"That's Evie Wyler, isn't it? She's one of my teachers."

"Yes, that's right. Did you meet with her a couple of weeks ago?"

"Yeah." Kimberly looked anxious. She shook her head. "I don't know what she's told you, but…"

"Actually, Miss Wyler hasn't told us anything. She died a few days ago."

Kimberly's eyes widened with shock. "She died? How? What happened?"

"It initially looked like an accident, but we are investigating whether it might have been homicide. We're hoping that you'll be able to help us with that."

Kimberly's mouth opened and closed. She didn't seem to be able to get the words out. Her face had gone very pale. Margie got up and, without asking, went to the little kitchenette and found a glass. She ran the cold faucet for a bit, then filled the glass. She took it over to Kimberly, who took it with a vague nod.

"Have a drink. It will help you to feel better," Margie encouraged.

Kimberly took a sip, then a longer gulp. She put the glass to the side, away from the computer. "How could she be dead?"

"When you met with Miss Wyler, I assume you talked with her about your essay," Jones said.

"How do you know about that?" Kimberly got out in a strangled voice.

"We have Miss Wyler's computer."

Kimberly breathed out a curse. She put her face in her hands, shaking her head.

"Would you like to tell us about it?"

"No! You think I want to end up dead, like her?"

"Have you been threatened?" Margie asked.

"Of course I have! Do you know what would happen to me if people found out what had happened?" Kimberly shook her head and breathed loudly into her hands, sobbing.

"You were a passenger, not the driver. You can't control what the driver does."

"He said that if I ever told anyone, they'd put me in prison too. I was… under the influence. I wasn't a credible witness. And if I said that he'd done it, they would say that I was the one behind the wheel."

"They?" Margie prodded.

"Hal and Vince." Kimberly swore again. "Why did you have to come here?"

"I know that doing the right thing is hard," Jones comforted. "But you'll feel better once everything is straightened out. I promise."

"I have a little girl. I can't go to prison. And I try to do things to help others out. I volunteer in the community. I take old people their meals. I try really hard to contribute to society."

She felt so guilty about the hit and run, she had bargained with herself, saying that she would make up for it. It wasn't the first time Margie had seen that behavior.

"Nobody has said anything about you going to prison," Jones assured her. "You need to talk about what happened. As a passenger, you are not responsible for what the driver did. You should have reported it, yes, but we can work with that."

"Hal said that I would go to prison." Kimberly was shaking. "He said if I breathed one word, I would go to prison. And then…" She sobbed, losing control. "I had to go and write that stupid essay!"

"You wanted to tell someone what had happened, didn't you?" Margie asked. "It has been such a heavy burden to bear; you hoped that it would be easier if you could tell someone else."

Kimberly nodded.

"Well, now we're here," Jones said. "Let's talk about it. Get it all off your chest."

Kimberly pulled her hands from her face and patted her pockets. Her face was wet, blotchy, and miserable. Margie had a couple of tissues ready and handed them to her. "Have another drink," she prompted.

Kimberly obediently blew her nose and drank more water, which seemed to steady her.

"When did this happen?" Jones asked. "Did you know Vince and Hal from somewhere?"

"From high school. They were buddies back then, Hal always taking Vince's crap and trying to do everything for him." Kimberly blotted the corners of her eyes. "Vince was always a bully. None of us came from money, and we kind of hung around together. The poor, unpopular kids. Vince was always trying to run some scam or another. To make money or to make the teachers think that he was such a great guy. They didn't see what he was like when it was just us. But I didn't have anyone else to hang out with, you know?"

"And this accident, did it happen during high school?" Jones asked.

So far, they didn't even have a name to put to the hit and run victim. It could have happened anywhere, any time.

"It was after school. A year or two, I guess. We didn't really hang out together anymore. Everybody had their own thing. But we thought we'd get together, have some fun. Just… relax and take a break from the rat race. From having to pretend to be something… something that we weren't."

Margie nodded encouragingly. "Take off the masks and just be yourself again. Relive those hey-days."

"We never had good times in school. It was all pretty miserable. Maybe Vince did, but the rest of us… we were just… trying to find something. Something that wasn't there. Not for us."

"So you went out together for a few drinks?" Jones suggested.

Kimberly blew her nose again. There was a tissue box nearby, and she pulled out a few more sheets. "Yeah. Drinks. Other stuff. We were all so wasted."

"Maybe you should have caught a cab or a bus."

"Not Vince. He was always so… arrogant and single-minded. He didn't *need* a cab or a bus. He could drink all night and it wouldn't affect him." Her sarcasm was biting.

"Do you remember where and when the incident happened?"

"Memorial Drive and… one of the bridges." She closed her eyes, forehead wrinkled. "I don't remember which one. In my dreams… sometimes it's one place, sometimes it's another. It was dark. I was dizzy, it's lucky I can remember anything considering how stupid drunk I was."

"And what happened?" Margie asked. "How much do you remember?"

"I remember it all. It was a red light. But Vince just blew through it. There were no other cars around, just us, so he didn't think he had to stop. But there was…" A loud sniff. Kimberly wiped her nose and pushed through, trying to get all the sickening details out. "There was a woman in the intersection. With a cart, you know, all of her stuff."

"Homeless?"

She nodded. "Yeah. Hal said…" Kimberly wiped her eyes, which were again streaming. "He said it didn't matter. No one would miss her. No one would be asking after her or care if she died. Because she was just some old bag lady. Like she didn't matter at all."

Margie wondered if her family knew what had happened to her. Whether the body had been matched to an identity, or whether she was a Jane Doe and the family had never been notified of her death.

"Okay." Jones's voice was calm and matter of fact. "Now we know what happened. Now I want to hear what happened afterward. Right after. Did they stop? Go back to see if she was okay?"

"No. I was screaming… I said we had to go back and help her. Call an ambulance. Vince was laughing. Hal said we couldn't go back. We couldn't be seen there. Vince said nobody saw us, we could still go back and report it. Pretend that we had seen someone else hit her. But Hal said… Hal said there would be a dent in the car where we had hit the woman and her cart. If the police saw that, they would know that we were the ones who had hit her."

Hal was probably the smartest of the bunch. He was still doing the same thing, warning and directing Skinner if he started to go off the rails. Trying to make sure they succeeded, because he wanted out. He wanted the life that he had been dreaming of—a nice house and car. Nice suits and prestige. A nice fat salary from the mayor.

But he knew that there was no way Vincent Skinner would make mayor if it were revealed that he was a cold-hearted killer. Calgary would elect a drunk, but not a killer.

So he had to stop anyone he thought was a liability.

"Did Hal threaten you?" Jones asked Kimberly.

She nodded. She cleared her throat, but her voice was still cracking. "He reminded me that I'd go to prison if I said anything. Said that they would both say that I was the one in the driver's seat and they had just been keeping quiet to protect me. Because they were gentlemen."

"And you said you'd stay quiet."

"Yeah. I didn't want to go to prison." She broke into fresh, racking sobs.

"Right," Jones agreed. "Now take a few deep breaths. We're going to go on and talk about Evie Wyler."

Kimberly obediently dragged in several long breaths. Margie found herself doing the same, whether to calm her own rapidly beating heart or to help comfort Kimberly, she didn't know. But it helped.

"How did she contact you?"

"She emailed me. Said that even though it wasn't a service that was included in my package, she liked to meet with the students who were local. To give them a chance to ask questions face to face and sort out anything we needed help with. But when I got there, to the coffee shop, that wasn't what it was. She started asking me about my essay. If it was true and who it was. Vince announcing that he was going to run for mayor really set me off. I was so mad that he could do something like that, pretending that he'd never done anything wrong. I was mad when I wrote that essay, or I would never..." Kimberly shook her head. "I should never have written it. I didn't want all this!" She made a motion that included her and the two detectives.

"It had to come out sooner or later," Jones said. "It was driving you crazy. You couldn't just forget it."

Kimberly nodded.

"So what did you tell Evie? Did you give her their names?"

"No... but I think she already knew. I guess it wouldn't be that hard to figure out who I went to school with. Even just picking the candidate who was closest to me in age."

"And she tried to persuade you to report the hit and run."

"Yeah. But I was too scared. I know Hal. I know he would do anything for Vince. I could never figure out why he was so devoted to

Vince. I mean, it wasn't like they were anything alike. But I knew Hal would do whatever it took to protect Vince. So I wasn't going to do anything. I couldn't."

"What did Evie say about that?"

"I don't know. She was disappointed in me. But she said it wouldn't affect my mark."

"Did she tell you that she was going to contact Vince or Hal directly?" Margie asked.

Kimberly shook her head, her eyes swimming in tears. "Why would she do that? Why?"

"I guess… she thought it was the right thing to do."

CHAPTER NINETEEN

It took most of the next day to verify everything they could about Kimberly's story and to get the warrants they needed but, once they had everything together, it wasn't too hard to track down Vincent Skinner. He was doing everything he could to keep the public's attention, including publishing his appearances on his campaign website and constantly live-tweeting events. So Jones and Margie went to the fundraiser and showed their police badges to get past the check-in table.

They scoped out the event, noting all the exits, as well as any security, and pinpointed both Skinner and Roberts. Since they were on opposite sides of the room initially, Margie and Jones bided their time, watching the events of the evening unfold.

Roberts went up on the stage first and, calling for everyone's attention, welcomed them and gave a little build-up to Skinner coming on-stage. After the intro, he motioned to Skinner, who joined him at the microphone, giving him hearty thanks and a perfunctory hug with a pat on his back. Roberts stood slightly to the side while Skinner made his pitch to the room. There was applause, and Skinner and Roberts started down the steps to leave the stage and schmooze with the guests. They slowed and stopped when they saw Jones and Margie waiting for them at the bottom.

Margie could see them trying to remember where they had seen the two unfamiliar women before. It was important for politicians to be able to remember faces, names, and details of their donors' lives. She smiled and motioned for them to come the rest of the way down the steps.

"We met at the Wildwood Stampede breakfast."

"Oh, of course," Skinner reached out his hand to shake with Margie, still not able to remember anything about her.

"Calgary Police Service," Margie added.

"Ah!"

She took Skinner's hand. "You're under arrest, Mr. Skinner." She swiftly handcuffed him without meeting any resistance. Skinner didn't understand what was going on.

Jones had a little more trouble with Roberts, but she was expecting it and was quick to restrain and handcuff him before he could begin to fight in earnest.

"What's going on here?" Skinner demanded. "Is this some kind of joke?" He looked at the baffled donors around him, looking for one who had arranged to make a mock arrest. Before COVID, there had been mock arrests on Law Day each year, with the arrestee having to raise money for bail, which would be given to the charity of choice, in order to be released.

But it wasn't Law Day and it wasn't a mock arrest.

Roberts's face was suffused with blood. He seemed to have a better idea of what was going on.

"You can't do this!" he growled. "What are your badge numbers? You can't just come into a private function and arrest us. Where's your warrant? Where's your cause? I want to talk to your boss!"

Margie flashed the arrest warrant at him. "Trust me, we made sure to get all our ducks in a row before coming here."

"What's going on here? What's this about?" one of the guests demanded. "I'm a lawyer. Do you really think that this is appropriate? I'm sure it could have been dealt with privately. Embarrassing a public figure could lose you your badge!"

"What area of law do you practice?" Jones asked, patting Roberts's pockets and waistband for a weapon.

"Securities," the lawyer sneered, looking down his substantial nose at her.

"Well, maybe you have a friend who is a criminal lawyer and could give these gentlemen some advice on defending a murder charge. Or rather, two murder charges."

Jones smiled at the shock on the lawyer's face.

"Murder?" Skinner repeated. "What are you talking about?"

"The murders of Kelly Forsythe,"—they'd been able to look up the name of the hit and run victim once they had the approximate date and location to work with and found that all of the details matched what Kimberly had said—"and Evie Wyler."

"Who are they? I've never heard of either one of them before."

"Let's go," Margie said, giving Skinner a little tug to get him on his way. He stumbled a little, but regained his balance again. He was reluctant to leave the event, but by the time he had reached the door had probably concluded that it was better to get out of there than for everyone to know the details of his dirty laundry. Outside, Margie pointed Skinner to one of the waiting squad cars. "You see? We could have come in with uniforms and a lot of noise. You should be grateful that Detective Jones and I figured we could make the arrests on our own."

Skinner scowled at her. "This is some kind of mistake. I'm not a murderer. I am a respected businessman."

"Well, you're actually not even that at this point." Though undoubtedly, he wished it were true. The guy hadn't been able to hold down a respectable job for more than a few months at a time. His whole campaign was smoke and mirrors. "To answer your question, Kelly Forsythe is the woman that you ran over a few years back and did not report. You were under the influence of alcohol at the time, so you might not remember it too clearly. And Evie Wyler is the ethics professor who was threatening to break the news about that death."

His jaw dropped. Margie had the uniformed officer standing by his car give Skinner a pat-down to ensure that he wasn't carrying a weapon. Though she was pretty sure that if either of them was armed, it would be Roberts. By the time he was finished and Skinner was facing Margie, he had regained his power of speech.

"Is this about Kimberly Martin? Do you have any idea of that woman's history?"

"Do I need to know more than the fact that she was there with you and saw the whole thing?"

"You should know better than to rely on the testimony of someone like her. That little tramp was higher than a kite. Any competent attorney will tear her apart on the stand."

Margie just smiled at him.

"And this other woman? Who is that? I've never even heard of her. How could I be guilty of doing anything to a woman I've never even heard of before?"

"Maybe you should ask your campaign manager about that one. I'm sure he'd be happy to give you all the details."

"Hal?" Skinner looked over at the other man, being placed in another squad car. He shook his head. "What are you talking about?"

"About the woman that he pushed off a cliff to save you having to face charges for Kelly Forsythe's death."

Skinner's face drained of color. "I don't know anything about that," he asserted. "I've never even heard of her."

Margie nodded. "I'm sure the Crown Prosecutor will be interested in anything you have to tell him about it."

CHAPTER TWENTY

Margie rolled her shoulders and massaged her neck before getting out of the car, trying to let go of any tension that lingered after the last few long days. She wanted to be relaxed and cheerful for Christina and able to enjoy the evening with her.

The lights were on—nearly every light in the house—so she knew that her daughter was home and not out with Tracy somewhere.

As she walked up to the front door, she could see Stella through the screen, tail waving like a flag, excited to see her. She opened the door and scratched Stella's ears as she walked in. "Who's a good girl? Hmm? Are you my good girl?"

She could tell by the smell that Christina had been cooking. She was surprised. Mostly, the two of them just warmed stuff up in the microwave or put a slice of bread in the toaster if they weren't making a meal together.

"Mmm, what smells so good?"

Christina turned to face her, smiling. "I made bannock. To take to Moushoom."

Margie felt a pang of disappointment. She had meant to make bannock with Christina. But she had been so busy with the Wyler case that she hadn't set aside the time to do it with her. She wished that Christina would have waited to do it with her. But she forced a smile.

"He is going to be so happy. You love him very much, don't you?"

Christina nodded. "I'm glad you got back early enough. We have time to go over and see him while it is still warm, right?"

Margie didn't look at the clock. "Yes. Definitely. We'll go right over so that we can catch him before bed."

"There's lots to go around, so you can have it for your supper too."

Carbs and jam might not be the best supper to lose weight on, but Margie would be sure to go for a run the next morning so that she didn't feel guilty about the indulgence. "You're the best. Thank you." She gave Christina a hug and they wrapped up the bannock.

"We'll zip over in the car today to save a bit of time."

"And the smoke has mostly cleared, so we can take Moushoom out for a walk."

"He'll like that. But most of all, he will like seeing you."

"And you," Christina pointed out.

Margie tucked a lock of hair behind Christina's ear, smiling.

MOUSHOOM HAD NOT GONE to bed yet and was eager to go out when they suggested it. Christina pushed his wheelchair up the hill and Margie held on to Stella's leash. Moushoom reached out to grab Margie's free hand. His hands, while thin, were still strong, like she remembered from when she was a girl. She squeezed his hand and smiled, walking in silence.

"You worry too much," Moushoom commented.

Margie chuckled. "Yes, I probably do."

"You need to let go to be at peace. Do your best, and then let go. We cannot control everything."

Margie had been thinking about little Ada, who would grow up without a mother. Or at least, without her first mother. Vance might find someone else he could share his life with, someone who would be happy to raise a child who hadn't come from her own body. But Ada would not remember Evie Wyler when she was grown.

That was one of those things that Margie could not control.

One of the many things she would have to just let go of.

EDWORTHY PARK

Created in 1962, Edworthy Park has been around for a while. There are picnic shelters and BBQ pits, plenty of washrooms, playgrounds, and trails. The trails are very popular for mountain bikers as well as walkers. The paved pathways join up with the Bow River Pathway and run all the way downtown to Princes Island Park and farther east all the way to Valleyview Park. It is hoped that one day a path will run from Edworthy to Haskayne Park, Glenbow Ranch Provincial Park, and through to Cochrane.

A longtime favourite for family reunions, school class trips, and throwing rocks into the river. Angel's Cafe is close to the north entrance if you're in the mood for a dinner not cooked over the campfire.

Did you enjoy this book? Reviews and recommendations are vital to making a book successful.

Please leave a review at your favorite book store or review site and share it with your friends.

Don't miss the following bonus material:
Sign up for mailing list to get a free ebook
Read a sneak preview chapter
Other books by P.D. Workman
Learn more about the author

Sign up for my mailing list at pdworkman.com and get
Gluten-Free Murder for free!

PREVIEW OF KNOWS THE HILLS

CHAPTER 1

Margie glanced at the phone on her desk again, even though it hadn't rung. She had an unsettled feeling. Something was in the air. Something was going to happen.

She wondered whether the feeling had been triggered by Christina. Her daughter hadn't seemed quite her normal self since going back to school. It had been a good summer for her. Her first summer in Calgary, finally able to go out with her friends since the social distancing and masking rules had been dispensed with. She had attended the Calgary Stampede, GlobalFest fireworks, Peters' Drive-in, and other places that Margie used to enjoy going to with her cousins when she had visited Calgary as a teen.

Of course, the kids were also into going to the mall shopping or staying home and streaming video, things she had not spent her summers doing, but it was nice for them to be able to spend the time with each other, whatever they decided to do.

Except then the delta variant had shut things down again, and Christina was once again wearing a mask at school and had been moody and sullen lately, walking around with a little storm cloud over her head. Margie hoped it was just because of the new rules and not because of anything personal Christina wasn't telling her about.

She always worried about whether Christina was spending too much time with her friend Tracy—a boy, not a girl—and Margie wasn't sure yet whether he was Christina's boyfriend or just a friend she liked to hang out with. Margie hadn't been much older than Christina when she had gotten pregnant, and that had changed the course of her life. She'd had to grow up pretty fast, and she wanted Christina to be able to grow up at her own pace, a little more slowly, taking the time to enjoy herself before she had to face adult responsibilities.

"Pat? Detective Patenaude…"

Margie was startled out of her thoughts of Christina. The phone still hadn't rung. Christina was in school; they hadn't called to say that she was absent or had gotten in any trouble. Margie would just have to wait and see how things turned out. She looked at Detective Jones, standing in the space between their desks in the bullpen. Jones's blond hair was pulled back into a bun, as usual, though there were a few curls escaping, also as usual. She held a Tim Hortons coffee cup toward Margie.

"You looked like you could use a little pick-me-up," Jones told her with a smile.

Margie took the coffee. "You didn't need to do that! But thank you." She took a sip of the piping hot coffee and swallowed, savoring it. "This is wonderful."

Jones sat down in her chair. "What's going on today? You seem worlds away. One of these cases bothering you?" She gestured to the files Margie had been working her way through. Cases that they had run out of leads on. She was hoping to find some thread that no one had thought to follow before. Some tip that had been called in that had not been followed up on, some theory that had not been pursued —anything to get one of them moving again and get them closer to the killer. Calgary Homicide had an excellent clearance rate, and she wanted to keep it up or even improve it if possible.

"No. Just thinking about the kid, actually."

Jones looked at the picture of Christina on Margie's desk. She had grown so much over the summer, topping Margie by a couple of inches now. Her long, sleek black hair and bronzed skin were gorgeous. She was much better looking than Margie had ever been. Margie suspected she got a lot of attention from the boys at school. Tracy probably had to beat them off with a stick.

"What's up with Christina?" Jones inquired.

"Nothing. Something. I don't know. She's moody, but she's a teenager, so what does that mean?" Margie shrugged. "If something is wrong, I wish she would talk to me about it. But kids don't go to their parents with their problems, do they? It's probably just hormones. Or having to go back to school and back to wearing a mask. It's scary, thinking that we were homefree and the danger was past, and now having to face it again, hospital ICU numbers climbing every day."

"She has to put up with stuff at school that we never had to," Jones agreed. "Imagine having all of this added onto the school stresses that we went through. It's not just homework, peer pressure, and weird teachers; they have to worry about not getting too close to anybody or catching this virus that could put them in hospital. A lot more young people are getting it this time around."

Margie shook her head. She couldn't put her finger on *why*, but she thought something else was wrong. Something that she should know about but didn't.

The phone rang, and it was a good thing that there was a plastic top on the coffee cup. She startled so violently the coffee would have been all over Margie's desk. As it was, she still managed to get a splash on her uniform through the drinking hole. Margie put the cup down on her desk and picked up the phone receiver with one hand while pulling several tissues out of the box on her desk with the other and dabbing at her uniform front and the edge of her desk. She was so distracted by the near catastrophe that she didn't even look at the caller ID before picking up the phone.

"Calgary Homicide, Detective Patenaude here."

"Detective Pat," Staff Sergeant MacDonald's tone was slightly amused by her formal answer, "join me in my office, please. Bring Jones with you."

"Yes, sir."

Margie hung up the phone and stood. She looked at Jones. "He wants both of us."

Jones stood. "Are we in trouble?" She gave Margie a mischievous smile. "What did you do?"

"It's not me. It must be you. Maybe he's onto your covert trip to Tim's."

"Nah. I already gave him a cup."

If MacDonald already had a cup of Tim's, Margie figured it was okay to take hers with her, so she picked it up. Jones picked up hers, and they walked across the bullpen to MacDonald's office. The door stood open. Margie knocked on the frame of the door to announce herself, and she and Jones walked in. MacDonald, tall, lean, and silver-haired, was looking at his computer and writing something down on the pad beside his keyboard. He looked up after a moment.

"It would appear we need Parks Pat's particular expertise," he informed them.

His use of the nickname could mean only one thing—another body in a park. Since everyone now associated Margie with murders in Calgary parks, she was the one who was called upon when a body was discovered. Even if it was an old homeless guy who stank to high heaven and obviously died of natural causes. She sighed.

"Happy to help, sir."

It wasn't really that she had any particular expertise in park settings. A murder in a park setting wasn't that different from a murder indoors or in the alley behind a biker bar. Homicide was homicide, and Margie didn't have any special genetic predisposition to solving murders that took place in a park setting as a result of her Métis ancestry or any special training or experience.

"What have we got?" Jones asked.

"Nose Hill Park. Reported as a slasher, but... well, I'll let you judge that by what you see. No need to plant anything into your mind ahead of time. Prepare yourself. Bloody scene."

Margie and Jones both nodded.

"Do we have a GPS location?" Margie asked. Some of the parks in Calgary were quite large, and she knew that Nose Hill Park was one of them, covering a large portion of the northwest. She didn't want to be wandering around for hours looking for the site.

"Sent it to your phone. Let me know if you run into any problems."

CHAPTER 2

They took Margie's car. Even though Margie had initially planned to bike from home to the downtown office, she had still not managed to do so. She was still driving and not getting that extra bit of exercise she had promised herself. But it was a lot handier to have a car when they had a murder scene to get to. Calgary was a huge urban sprawl, and it could take an hour to drive from one end to the other. Not like the cute little English villages on TV that a copper could patrol on his bicycle.

"Have you ever been to Nose Hill?" Jones asked.

"No." Margie couldn't see the big hill yet, but she looked in that direction anyway. "It looked like it's pretty bare. Just grassland."

"That's only the part that you can see from the road. There are valleys full of trees. Great view of the city skyline. Wildflowers in the spring. Lots of people walk their dogs there."

Jones had been to Margie's house and met not only Christina, but also their dog Stella. She knew they enjoyed taking her for walks in Calgary's numerous green spaces. Though it was September, so most of the grassy areas had been scorched brown and yellow by the sun, and the leaves were losing their chlorophyll as winter approached. The nights were getting chilly, and though it hadn't been below zero yet, the trees knew that winter was on its way.

"Maybe we'll take Stella out there to explore," Margie said.

Margie had input the coordinates of the body into her GPS unit, so she followed the directions of the electronic voice the best she could, with Jones giving her a few warnings or lane changes she needed to make or turns that were coming up sooner than they appeared to be on the GPS screen. Eventually, they pulled into a dusty parking lot. A couple of marked Calgary Police Service cars were parked already, which told Margie they were in the right place. They took off their office-appropriate blazers, which would be far too warm for walking through the park and left them in the car. Margie grabbed her scene-of-crime kit and they headed into the park.

The yellow-brown hills were speckled here and there with trees or large sandstone rocks. There were scrubby rose bushes and small clumps of wildflowers past their bloom. There were not many people on the trail that Margie and Jones began to walk up together. The hill was steeper than it looked, and they were both slightly out of breath before long. Margie slowed. She didn't want to be huffing and puffing when they got to the scene. And Jones was heavier than Margie and not having the easiest time with the climb.

"We came here a few times as kids in elementary school," Jones puffed. "It didn't seem like such a climb then! As kids, we just ran up it."

"Did you come as a class?"

"Field trip," Jones agreed. "End of the year. A special treat."

Margie looked around. There weren't any playgrounds or picnic areas that she could see. Not really the type of place that she would have expected the school kids to see as a treat.

"It was fun." Jones shrugged. "Anything to get out of the classroom."

"I guess so."

Margie could see a couple of police officers down in a coulee below. As Jones had said, plenty of trees grew in the more protected areas between the hills. They reached a footpath worn in the grass and followed it down into the valley to meet with the law enforcement officers below.

"Parks Pat?" one of the masked constables asked with a smile in his voice and a fan of wrinkles around the corners of his eyes.

"That's me," Margie agreed. "How far do we have to go?"

"Not far. It's just around the edge of the wooded area here."

They led Margie and Jones through the trees until they arrived at an area that had been cordoned off with yellow tape. A couple more officers were guarding the scene.

"So, what have we got?" Margie asked, getting closer but staying outside of the perimeter. "The sergeant said a slasher?"

"Mmm." The constable made a noise that was neither agreement nor denial.

Margie got to an angle where she could see one side of the body. It was, as MacDonald had warned, a bloody scene. Margie could see long gashes down the woman's arm. Slasher certainly seemed apt, despite MacDonald's suggestion that it might be something else. She shrugged at Jones and put down her scene-of-crime kit. She unzipped it and they each pulled on protective suits and booties to reduce any contamination of the scene. They crossed the yellow tape and picked their way carefully across the area to get a close look at the victim.

It was a woman, as Margie had discerned from outside the perimeter. A slim woman with Asian features. Hair just longer than her shoulders. Young, an older teen or young adult. Margie's stomach clenched, immediately associating the victim with Christina. What had happened? Why had she been down in the coulee and who had attacked her? Was it just a chance thing? Had she been chased or stalked?

There were numerous gashes and slashes, but as Margie got closer, she could see that there were also puncture marks and flesh had been torn away. She shook her head, shooting a look at one of the CPS officers standing outside the cordon.

"This is an animal attack."

He gave a nod of agreement.

Margie rolled her eyes. She and Jones stepped back from the body, returning the way they had come.

"No need for homicide here," Margie said, somewhat exasperated. Those bites and slashes were not caused by a human.

"Not a homicide," the cop agreed. "But it was called in as one, so…"

"So I need to sign off. Fine. I agree. Not a homicide. Is the medical examiner on the way?"

"Should be here any minute."

"And we really don't need crime scene to collect anything, since this is not a crime scene. Who else? Do we call Alberta Fish and Wildlife?"

"Calgary Parks. They've been informed and will send someone over to investigate. Then they'll probably call Alberta, and they will determine the best response."

Margie looked regretfully at the woman who had been killed. "What was it? A cougar? Bear?"

"Don't think so," said a smaller officer, who had been quiet until that point. "Looks like coyote."

"Really? I thought coyotes were shy. Avoided people."

The man stepped forward so they could converse more easily. Margie realized he was not just small, but he must be fresh out of the academy. And the academy appeared to be recruiting babies now. His name bar said Young, and Margie suppressed a chuckle at the appropriateness of his name.

"There have been a number of coyote attacks in the city," Young offered. "They get habituated to people, and then they aren't afraid enough to stay away anymore."

"And a coyote could do *that?*" Margie glanced in the direction of the body.

"Maybe more than one of them. Usually, it's just a bite or two and then they run. But in this case…" Young trailed off. Obviously, that hadn't happened. They had attacked viciously and not been deterred by the victim screaming and fighting back.

"Could they be rabid?" Margie speculated.

"Could be. Not that it's going to make any difference to our victim."

No, she was past being worried about getting rabies. But they would want to protect the public if the animals were rabid.

"Do you have an ID on her yet?"

"We'll wait for the ME or a matching missing person report. Haven't searched her pockets."

As Young said, it was best to wait and let the ME's death investigators handle it. They were the best positioned to see what trace evidence needed to be preserved. Margie could check for a missing person report when she returned to the office. It seemed like someone should have noticed the young woman was missing. She appeared to be clean and well cared for. Not homeless, with a camp set up somewhere in the trees. However, there might be others around who did.

"Are there any homeless camps around here?" She addressed her question to all of the police officers there. They were presumably assigned to the area and would know whether there was a problem with people camping out in the park.

"Not that I'm aware of," one of the older cops answered. "Residents in the area are pretty quick to call it in if someone sets up a tent. They're not allowed to camp in the park. We move them along. Why?" He shook his head. "It's pretty obvious this was an animal attack, not a human."

"Oh, I know. I just thought that there might be witnesses. If someone was camping out here, they might have seen or heard something that would be helpful."

"Suppose so. But we don't really need to know anything else. What difference will it make to know when she was attacked or how long it took? Or if she screamed?" He shook his head heavily. "No witness statement will make any difference to this case."

"I suppose not." Margie scratched the back of her neck. "I'm just too used to dealing with homicides. An animal attack is a new one for me."

"What makes you think it was a coyote?" Jones asked Young, turning back to face him after gazing at the woman's body. "Are you that familiar with the difference between bite marks or claws?"

Young shook his head. "Coyote scat."

Jones looked at him blankly. Margie could see her trying to process this concise explanation. For someone unused to dealing with wildlife, scat was a verb, not a noun, and Jones was probably trying to come up with a full sentence or explanation that made sense to her.

"Their droppings," Margie informed her, looking around at the ground. Within the yellow-taped barrier were a couple of piles of coyote scat. "Like that."

Jones leaned closer to study one of the deposits, her nose wrinkling in distaste. "And how do you know that's coyote and not... bear? It looks like there are berries in it. Coyotes don't eat berries, do they? But bears do."

"Coyotes are very opportunistic," Young told her. "Berries, small animals, garbage. Their droppings don't look like dog crap. A dog that just eats dog food out of a can, their turds are all smooth and evenly colored. Not like these."

The ropy, knotted-looking coyote scat, full of berries and bits of fur and debris, was quite different from what Margie picked up after Stella did her business. She wouldn't have identified it as belonging to an animal in the dog family at all. She probably would have gone with bear, as Jones had suggested.

"Coyote, then," she agreed with a shrug.

The medical examiner's van appeared, some distance away and making its way very carefully over the rough terrain with no proper access route. It eventually crawled to a stop a few feet back from the tape, and one of the investigators climbed out to have a look.

"Once you've confirmed that the victim is dead and this doesn't appear to be a homicide, I can be on my way," Margie offered. Despite the nice weather, she didn't really want to hang out at a death scene all day.

Knows the Hills, Book #7 of the *Parks Pat Mysteries* series by P.D. Workman can be purchased at pdworkman.com

ABOUT THE AUTHOR

P.D. Workman is a USA Today Bestselling author, winner of several awards from Library Services for Youth in Custody and the InD'tale Magazine's Crowned Heart award, and has published over 90 mystery/suspense/thriller and young adult books, including stand alones and these series: Auntie Clem's Bakery cozy mysteries, Reg Rawlins Psychic Investigator paranormal mysteries, Zachary Goldman Mysteries (PI), Kenzie Kirsch Medical Thrillers, Parks Pat Mysteries (police procedural), and YA series: Tamara's Teardrops, Between the Cracks, and Breaking the Pattern.

Workman loves writing about the underdog, who the reader may love or hate. She has been praised for her realistic details, deep characterization, and sensitive handling of the serious social issues that appear in all of her stories, from light cozy mysteries through to darker, grittier young adult and mystery/suspense books.

> P. D. Workman, does not shy from probing the deep psychological scars of childhood trauma, mental illness, and addiction. Also characteristic of this author, these extremely sensitive issues are explored with extensive empathy, described with incredible clarity, and portrayed with profound insight.
>
> — —KIM, GOODREADS REVIEWER

Some of Workman's titles have been translated into Spanish, French, Portuguese, German, and Italian.

Workman began writing at an early age and is a prolific reader as well as writer. She is also passionate about teaching and learning, expresses her creativity through art and cooking, and loves exploring the Calgary parks and green spaces where the Parks Pat Mysteries are set. She was a legal assistant for many years and has done extensive charitable work.

Workman was born and raised in Alberta, Canada, and is married with one adult son.

§&

Please visit P.D. Workman at pdworkman.com to see what else she is working on, to join her mailing list, and to link to her social networks.

§&

If you enjoyed this book, please take the time to recommend it to other purchasers with a review or star rating and share it with your friends!

tiktok.com/@pdworkmanauthor

facebook.com/pdworkmanauthor

twitter.com/pdworkmanauthor

instagram.com/pdworkmanauthor

amazon.com/author/pdworkman

bookbub.com/authors/p-d-workman

goodreads.com/pdworkman

linkedin.com/in/pdworkman

pinterest.com/pdworkmanauthor

youtube.com/pdworkman

Find P.D. Workman's books at

PDWORKMAN.COM

Scan the QR code below